I0573930

John Dryden

Plutarch's Lives

The translation called Dryden's. Vol. 1

John Dryden

Plutarch's Lives
The translation called Dryden's. Vol. 1

ISBN/EAN: 9783337426491

Printed in Europe, USA, Canada, Australia, Japan

Cover: Foto ©Andreas Hilbeck / pixelio.de

More available books at **www.hansebooks.com**

PLUTARCH'S LIVES.

THE

TRANSLATION CALLED DRYDEN'S.

Corrected from the Greek and Revised

BY

A. H. CLOUGH,

SOMETIME FELLOW AND TUTOR OF ORIEL COLLEGE, OXFORD, AND LATE
PROFESSOR OF THE ENGLISH LANGUAGE AND LITERATURE
AT UNIVERSITY COLLEGE, LONDON.

VOL. I.

BOSTON:
LITTLE, BROWN, AND COMPANY.
1865.

Entered according to Act of Congress, in the year 1859, by
LITTLE, BROWN, AND COMPANY,
in the Clerk's Office of the District Court for the District of Massachusetts.

One Hundred copies printed.

UNIVERSITY PRESS:
WELCH, BIGELOW, AND COMPANY,
CAMBRIDGE.

GENERAL TABLE OF CONTENTS.

VOLUME I.

VOLUME II.

(3)

VOLUME III.

VOLUME IV.

GENERAL TABLE OF CONTENTS.

VOLUME V.

ALPHABETICAL INDEX OF THE LIVES.

ALPHABETICAL INDEX OF THE COMPARISONS.

PREFACE,

CONTAINING A LIFE OF PLUTARCH.

———

THE collection so well known as " Plutarch's Lives," is nei-ther in form nor in arrangement what its author left behind him.

To the proper work, the Parallel Lives, narrated in a series of Books, each containing the accounts of one Greek and one Roman, followed by a Comparison, some single lives have been appended, for no reason but that they are also biographies. Otho and Galba belonged, probably, to a series of Roman Em-perors from Augustus to Vitellius. Artaxerxes and Aratus the statesman, are detached narratives, like others which once, we are told, existed, Hercules, Aristomenes, Hesiod, Pindar, Dai-phantus, Crates the cynic, and Aratus the poet.

In the Parallel Lives themselves there are gaps. There was a Book containing those of Epaminondas and Scipio the younger. Many of the comparisons are wanting, have either been lost, or were not completed. And the reader will notice for himself that references made here and there in the extant lives, show that their original order was different from the present. In the very first page, for example, of the book, in the life of Theseus, mention occurs of the lives of Lycurgus and Numa, as already written.

VOL. I.   *a*   (v)

The plain facts of Plutarch's own life may be given in a very short compass. He was born, probably, in the reign of Claudius, about A. D. 45 or 50. His native place was Chæronea, in Bœotia, where his family had long been settled and was of good standing and local reputation. He studied at Athens under a philosopher named Ammonius. He visited Egypt. Later in life, some time before A. D. 90, he was at Rome "on public business," a deputation, perhaps, from Chæronea. He continued there long enough to give lectures which attracted attention. Whether he visited Italy once only, or more often, is uncertain.

He was intimate with Sosius Senecio, to all appearances the same who was four times consul. The acquaintance may have sprung up at Rome, where Sosius, a much younger man than himself,* may have first seen him as a lecturer; or they may have previously known each other in Greece.

To Greece and to Chæronea he returned, and appears to have spent in the little town, which he was loth "to make less by the withdrawal of even one inhabitant," the remainder of his life. He took part in the public business of the place and the neighborhood. He was archon in the town, and officiated many years as a priest of Apollo, apparently at Delphi.

He was married, and was the father of at least five children, of whom two sons, at any rate, survived to manhood. His greatest work, his Biographies, and several of his smaller writings, belong to this later period of his life, under the reign of Trajan. Whether he survived to the time of Hadrian is doubtful. If A. D. 45 be taken by way of conjecture for the date of his birth, A. D. 120, Hadrian's fourth year, may be assumed, in like manner, as pretty nearly that of his death. All that is certain is that he lived to be old; that in one of his fictitious

---

* Unless the expression "my sons your companions" ought to be taken as a piece of pleasantry.

.dialogues he describes himself as a young man conversing on philosophy with Ammonius in the time of Nero's visit to Greece, A. D. 66–67; and that he was certainly alive and still writing in A. D. 106, the winter which Trajan, after building his bridge over the Danube, passed in Dacia. " We are told," he says, in his Inquiry into the Principle of Cold, "by those who are now wintering with the Emperor on the Danube, that the freezing of water will crush boats to pieces."

To this bare outline of certainties, several names and circumstances may be added from his writings; on which indeed alone we can safely rely for the very outline itself. There are a few allusions and anecdotes in the Lives, and from his miscellaneous compositions, his Essays, Lectures, Dialogues, Table-Talk, etc., the imagination may furnish itself with a great variety of curious and interesting suggestions.

The name of his great-grandfather, Nicarchus, is incidentally recorded in the life of Antony. " My great-grandfather used," ne says, " to tell, how in Antony's last war the whole of the citizens of Chæronea were put in requisition to bring down corn to the coast of the gulf of Corinth, each man carrying a certain load, and soldiers standing by to urge them on with the lash." One such journey was made, and they had measured out their burdens for the second, when news arrived of the defeat at Actium.* Lamprias, his grandfather, is also mentioned in the same life. Philotas, the physician, had told him an anecdote illustrating the luxuriousness of Antony's life in Egypt. His father is more than once spoken of in the minor works, but never mentioned by his name.

The name of Ammonius, his teacher and preceptor at Athens,

* There appears, however, to be no sure reason for saying that Plutarch himself remembered seeing his great-grandfather, and hearing him tell the story.

occurs repeatedly in the minor works, and is once specially mentioned in the Lives; a descendant of Themistocles had studied with Plutarch under Ammonius. We find it mentioned that he three times held the office, once so momentous in the world's history, of *strategus* at Athens.* This, like that of the Bœotarchs in Bœotia, continued under the Empire to be intrusted to native citizens, and judging from what is said in the little treatise of Political Precepts, was one of the more important places under the Roman provincial governor.

" Once," Plutarch tells us, " our teacher, Ammonius, observing at his afternoon lecture that some of his auditors had been indulging too freely at breakfast, gave directions, in our presence, for chastisement to be administered to his own son, *because*, he said, *the young man has declined to take his breakfast unless he has sour wine with it*, fixing his eyes at the same time on the offending members of the class."

The following anecdote appears to belong to some period a little later than that of his studies at Athens. " I remember, when I myself was still a young man, I was sent in company with another on a deputation to the proconsul; my colleague, it so happened, was unable to proceed, and I saw the proconsul and performed the commission alone. Upon my return, when I was about to lay down my office, and to give an account of its discharge, my father got up in the assembly and bade me privately to take care not to say *I* went, but *we* went, nor *I* said, but *we* said, and in the whole narration to give my companion his share."

---

* This may throw some doubt on the statement (with which, however, it is perhaps not absolutely incompatible) made by the Byzantine historian Eunapius, that " Ammonius, the teacher of the divine Plutarch, was an Egyptian."

Plutarch was certainly skilled in all the wisdom of the Græco-Egyptians; see his treatise addressed to the learned lady Clea, on Isis and Osiris; but he may, for any thing we know, have staid long and studied much at Alexandria.

Of his stay in Italy, his visit to or residence in Rome, we know little beyond the statement which he gives us in the life of Demosthenes, that public business and visitors who came to see him on subjects of philosophy, took up so much of his time that he learned, at that time, but little of the Latin language. He must have travelled about, for he saw the bust or statue of Marius at Ravenna, as he informs us in the beginning of Marius's life. He undertook, he tells us in his essay on Brotherly Affection, the office, whilst he was in Rome, of arbitrating between two brothers, one of whom was considered to be a lover of philosophy. "But he had," he says, "in reality, no legitimate title to the name either of brother or of philosopher. When I told him I should expect from him the behavior of a philosopher towards one, who was, first of all, an ordinary person making no such profession, and, in the second place, a brother, *as for the first point,* replied he, *it may be well enough, but I don't attach any great importance to the fact of two people having come from the same pair of bodies;*" an impious piece of freethinking which met, of course, with Plutarch's indignant rebuke and reprobation.

A more remarkable anecdote is related in his discourse on Inquisitiveness. Among other precepts for avoiding or curing the fault, "We should habituate ourselves," he says, "when letters are brought to us, not to open them instantly and in a hurry, not to bite the strings in two, as many people will, if they do not succeed at once with their fingers; when a messenger comes, not to run to meet him; not to jump up, when a friend says he has something new to tell us; rather, if he has some good or useful advice to give us. Once when I was lecturing at Rome, Rusticus, whom Domitian afterwards, out of jealousy of his reputation, put to death, was one of my hearers; and while I was going on, a soldier came in and brought him a letter from the Emperor. And when every one was silent, and I stopped in order to let him read the letter, he declined to do so, and put it aside until I had finished and the audience withdrew; an example of serious and dignified behavior which excited much admiration."

L. Junius Arulenus Rusticus, the friend of Pliny and Tacitus, glorified among the Stoic martyrs whose names are written in the life of Agricola, was in youth the ardent disciple of Thrasea Pætus; and when Pætus was destined by Nero for death, and the Senate was prepared to pass the decree for his condemnation, Rusticus, in the fervor of his feelings, was eager to interpose the veto still attaching in form to the office, which he happened then to hold, of tribune, and was scarcely withheld by his master from a demonstration which would but have added him, before his time, to the catalogue of victims. After performing, in the civil wars ensuing on the death of Nero, the duties of prætor, he published in Domitian's time a life of Thrasea, as did Senecio one of Helvidius, and Tacitus, probably, himself, that of Agricola: the bold language of which insured his death. Among the teachers who afterwards gave instruction to the youthful Marcus Aurelius, we read the name of an Arulenus Rusticus, probably his grandson, united with that of Sextus of Chæronea, Plutarch's nephew, " who taught me," says the virtuous Emperor, " by his own example, the just and wise habits he recommended," and to whose door, in late life, he was still seen to go, still desirous, as he said, to be a learner.

It does not, of course, follow from the terms in which the story is related, that the incident occurred in Domitian's time, and that it was to Domitian's letter that Plutarch's discourse was preferred. But that Plutarch was at Rome in or after Domitian's reign, seems to be fairly inferred from the language in which he speaks of the absurd magnificence of Domitian's palaces and other imperial buildings.

His two brothers, Timon and Lamprias, are frequently mentioned in his Essays and Dialogues. They, also, appear to have
been pupils of Ammonius. In the treatise on Affection between
Brothers, after various examples of the strength of this feeling,
occurs the following passage: "And for myself," he says,
"that among the many favors for which I have to thank the
kindness of fortune, my brother Timon's affection to me is one,
past and present, that may be put in the balance against all the
rest, is what every one that has so much as met with us must
be aware of, and our friends, of course, know well."

His wife was Timoxena, the daughter of Alexion. The circumstances of his domestic life receive their best illustration
from his letter addressed to this wife, on the loss of their one
daughter, born to them, it would appear, late in life, long after
her brothers. "Plutarch to his wife, greeting. The messengers
you sent to announce our child's death, apparently missed the
road to Athens. I was told about my daughter on reaching
Tanagra. Every thing relating to the funeral I suppose to have
been already performed; my desire is that all these arrangements may have been so made, as will now and in the future
be most consoling to yourself. If there is any thing which you
have wished to do and have omitted, awaiting my opinion, and
think would be a relief to you, it shall be attended to, apart
from all excess and superstition, which no one would like less
than yourself. Only, my wife, let me hope, that you will maintain both me and yourself within the reasonable limits of grief.
What our loss really amounts to, I know and estimate for myself. But should I find your distress excessive, my trouble on
your account will be greater than on that of our loss. I am
not a 'stock or stone,' as you, my partner in the care of our
numerous children, every one of whom we have ourselves
brought up at home, can testify. And this child, a daughter,
born to your wishes after four sons, and affording me the oppor-

tunity of recording your name, I am well aware was a special object of affection."

The sweet temper and the pretty ways of the child, he proceeds to say, make the privation peculiarly painful. " Yet why," he says, " should we forget the reasonings we have often addressed to others, and regard our present pain as obliterating and effacing our former joys ? " Those who had been present had spoken to him in terms of admiration of the calmness and simplicity of her behavior. The funeral had been devoid of any useless and idle sumptuosity, and her own house of all display of extravagant lamentation. This was indeed no wonder to him, who knew how much her plain and unluxurious living had surprised his philosophical friends and visitors, and who well remembered her composure under the previous loss of the eldest of her children, and again, " when our beautiful Charon left us." " I recollect," he says, " that some acquaintance from abroad were coming up with me from the sea when the tidings of the child's decease were brought, and they followed with our other friends to the house ; but the perfect order and tranquillity they found there made them believe, as I afterwards was informed they had related, that nothing had happened, and that the previous intelligence had been a mistake."

The Consolation (so the letter is named) closes with expressions of belief in the immortality of each human soul; in which the parents are sustained and fortified by the tradition of their ancestors, and the revelations to which they had both been admitted, conveyed in the mystic Dionysian ceremonies.

There is a phrase in the letter which might be taken to imply that, at the time of this domestic misfortune, Plutarch and Timoxena were already grandparents. The marriage of their son Autobulus is the occasion of one of the dinner parties recorded in the Symposiac Questions ; and in one of the dia-

logues, there is a distinct allusion to Autobulus's son. Plutarch
inscribes the little treatise in explanation of the Timæus to his
two sons, Autobulus and Plutarch. They must certainly have
been grown up men, to have any thing to do with so difficult a
subject. In his Inquiry as to the Way in which the Young
should read the Poets, "It is not easy," he says, addressing Marcus Sedatus, "to restrain altogether from such reading young
people of the age of my Soclarus and your Cleander." But
whether Soclarus was a son, or a grandson, or some more distant relative, or, which is possible, a pupil, does not appear.
Eurydice, to whom and to Pollianus, her newly espoused husband, he addresses his Marriage Precepts, seems to be spoken
of as a recent inmate of his house; but it cannot be inferred
that she was a daughter, nor does it seem likely that the little
Timoxena's place was ever filled up.*

The office of Archon, which Plutarch held in his native mu-
nicipality, was probably only an annual one; but very likely
he served it more than once. He seems to have busied himself
about all the little matters of the town, and to have made it a
point to undertake the humblest duties. After relating the
story of Epaminondas giving dignity to the office of Chief
Scavenger, "And I, too, for that matter," he says, "am often a
jest to my neighbors, when they see me, as they frequently do,
in public, occupied on very similar duties; but the story told
about Antisthenes comes to my assistance. When some one
expressed surprise at his carrying home some pickled fish from
market in his own hands, *It is*, he answered, *for myself.* Con-
versely, when I am reproached with standing by and watching
while tiles are measured out, and stone and mortar brought up,
This service, I say, *is not for myself*, it is for my country."

* That he had more than two sons who grew up, at any rate, to youth, appears from a passage where he speaks of his *younger sons* having staid too long at the theatre, and being, in consequence, too late at supper.

In the little essay on the question, Whether an Old Man should continue in Public Life, written in the form of an exhortation to Euphanes, an ancient and distinguished member of the Areopagus at Athens, and of the Amphictyonic council, not to relinquish his duties, " Let there be no severance," he says, "in our long companionship, and let neither the one nor the other of us forsake the life that was our choice." And, alluding to his own functions as priest of Apollo at Delphi, " You know," he adds in another place, " that I have served the Pythian God for many *pythiads** past, yet you would not now tell me, *you have taken part enough in the sacrifices, processions, and dances, and it is high time, Plutarch, now you are an old man, to lay aside your garland, and retire as superannuated from the oracle.*"

Even in these, the comparatively few, more positive and matter-of-fact passages of allusion and anecdote, there is enough to bring up something of a picture of a happy domestic life, half academic, half municipal, passed among affectionate relatives and well-known friends, inclining most to literary and moral studies, yet not cut off from the duties and avocations of the citizen. We cannot, of course, to go yet further, accept the scenery of the fictitious Dialogues as historical; yet there is much of it which may be taken as, so to say, pictorially just; and there is, probably, a good deal here and there that is literally true to the fact. The Symposiac, or After-Dinner Questions, collected in nine books, and dedicated to Sosius Senecio, were discussed, we are told, many of them, in the company of Sosius himself, both at Rome and in Greece, as, for example, when he was with them at the marriage festivities of Autobulus. Lamprias and Timon, the author's brothers, are frequent speakers,

---

* Periods of four years elapsing between the celebrations of the Pythian games, like the Olympiads for the Olympic games.

each with a distinctly traced character, in these conversations; the father, and the elder Lamprias, the grandfather, both take an occasional, and the latter a lively part; there is one whole book in which Ammonius predominates; the scene is now at Delphi, and now at Athens, sometimes perhaps, but rarely, at Rome, sometimes at the celebrations of the Games. Plutarch, in his priestly capacity, gives an entertainment in honor of a poetic victor at the Pythia, there is an Isthmian dinner at Corinth, and an Olympian party at Elis. As an adopted Athenian citizen of the Leontid tribe, he attends the celebration of the success of his friend, the philosophic poet Serapion. The *dramatis personæ* of the various little pieces form a company, when put together, of more than eighty names, philosophers, rhetoricians, and grammarians, several physicians, Euthydemus his colleague in the priesthood, Alexion his father-in-law, and four or five other connections by marriage, Favorinus the philosopher of Arles in Provence, afterwards favored by Hadrian, to whom he dedicates one of his treatises, and who in return wrote an essay called Plutarchus, on the Academic Philosophy. Serapion entertains them in a garden on the banks of the Cephisus. They dine with a friendly physician on the heights of Hyampolis, and meet in a party at the baths of Ædepsus. The questions are of the most miscellaneous description, grave sometimes, and moral, grammatical and antiquarian, and often festive and humorous. *In what sense does Plato say that God uses geometry? Why do we hear better by night than by day? Why are dreams least true in autumn? Which existed first, the hen or the egg? Which of Venus's hands did Diomed wound?* Lamprias, the grandfather, finds fault with his son, Plutarch's father, for *inviting too many guests* to the parties given " when we came home from Alexandria." Ammonius, in office as general at Athens, gives a dinner to the young men who had distinguished themselves at a trial of skill in grammar, rhetoric, geometry, and poetry; and anecdotes are told on the occasion *of verses aptly or inaptly quoted.*

Of the other minor works, some look a good deal like lectures delivered at Rome, and afterwards published with little dedications prefixed. We have a disquisition on the Advantages we can derive from our Enemies, addressed to Cornelius Pulcher, a discourse On Fate, to Piso, and On Brotherly Affection, to Nigrinus and Quintus. Many, however, are dialogues and conversations, with a good deal of the same varied scenery and exuberant detail which embellish the Table-Talk.

In a conversation which he had been present at, " long ago, when Nero was staying in Greece," between Ammonius and some other friends, the meaning of the strange inscription at Delphi, the two letters EI, is debated. A visitor is conducted by some of Plutarch's friends over the sacred buildings at Delphi, and in the intervals between the somewhat tedious speeches of the professional guides, who showed the sights, a discussion takes place on the Nature of the Oracles. " It happened a little before the Pythian games in the time of Callistratus, there met us at Delphi two travellers, from the extremities of the world, Demetrius, the grammarian, on his way home to Tarsus from Britain, and Cleombrotus, the Lacedæmonian, just returned from a journey he had made for his pleasure and instruction in Upper Egypt, and far out into the Erythræan Sea." The question somehow or other occurs, and the dialogue, Of the Cessation of Oracles, ensues; one passage of which is the famous story of the voice that proclaimed the death of the great Pan. Autobulus is talking with Soclarus, the companion of his son, about an encomium which they had heard on hunting; the best praise they can give it is, that it diverts into a less objectionable course the passion which finds one vent in seeing the contests of gladiators. Up come presently a large party of young men, lovers of hunting and fishing, and the question of the Superior Sagacity of ·Land or of Water Animals is formally pleaded by two selected orators. Stories are told of elephants; and Aristotimus, the advocate of the land animals, relates a sight (of the dog imitating in a play the effects of poison) which he himself, he says, saw in Rome, and which was so perfectly acted as to cause emotion in the spectators, the Emperor included; the aged Vespasian himself being present, in the theatre of Marcellus. It reads very much as if Plutarch, and not Aristotimus, had been the eye-witness.*

Autobulus occurs again in the Dialogue on Love. At the request of his friend Flavianus, he repeats a long conversation, attended with curious incidents, in which his father had taken part on Mount Helicon, "once long ago, before we were born, when he brought our mother, after the dispute and variance which had arisen between their parents, that she might offer a sacrifice to Love at the feast held at Thespiæ."

The variance alluded to must clearly have been a fact. And, in general, though these playful fictions or semi-fictions, which form the machinery of the dialogues, are not indeed to be accepted in a literal way, they possess an authenticity which we cannot venture to attribute to the professedly historical statements about their author, given in later writers. Suidas, the lexicographer, repeats a mere romance when he tells us that Trajan gave him the dignity of consul, and issued orders that none of the magistrates in Illyria should do any thing without

---

* Something also of a personal remembrance of Vespasian's unrelentingly severe temper may be thought to appear in the story, related in the Dialogue on Love, of the Gaulish rebel Sabinus, and his wife Eponina, mentioned by Tacitus in his Histories, who, after living in an underground concealment several years, were discovered and put to death. Two sons were born to them in their hiding-place, "one of whom, says Plutarch, "was here with us in Delphi only a little while ago," and he is disposed, he adds, to attribute the subsequent extinction of the race of Vespasian to divine displeasure at this cruel and unfeeling act.

consulting him. Syncellus, the Byzantine historian, under the record of one of the first years of Hadrian's reign, is equally or even more extravagant, relating that Plutarch, the philosopher of Chæronea, was in his old age appointed by the emperor to the office of governor of Greece. Though the period of Trajan and the Antonines was the golden age of philosophers, whose brief persecution under Domitian seems to have won them for a while a sort of spiritual supremacy, similar to that which, after Diocletian, was wrested from them by the ministers of the new religion, still these assertions are on the face of them entirely incredible.

There is a letter, indeed, given among Plutarch's printed works, in which a collection of Sayings of Kings and Commanders is dedicated to Trajan; and though much doubt is entertained, it is not at all improbable that it is Plutarch's own writing. There is nothing remarkable in its contents, and it is most noticeable for the contrast in tone which it presents to another letter, undoubtedly spurious, first published in Latin by John of Salisbury, which is a very preceptorial lecture to Trajan, his pupil, by Plutarch, his supposed former teacher.

A list of Plutarch's works, including many of which nothing remains, is also given by Suidas, as made by Lamprias, Plutarch's son; and a little prefatory letter to a friend, whom he had known in Asia, and who had written to ask for the information, is prefixed to the catalogue. The catalogue itself may be correct enough, but the name of Lamprias occurs nowhere in all Plutarch's extant works as that of one of his sons; and it cannot but be suspected that this family name was adopted, and this letter to the nameless friend in Asia composed, by some grammarian long after, who desired to give interest to an ordinary list of the author's extant writings.

In reading Plutarch, the following points should be remembered. He is a moralist rather than a historian. His interest is less for politics and the changes of empires, and much more for personal character and individual actions and motives to action; duty performed and rewarded; arrogance chastised, hasty anger corrected; humanity, fair dealing, and generosity triumphing in the visible, or relying on the invisible world. His mind in his biographic memoirs is continually running on the Aristotelian Ethics and the high Platonic theories, which formed the religion of the educated population of his time.

The time itself is a second point; that of . Nerva, Trajan, and Hadrian; the commencement of the best and happiest age of the great Roman imperial period. The social system, spreading over all the coasts of the Mediterranean Sea, of which Greece and Italy were the centres, and to which the East and the furthest known West were brought into relation, had then reached its highest mark of advance and consummation. The laws of Rome and the philosophy of Greece were powerful from the Tigris to the British islands. It was the last great era of Greek and Roman literature. Epictetus was teaching in Greek the virtues which Marcus Aurelius was to illustrate as emperor. Dio Chrysostom and Arrian were recalling the memory of the most famous Attic rhetoricians and historians, and while Plutarch wrote in Chæronea, Tacitus, Pliny the Younger, Martial, and Juvenal were writing at Rome. It may be said too, perhaps, not untruly, that the Latin, the metropolitan writers, less faithfully represent the general spirit and character of the time, than what came from the pen of a simple Bœotian provincial, writing in a more universal language, and unwarped by the strong local reminiscences of the old home of the Senate and the Republic. Tacitus and Juvenal have more, perhaps, of the "antique Roman" than of the citizen of the great Mediterranean Empire. The evils of the imperial government, as felt in the capital city, are depicted in the Roman prose and verse more vividly and more vehemently than suits a general representation of the state of the imperial world, even under the rule of Domitian himself.

It is, at any rate, the serener aspect and the better era that the life and writings of Plutarch reflect. His language is that of a man happy in himself and in what is around him. His natural cheerfulness is undiminished, his easy and joyous simplicity is unimpaired, his satisfactions are not saddened or imbittered by any overpowering recollections of years passed under the immediate present terrors of imperial wickedness. Though he also could remember Nero, and had been a man when Domitian was an emperor, the utmost we can say is, that he shows, perhaps, the instructed happiness of one who had lived into good times out of evil, and that the very vigor of his content proves that its roots were fixed amongst circumstances not too indulgent or favorable.

Much has been said of Plutarch's inaccuracy; and it cannot be denied that he is careless about numbers, and occasionally contradicts his own statements. A greater fault, perhaps, is his passion for anecdote; he cannot forbear from repeating stories, the improbability of which he is the first to recognize; which, nevertheless, by mere repetition, leave unjust impressions. He is unfair in this way to Demosthenes and to Pericles, against the latter of whom, however, he doubtless inherited the prejudices which Plato handed down to the philosophers.

It is true, also, that his unhistorical treatment of the subjects of his biography makes him often unsatisfactory and imperfect in the portraits he draws. Much, of course, in the public lives of statesmen can find its only explanation in their political position; and of this Plutarch often knows and thinks little. So far as the researches of modern historians have succeeded in really recovering a knowledge of relations of this sort, so far, undoubtedly, these biographies stand in need of their correction. Yet in the uncertainty which must attend all modern restorations, it is agreeable, and surely, also, profitable, to recur to portraits drawn ere new thoughts and views had occupied the civilized world, without reference to such disputable grounds of judgment, simply upon the broad principles of the ancient moral code of right and wrong.

Making some little deductions in cases such as those that have been mentioned, allowing for a little over-love of story, and for some considerable quasi-religious hostility to the democratic leaders who excited the scorn of Plato, if we bear in mind, also, that in narratives like that of Theseus, he himself confesses his inability to disengage fact from fable, it may be said that in Plutarch's Lives the readers of all ages will find instructive and faithful biographies of the great men of Greece and Rome. Or, at any rate, if in Plutarch's time it was too late to think of really faithful biographies, we have here the faithful record of the historical tradition of his age. This is what, in the second century of our era, Greeks and Romans loved to believe about their warriors and statesmen of the past. As a picture, at least, of the best Greek and Roman moral views and moral judgments, as a presentation of the results of Greek and Roman moral thought, delivered not under the pressure of calamity, but as they existed in ordinary times, and actuated plain-living people in country places in their daily life, Plutarch's writings are of indisputable value; and it may be said, also, that Plutarch's character, as depicted in them, possesses a natural charm of pleasantness and amiability which it is not easy to match among all extant classical authors.

The present translation is a revision of that published at the end of the seventeenth century, with a life of Plutarch written by Dryden, whose name, it was presumed, would throw some reflected lustre on the humbler workmen who performed, better or worse, the more serious labor. There is, of course, a great inequality in their work. But the translation by Langhorne, for which, in the middle of the last century, the older volumes were discarded, is so inferior in liveliness, and is in fact so dull and heavy a book, that, in default of an entirely new translation, some advantage, it is hoped, may be gained by the revival here attempted. It would not have been needed, had Mr. Long not limited the series which he published, with very useful notes, in Mr. Knight's Shilling Library, to the lives connected with the Civil Wars of Rome.

Dryden's Life of Plutarch is, like many of Dryden's writings, hasty yet well written, inaccurate but agreeable to read ; that by Dacier, printed in the last volume of his French translation, is, in many respects, very good. The materials for both were collected, and the references accumulated, by Rualdus, in his laborious Life appended to the old Paris folios of 1624. But every thing that is of any value is given in the articles in Fabricius's Bibliotheca Græca, and, with the most recent additions, in Pauly's German Cyclopædia. Much that is useful is found, as might be expected, in Clinton's Fasti Romani, from which the following table is taken : —

Date. A. D.	OCCURRENCES.	AUTHORS.
41	Accession of Claudius.	
54	Accession of Nero.	
66	Nero comes into Greece; alluded to in Plutarch's Dialogue, On the EI at Delphi.	Seneca. Lucan. Persius.
67	Nero celebrates the Isthmian Games ; alluded to in Plutarch's life of Flamininus.	
68	Galba is Emperor. Civil wars.	
69	Vitellius, Otho, Vespasian.	
70	Taking of Jerusalem.	
74	The Philosophers are expelled from Rome.	
79	Death of Sabinus, the Gaul. Death of Vespasian, and accession of Titus. Eruption of Vesuvius; alluded to by Plutarch, as a recent occurrence, in his Enquiry why the Pythian Oracles are no longer delivered in verse.	Death of Pliny the Elder.

Date. A.D.	OCCURRENCES.	AUTHORS.
81	Accession of Domitian.	Quintilian.
90	The Philosophers are again expelled from Rome, after the death of Rusticus.	Statius. Silius Italicus. Martial.
96	Accession of Nerva.	*Dio Chrysostom.*
98	Accession of Trajan.	Tacitus, born
100	Pliny's Panegyric.	about A.D. 60.
103	Epictetus is teaching at Nicopolis, Arrian attending him.	*Plutarch.* *Epictetus.*
104	Pliny in Bithynia.	*Arrian.*
106	Trajan winters on the Danube; alluded to by Plutarch, On the Principle of Cold.	Pliny the Younger, born, A.D.
113	Erection of Trajan's Column.	61.
114	Trajan's Parthian Victories. Plutarch had written his life of Antony before these.	Juvenal, born A.D. 59.
117	Accession of Hadrian.	*Favorinus.*
	In Hadrian's third year, Plutarch, according to Eusebius, was still alive.	Suetonius, born about A.D. 70.
		Ptolemy.
138	Accession of Antoninus.	*Appian.* *Pausanias.*
161	Accession of Marcus Aurelius.	*Galen.* *Lucian.*
181	Accession of Commodus.	*Athenæus.* *Dion Cassius.*

NOTE. — *The authors whose names are printed in italics are Greek writers.*

The fault which runs through all the earlier biographies, from that of Rualdus downward, is the assumption, wholly untenable, that Plutarch passed many years, as many, perhaps as forty, at Rome. The entire character of his life is of course altered by such an impression. It is, therefore, not worth while reprinting here the life originally prefixed by Dryden to the translations which, with more or less of alteration, follow in the present volumes. One or two characteristic extracts may be sufficient. The first may throw some light on a subject which to modern readers is a little obscure. Dryden is wrong in one or two less important points, but his general view of the *dæmonic* belief which pervades Plutarch's writings is tolerably to the purpose.

" We can only trace the rest of his opinions from his philoso-phy, which we have said in the general to be Platonic, though it cannot also be denied that there was a tincture in it of the Electic * sect, which was begun by Potamon under the empire of Augustus, and which selected from all the other sects what seemed most probable in their opinions, not adher-ing singularly to any of them, nor rejecting every thing. I will only touch his belief of Spirits. In his two Treatises of Oracles, the one concerning the Reason of their Cessation, the other inquiring Why they were not given in Verse as in former times, he seems to assert the Pythagorean doctrine of Trans-migration of Souls. We have formerly shown that he owned the unity of a Godhead; whom, according to his attributes, he calls by several names, as Jupiter from his almighty power, Apollo from his wisdom, and so of the rest; but under him he places those beings whom he styles *Genii* or *Dæmons*, of a middle nature, between divine and human; for he thinks it ab-surd that there should be no mean between the two extremes of an immortal and a mortal being; that there cannot be in nature so vast a flaw, without some intermedial kind of life, partaking of them both. As, therefore, we find the intercourse between the soul and body to be made by the animal spirits, so between divinity and humanity there is this species of dæ-mons. Who,† having first been men, and followed the strict rules of virtue, have purged off the grossness and feculency of their earthly being, are exalted into these genii; and are from thence either raised higher into an ethereal life, if they still continue virtuous, or tumbled down again into mortal bodies, and sinking into flesh after they have lost that purity which constituted their glorious being. And this sort of Genii are

---

* He means the Eclectic, as it is more usually called.

† He means, I believe, *Those who* ;

apparently the word *and* should be omitted in line 29, before *sinking into flesh.*

those who, as our author imagines, presided over oracles ; spirits which have so much of their terrestrial principles remaining in them as to be subject to passions and inclinations; usually beneficent, sometimes malevolent to mankind, according as they refine themselves, or gather dross, and are declining into mortal bodies. The cessation, or rather the decrease of oracles, (for some of them were still remaining in Plutarch's time,) he attributes either to the death of those dæmons, as appears by the story of the Egyptian Thamus, who was commanded to declare that the great god Pan was dead, or to their forsaking of those places where they formerly gave out their oracles, from whence they were driven by stronger Genii into banishment for a certain revolution of ages. Of this last nature were the war of the giants against the gods, the dispossession of Saturn by Jupiter, the banishment of Apollo from heaven, the fall of Vulcan, and many others; all which, according to our author, were the battles of these Genii or Dæmons amongst themselves. But supposing, as Plutarch evidently does, that these spirits administered, under the Supreme Being, the affairs of men, taking care of the virtuous, punishing the bad, and sometimes communicating with the best, as, particularly, the Genius of Socrates always warned him of approaching dangers, and taught him to avoid them, I cannot but wonder that every one who has hitherto written Plutarch's Life, and particularly Rualdus, the most knowing of them all, should so confidently affirm that these oracles were given by bad spirits, according to Plutarch. As Christians, indeed, we may think them so ; but that Plutarch so thought is a most apparent falsehood. 'Tis enough to convince a reasonable man, that our author in his old age, (and that then he doted not, we may see by the treatise he has written, That old men ought to have the management of public affairs,) I say that then he initiated himself in the sacred rites of Delphos, and died, for ought we know, Apollo's priest. Now it is not to be imagined that he thought the God he served a *Cacodæmon*, or, as we call him, a devil. Nothing could be further from the opinion and practice of this holy philosopher than so gross an impiety. The story of the Pythias, or priestess of Apollo, which he relates immediately before the ending of that treatise, concerning the Cessation of Oracles, confirms my assertion rather than shakes it; for 'tis there delivered, 'That going with great reluctation into the sacred place to be inspired, she came out foaming at the mouth, her eyes goggling, her breast heaving, her voice undistinguishable and shrill, as if she had an earthquake within her, laboring for vent; and, in short, that thus tormented with the god, whom she was not able to support, she died distracted in a few days after. For he had said before that the divineress ought to have no perturbations of mind or impure passions at the time when she was to consult the oracle, and if she had, she was no more fit to be inspired than an instrument untuned to render an harmonious sound.' And he gives us to suspect, by what he says at the close of this relation, 'That this Pythias had not lived chastely for some time before it; so that her death appears more like a punishment inflicted for loose living, by some holy Power, than the mere malignancy of a Spirit delighted naturally in mischief.' There is another observation which indeed comes nearer to their purpose; which I will digress so far as to relate, because it somewhat appertains to our own country. 'There are many islands,' says he, 'which lie scattering about Britain, after the manner of our Sporades; they are unpeopled, and some of them are called the Islands of the Heroes, or the Genii.' One Demetrius was sent by the emperor (who by computation of the time must either be Caligula or Claudius*) to discover those parts, and arriving at one of the islands next

---

* Undoubtedly much later.

adjoining to the before mentioned, which was inhabited by some few Britons, (but those held sacred and inviolable by all their countrymen,) immediately after his arrival, the air grew black and troubled, strange apparitions were seen, the winds raised a tempest, and fiery spouts or whirlwinds appeared dancing towards the earth. When these prodigies were ceased, the islanders informed him that some one of the aerial beings, superior to our nature, then ceased to live. For as a taper, while yet burning, affords a pleasant, harmless light, but is noisome and offensive when extinguished, so those heroes shine benignly on us and do us good, but at their death turn all things topsy-turvy, raise up tempests, and infect the air with pestilential vapors. By those holy and inviolable men, there is no question but he means our Druids, who were nearest to the Pythagoreans of any sect; and this opinion of the Genii might probably be one of theirs. Yet it proves not that all dæmons were thus malicious, only those who were to be condemned hereafter into human bodies, for their misdemeanors in their aerial being. But 'tis time to leave a subject so very fanciful, and so little reasonable as this. I am apt to imagine the natural vapors, arising in the cave where the temple afterwards was built, might work upon the spirits of those who entered the holy place, as they did on the shepherd Coretas, who first found it out by accident, and incline them to Enthusiasm and prophetic madness; that as the strength of those vapors diminished, (which were generally in caverns, as that of Mopsus, of Trophonius, and this of Delphos,) so the inspiration decreased by the same measures; that they happened to be stronger when they killed the Pythias, who being conscious of this, was so unwilling to enter; that the oracles ceased to be given in verse when poets ceased to be the priests, and that the Genius of Socrates (whom he confessed never to have seen, but only to have heard inwardly, and unperceived by others,) was no more than the strength of his imagination; or, to speak in the language of a Christian Platonist, his guardian angel."

The concluding passage of the life may serve as a conclusion to this prefatory essay. It is as follows: "And now, with the usual vanity of Dutch prefacers, I could load our author with the praises and commemorations of writers; for both ancient and modern have made honorable mention of him. But to cumber pages with this kind of stuff were to raise a distrust in common readers that Plutarch wants them. Rualdus, indeed, has collected ample testimonies of them; but I will only recite the names of some, and refer you to him for the particular quotations. He reckons Gellius, Eusebius, Himerius the Sophister, Eunapius, Cyrillus of Alexandria, Theodoret, Agathias, Photius and Xiphilin, patriarchs of Constantinople, Johannes Sarisberiensis, the famous Petrarch, Petrus Victorius, and Justus Lipsius.

"But Theodorus Gaza, a man learned in the Latin tongue, and a great restorer of the Greek, who lived above two hundred years ago, deserves to have his suffrage set down in words at length; for the rest have only commended Plutarch more than any single author, but he has extolled him above all together.

"'Tis said that, having this extravagant question put to him by a friend, that if learning must suffer a general shipwreck, and he had only his choice left him of preserving one author, who should be the man he would preserve, he answered, Plutarch; and probably might give this reason, that in saving him, he should secure the best collection of them all.

"The epigram of Agathias deserves also to be remembered. This author flourished about the year five hundred, in the reign of the Emperor Justinian. The verses are extant in the Anthologia, and with the translation of them I will conclude the praises of our author; having first admonished you, that they are supposed to be written on a statue erected by the Romans to his memory.

> " Chæronean Plutarch, to thy deathless praise
> Does martial Rome this grateful statue raise,
> Because both Greece and she thy fame have shared,
> (Their heroes written, and their lives compared).
> But thou thyself couldst never write thy own ;
> Their lives have parallels, but thine has none."

PLUTARCH'S LIVES.

THESEUS.

As geographers, Sosius,* crowd into the edges of their maps parts of the world which they do not know about, adding notes in the margin to the effect, that beyond this lies nothing but sandy deserts full of wild beasts, unapproachable bogs, Scythian ice, or a frozen sea, so, in this work of mine, in which I have compared the lives of the greatest men with one another, after passing through those periods which probable reasoning can reach to and real history find a footing in, I might very well say of those that are farther off, Beyond this there is nothing but prodigies and fictions, the only inhabitants are the poets and inventors of fables; there is no credit, or certainty any farther. Yet, after publishing an account of Lycurgus the lawgiver and Numa the king, I thought I might, not without reason, ascend as high as to Romulus, being brought by my history so near to his time. Considering therefore with myself

> Whom shall I set so great a man to face?
> Or whom oppose? who's equal to the place?

(as Æschylus expresses it), I found none so fit as him that peopled the beautiful and far-famed city of Athens, to be

* Sosius Senecio, Plutarch's friend at Rome, whom he addresses.

set in opposition with the father of the invincible and
renowned city of Rome.   Let us hope that Fable may, in
what shall follow, so submit to the purifying processes of
Reason as to take the character of exact history.   In any
case, however, where it shall be found contumaciously
slighting credibility, and refusing to be reduced to any
thing like probable fact, we shall beg that we may meet
with candid readers, and such as will receive with indulgence the stories of antiquity.

Theseus seemed to me to resemble Romulus in many
particulars.   Both of them, born out of wedlock and of
uncertain parentage, had the repute of being sprung from
the gods.

> Both warriors; that by all the world's allowed.

Both of them united with strength of body an equal vigor
of mind; and of the two most famous cities of the world,
the one built Rome, and the other made Athens be inhabited.   Both stand charged with the rape of women;
neither of them could avoid domestic misfortunes nor
jealousy at home; but towards the close of their lives are
both of them said to have incurred great odium with their
countrymen, if, that is, we may take the stories least like
poetry as our guide to the truth.

The lineage of Theseus, by his father's side, ascends as
high as to Erechtheus and the first inhabitants of Attica.
By his mother's side he was descended of Pelops.   For
Pelops was the most powerful of all the kings of Peloponnesus, not so much by the greatness of his riches as
the multitude of his children, having married many
daughters to chief men, and put many sons in places of
command in the towns round about him.   One of whom,
named Pittheus, grandfather to Theseus, was governor
of the small city of the Trœzenians, and had the repute
of a man of the greatest knowledge and wisdom of his

time; which then, it seems, consisted chiefly in grave maxims, such as the poet Hesiod got his great fame by, in his book of Works and Days. And, indeed, among these is one that they ascribe to Pittheus, —

Unto a friend suffice
A stipulated price; *

which, also, Aristotle mentions. And Euripides, by calling Hippolytus "scholar of the holy Pittheus," shows the opinion that the world had of him.

Ægeus, being desirous of children, and consulting the oracle of Delphi, received the celebrated answer which forbade him the company of any woman before his return to Athens. But the oracle being so obscure as not to satisfy him that he was clearly forbid this, he went to Trœzen, and communicated to Pittheus the voice of the god, which was in this manner, —

Loose not the wine-skin foot, thou chief of men,
Until to Athens thou art come again.

Pittheus, therefore, taking advantage from the obscurity of the oracle, prevailed upon him, it is uncertain whether by persuasion or deceit, to lie with his daughter Æthra. Ægeus afterwards, knowing her whom he had lain with to be Pittheus's daughter, and suspecting her to be with child by him, left a sword and a pair of shoes, hiding them under a great stone that had a hollow in it exactly fitting them; and went away making her only

* In the Works and Days this proverb, as it now stands, certainly means, "Stipulate your price beforehand with your friend." "Even," adds the following line, "in a bargain with your brother, laugh, and call in a witness." Aristotle understood it to say, that no one can claim, in justice, more than the sum that had been first agreed upon. Before Hesiod, however, and perhaps originally in Hesiod, it may have simply been an injunction to *pay a friend fairly and fully the price that at first was appointed.*

privy to it, and commanding her, if she brought forth a
son who, when he came to man's estate, should be able to
lift up the stone and take away what he had left there,
she should send him away to him with those things with
all secrecy, and with injunctions to him as much as possible to conceal his journey from every one; for he greatly
feared the Pallantidæ, who were continually mutinying
against him, and despised him for his want of children,
they themselves being fifty brothers, all sons of Pallas.*

When Æthra was delivered of a son, some say that
he was immediately named Theseus, from the tokens
which his father had *put†* under the stone; others that
he received his name afterwards at Athens, when Ægeus
acknowledged† him for his son. He was brought up under
his grandfather Pittheus, and had a tutor and attendant
set over him named Connidas, to whom the Athenians,
even to this time, the day before the feast that is dedicated to Theseus, sacrifice a ram, giving this honor to his
memory upon much juster grounds than to Silanio and
Parrhasius, for making pictures and statues of Theseus.
There being then a custom for the Grecian youth, upon
their first coming to man's estate, to go to Delphi and
offer first-fruits of their hair to the god, Theseus also
went thither, and a place there to this day is yet named
Thesea, as it is said, from him. He clipped only the fore
part of his head, as Homer says the Abantes did.‡ And
this sort of tonsure was from him named Theseis. The
Abantes first used it, not in imitation of the Arabians,
as some imagine, nor of the Mysians, but because they
were a warlike people, and used to close fighting, and
above all other nations accustomed to engage hand to
hand; as Archilochus testifies in these verses: —

* Brother to Ægeus.
† Thésis, putting: Thesthai, to take to oneself, to adopt or ac-
knowledge, as a son.
‡ The Euboeans of the Iliad.

Slings shall not whirl, nor many arrows fly,
   When on the plain the battle joins; but swords,
Man against man, the deadly conflict try,
   As is the practice of Eubœa's lords
Skilled with the spear. ——

Therefore that they might not give their enemies a hold by their hair, they cut it in this manner. They write also that this was the reason why Alexander gave command to his captains that all the beards of the Macedonians should be shaved, as being the readiest hold for an enemy.

Æthra for some time concealed the true parentage of Theseus, and a report was given out by Pittheus that he was begotten by Neptune; for the Trœzenians pay Neptune the highest veneration. He is their tutelar god, to him they offer all their first-fruits, and in his honor stamp their money with a trident.

Theseus displaying not only great strength of body, but equal bravery, and a quickness alike and force of understanding, his mother Æthra, conducting him to the stone, and informing him who was his true father, commanded him to take from thence the tokens that Ægeus had left, and to sail to Athens. He without any difficulty set himself to the stone and lifted it up; but refused to take his journey by sea, though it was much the safer way, and though his mother and grandfather begged him to do so. For it was at that time very dangerous to go by land on the road to Athens, no part of it being free from robbers and murderers. That age produced a sort of men, in force of hand, and swiftness of foot, and strength of body, excelling the ordinary rate, and wholly incapable of fatigue; making use, however, of these gifts of nature to no good or profitable purpose for mankind, but rejoicing and priding themselves in insolence, and taking the benefit of their superior strength in the exercise of inhu-

manity and cruelty, and in seizing, forcing, and commit-
ting all manner of outrages upon every thing that fell into
their hands; all respect for others, all justice, they thought,
all equity and humanity, though naturally lauded by
common people, either out of want of courage to commit
injuries or fear to receive them, yet no way concerned
those who were strong enough to win for themselves.
Some of these, Hercules destroyed and cut off in his passage through these countries, but some, escaping his notice
while he was passing by, fled and hid themselves, or else
were spared by him in contempt of their abject submission ; and after that Hercules fell into misfortune, and,
having slain Iphitus, retired to Lydia, and for a long time
was there slave to Omphale, a punishment which he had
imposed upon himself for the murder, then, indeed,
Lydia enjoyed high peace and security, but in Greece
and the countries about it the like villanies again re-
vived and broke out, there being none to repress or chastise them.   It was therefore a very hazardous journey to
travel by land from Athens to Peloponnesus; and Pittheus, giving him an exact account of each of these robbers and villains, their strength, and the cruelty they used
to all strangers, tried to persuade Theseus to go by sea.
But he, it seems, had long since been secretly fired by
the glory of Hercules, held him in the highest estima-
tion, and was never more satisfied than in listening to any
that gave an account of him ; especially those that had
seen him, or had been present at any action or saying of
his.   So that he was altogether in the same state of feeling as, in after ages, Themistocles was, when he said that
he could not sleep for the trophy of Miltiades ; entertaining such admiration for the virtue of Hercules, that in
the night his dreams were all of that hero's actions, and in
the day a continual emulation stirred him up to perform

the like. Besides, they were related, being born of cousins german. For Æthra was daughter of Pittheus, and Alcmena of Lysidice; and Lysidice and Pittheus were brother and sister, children of Hippodamia and Pelops. He thought it therefore a dishonorable thing, and not to be endured, that Hercules should go out everywhere, and purge both land and sea from wicked men, and he himself should fly from the like adventures that actually came in his way; disgracing his reputed father by a mean flight by sea, and not showing his true one as good evidence of the greatness of his birth by noble and worthy actions, as by the tokens that he brought with him, the shoes and the sword.

With this mind and these thoughts, he set forward with a design to do injury to nobody, but to repel and revenge himself of all those that should offer any. And first of all, in a set combat, he slew Periphetes, in the neighborhood of Epidaurus, who used a club for his arms, and from thence had the name of Corynetes, or the club-bearer; who seized upon him, and forbade him to go forward in his journey. Being pleased with the club, he took it, and made it his weapon, continuing to use it as Hercules did the lion's skin, on whose shoulders that served to prove how huge a beast he had killed; and to the same end Theseus carried about him this club; overcome indeed by him, but now, in his hands, invincible.

Passing on further towards the Isthmus of Peloponnesus, he slew Sinnis, often surnamed the Bender of Pines, after the same manner in which he himself had destroyed many others before. And this he did without having either practised or ever learnt the art of bending these trees, to show that natural strength is above all art. This Sinnis had a daughter of remarkable beauty and stature, called Perigune, who, when her father was killed, fled, and was sought after everywhere by Theseus; and coming into a place overgrown with brushwood, shrubs,

and asparagus-thorn, there, in a childlike, innocent manner,
prayed and begged them, as if they understood her, to
give her shelter, with vows that if she escaped she would
never cut them down nor burn them.   But Theseus calling upon her, and giving her his promise that he would
use her with respect, and offer her no injury, she came
forth, and in due time bore him a son, named Melanippus; but afterwards was married to Deioneus, the son of
Eurytus, the Œchalian, Theseus himself giving her to
him.   Ioxus, the son of this Melanippus who was born to
Theseus, accompanied Ornytus in the colony that he
carried with him into Caria, whence it is a family usage
amongst the people called Ioxids, both male and female,
never to burn either shrubs or asparagus-thorn, but to
respect and honor them.

The Crommyonian sow, which they called Phæa, was a
savage and formidable wild beast, by no means an enemy
to be despised.   Theseus killed her, going out of his way
on purpose to meet and engage her, so that he might not
seem to perform all his great exploits out of mere necessity; being also of opinion that it was the part of a brave
man to chastise villanous and wicked men when attacked
by them, but to seek out and overcome the more noble
wild beasts.   Others relate that Phæa was a woman, a
robber full of cruelty and lust, that lived in Crommyon,
and had the name of Sow given her from the foulness of
her life and manners, and afterwards was killed by Theseus.   He slew also Sciron, upon the borders of Megara,
casting him down from the rocks, being, as most report, a
notorious robber of all passengers, and, as others add, accustomed, out of insolence and wantonness, to stretch forth
his feet to strangers, commanding them to wash them,
and then while they did it, with a kick to send them down
the rock into the sea.   The writers of Megara, however,
in contradiction to the received report, and, as Simonides

expresses it, "fighting with all antiquity," contend that Sciron was neither a robber nor doer of violence, but a punisher of all such, and the relative and friend of good and just men; for Æacus, they say, was ever esteemed a man of the greatest sanctity of all the Greeks; and Cychreus, the Salaminian, was honored at Athens with divine worship; and the virtues of Peleus and Telamon were not unknown to any one. Now Sciron was son-in-law to Cychreus, father-in-law to Æacus, and grandfather to Peleus and Telamon, who were both of them sons of Endeis, the daughter of Sciron and Chariclo; it was not probable, therefore, that the best of men should make these alliances with one who was worst, giving and receiving mutually what was of greatest value and most dear to them. Theseus, by their account, did not slay Sciron in his first journey to Athens, but afterwards, when he took Eleusis, a city of the Megarians, having circumvented Diocles, the governor. Such are the contradictions in this story. In Eleusis he killed Cercyon, the Arcadian, in a wrestling match. And going on a little farther, in Erineus, he slew Damastes, otherwise called Procrustes, forcing his body to the size of his own bed, as he himself was used to do with all strangers; this he did in imitation of Hercules, who always returned upon his assailants the same sort of violence that they offered to him; sacrificed Busiris, killed Antæus in wrestling, and Cycnus in single combat, and Termerus by breaking his skull in pieces (whence, they say, comes the proverb of "a Termerian mischief"), for it seems Termerus killed passengers that he met, by running with his head against them. And so also Theseus proceeded in the punishment of evil men, who underwent the same violence from him which they had inflicted upon others, justly suffering after the manner of their own injustice.

As he went forward on his journey, and was come as far as the river Cephisus, some of the race of the Phytalidæ met him and saluted him, and, upon his desire to use the purifications, then in custom, they performed them with all the usual ceremonies, and, having offered propitiatory sacrifices to the gods, invited him and entertained him at their house, a kindness which, in all his journey hitherto, he had not met.

On the eighth day of Cronius, now called Hecatombæon, he arrived at Athens, where he found the public affairs full of all confusion, and divided into parties and factions, Ægeus also, and his whole private family, laboring under the same distemper; for Medea, having fled from Corinth, and promised Ægeus to make him, by her art, capable of having children, was living with him. She first was aware of Theseus, whom as yet Ægeus did not know, and he being in years, full of jealousies and suspicions, and fearing every thing by reason of the faction that was then in the city, she easily persuaded him to kill him by poison at a banquet, to which he was to be invited as a stranger. He, coming to the entertainment, thought it not fit to discover himself at once, but, willing to give his father the occasion of first finding him out, the meat being on the table, he drew his sword as if he designed to cut with it; Ægeus, at once recognizing the token, threw down the cup of poison, and, questioning his son, embraced him, and, having gathered together all his citizens, owned him publicly before them, who, on their part, received him gladly for the fame of his greatness and bravery; and it is said, that when the cup fell, the poison was spilt there where now is the enclosed space in the Delphinium; for in that place stood Ægeus's house, and the figure of Mercury on the east side of the temple is called the Mercury of Ægeus's gate.

The sons of Pallas, who before were quiet, upon expectation of recovering the kingdom after Ægeus's death, who was without issue, as soon as Theseus appeared and was acknowledged the successor, highly resenting that Ægeus first, an adopted son only of Pandion, and not at all related to the family of Erechtheus, should be holding the kingdom, and that after him, Theseus, a visitor and stranger, should be destined to succeed to it, broke out into open war. And, dividing themselves into two companies, one part of them marched openly from Sphettus, with their father, against the city, the other, hiding themselves in the village of Gargettus, lay in ambush, with a design to set upon the enemy on both sides. They had with them a crier of the township of Agnus, named Leos, who discovered to Theseus all the designs of the Pallantidæ. He immediately fell upon those that lay in ambuscade, and cut them all off; upon tidings of which Pallas and his company fled and were dispersed.

From hence they say is derived the custom among the people of the township of Pallene to have no marriages or any alliance with the people of Agnus, nor to suffer the criers to pronounce in their proclamations the words used in all other parts of the country, Acouĕtĕ Leoi (Hear ye people), hating the very sound of Leo, because of the treason of Leos.

Theseus, longing to be in action, and desirous also to make himself popular, left Athens to fight with the bull of Marathon, which did no small mischief to the inhabitants of Tetrapolis. And having overcome it, he brought it alive in triumph through the city, and afterwards sacrificed it to the Delphinian Apollo. The story of Hecale, also, of her receiving and entertaining Theseus in this expedition, seems to be not altogether void of truth; for the townships round about, meeting upon a certain day,

used to offer a sacrifice, which they called Hecalesia, to
Jupiter Hecaleius, and to pay honor to Hecale, whom, by
a diminutive name, they called Hecalene, because she,
while entertaining Theseus, who was quite a youth, addressed him, as old people do, with similar endearing
diminutives ; and having made a vow to Jupiter for him
as he was going to the fight, that, if he returned in safety,
she would offer sacrifices in thanks of it, and dying before
he came back, she had these honors given her by way
of return for her hospitality, by the command of Theseus,
as Philochorus tells us.

Not long after arrived the third time from Crete the
collectors of the tribute which the Athenians paid them
upon the following occasion. Androgeus having been
treacherously murdered in the confines of Attica, not only
Minos, his father, put the Athenians to extreme distress by
a perpetual war, but the gods also laid waste their country ; both famine and pestilence lay heavy upon them, and
even their rivers were dried up.   Being told by the oracle
that, if they appeased and reconciled Minos, the anger of
the gods would cease and they should enjoy rest from the
miseries they labored under, they sent heralds, and with
much supplication were at last reconciled, entering into
an agreement to send to Crete every nine years a tribute
of seven young men and as many virgins, as most writers
agree in stating ; and the most poetical story adds, that
the Minotaur destroyed them, or that, wandering in the
labyrinth, and finding no possible means of getting out,
they miserably ended their lives there ; and that this
Minotaur was (as Euripides hath it)

> A mingled form, where two strange shapes combined,
> And different natures, bull and man, were joined.

But Philochorus says that the Cretans will by no means

allow the truth of this, but say that the labyrinth was only an ordinary prison, having no other bad quality but that it secured the prisoners from escaping, and that Minos, having instituted games in honor of Androgeus, gave, as a reward to the victors, these youths, who in the mean time were kept in the labyrinth ; and that the first that overcame in those games was one of the greatest power and command among them, named Taurus, a man of no merciful or gentle disposition, who treated the Athenians that were made his prize in a proud and cruel manner. Also Aristotle himself, in the account that he gives of the form of government of the Bottiæans, is manifestly of opinion that the youths were not slain by Minos, but spent the remainder of their days in slavery in Crete ; that the Cretans, in former times, to acquit themselves of an ancient vow which they had made, were used to send an offering of the first-fruits of their men to Delphi, and that some descendants of these Athenian slaves were mingled with them and sent amongst them, and, unable to get their living there, removed from thence, first into Italy, and settled about Japygia; from thence again, that they removed to Thrace, and were named Bottiæans ; and that this is the reason why, in a certain sacrifice, the Bottiæan girls sing a hymn beginning *Let us go to Athens.* This may show us how dangerous a thing it is to incur the hostility of a city that is mistress of eloquence and song. For Minos was always ill spoken of, and represented ever as a very wicked man, in the Athenian theatres ; neither did Hesiod avail him by calling him "the most royal Minos," nor Homer, who styles him " *Jupiter's familiar friend ;* " the tragedians got the better, and from the vantage ground of the stage showered down obloquy upon him, as a man of cruelty and violence ; whereas, in fact, he appears to have been a king and a lawgiver, and

Rhadamanthus a judge under him, administering the statutes that he ordained.

Now when the time of the third tribute was come, and the fathers who had any young men for their sons were to proceed by lot to the choice of those that were to be sent, there arose fresh discontents and accusations against Ægeus among the people, who were full of grief and indignation that he, who was the cause of all their miseries, was the only person exempt from the punishment; adopting and settling his kingdom upon a bastard and foreign son, he took no thought, they said, of their destitution and loss, not of bastards, but lawful children. These things sensibly affected Theseus, who, thinking it but just not to disregard, but rather partake of, the sufferings of his fellow citizens, offered himself for one without any lot. All else were struck with admiration for the nobleness and with love for the goodness of the act; and Ægeus, after prayers and entreaties, finding him inflexible and not to be persuaded, proceeded to the choosing of the rest by lot. Hellanicus, however, tells us that the Athenians did not send the young men and virgins by lot, but that Minos himself used to come and make his own choice, and pitched upon Theseus before all others; according to the conditions agreed upon between them, namely, that the Athenians should furnish them with a ship, and that the young men that were to sail with him should carry no weapon of war; but that if the Minotaur was destroyed, the tribute should cease.

On the two former occasions of the payment of the tribute, entertaining no hopes of safety or return, they sent out the ship with a black sail, as to unavoidable destruction; but now, Theseus encouraging his father and speaking greatly of himself, as confident that he should kill the Minotaur, he gave the pilot another sail, which was white, commanding him, as he returned, if Theseus were safe, to make use of that; but if not, to sail with the black one, and to hang out that sign of his misfortune. Simonides says that the sail which Ægeus delivered to the pilot was not white, but

> Scarlet, in the juicy bloom
> Of the living oak-tree steeped,*

and that this was to be the sign of their escape. Phereclus, son of Amarsyas, according to Simonides, was pilot of the ship. But Philochorus says Theseus had sent him by Scirus, from Salamis, Nausithoüs to be his steersman, and Phæax his look-out-man in the prow, the Athenians having as yet not applied themselves to navigation; and that Scirus did this because one of the young men, Menesthes, was his daughter's son; and this the chapels of Nausithoüs and Phæax, built by Theseus near the temple of Scirus, confirm. He adds, also, that the feast named Cybernesia † was in honor of them. The lot being cast, and Theseus having received out of the Prytaneüm those upon whom it fell, he went to the Delphinium, and made an offering for them to Apollo of his suppliant's badge, which was a bough of a consecrated olive tree, with white wool tied about it.

Having thus performed his devotion, he went to sea, the sixth day of Munychion, on which day even to this time the Athenians send their virgins to the same temple to make supplication to the gods. It is farther reported that he was commanded by the oracle at Delphi to make Venus his guide, and to invoke her as the companion and conductress of his voyage, and that, as he was sacrificing a she goat to her by the seaside, it was suddenly changed into a he, and for this cause that goddess had the name of Epitragia. ‡

---

* Prinus, the scarlet-oak.   ‡ Trăgos, a he goat.
† Pilots' feast.

When he arrived at Crete, as most of the ancient historians as well as poets tell us, having a clue of thread
given him by Ariadne, who had fallen in love with him,
and being instructed by her how to use it so as to con
duct him through the windings of the labyrinth, he
escaped out of it and slew the Minotaur, and sailed back,
taking along with him Ariadne and the young Athenian
captives. Pherecydes adds that he bored holes in the bot-
toms of the Cretan ships to hinder their pursuit. Demon
writes that Taurus, the chief captain of Minos, was slain
by Theseus at the mouth of the port, in a naval combat,
as he was sailing out for Athens. But Philochorus gives
us the story thus: That at the setting forth of the yearly
games by king Minos, Taurus was expected to carry away
the prize, as he had done before; and was much grudged
the honor. His character and manners made his power
hateful, and he was accused moreover of too near familiarity with Pasiphae, for which reason, when Theseus
desired the combat, Minos readily complied. And as it
was a custom in Crete that the women also should be
admitted to the sight of these games, Ariadne, being present, was struck with admiration of the manly beauty of
Theseus, and the vigor and address which he showed in
the combat, overcoming all that encountered with him.
Minos, too, being extremely pleased with him, especially
because he had overthrown and disgraced Taurus, voluntarily gave up the young captives to Theseus, and remitted the tribute to the Athenians. Clidemus gives an
account peculiar to himself, very ambitiously, and beginning a great way back: That it was a decree consented
to by all Greece, that no vessel from any place, containing
above five persons, should be permitted to sail, Jason only
excepted, who was made captain of the great ship Argo,
to sail about and scour the sea of pirates. But Dædalus
having escaped from Crete, and flying by sea to Athens,

Minos, contrary to this decree, pursued him with his ships of war, was forced by a storm upon Sicily, and there ended his life. After his decease, Deucalion, his son, desiring a quarrel with the Athenians, sent to them, demanding that they should deliver up Dædalus to him, threatening, upon their refusal, to put to death all the young Athenians whom his father had received as hostages from the city. To this angry message Theseus returned a very gentle answer, excusing himself that he could not deliver up Dædalus, who was nearly related to him, being his cousin-german, his mother being Merope, the daughter of Erechtheus. In the mean while he secretly prepared a navy, part of it at home near the village of the Thymœtadæ, a place of no resort, and far from any common roads, the other part by his grandfather Pittheus's means at Trœzen, that so his design might be carried on with the greatest secrecy. As soon as ever his fleet was in readiness, he set sail, having with him Dædalus and other exiles from Crete for his guides; and none of the Cretans having any knowledge of his coming, but imagining, when they saw his fleet, that they were friends and vessels of their own, he soon made himself master of the port, and, immediately making a descent, reached Gnossus before any notice of his coming, and, in a battle before the gates of the labyrinth, put Deucalion and all his guards to the sword. The government by this means falling to Ariadne, he made a league with her, and received the captives of her, and ratified a perpetual friendship between the Athenians and the Cretans, whom he engaged under an oath never again to commence any war with Athens.

There are yet many other traditions about these things, and as many concerning Ariadne, all inconsistent with each other. Some relate that she hung herself, being deserted by Theseus. Others that she was carried away by his sailors to the isle of Naxos, and married to Œnarus, priest of Bacchus; and that Theseus left her because he fell in love with another,

> For Ægle's love was burning in his breast;

a verse which Hereas, the Megarian, says, was formerly in the poet Hesiod's works, but put out by Pisistratus, in like manner as he added in Homer's Raising of the Dead, to gratify the Athenians, the line

> Theseus, Pirithous, mighty sons of gods.

Others say Ariadne had sons also by Theseus, Œnopion and Staphylus; and among these is the poet Ion of Chios, who writes of his own native city

> Which once Œnopion, son of Theseus, built.

But the more famous of the legendary stories everybody (as I may say) has in his mouth. In Pæon, however, the Amathusian, there is a story given, differing from the rest. For he writes that Theseus, being driven by a storm upon the isle of Cyprus, and having aboard with him Ariadne, big with child, and extremely discomposed with the rolling of the sea, set her on shore, and left her there alone, to return himself and help the ship, when, on a sudden, a violent wind carried him again out to sea. That the women of the island received Ariadne very kindly, and did all they could to console and alleviate her distress at being left behind. That they counterfeited kind letters, and delivered them to her, as sent from Theseus, and, when she fell in labor, were diligent in performing to her every needful service; but that she died before she could be delivered, and was honorably interred. That soon after Theseus returned, and was greatly afflicted for her loss, and at his departure left a sum of money among the people of the island, ordering them to do sacrifice to Ariadne; and caused two little images to be made and dedicated to her, one of silver and the other of brass. Moreover, that on the second day of Gorpiæus,* which is sacred to Ariadne, they have this ceremony among their sacrifices, to have a youth lie down and with his voice and gesture represent the pains of a woman in travail; and that the Amathusians call the grove in which they show her tomb, the grove of Venus Ariadne.

Differing yet from this account, some of the Naxians write that there were two Minoses and two Ariadnes, one of whom, they say, was married to Bacchus, in the isle of Naxos, and bore the children Staphylus and his brother; but that the other, of a later age, was carried off by Theseus, and, being afterwards deserted by him, retired to Naxos with her nurse Corcyna, whose grave they yet show. That this Ariadne also died there, and was worshipped by the island, but in a different manner from the former; for her day is celebrated with general joy and revelling, but all the sacrifices performed to the latter are attended with mourning and gloom.

.Now Theseus, in his return from Crete, put in at Delos, and, having sacrificed to the god of the island, dedicated to the temple the image of Venus which Ariadne had given him, and danced with the young Athenians a dance that, in memory of him, they say is still preserved among the inhabitants of Delos, consisting in certain measured turnings and returnings, imitative of the windings and twistings of the labyrinth. And this dance, as Dicæarchus writes, is called among the Delians, the Crane. This he danced round the Ceratonian Altar,† so called from its consisting of horns taken from the left side of the head. They say also that he instituted games in Delos, where

* September.　　　† Kĕras, a horn.

he was the first that began the custom of giving a palm
to the victors.

When they were come near the coast of Attica, so great
was the joy for the happy success of their voyage, that
neither Theseus himself nor the pilot remembered to hang
out the sail which should have been the token of their
safety to Ægeus, who, in despair at the sight, threw himself
headlong from a rock, and perished in the sea. But Theseus, being arrived at the port of Phalerum, paid there the
sacrifices which he had vowed to the gods at his setting
out to sea, and sent a herald to the city to carry the news
of his safe return. At his entrance, the herald found the
people for the most part full of grief for the loss of their
king, others, as may well be believed, as full of joy for
the tidings that he brought, and eager to welcome him
and crown him with garlands for his good news, which he
indeed accepted of, but hung them upon his herald's
staff; and thus returning to the seaside before Theseus
had finished his libation to the gods, he stayed apart for
fear of disturbing the holy rites, but, as soon as the libation was ended, went up and related the king's death,
upon the hearing of which, with great lamentations and
a confused tumult of grief, they ran with all haste to the
city. And from hence, they say, it comes that at this day,
in the feast of Oschophoria, the herald is not crowned, but
his staff, and all who are present at the libation cry out
eleleu, iou, iou, the first of which confused sounds is commonly used by men in haste, or at a triumph, the other
is proper to people in consternation or disorder of mind.

Theseus, after the funeral of his father, paid his vows
to Apollo the seventh day of Pyanepsion; for on that day
the youth that returned with him safe from Crete made
their entry into the city. They say, also, that the custom
of boiling pulse at this feast is derived from hence; because the young men that escaped put all that was left

of their provision together, and, boiling it in one common pot, feasted themselves with it, and ate it all up together. Hence, also, they carry in procession an olive branch bound about with wool (such as they then made use of in their supplications), which they call Eiresione, crowned with all sorts of fruits, to signify that scarcity and barrenness was ceased, singing in their procession this song:

Eiresione bring figs, and Eiresione bring loaves;
Bring us honey in pints, and oil to rub on our bodies,
And a strong flagon of wine, for all to go mellow to bed on.

Although some hold opinion that this ceremony is retained in memory of the Heraclidæ, who were thus entertained and brought up by the Athenians. But most are of the opinion which we have given above.

The ship wherein Theseus and the youth of Athens returned had thirty oars, and was preserved by the Athenians down even to the time of Demetrius Phalereus, for they took away the old planks as they decayed, putting in new and stronger timber in their place, insomuch that this ship became a standing example among the philosophers, for the logical question as to things that grow;* one side holding that the ship remained the same, and the other contending that it was not the same.

The feast called Oschophoria, or the feast of boughs, which to this day the Athenians celebrate, was then first instituted by Theseus. For he took not with him the full number of virgins which by lot were to be carried away, but selected two youths of his acquaintance, of fair and womanish faces, but of a manly and forward spirit, and having, by frequent baths, and avoiding the

---

* The Problem called Auxano-měnos, the grower, like the more famous one called Pseudoměnos, the liar.

heat and scorching of the sun, with a constant use of all
the ointments and washes and dresses that serve to the
adorning of the head or smoothing the skin or improving
the complexion, in a manner changed them from what
they were before, and having taught them farther to
counterfeit the very voice and carriage and gait of virgins,
so that there could not be the least difference perceived;
he, undiscovered by any, put them into the number of
the Athenian maids designed for Crete. At his return,
he and these two youths led up a solemn procession, in
the same habit that is now worn by those who carry the
vine-branches. These branches they carry in honor of
Bacchus and Ariadne, for the sake of their story before
related; or rather because they happened to return in autumn, the time of gathering the grapes. The women
whom they call Deipnopheræ, or supper-carriers, are taken
into these ceremonies, and assist at the sacrifice, in remembrance and imitation of the mothers of the young
men and virgins upon whom the lot fell, for thus they ran
about bringing bread and meat to their children; and
because the women then told their sons and daughters
many tales and stories, to comfort and encourage them
under the danger they were going upon, it has still continued a custom that at this feast old fables and tales
should be told. For these particularities we are indebted
to the history of Demon. There was then a place chosen
out, and a temple erected in it to Theseus, and those families out of whom the tribute of the youth was gathered
were appointed to pay a tax to the temple for sacrifices
to him. And the house of the Phytalidæ had the over-
seeing of these sacrifices, Theseus doing them that honor
in recompense of their former hospitality.

Now, after the death of his father Ægeus, forming in
his mind a great and wonderful design, he gathered to-

gether all the inhabitants of Attica into one town, and
made them one people of one city, whereas before they
lived dispersed, and were not easy to assemble upon any
affair for the common interest. Nay, differences and even
wars often occurred between them, which he by his persuasions appeased, going from township to township, and
from tribe to tribe. And those of a more private and
mean condition readily embracing such good advice, to
those of greater power he promised a commonwealth
without monarchy, a democracy, or people's government,
in which he should only be continued as their commander
in war and the protector of their laws, all things else
being equally distributed among them; — and by this
means brought a part of them over to his proposal. The
rest, fearing his power, which was already grown very formidable, and knowing his courage and resolution, chose
rather to be persuaded than forced into a compliance.
He then dissolved all the distinct state-houses, council
halls, and magistracies, and built one common state-house *
and council hall on the site of the present upper town,
and gave the name of Athens to the whole state, ordaining a common feast and sacrifice, which he called Panathenæa, or the sacrifice of all the united Athenians. He
instituted also another sacrifice, called Metœcia, or Feast
of Migration, which is yet celebrated on the sixteenth
day of Hecatombæon. Then, as he had promised, he laid
down his regal power and proceeded to order a commonwealth, entering upon this great work not without advice
from the gods. For having sent to consult the oracle of
Delphi concerning the fortune of his new government
and city, he received this answer:

> Son of the Pitthean maid,
> To your town the terms and fates,

* Prytaneum.

My father gives of many states.
Be not anxious nor afraid ;
The bladder will not fail to swim
On the waves that compass him.

Which oracle, they say, one of the sibyls long after did in a manner repeat to the Athenians, in this verse,

The bladder may be dipt, but not be drowned.

Farther yet designing to enlarge his city, he invited all strangers to come and enjoy equal privileges with the natives, and it is said that the common form, *Come hither all ye people,* was the words that Theseus proclaimed when he thus set up a commonwealth, in a manner, for all nations. Yet he did not suffer his state, by the promiscuous multitude that flowed in, to be turned into confusion and be left without any order or degree, but was the first that divided the Commonwealth into three distinct ranks, the noblemen, the husbandmen, and artificers.* To the nobility he committed the care of religion, the choice of magistrates, the teaching and dispensing of the laws, and interpretation and direction in all sacred matters; the whole city being, as it were, reduced to an exact equality, the nobles excelling the rest in honor, the husbandmen in profit, and the artificers in number. And that Theseus was the first, who, as Aristotle says, out of an inclination to popular government, parted with the regal power, Homer also seems to testify, in his catalogue of the ships, where he gives the name of *People* to the Athenians only.

He also coined money, and stamped it with the image of an ox, either in memory of the Marathonian bull, or of Taurus, whom he vanquished, or else to put his people in mind to follow husbandry; and from this coin came

* Eupatridæ, Geomŏri, Demiurgi.

the expression so frequent among the Greeks, of a thing being worth ten or a hundred oxen. After this he joined Megara to Attica, and erected that famous pillar on the Isthmus, which bears an inscription of two lines, showing the bounds of the two countries that meet there. On the east side the inscription is, —

Peloponnesus there, Ionia here,

and on the west side, —

Peloponnesus here, Ionia there.

He also instituted the games, in emulation of Hercules, being ambitious that as the Greeks, by that hero's appointment, celebrated the Olympian games to the honor of Jupiter, so, by his institution, they should celebrate the Isthmian to the honor of Neptune. For those that were there before observed, dedicated to Melicerta, were performed privately in the night, and had the form rather of a religious rite than of an open spectacle or public feast. There are some who say that the Isthmian games were first instituted in memory of Sciron, Theseus thus making expiation for his death, upon account of the nearness of kindred between them, Sciron being the son of Canethus and Heniocha, the daughter of Pittheus; though others write that Sinnis, not Sciron, was their son, and that to his honor, and not to the other's, these games were ordained by Theseus. At the same time he made an agreement with the Corinthians, that they should allow those that came from Athens to the celebration of the Isthmian games as much space of honor before the rest to behold the spectacle in, as the sail of the ship that brought them thither, stretched to its full extent, could cover; so Hellanicus and Andro of Halicarnassus have established.

Concerning his voyage into the Euxine Sea, Philochorus

and some others write that he made it with Hercules, offering him his service in the war against the Amazons, and had Antiope given him for the reward of his valor; but the greater number, of whom are Pherecydes, Hellanicus, and Herodorus, write that he made this voyage many years after Hercules, with a navy under his own command, and took the Amazon prisoner, — the more probable story, for we do not read that any other, of all those that accompanied him in this action, took any Amazon prisoner. Bion adds, that, to take her, he had to use deceit and fly away; for the Amazons, he says, being naturally lovers of men, were so far from avoiding Theseus when he touched upon their coasts, that they sent him presents to his ship; but he, having invited Antiope, who brought them, to come aboard, immediately set sail and carried her away. An author named Menecrates, that wrote the History of Nicæa in Bithynia, adds, that Theseus, having Antiope aboard his vessel, cruised for some time about those coasts, and that there were in the same ship three young men of Athens, that accompanied him in this voyage, all brothers, whose names were Euneos, Thoas, and Soloon. The last of these fell desperately in love with Antiope; and, escaping the notice of the rest, revealed the secret only to one of his most intimate acquaintance, and employed him to disclose his passion to Antiope, she rejected his pretences with a very positive denial, yet treated the matter with much gentleness and discretion, and made no complaint to Theseus of any thing that had happened; but Soloon, the thing being desperate, leaped into a river near the seaside and drowned himself. As soon as Theseus was acquainted with his death, and his unhappy love that was the cause of it, he was extremely distressed, and, in the height of his grief, an oracle which he had formerly received at Delphi came into his mind; for he had been commanded by the priestess of Apollo Pythius, that, wherever in a strange land he was most sorrowful and under the greatest affliction, he should build a city there, and leave some of his followers to be governors of the place. For this cause he there founded a city, which he called, from the name of Apollo, Pythopolis, and, in honor of the unfortunate youth, he named the river that runs by it Soloon, and left the two surviving brothers intrusted with the care of the government and laws, joining with them Hermus, one of the nobility of Athens, from whom a place in the city is called the House of Hermus; though by an error in the accent * it has been taken for the House of Hermes, or Mercury, and the honor that was designed to the hero, transferred to the god.

This was the origin and cause of the Amazonian invasion of Attica, which would seem to have been no slight or womanish enterprise. For it is impossible that they should have placed their camp in the very city, and joined battle close by the Pnyx and the hill called Museum, unless, having first conquered the country round about, they had thus with impunity advanced to the city. That they made so long a journey by land, and passed the Cimmerian Bosphorus when frozen, as Hellanicus writes, is difficult to be believed. That they encamped all but in the city is certain, and may be sufficiently confirmed by the names that the places thereabout yet retain, and the graves and monuments of those that fell in the battle. Both armies being in sight, there was a long pause and doubt on each side which should give the first onset; at last Theseus, having sacrificed to Fear, in obedience to the command of an oracle he had received, gave them battle; and this happened in the month of Boedromion, in which to this very day the Athenians celebrate the Feast Boedromia. Clidemus, desirous to be very circum-

* Hermoû, genitive case of Hermes, instead of Hérmou, that of Hermus.

stantial, writes that the left wing of the Amazons moved towards the place which is yet called Amazonium and the right towards the Pnyx, near Chrysa,* that with this wing the Athenians, issuing from behind the Museum, engaged, and that the graves of those that were slain are to be seen in the street that leads to the gate called the Piraic, by the chapel of the hero Chalcodon ; and that here the Athenians were routed, and gave way before the women, as far as to the temple of the Furies, but, fresh supplies coming in from the Palladium, Ardettus, and the Lyceum, they charged their right wing, and beat them back into their tents, in which action a great number of the Amazons were slain. At length, after four months, a peace was concluded between them by the mediation of Hippolyta (for so this historian calls the Amazon whom Theseus married, and not Antiope), though others write that she was slain with a dart by Molpadia, while fighting by Theseus's side, and that the pillar which stands by the temple of Olympian Earth was erected to her honor. Nor is it to be wondered at, that in events of such antiquity, history should be in disorder. For indeed we are also told that those of the Amazons that were wounded were privately sent away by Antiope to Chalcis, where many by her care recovered, but some that died were buried there in the place that is to this time called Amazonium. That this war, however, was ended by a treaty is evident, both from the name of the place adjoining to the temple of Theseus, called, from the solemn oath there taken, Horcomosium ; † and also from the ancient sacrifice which used to be celebrated to the Amazons the day before the Feast of Theseus. The Megarians also show a spot in their city where some Amazons were buried, on the way from the market to a place called

* Or near the golden figure of Victory.   † Horcos, oath ; omŏsai, to swear.

Rhus, where the building in the shape of a lozenge stands.
It is said, likewise, that others of them were slain near
Chæronea, and buried near the little rivulet, formerly
called Thermodon, but now Hæmon, of which an account
is given in the life of Demosthenes. It appears further
that the passage of the Amazons through Thessaly was
not without opposition, for there are yet shown many
tombs of them near Scotussa and Cynoscephalæ.

This is as much as is worth telling concerning the
Amazons. For the account which the author of the poem
called the Theseid gives of this rising of the Amazons, how
Antiope, to revenge herself upon Theseus for refusing
her and marrying Phædra, came down upon the city
with her train of Amazons, whom Hercules slew, is manifestly nothing else but fable and invention. It is true,
indeed, that Theseus married Phædra, but that was after
the death of Antiope, by whom he had a son called Hippolytus, or, as Pindar writes, Demophon. The calamities
which befell Phædra and this son, since none of the historians have contradicted the tragic poets that have written
of them, we must suppose happened as represented uni-
formly by them.

There are also other traditions of the marriages of
Theseus, neither honorable in their occasions nor fortunate in their events, which yet were never represented in
the Greek plays. For he is said to have carried off Anaxo,
a Trœzenian, and, having slain Sinnis and Cercyon, to have
ravished their daughters; to have married Periboœa, the
mother of Ajax, and then Phereboœa, and then Iope, the
daughter of Iphicles. And further, he is accused of deserting Ariadne (as is before related), being in love with Ægle
the daughter of Panopeus, neither justly nor honorably;
and lastly, of the rape of Helen, which filled all Attica
with war and blood, and was in the end the occasion of
his banishment and death, as will presently be related.

Herodorus is of opinion, that though there were many famous expeditions undertaken by the bravest men of his time, yet Theseus never joined in any of them, once only excepted, with the Lapithæ, in their war against the Centaurs; but others say that he accompanied Jason to Colchis and Meleager to the slaying of the Calydonian boar, and that hence it came to be a proverb, *Not without Theseus;* that he himself, however, without aid of any one, performed many glorious exploits, and that from him began the saying, *He is a second Hercules.* He also joined Adrastus in recovering the bodies of those that were slain before Thebes, but not as Euripides in his tragedy says, by force of arms, but by persuasion and mutual agreement and composition, for so the greater part of the historians write; Philochorus adds further that this was the first treaty that ever was made for the recovering the bodies of the dead, but in the history of Hercules it is shown that it was he who first gave leave to his enemies to carry off their slain. The burying-places of the most part are yet to be seen in the village called Eleutheræ; those of the commanders, at Eleusis, where Theseus allotted them a place, to oblige Adrastus. The story of Euripides in his Suppliants is disproved by Æschylus in his Eleusinians, where Theseus himself relates the facts as here told.

The celebrated friendship. between Theseus and Pirithoüs is said to have been thus begun : the fame of the strength and valor of Theseus being spread through Greece, Pirithoüs was desirous to make a trial and proof of it himself, and to this end seized a herd of oxen which belonged to Theseus, and was driving them away from Marathon, and, when news was brought that Theseus pursued him in arms, he did not fly, but turned back and went to meet him. But as soon as they had viewed one another, each so admired the gracefulness and beauty, and was seized with such a respect for the courage, of the other, that they forgot all thoughts of fighting; and Pirithoüs, first stretching out his hand to Theseus, bade him be judge in this case himself, and promised to submit willingly to any penalty he should impose. But Theseus not only forgave him all, but entreated him to be his friend and brother in arms; and they ratified their friendship by oaths. After this Pirithoüs married Deidamia, and invited Theseus to the wedding, entreating him to come and see his country, and make acquaintance with the Lapithæ; he had at the same time invited the Centaurs to the feast, who growing hot with wine and beginning to be insolent and wild, and offering violence to the women, the Lapithæ took immediate revenge upon them, slaying many of them upon the place, and afterwards, having overcome them in battle, drove the whole race of them out of their country, Theseus all along taking their part and fighting on their side. But Herodorus gives a different relation of these things: that Theseus came not to the assistance of the Lapithæ till the war was already begun; and that it was in this journey that he had the first sight of Hercules, having made it his business to find him out at Trachis, where he had chosen to rest himself after all his wanderings and his labors; and that this interview was honorably performed on each part, with extreme respect, good-will, and admiration of each other. Yet it is more credible, as others write, that there were, before, frequent interviews between them, and that it was by the means of Theseus that Hercules was initiated at Eleusis, and purified before initiation, upon account of several rash actions of his former life.

Theseus was now fifty years old, as Hellanicus states, when he carried off Helen, who was yet too young to be married. Some writers, to take away this accusation of one of the greatest crimes laid to his charge, say, that he

did not steal away Helen himself, but that Idas and Lyn-
ceus were the ravishers, who brought her to him, and
committed her to his charge, and that, therefore, he refused to restore her at the demand of Castor and Pollux;
or, indeed, they say her own father, Tyndarus, had sent
her to be kept by him, for fear of Enarophorus, the son
of Hippocoün, who would have carried her away by force
when she was yet a child. But the most probable account,
and that which has most witnesses on its side, is this:
Theseus and Pirithoüs went both together to Sparta, and,
having seized the young lady as she was dancing in the
temple of Diana Orthia, fled away with her. There were
presently men in arms sent to pursue, but they followed
no further than to Tegea; and Theseus and Pirithoüs,
being now out of danger, having passed through Peloponnesus, made an agreement between themselves, that he
to whom the lot should fall should have Helen to his
wife, but should be obliged to assist in procuring another
for his friend. The lot fell upon Theseus, who conveyed
her to Aphidnæ, not being yet marriageable, and delivered her to one of his allies, called Aphidnus, and, having
sent his mother Æthra after to take care of her, desired
him to keep them so secretly, that none might know
where they were; which done, to return the same service
to his friend Pirithoüs, he accompanied him in his journey to Epirus, in order to steal away the king of the
Molossians' daughter. The king, his own name being
Aïdoneus, or Pluto, called his wife Proserpina, and his
daughter Cora, and a great dog which he kept Cerberus,
with whom he ordered all that came as suitors to his
daughter to fight, and promised her to him that should
overcome the beast. But having been informed that the
design of Pirithoüs and his companion was not to court
his daughter, but to force her away, he caused them both

to be seized, and threw Pirithoüs to be torn in pieces by his dog, and put Theseus into prison, and kept him.

About this time, Menestheus, the son of Peteus, grandson of Orneus, and great-grandson to Erechtheus, the first man that is recorded to have affected popularity and ingratiated himself with the multitude, stirred up and exasperated the most eminent men of the city, who had long borne a secret grudge to Theseus, conceiving that he had robbed them of their several little kingdoms and lordships, and, having pent them all up in one city, was using them as his subjects and slaves. He put also the meaner people into commotion, telling them, that, deluded with a mere dream of liberty, though indeed they were deprived both of that and of their proper homes and religious usages, instead of many good and gracious kings of their own, they had given themselves up to be lorded over by a new-comer and a stranger. Whilst he was thus busied in infecting the minds of the citizens, the war that Castor and Pollux brought against Athens came very opportunely to further the sedition he had been promoting, and some say that he by his persuasions was wholly the cause of their invading the city. At their first approach, they committed no acts of hostility, but peaceably demanded their sister Helen; but the Athenians returning answer that they neither had her there nor knew where she was disposed of, they prepared to assault the city, when Academus, having, by whatever means, found it out, disclosed to them that she was secretly kept at Aphidnæ. For which reason he was both highly honored during his life by Castor and Pollux, and the Lacedæmonians, when often in aftertimes they made incursions into Attica, and destroyed all the country round about, spared the Academy for the sake of Academus. But Dicæarchus writes that there were two Arcadians in the army of Castor and Pollux, the one called Echedemus, and the other Marathus;

from the first that which is now called Academia was then named Echedemia, and the village Marathon had its name from the other, who, to fulfil some oracle, voluntarily offered himself to be made a sacrifice before battle. As soon as they were arrived at Aphidnæ, they overcame their enemies in a set battle, and then assaulted and took the town. And here, they say, Alycus, the son of Sciron, was slain, of the party of the Dioscuri (Castor and Pollux), from whom a place in Megara, where he was buried, is called Alycus to this day. And Hereas writes that it was Theseus himself that killed him, in witness of which he cites these verses concerning Alycus,

> And Alycus, upon Aphidna's plain
> By Theseus in the cause of Helen slain.

Though it is not at all probable that Theseus himself was there when both the city and his mother were taken.

Aphidnæ being won by Castor and Pollux, and the city of Athens being in consternation, Menestheus persuaded the people to open their gates, and receive them with all manner of friendship, for they were, he told them, at enmity with none but Theseus, who had first injured them, and were benefactors and saviors to all mankind beside. And their behavior gave credit to those promises; for, having made themselves absolute masters of the place, they demanded no more than to be initiated, since they were as nearly related to the city as Hercules was, who had received the same honor. This their desire they easily obtained, and were adopted by Aphidnus, as Hercules had been by Pylius. They were honored also like gods, and were called by a new name, Anaces, either from the *cessation* * of the war, or from the *care* they took that none should suffer any injury, though there was so great an army within the walls; for the phrase *anăkōs ĕkhein* is

* Anŏkhē.

used of those who look to or care for any thing; kings for this reason, perhaps, are called *anactes*. Others say, that from the appearance of their star in the heavens, they were thus called, for in the Attic dialect this name comes very near the words that signify *above*.*

Some say that Æthra, Theseus's mother, was here taken prisoner, and carried to Lacedæmon, and from thence went away with Helen to Troy, alleging this verse of Homer, to prove that she waited upon Helen,

Æthra of Pittheus born, and large-eyed Clymene.

Others reject this verse as none of Homer's, as they do likewise the whole fable of Munychus, who, the story says, was the son of Demophon and Laodice, born secretly, and brought up by Æthra at Troy. But Ister, in the thirteenth book of his Attic History, gives us an account of Æthra, different yet from all the rest: that Achilles and Patroclus overcame Paris in Thessaly, near the river Sperchius, but that Hector took and plundered the city of the Trœzenians, and made Æthra prisoner there. But this seems a groundless tale.

Now Hercules, passing by the Molossians, was entertained in his way by Aidoneus the king, who, in conversation, accidentally spoke of the journey of Theseus and Pirithoüs into his country, of what they had designed to do, and what they were forced to suffer. Hercules was much grieved for the inglorious death of the one and the miserable condition of the other. As for Pirithoüs, he thought it useless to complain; but begged to have Theseus released for his sake, and obtained that favor from the king. Theseus, being thus set at liberty, returned to Athens, where his friends were not yet wholly suppressed, and dedicated to Hercules all the sacred places which the city had set apart for himself, changing their names from

* Anĕkas, anecathen.

Thesea to Heraclea, four only excepted, as Philochorus
writes. And wishing immediately to resume the first
place in the commonwealth, and manage the state as before, he soon found himself involved in factions and
troubles; those who long had hated him had now added
to their hatred contempt; and the minds of the people
were so generally corrupted, that, instead of obeying
commands with silence, they expected to be flattered into
their duty. He had some thoughts to have reduced them
by force, but was overpowered by demagogues and factions. And at last, despairing of any good success of his
affairs in Athens, he sent away his children privately to
Euboea, commending them to the care of Elephenor, the
son of Chalcodon; and he himself, having solemnly cursed
the people of Athens in the village of Gargettus, in which
there yet remains the place called Araterion, or the place
of cursing, sailed to Scyros, where he had lands left him
by his father, and friendship, as he thought, with those of
the island. Lycomedes was then king of Scyros. Theseus, therefore, addressed himself to him, and desired to
have his lands put into his possession, as designing to
settle and to dwell there, though others say that he came
to beg his assistance against the Athenians. But Lycomedes, either jealous of the glory of so great a man, or
to gratify Menestheus, having led him up to the highest
cliff of the island, on pretence of showing him from thence
the lands that he desired, threw him headlong down
from the rock, and killed him. Others say he fell down
of himself by a slip of his foot, as he was walking there,
according to his custom, after supper. At that time there
was no notice taken, nor were any concerned for his
death, but Menestheus quietly possessed the kingdom of
Athens. His sons were brought up in a private condition,
and accompanied Elephenor to the Trojan war, but, after
the decease of Menestheus in that expedition, returned to

Athens, and recovered the government. But in succeeding ages, beside several other circumstances that moved
the Athenians to honor Theseus as a demigod, in the
battle which was fought at Marathon against the Medes,
many of the soldiers believed they saw an apparition of
Theseus in arms, rushing on at the head of them against
the barbarians. And after the Median war, Phædo being
archon of Athens, the Athenians, consulting the oracle at
Delphi, were commanded to gather together the bones of
Theseus, and, laying them in some honorable place, keep
them as sacred in the city. But it was very difficult to
recover these relics, or so much as to find out the place
where they lay, on account of the inhospitable and savage
temper of the barbarous people that inhabited the island.
Nevertheless, afterwards, when Cimon took the island (as
is related in his life), and had a great ambition to find out
the place where Theseus was buried, he, by chance, spied
an eagle upon a rising ground pecking with her beak
and tearing up the earth with her talons, when on the
sudden it came into his mind, as it were by some divine
inspiration, to dig there, and search for the bones of Theseus. There were found in that place a coffin of a man of
more than ordinary size, and a brazen spear-head, and a
sword lying by it, all which he took aboard his galley
and brought with him to Athens. Upon which the Athenians, greatly delighted, went out to meet and receive
the relics with splendid processions and with sacrifices, as
if it were Theseus himself returning alive to the city. He
lies interred in the middle of the city, near the present
gymnasium. His tomb is a sanctuary and refuge for slaves,
and all those of mean condition that fly from the persecution of men in power, in memory that Theseus while
he lived was an assister and protector of the distressed,
and never refused the petitions of the afflicted that fled
to him. The chief and most solemn sacrifice which they

celebrate to him is kept on the eighth day of Pyanepsion,
on which he returned with the Athenian young men from
Crete. Besides which, they sacrifice to him on the eighth
day of every month, either because he returned from
Trœzen the eighth day of Hecatombæon, as Diodorus the
geographer writes, or else thinking that number to be
proper to him, because he was reputed to be born of Neptune, because they sacrifice to Neptune on the eighth
day of every month. The number eight being the first
cube of an even number, and the double of the first
square, seemed to be an emblem of the steadfast and immovable power of this god, who from thence has the
names of Asphalius and Gæiochus, that is, the establisher
and stayer of the earth.

ROMULUS.

FROM whom, and for what reason, the city of Rome, a name so great in glory, and famous in the mouths of all men, was so first called, authors do not agree. Some are of opinion that the Pelasgians, wandering over the greater part of the habitable world, and subduing numerous nations, fixed themselves here, and, from their own great *strength* * in war, called the city Rome. Others, that at the taking of Troy, some few that escaped and met with shipping, put to sea, and, driven by winds, were carried upon the coasts of Tuscany, and came to anchor off the mouth of the river Tiber, where their women, out of heart and weary with the sea, on its being proposed by one of the highest birth and best understanding amongst them, whose name was Roma, burnt the ships. With which act the men at first were angry, but afterwards, of necessity, seating themselves near Palatium, where things in a short while succeeded far better than they could hope, in that they found the country very good, and the people courteous, they not only did the lady Roma other honors, but added also this, of calling after her name the city which she had been the occasion of their founding. From this, they say, has come down that custom at Rome for women to

* Rome, strength.

salute their kinsmen and husbands with kisses; because
these women, after they had burnt the ships, made use
of such endearments when entreating and pacifying their
husbands.

Some again say that Roma, from whom this city was
so called, was daughter of Italus and Leucaria; or, by
another account, of Telephus, Hercules's son, and that
she was married to Æneas, or, according to others again,
to Ascanius, Æneas's son. Some tell us that Romanus,
the son of Ulysses and Circe, built it; some, Romus, the
son of Emathion, Diomede having sent him from Troy;
and others, Romus, king of the Latins, after driving out
the Tyrrhenians, who had come from Thessaly into Lydia,
and from thence into Italy. Those very authors, too,
who, in accordance with the safest account, make Romulus give the name to the city, yet differ concerning
his birth and family. For some say, he was son to Æneas
and Dexithea, daughter of Phorbas, and was, with his
brother Remus, in their infancy, carried into Italy, and
being on the river when the waters came down in a flood,
all the vessels were cast away except only that where
the young children were, which being gently landed on
a level bank of the river, they were both unexpectedly
saved, and from them the place was called Rome. Some
say, Roma, daughter of the Trojan lady above mentioned,
was married to Latinus, Telemachus's son, and became mother to Romulus; others, that Æmilia, daughter of Æneas
and Lavinia, had him by the god Mars; and others give
you mere fables of his origin. For to Tarchetius, they
say, king of Alba, who was a most wicked and cruel man,
there appeared in his own house a strange vision, a male
figure that rose out of a hearth, and stayed there for
many days. There was an oracle of Tethys in Tuscany
which Tarchetius consulted, and received an answer that
a virgin should give herself to the apparition, and that a

son should be born of her, highly renowned, eminent for valor, good fortune, and strength of body. Tarchetius told the prophecy to one of his own daughters, and commanded her to do this thing; which she avoiding as an indignity, sent her handmaid. Tarchetius, hearing this, in great anger imprisoned them both, purposing to put them to death; but being deterred from murder by the goddess Vesta in a dream, enjoined them for their punishment the working a web of cloth, in their chains as they were, which when they finished, they should be suffered to marry; but whatever they worked by day, Tarchetius commanded others to unravel in the night. In the mean time, the waiting-woman was delivered of two boys, whom Tarchetius gave into the hands of one Teratius, with command to destroy them; he, however, carried and laid them by the river side, where a wolf came and continued to suckle them, while birds of various sorts brought little morsels of food, which they put into their mouths; till a cow-herd, spying them, was first strangely surprised, but, venturing to draw nearer, took the children up in his arms. Thus they were saved, and, when they grew up, set upon Tarchetius and overcame him. This one Promathion says, who compiled a history of Italy.

But the story which is most believed and has the greatest number of vouchers was first published, in its chief particulars, amongst the Greeks by Diocles of Peparethus, whom Fabius Pictor also follows in most points. Here again there are variations, but in general outline it runs thus: the kings of Alba reigned in lineal descent from Æneas, and the succession devolved at length upon two brothers, Numitor and Amulius. Amulius proposed to divide things into two equal shares, and set as equivalent to the kingdom the treasure and gold that were brought from Troy. Numitor chose the kingdom; but Amulius, having the money, and being

able to do more with that than Numitor, took his kingdom from him with great ease, and, fearing lest his daughter might have children, made her a Vestal, bound in
that condition forever to live a single and maiden life.
This lady some call Ilia, others Rhea, and others Silvia;
however, not long after, she was, contrary to the established laws of the Vestals, discovered to be with child,
and should have suffered the most cruel punishment, had
not Antho, the king's daughter, mediated with her father
for her; nevertheless, she was confined, and debarred all
company, that she might not be delivered without the
king's knowledge. In time she brought forth two boys,
of more than human size and beauty, whom Amulius,
becoming yet more alarmed, commanded a servant to
take and cast away; this man some call Faustulus,
others say Faustulus was the man who brought them up.
He put the children, however, in a small trough, and
went towards the river with a design to cast them in;
but, seeing the waters much swollen and coming violently
down, was afraid to go nearer, and, dropping the children
near the bank, went away. The river overflowing, the
flood at last bore up the trough, and, gently wafting it,
landed them on a smooth piece of ground, which they
now call Cermanus,* formerly Germanus, perhaps from
Germani, which signifies brothers.

Near this place grew a wild fig-tree, which they called
Rumiualis, either from Romulus (as it is vulgarly thought),
or from *ruminating*, because cattle did usually in the
heat of the day seek cover under it, and there chew the
cud; or, better, from the suckling of these children there,
for the ancients called the dug or teat of any creature
ruma; and there is a tutelar goddess of the rearing of
children whom they still call Rumilia, in sacrificing to
whom they use no wine, but make libations of milk.

* More correctly Cermalus.

While the infants lay here, history tells us, a she-wolf nursed them, and a woodpecker constantly fed and watched them; these creatures are esteemed holy to the god Mars, the woodpecker the Latins still especially worship and honor. Which things, as much as any, gave credit to what the mother of the children said, that their father was the god Mars: though some say that it was a mistake put upon her by Amulius, who himself had come to her dressed up in armor.

Others think that the first rise of this fable came from the children's nurse, through the ambiguity of her name; for the Latins not only called wolves *lupæ*, but also women of loose life; and such an one was the wife of Faustulus, who nurtured these children, Acca Larentia by name. To her the Romans offer sacrifices, and in the month of April the priest of Mars makes libations there; it is called the Larentian Feast. They honor also another Larentia, for the following reason: the keeper of Hercules's temple having, it seems, little else to do, proposed to his deity a game at dice, laying down that, if he himself won, he would have something valuable of the god; but if he were beaten, he would spread him a noble table, and procure him a fair lady's company. Upon these terms, throwing first for the god and then for himself, he found himself beaten. Wishing to pay his stakes honorably, and holding himself bound by what he had said, he both provided the deity a good supper, and, giving money to Larentia, then in her beauty, though not publicly known, gave her a feast in the temple, where he had also laid a bed, and after supper locked her in, as if the god were really to come to her. And indeed, it is said, the deity did truly visit her, and commanded her in the morning to walk to the market-place, and, whatever man she met first, to salute him, and make him her friend. She met one named

Tarrutius, who was a man advanced in years, fairly rich,
without children, and had always lived a single life. He
received Larentia, and loved her well, and at his death
left her sole heir of all his large and fair possessions, most
of which she, in her last will and testament, bequeathed
to the people. It was reported of her, being now celebrated and esteemed the mistress of a god, that she suddenly disappeared near the place where the first Larentia
lay buried; the spot is at this day called Velabrum,
because, the river frequently overflowing, they went over
in ferry-boats somewhere hereabouts to the forum, the
Latin word for ferrying being *velatura*. Others derive
the name from *velum*, a sail; because the exhibitors of
public shows used to hang the road that leads from the
forum to the Circus Maximus with sails, beginning at
this spot. Upon these accounts the second Larentia
is honored at Rome.

Meantime Faustulus, Amulius's swineherd, brought up
the children without any man's knowledge; or, as those
say who wish to keep closer to probabilities, with the
knowledge and secret assistance of Numitor; for it is
said, they went to school at Gabii, and were well instructed in letters, and other accomplishments befitting
their birth. And they were called Romulus and Remus,
(from *ruma*, the dug,) as we had before, because they were
found sucking the wolf. In their very infancy, the size
and beauty of their bodies intimated their natural superiority; and when they grew up, they both proved brave
and manly, attempting all enterprises that seemed hazardous, and showing in them a courage altogether undaunted.
But Romulus seemed rather to act by counsel, and to
show the sagacity of a statesman, and in all his dealings
with their neighbors, whether relating to feeding of flocks
or to hunting, gave the idea of being born rather to rule
than to obey. To their comrades and inferiors they were

therefore dear; but the king's servants, his bailiffs and overseers, as being in nothing better men than themselves, they despised and slighted, nor were the least concerned at their commands and menaces. They used honest pastimes and liberal studies, not esteeming sloth and idleness honest and liberal, but rather such exercises as hunting and running, repelling robbers, taking of thieves, and delivering the wronged and oppressed from injury. For doing such things they became famous.

A quarrel occurring betwixt Numitor's and Amulius's cowherds, the latter, not enduring the driving away of their cattle by the others, fell upon them and put them to flight, and rescued the greatest part of the prey. At which Numitor being highly incensed, they little regarded it, but collected and took into their company a number of needy men and runaway slaves, — acts which looked like the first stages of rebellion. It so happened, that when Romulus was attending a sacrifice, being fond of sacred rites and divination, Numitor's herdsmen, meeting with Remus on a journey with few companions, fell upon him, and, after some fighting, took him prisoner, carried him before Numitor, and there accused him. Numitor would not punish him himself, fearing his brother's anger, but went to Amulius, and desired justice, as he was Amulius's brother and was affronted by Amulius's servants. The men of Alba likewise resenting the thing, and thinking he had been dishonorably used, Amulius was induced to deliver Remus up into Numitor's hands, to use him as he thought fit. He therefore took and carried him home, and, being struck with admiration of the youth's person, in stature and strength of body exceeding all men, and perceiving in his very countenance the courage and force of his mind, which stood unsubdued and unmoved by his present circumstances, and hearing further that all the enterprises and actions of his life were answerable to what he saw of him, but chiefly, as it seemed, a divine influence aiding and directing the first steps that were to lead to great results, out of the mere thought of his mind, and casually, as it were, he put his hand upon the fact, and, in gentle terms and with a kind aspect, to inspire him with confidence and hope, asked him who he was, and whence he was derived. He, taking heart, spoke thus: "I will hide nothing from you, for you seem to be of a more princely temper than Amulius, in that you give a hearing and examine before you punish, while he condemns before the cause is heard. Formerly, then, we (for we are twins) thought ourselves the sons of Faustulus and Larentia, the king's servants; but since we have been accused and aspersed with calumnies, and brought in peril of our lives here before you, we hear great things of ourselves, the truth of which my present danger is likely to bring to the test. Our birth is said to have been secret, our fostering and nurture in our infancy still more strange; by birds and beasts, to whom we were cast out, we were fed, by the milk of a wolf, and the morsels of a woodpecker, as we lay in a little trough by the side of the river. The trough is still in being, and is preserved, with brass plates round it, and an inscription in letters almost effaced, which may prove hereafter unavailing tokens to our parents when we are dead and gone." Numitor, upon these words, and computing the dates by the young man's looks, slighted not the hope that flattered him, but considered how to come at his daughter privately (for she was still kept under restraint), to talk with her concerning these matters.

Faustulus, hearing Remus was taken and delivered up, called on Romulus to assist in his rescue, informing him then plainly of the particulars of his birth, not but he had before given hints of it, and told as much as an atten-

tive man might make no small conclusions from; he himself, full of concern and fear of not coming in time, took
the trough, and ran instantly to Numitor; but giving a
suspicion to some of the king's sentry at his gate, and
being gazed upon by them and perplexed with their
questions, he let it be seen that he was hiding the trough
under his cloak. By chance there was one among them
who was at the exposing of the children, and was one
employed in the office; he, seeing the trough and knowing it by its make and inscription, guessed at the business,
and, without further delay, telling the king of it, brought
in the man to be examined. Faustulus, hard beset, did
not show himself altogether proof against terror; nor
yet was he wholly forced out of all; confessed indeed
the children were alive, but lived, he said, as shepherds,
a great way from Alba; he himself was going to
carry the trough to Ilia, who had often greatly desired to
see and handle it, for a confirmation of her hopes of her
children. As men generally do who are troubled in mind
and act either in fear or passion, it so fell out Amulius
now did; for he sent in haste as a messenger, a man, otherwise honest, and friendly to Numitor, with commands
to learn from Numitor whether any tidings were come to
him of the children's being alive. He, coming and seeing
how little Remus wanted of being received into the arms
and embraces of Numitor, both gave him surer confidence
in his hope, and advised them, with all expedition, to proceed to action; himself too joining and assisting them,
and indeed, had they wished it, the time would not have
let them demur. For Romulus was now come very near,
and many of the citizens, out of fear and hatred of Amulius, were running out to join him; besides, he brought
great forces with him, divided into companies, each of an
hundred men, every captain carrying a small bundle of
grass and shrubs tied to a pole. The Latins call such

bundles *manipuli,* and from hence it is that in their armies
still they call their captains *manipulares.* Remus rousing
the citizens within to revolt, and Romulus making attacks
from without, the tyrant, not knowing either what to do,
or what expedient to think of for his security, in this per-
plexity and confusion was taken and put to death. This
narrative, for the most part given by Fabius and Diocles
of Peparethus, who seem to be the earliest historians of
the foundation of Rome, is suspected by some, because of
its dramatic and fictitious appearance; but it would not
wholly be disbelieved, if men would remember what a
poet fortune sometimes shows herself, and consider that
the Roman power would hardly have reached so high a
pitch without a divinely ordered origin, attended with
great and extraordinary circumstances.

Amulius now being dead and matters quietly disposed,
the two brothers would neither dwell in Alba without
governing there, nor take the government into their own
hands during the life of their grandfather. Having
therefore delivered the dominion up into his hands, and
paid their mother befitting honor, they resolved to live
by themselves, and build a city in the same place where
they were in their infancy brought up. This seems the
most honorable reason for their departure; though perhaps it was necessary, having such a body of slaves and
fugitives collected about them, either to come to nothing
by dispersing them, or if not so, then to live with them
elsewhere. For that the inhabitants of Alba did not
think fugitives worthy of being received and incorporated
as citizens among them plainly appears from the matter of
the women, an attempt made not wantonly but of necessity, because they could not get wives by good-will.
For they certainly paid unusual respect and honor to
those whom they thus forcibly seized.

Not long after the first foundation of the city, they

opened a sanctuary of refuge for all fugitives, which they called the temple of the god Asylæus, where they received and protected all, delivering none back, neither the servant to his master, the debtor to his creditor, nor the murderer into the hands of the magistrate, saying it was a privileged place, and they could so maintain it by an order of the holy oracle; insomuch that the city grew presently very populous, for, they say, it consisted at first of no more than a thousand houses. But of that hereafter.

Their minds being fully bent upon building, there arose presently a difference about the place where. Romulus chose what was called Roma Quadrata, or the Square Rome, and would have the city there. Remus laid out a piece of ground on the Aventine. Mount, well fortified by nature, which was from him called Remonium, but now Rignarium. Concluding at last to decide the contest by a divination from a flight of birds, and placing themselves apart at some distance, Remus, they say, saw six vultures, and Romulus double the number; others say Remus did truly see his number, and that Romulus feigned his, but, when Remus came to him, that then he did, indeed, see twelve. Hence it is that the Romans, in their divinations from birds, chiefly regard the vulture, though Herodorus Ponticus relates that Hercules was always very joyful when a vulture appeared to him upon any action. For it is a creature the least hurtful of any, pernicious neither to corn, fruit-tree, nor cattle; it preys only upon carrion, and never kills or hurts any living thing; and as for birds, it touches not them, though they are dead, as being of its own species, whereas eagles, owls, and hawks mangle and kill their own fellow-creatures; yet, as Æschylus says, —

What bird is clean that preys on fellow bird?

Besides, all other birds are, so to say, never out of our

eyes; they let themselves be seen of us continually; but
a vulture is a very rare sight, and you can seldom meet
with a man that has seen their young; their rarity and
infrequency has raised a strange opinion in some, that
they come to us from some other world; as soothsayers
ascribe a divine origination to all things not produced
either of nature or of themselves.

When Remus knew the cheat, he was much displeased;
and as Romulus was casting up a ditch, where he designed
the foundation of the city-wall, he turned some pieces of
the work to ridicule, and obstructed others: at last, as he
was in contempt leaping over it, some say Romulus himself struck him, others Celer, one of his companions; he
fell, however, and in the scuffle Faustulus also was slain,
and Plistinus, who, being Faustulus's brother, story tells
us, helped to bring up Romulus. Celer upon this fled
instantly into Tuscany, and from him the Romans call all
men that are swift of foot Celeres; and because Quintus
Metellus, at his father's funeral, in a few days' time gave
the people a show of gladiators, admiring his expedition
in getting it ready, they gave him the name of Celer.

Romulus, having buried his brother Remus, together
with his two foster-fathers, on the mount Remonia, set to
building his city; and sent for men out of Tuscany, who
directed him by sacred usages and written rules in all the
ceremonies to be observed, as in a religious rite. First,
they dug a round trench about that which is now the
Comitium, or Court of Assembly, and into it solemnly
threw the first-fruits of all things either good by custom
or necessary by nature; lastly, every man taking a small
piece of earth of the country from whence he came, they
all threw them in promiscuously together. This trench
they call, as they do the heavens, Mundus; making
which their centre, they described the city in a circle
round it. Then the founder fitted to a plough a brazen

ploughshare, and, yoking together a bull and a cow, drove himself a deep line or furrow round the bounds; while the business of those that followed after was to see that whatever earth was thrown up should be turned all inwards towards the city, and not to let any clod lie outside. With this line they described the wall, and called it, by a contraction, Pomœrium, that is, *post murum*, after or beside the wall; and where they designed to make a gate, there they took out the share, carried the plough over, and left a space; for which reason they consider the whole wall as holy, except where the gates are; for had they adjudged them also sacred, they could not, without offence to religion, have given free ingress and egress for the necessaries of human life, some of which are in themselves unclean.

As for the day they began to build the city, it is universally agreed to have been the twenty-first of April, and that day the Romans annually keep holy, calling it their country's birth-day. At first, they say, they sacrificed no living creature on this day, thinking it fit to preserve the feast of their country's birth-day pure and without stain of blood. Yet before ever the city was built, there was a feast of herdsmen and shepherds kept on this day, which went by the name of Palilia. The Roman and Greek months have now little or no agreement; they say, however, the day on which Romulus began to build was quite certainly the thirtieth of the month, at which time there was an eclipse of the sun which they conceive to be that seen by Antimachus, the Teian poet, in the third year of the sixth Olympiad. In the times of Varro the philosopher, a man deeply read in Roman history, lived one Tarrutius, his familiar acquaintance, a good philosopher and mathematician, and one, too, that out of curiosity had studied the way of drawing schemes and tables, and was thought to be a proficient in the art; to him Varro propounded to cast Romulus's

nativity, even to the first day and hour, making his
deductions from the several events of the man's life which
he should be informed of, exactly as in working back a
geometrical problem; for it belonged, he said, to the same
science both to foretell a man's life by knowing the time
of his birth, and also to find out his birth by the knowledge of his life. This task Tarrutius undertook, and first
looking into the actions and casualties of the man, together with the time of his life and manner of his death,
and then comparing all these remarks together, he very
confidently and positively pronounced that Romulus was
conceived in his mother's womb the first year of the
second Olympiad, the twenty-third day of the month the
Ægyptians call Chœac, and the third hour after sunset,
at which time there was a total eclipse of the sun; that
he was born the twenty-first day of the month Thoth,
about sun-rising; and that the first stone of Rome was
laid by him the ninth day of the month Pharmuthi, between the second and third hour. For the fortunes of
cities as well as of men, they think, have their certain
periods of time prefixed, which may be collected and fore-
known from the position of the stars at their first foundation. But these and the like relations may perhaps not
so much take and delight the reader with their novelty
and curiosity, as offend him by their extravagance.

The city now being built, Romulus enlisted all that
were of age to bear arms into military companies, each
company consisting of three thousand footmen and three
hundred horse. These companies were called legions,
because they were the choicest and most select of the
people for fighting men. The rest of the multitude he
called the people; an hundred of the most eminent he
chose for counsellors; these he styled patricians, and
their assembly the senate, which signifies a council of
elders. The patricians, some say, were so called because

they were the fathers of lawful children; others, because
they could give a good account who their own fathers
were, which not every one of the rabble that poured into
the city at first could do; others, from patronage, their
word for protection of inferiors, the origin of which they
attribute to Patron, one of those that came over with Evander, who was a great protector and defender of the weak
and needy. But perhaps the most probable judgment
might be, that Romulus, esteeming it the duty of the
chiefest and wealthiest men, with a fatherly care and concern to look after the meaner, and also encouraging the
commonalty not to dread or be aggrieved at the honors
of their superiors, but to love and respect them, and to
think and call them their fathers, might from hence give
them the name of patricians. For at this very time all
foreigners give senators the style of lords; but the Romans, making use of a more honorable and less invidious
name, call them Patres Conscripti; at first indeed simply
Patres, but afterwards, more being added, Patres Conscripti. By this more imposing title he distinguished the
senate from the populace; and in other ways also separated the nobles and the commons, — calling them patrons, and these their clients, — by which means he created
wonderful love and amity betwixt them, productive of
great justice in their dealings. For they were always
their clients' counsellors in law cases, their advocates in
courts of justice, in fine their advisers and supporters in
all affairs whatever. These again faithfully served their
patrons, not only paying them all respect and deference,
but also, in case of poverty, helping them to portion their
daughters and pay off their debts; and for a patron to
witness against his client, or a client against his patron,
was what no law nor magistrate could enforce. In after-
times, all other duties subsisting still between them, it
was thought mean and dishonorable for the better sort

to take money from their inferiors. And so much of these matters.

In the fourth month, after the city was built, as Fabius writes, the adventure of stealing the women was attempted; and some say Romulus himself, being naturally a martial man, and predisposed too, perhaps, by certain oracles, to believe the fates had ordained the future growth and greatness of Rome should depend upon the benefit of war, upon these accounts first offered violence to the Sabines, since he took away only thirty virgins, more to give an occasion of war than out of any want of women. But this is not very probable; it would seem rather that, observing his city to be filled by a confluence of foreigners, few of whom had wives, and that the multitude in general, consisting of a mixture of mean and obscure men, fell under contempt, and seemed to be of no long continuance together, and hoping farther, after the women were appeased, to make this injury in some measure an occasion of confederacy and mutual commerce with the Sabines, he took in hand this exploit after this manner. First, he gave it out as if he had found an altar of a certain god hid under ground; the god they called Consus, either the god of counsel (for they still call a consultation *consilium*, and their chief magistrates *consules*, namely, counsellors), or else the equestrian Neptune, for the altar is kept covered in the circus maximus at all other times, and only at horse-races is exposed to public view; others merely say that this god had his altar hid under ground because counsel ought to be secret and concealed. Upon discovery of this altar, Romulus, by proclamation, appointed a day for a splendid sacrifice, and for public games and shows, to entertain all sorts of people; many flocked thither, and he himself sate in front, amidst his nobles, clad in purple. Now the signal for their falling on was to be whenever he rose and gathered up his robe and threw it over his body; his men stood all ready armed, with their eyes intent upon him, and when the sign was given, drawing their swords and falling on with a great shout, they ravished away the daughters of the Sabines, they themselves flying without any let or hindrance. They say there were but thirty taken, and from them the Curiæ or Fraternities were named; but Valerius Antias says five hundred and twenty-seven, Juba, six hundred and eighty-three virgins; which was indeed the greatest excuse Romulus could allege, namely, that they had taken no married woman, save one only, Hersilia by name, and her too unknowingly; which showed they did not commit this rape wantonly, but with a design purely of forming alliance with their neighbors by the greatest and surest bonds. This Hersilia some say Hostilius married, a most eminent man among the Romans; others, Romulus himself, and that she bore two children to him, a daughter, by reason of primogeniture called Prima, and one only son, whom, from the great concourse of citizens to him at that time, he called Aollius,* but after ages Abillius. But Zenodotus the Trœzenian, in giving this account, is contradicted by many.

Among those who committed this rape upon the virgins, there were, they say, as it so then happened, some of the meaner sort of men, who were carrying off a damsel, excelling all in beauty and comeliness of stature, whom when some of superior rank that met them attempted to take away, they cried out they were carrying her to Talasius, a young man, indeed, but brave and worthy; hearing that, they commended and applauded them loudly, and also some, turning back, accompanied them with good-will and pleasure, shouting out the name of Talasius. Hence the Romans to this very time, at their

---

* Aollein, Gr., to collect a multitude.

weddings, sing Talasius for their nuptial word, as the Greeks do Hymenæus, because, they say, Talasius was very happy in his marriage. But Sextius Sylla the Carthaginian, a man wanting neither learning nor ingenuity, told me Romulus gave this word as a sign when to begin the onset; everybody, therefore, who made prize of a maiden, cried out, Talasius; and for that reason the custom continues so now at marriages. But most are of opinion (of whom Juba particularly is one) that this word was used to new-married women by way of incitement to good housewifery and *talasia* (spinning), as we say in Greek, Greek words at that time not being as yet overpowered by Italian. But if this be the case, and if the Romans did at that time use the word *talasia* as we do, a man might fancy a more probable reason of the custom. For when the Sabines, after the war against the Romans, were reconciled, conditions were made concerning their women, that they should be obliged to do no other servile offices to their husbands but what concerned spinning; it was customary, therefore, ever after, at weddings, for those that gave the bride or escorted her or otherwise were present, sportingly to say Talasius, intimating that she was henceforth to serve in spinning and no more. It continues also a custom at this very day for the bride not of herself to pass her husband's threshold, but to be lifted over, in memory that the Sabine virgins were carried in by violence, and did not go in of their own will. Some say, too, the custom of parting the bride's hair with the head of a spear was in token their marriages began at first by war and acts of hostility, of which I have spoken more fully in my book of Questions.

This rape was committed on the eighteenth day of the month Sextilis, now called August, on which the solemnities of the Consualia are kept.

The Sabines were a numerous and martial people, but

lived in small, unfortified villages, as it befitted, they
thought, a colony of the Lacedæmonians to be bold and
fearless; nevertheless, seeing themselves bound by such
hostages to their good behavior, and being solicitous for
their daughters, they sent ambassadors to Romulus with
fair and equitable requests, that he would return their
young women and recall that act of violence, and afterwards, by persuasion and lawful means, seek friendly correspondence between both nations. Romulus would not
part with the young women, yet proposed to the Sabines
to enter into an alliance with them; upon which point
some consulted and demurred long, but Acron, king of
the Ceninenses, a man of high spirit and a good warrior,
who had all along a jealousy of Romulus's bold attempts,
and considering particularly from this exploit upon the
women that he was growing formidable to all people, and
indeed insufferable, were he not chastised, first rose up in
arms, and with a powerful army advanced against him.
Romulus likewise prepared to receive him; but when
they came within sight and viewed each other, they
made a challenge to fight a single duel, the armies standing by under arms, without participation. And Romulus,
making a vow to Jupiter, if he should conquer, to carry,
himself, and dedicate his adversary's armor to his honor,
overcame him in combat, and, a battle ensuing, routed
his army also, and then took his city; but did those he
found in it no injury, only commanded them to demolish
the place and attend him to Rome, there to be admitted
to all the privileges of citizens. And indeed there was
nothing did more advance the greatness of Rome, than
that she did always unite and incorporate those whom
she conquered into herself. Romulus, that he might
perform his vow in the most acceptable manner to Jupiter, and withal make the pomp of it delightful to the
eye of the city, cut down a tall oak which he saw grow-

ing in the camp, which he trimmed to the shape of a
trophy, and fastened on it Acron's whole suit of armor
disposed in proper form; then he himself, girding his
clothes about him, and crowning his head with a laurel-
garland, his hair gracefully flowing, carried the trophy
resting erect upon his right shoulder, and so marched on,
singing songs of triumph, and his whole army following
after, the citizens all receiving him with acclamations of
joy and wonder. The procession of this day was the
origin and model of all after triumphs. This trophy was
styled an offering to Jupiter Feretrius, from *ferire*, which
in Latin is to smite; for Romulus prayed he might smite
and overthrow his enemy; and the spoils were called
opima, or royal spoils, says Varro, from their richness,
which the word *opes* signifies; though one would more
probably conjecture from *opus*, an act; for it is only to
the general of an army who with his own hand kills his
enemies' general that this honor is granted of offering
the *opima spolia*. And three only of the Roman captains
have had it conferred on them: first, Romulus, upon
killing Acron the Ceninensian; next, Cornelius Cossus,
for slaying Tolumnius the Tuscan; and lastly, Claudius
Marcellus, upon his conquering Viridomarus, king of the
Gauls. The two latter, Cossus and Marcellus, made their
entries in triumphant chariots, bearing their trophies
themselves; but that Romulus made use of a chariot,
Dionysius is wrong in asserting. History says, Tarquinius,
Damaratus's son, was the first that brought triumphs to
this great pomp and grandeur; others, that Publicola was
the first that rode in triumph. The statues of Romulus
in triumph are, as may be seen in Rome, all on foot.

After the overthrow of the Ceninensians, the other
Sabines still protracting the time in preparations, the
people of Fidenæ, Crustumerium, and Antemna, joined
their forces against the Romans; they in like manner

were defeated in battle, and surrendered up to Romulus their cities to be seized, their lands and territories to be divided, and themselves to be transplanted to Rome. All the lands which Romulus acquired, he distributed among the citizens, except only what the parents of the stolen virgins had; these he suffered to possess their own. The rest of the Sabines, enraged hereat, choosing Tatius their captain, marched straight against Rome. The city was almost inaccessible, having for its fortress that which is now the Capitol, where a strong guard was placed, and Tarpeius their captain; not Tarpeia the virgin, as some say who would make Romulus a fool. But Tarpeia, daughter to the captain, coveting the golden bracelets she saw them wear, betrayed the fort into the Sabines' hands, and asked, in reward of her treachery, the things they wore on their left arms. Tatius conditioning thus with her, in the night she opened one of the gates, and received the Sabines in. And truly Antigonus, it would seem, was not solitary in saying, he loved betrayers, but hated those who had betrayed; nor Cæsar, who told Rhymitalces the Thracian, that he loved the treason, but hated the traitor; but it is the general feeling of all who have occasion for wicked men's service, as people have for the poison of venomous beasts; they are glad of them while they are of use, and abhor their baseness when it is over. And so then did Tatius behave towards Tarpeia, for he commanded the Sabines, in regard to their contract, not to refuse her the least part of what they wore on their left arms; and he himself first took his bracelet off his arm, and threw that, together with his buckler, at her; and all the rest following, she, being borne down and quite buried with the multitude of gold and their shields, died under the weight and pressure of them; Tarpeius also himself, being prosecuted by Romulus, was found guilty of treason, as Juba says Sulpicius Galba relates. Those who write otherwise concerning Tarpeia, as that she was the daughter of Tatius, the Sabine captain, and, being forcibly detained by Romulus, acted and suffered thus by her father's contrivance, speak very absurdly, of whom Antigonus is one. And Simylus, the poet, who thinks Tarpeia betrayed the Capitol, not to the Sabines, but the Gauls, having fallen in love with their king, talks mere folly, saying thus : —

> Tarpeia 't was, who, dwelling close thereby,
> Laid open Rome unto the enemy.
> She, for the love of the besieging Gaul,
> Betrayed the city's strength, the Capitol.

And a little after, speaking of her death : —

> The numerous nations of the Celtic foe
> Bore her not living to the banks of Po ;
> Their heavy shields upon the maid they threw,
> And with their splendid gifts entombed at once and slew.

Tarpeia afterwards was buried there, and the hill from her was called Tarpeius, until the reign of king Tarquin, who dedicated the place to Jupiter, at which time her bones were removed, and so it lost her name, except only that part of the Capitol which they still call the Tarpeian Rock, from which they used to cast down malefactors.

The Sabines being possessed of the hill, Romulus, in great fury, bade them battle, and Tatius was confident to accept it, perceiving, if they were overpowered, that they had behind them a secure retreat. The level in the middle, where they were to join battle, being surrounded with many little hills, seemed to enforce both parties to a sharp and desperate conflict, by reason of the difficulties of the place, which had but a few outlets, inconvenient either for refuge or pursuit. It happened, too, the river having overflowed not many days before, there was left

behind in the plain, where now the forum stands, a deep
blind mud and slime, which, though it did not appear
much to the eye, and was not easily avoided, at bottom
was deceitful and dangerous; upon which the Sabines being unwarily about to enter, met with a piece of good fortune; for Curtius, a gallant man, eager of honor, and of
aspiring thoughts, being mounted on horseback, was gal-
loping on before the rest, and mired his horse here, and,
endeavoring for awhile by whip and spur and voice to
disentangle him, but finding it impossible, quitted him and
saved himself; the place from him to this very time is
called the Curtian Lake. The Sabines, having avoided
this danger, began the fight very smartly, the fortune of
the day being very dubious, though many were slain;
amongst whom was Hostilius, who, they say, was husband
to Hersilia, and grandfather to that Hostilius who reigned
after Numa. There were many other brief conflicts, we
may suppose, but the most memorable was the last, in
which Romulus having received a wound on his head by
a stone, and being almost felled to the ground by it, and
disabled, the Romans gave way, and, being driven out of
the level ground, fled towards the Palatium. Romulus, by
this time recovering from his wound a little, turned about
to renew the battle, and, facing the fliers, with a loud voice
encouraged them to stand and fight. But being overborne
with numbers, and nobody daring to face about, stretching
out his hands to heaven, he prayed to Jupiter to stop the
army, and not to neglect but maintain the Roman cause,
now in extreme danger. The prayer was no sooner made,
than shame and respect for their king checked many;
the fears of the fugitives changed suddenly into confidence. The place they first stood at was where now is
the temple of Jupiter Stator (which may be translated
the Stayer); there they rallied again into ranks, and repulsed the Sabines to the place called now Regia, and to

the temple of Vesta ; where both parties, preparing to begin a second battle, were prevented by a spectacle, strange to behold, and defying description. For the daughters of the Sabines, who had been carried off, came running, in great confusion, some on this side, some on that, with miserable cries and lamentations, like creatures possessed, in the midst of the army, and among the dead bodies, to come at their husbands and their fathers, some with their young babes in their arms, others their hair loose about their ears, but all calling, now upon the Sabines, now upon the Romans, in the most tender and endearing words. Hereupon both melted into compassion, and fell back, to make room for them betwixt the armies. The sight of the women carried sorrow and commiseration upon both sides into the hearts of all, but still more their words, which began with expostulation and upbraiding, and ended with entreaty and supplication.

"Wherein," say they, "have we injured or offended you, as to deserve such sufferings, past and present ? We were ravished away unjustly and violently by those whose now we are ; that being done, we were so long neglected by our fathers, our brothers, and countrymen, that time, having now by the strictest bonds united us to those we once mortally hated, has made it impossible for us not to tremble at the danger and weep at the death of the very men who once used violence to us. You did not come to vindicate our honor, while we were virgins, against our assailants ; but do come now to force away wives from their husbands and mothers from their children, a succor more grievous to its wretched objects than the former betrayal and neglect of them. Which shall we call the worst, their love-making or your compassion ? If you were making war upon any other occasion, for our sakes you ought to withhold your hands from those to whom we have made you fathers-in-law and grandsires.

If it be for our own cause, then take us, and with us your sons-in-law and grandchildren. Restore to us our parents and kindred, but do not rob us of our children and husbands. Make us not, we entreat you, twice captives." Hersilia having spoken many such words as these, and the others earnestly praying, a truce was made, and the chief officers came to a parley ; the women, in the mean time, brought and presented their husbands and children to their fathers and brothers ; gave those that wanted, meat and drink, and carried the wounded home to be cured, and showed also how much they governed within doors, and how indulgent their husbands were to them, in demeaning themselves towards them with all kindness and respect imaginable. Upon this, conditions were agreed upon, that what women pleased might stay where they were, exempt, as aforesaid, from all drudgery and labor but spinning; that the Romans and Sabines should inhabit the city together ; that the city should be called Rome, from Romulus; but the Romans, Quirites, from the country of Tatius ; and that they both should govern and command in common. The place of the ratification is still called Comitium, from *coire*, to meet.

The city being thus doubled in number, an hundred of the Sabines were elected senators, and the legions were increased to six thousand foot and six hundred horse ; then they divided the people into three tribes; the first, from Romulus, named Ramnenses ; the second, from Tatius, Tatienses ; the third, Luceres, from the *lucus*, or grove, where the Asylum stood, whither many fled for sanctuary, and were received into the city. And that they were just three, the very name of *tribe* and *tribune* seems to show ; each tribe contained ten curiæ, or brotherhoods, which, some say, took their names from the Sabine women ; but that seems to be false, because many had their names from various places. Though it is

true, they then constituted many things in honor to the
women ; as to give them the way wherever they met
them ; to speak no ill word in their presence ; not to appear naked before them, or else be liable to prosecution
before the judges of homicide ; that their children should
wear an ornament about their necks called the *bulla*
(because it was like a bubble), and the *prætexta*, a gown
edged with purple.

The princes did not immediately join in council together, but at first each met with his own hundred ;
afterwards all assembled together. Tatius dwelt where
now the temple of Moneta stands, and Romulus, close by
the steps, as they call them, of the Fair Shore, near the
descent from the Mount Palatine to the Circus Maximus.
There, they say, grew the holy cornel tree, of which they
report, that Romulus once, to try his strength, threw a
dart from the Aventine Mount, the staff of which was made
of cornel, which struck so deep into the ground, that no
one of many that tried could pluck it up ; and the soil,
being fertile, gave nourishment to the wood, which sent
forth branches, and produced a cornel-stock of considerable
bigness. This did posterity preserve and worship as one
of the most sacred things ; and, therefore, walled it about ;
and if to any one it appeared not green nor flourishing,
but inclining to pine and wither, he immediately made
outcry to all he met, and they, like people hearing of a
house on fire, with one accord would cry for water, and
run from all parts with buckets full to the place. But
when Caius Cæsar, they say, was repairing the steps about
it, some of the laborers digging too close, the roots were
destroyed, and the tree withered.

The Sabines adopted the Roman months, of which
whatever is remarkable is mentioned in the Life of
Numa. Romulus, on the other hand, adopted their long
shields, and changed his own armor and that of all the

Romans, who before wore round targets of the Argive pattern. Feasts and sacrifices they partook of in common, not abolishing any which either nation observed before, and instituting several new ones; of which one was the Matronalia, instituted in honor of the women, for their extinction of the war; likewise the Carmentalia. This Carmenta some think a deity presiding over human birth; for which reason she is much honored by mothers. Others say she was the wife of Evander, the Arcadian, being a prophetess, and went to deliver her oracles in verse, and from *carmen*, a verse, was called Carmenta; her proper name being Nicostrata. Others more probably derive Carmenta from *carens mente*, or insane, in allusion to her prophetic frenzies. Of the Feast of Palilia we have spoken before. The Lupercalia, by the time of its celebration, may seem to be a feast of purification, for it is solemnized on the *dies nefasti*, or non-court days, of the month February, which name signifies purification, and the very day of the feast was anciently called Februata; but its name is equivalent to the Greek Lycæa; and it seems thus to be of great antiquity, and brought in by the Arcadians who came with Evander. Yet this is but dubious, for it may come as well from the wolf that nursed Romulus; and we see the Luperci, the priests, begin their course from the place where they say Romulus was exposed. But the ceremonies performed in it render the origin of the thing more difficult to be guessed at; for there are goats killed, then, two young noblemen's sons being brought, some are to stain their foreheads with the bloody knife, others presently to wipe it off with wool dipped in milk; then the young boys must laugh after their foreheads are wiped; that done, having cut the goats' skins into thongs, they run about naked, only with something about their middle, lashing all they meet; and the young wives do not avoid their strokes, fancying they

will help conception and child-birth.   Another thing peculiar to this feast is for the Luperci to sacrifice a dog.
But as, a certain poet who wrote fabulous explanations of
Roman customs in elegiac verses, says, that Romulus and
Remus, after the conquest of Amulius, ran joyfully to the
place where the wolf gave them suck ; and that in imitation of that, this feast was held, and two young noblemen
ran —

> Striking at all, as when from Alba town,
> With sword in hand, the twins came hurrying down;

and that the bloody knife applied to their foreheads
was a sign of the danger and bloodshed of that day ; the
cleansing of them in milk, a remembrance of their food
and nourishment.   Caius Acilius writes, that, before the
city was built, the cattle of Romulus and Remus one day
going astray, they, praying to the god Faunus, ran out
to seek them naked, wishing not to be troubled with
sweat, and that this is why the Luperci run naked.   If the
sacrifice be by way of purification, a dog might very well
be sacrificed ; for the Greeks, in their lustrations, carry
out young dogs, and frequently use this ceremony of
periscylacismus, as they call it.   Or if again it is a sacrifice of gratitude to the wolf that nourished and preserved
Romulus, there is good reason in killing a dog, as being
an enemy to wolves.   Unless indeed, after all, the creature
is punished for hindering the Luperci in their running.

They say, too, Romulus was the first that consecrated holy fire, and instituted holy virgins to keep it,
called vestals ; others ascribe it to Numa Pompilius ;
agreeing, however, that Romulus was otherwise eminently
religious, and skilled in divination, and for that reason
carried the *lituus*, a crooked rod with which soothsayers
describe the quarters of the heavens, when they sit to
observe the flights of birds.   This of his, being kept in

the Palatium, was lost when the city was taken by the Gauls; and afterwards, that barbarous people being driven out, was found in the ruins, under a great heap of ashes, untouched by the fire, all things about it being consumed and burnt. He instituted also certain laws, one of which is somewhat severe, which suffers not a wife to leave her husband, but grants a husband power to turn off his wife, either upon poisoning her children, or counterfeiting his keys, or for adultery; but if the husband upon any other occasion put her away, he ordered one moiety of his estate to be given to the wife, the other to fall to the goddess Ceres; and whoever cast off his wife, to make an atonement by sacrifice to the gods of the dead. This, too, is observable as a singular thing in Romulus, that he appointed no punishment for real parricide, but called all murder so, thinking the one an accursed thing, but the other a thing impossible; and, for a long time, his judgment seemed to have been right; for in almost six hundred years together, nobody committed the like in Rome; and Lucius Hostius, after the wars of Hannibal, is recorded to have been the first parricide. Let thus much suffice concerning these matters.

In the fifth year of the reign of Tatius, some of his friends and kinsmen, meeting ambassadors coming from Laurentum to Rome, attempted on the road to take away their money by force, and, upon their resistance, killed them. So great a villany having been committed, Romulus thought the malefactors ought at once to be punished, but Tatius shuffled off and deferred the execution of it; and this one thing was the beginning of open quarrel betwixt them; in all other respects they were very careful of their conduct, and administered affairs together with great unanimity. The relations of the slain, being debarred of lawful satisfaction by reason of Tatius, fell upon him as he was sacrificing with Romulus at Lavinium,

and slew him; but escorted Romulus home, commending
and extolling him for a just prince. Romulus took the
body of Tatius, and buried it very splendidly in the Aventine Mount, near the place called Armilustrium, but
altogether neglected revenging his murder. Some authors write, the city of Laurentum, fearing the consequence, delivered up the murderers of Tatius; but Romulus dismissed them, saying, one murder was requited
with another. This gave occasion of talk and jealousy,
as if he were well pleased at the removal of his copartner
in the government. Nothing of these things, however,
raised any sort of feud or disturbance among the Sabines;
but some out of love to him, others out of fear of his
power, some again reverencing him as a god, they all
continued living peacefully in admiration and awe of him;
many foreign nations, too, showed respect to Romulus;
the Ancient Latins sent, and entered into league and confederacy with him. Fidenæ he took, a neighboring city
to Rome, by a party of horse, as some say, whom he sent
before with commands to cut down the hinges of the
gates, himself afterwards unexpectedly coming up. Others say, they having first made the invasion, plundering
and ravaging the country and suburbs, Romulus lay in
ambush for them, and, having killed many of their men,
took the city; but, nevertheless, did not raze or demolish
it, but made it a Roman colony, and sent thither, on the
Ides of April, two thousand five hundred inhabitants.

Soon after a plague broke out, causing sudden death
without any previous sickness; it infected also the corn
with unfruitfulness, and cattle with barrenness; there
rained blood, too, in the city; so that, to their actual sufferings, fear of the wrath of the gods was added. But
when the same mischiefs fell upon Laurentum, then everybody judged it was divine vengeance that fell upon both
cities, for the neglect of executing justice upon the mur-

der of Tatius and the ambassadors. But the murderers
on both sides being delivered up and punished, the pestilence visibly abated; and Romulus purified the cities
with lustrations, which, they say, even now are performed
at the wood called Ferentina. But before the plague
ceased, the Camertines invaded the Romans and overran
the country, thinking them, by reason of the distemper,
unable to resist; but Romulus at once made head against
them, and gained the victory, with the slaughter of six
thousand men; then took their city, and brought half of
those he found there to Rome; sending from Rome to
Camerium double the number he left there. This was
done the first of August. So many citizens had he to
spare, in sixteen years' time from his first founding Rome.
Among other spoils, he took a brazen four-horse chariot
from Camerium, which he placed in the temple of Vulcan,
setting on it his own statue, with a figure of Victory
crowning him.

The Roman cause thus daily gathering strength, their
weaker neighbors shrunk away, and were thankful to be
left untouched; but the stronger, out of fear or envy,
thought they ought not to give way to Romulus, but to
curb and put a stop to his growing greatness. The first
were the Veientes, a people of Tuscany, who had large
possessions, and dwelt in a spacious city; they took occasion to commence a war, by claiming Fidenæ as belonging
to them; a thing not only very unreasonable, but very
ridiculous, that they, who did not assist them in the greatest extremities, but permitted them to be slain, should
challenge their lands and houses when in the hands of
others. But being scornfully retorted upon by Romulus
in his answers, they divided themselves into two bodies;
with one they attacked the garrison of Fidenæ, the other
marched against Romulus; that which went against Fidenæ got the victory, and slew two thousand Romans; the

other was worsted by Romulus, with the loss of eight thousand men. A fresh battle was fought near Fidenæ, and here all men acknowledge the day's success to have been chiefly the work of Romulus himself, who showed the highest skill as well as courage, and seemed to manifest a strength and swiftness more than human. But what some write, that, of fourteen thousand that fell that day, above half were slain by Romulus's own hand, verges too near to fable, and is, indeed, simply incredible; since even the Messenians are thought to go too far in saying that Aristomenes three times offered sacrifice for the death of a hundred enemies, Lacedæmonians, slain by himself. The army being thus routed, Romulus, suffering those that were left to make their escape, led his forces against the city; they, having suffered such great losses, did not venture to oppose, but, humbly suing to him, made a league and friendship for an hundred years; surrendering also a large district of land called Septempagium, that is, the seven parts, as also their salt-works upon the river, and fifty noblemen for hostages. He made his triumph for this on the Ides of October, leading, among the rest of his many captives, the general of the Veientes, an elderly man, but who had not, it seemed, acted with the prudence of age; whence even now, in sacrifices for victories, they lead an old man through the market-place to the Capitol, apparelled in purple, with a *bulla*, or child's toy, tied to it, and the crier cries, *Sardians to be sold;* for the Tuscans are said to be a colony of the Sardians, and the Veientes are a city of Tuscany.

This was the last battle Romulus ever fought; afterwards he, as most, nay all men, very few excepted, do, who are raised by great and miraculous good-haps of fortune to power and greatness, so, I say, did he; relying upon his own great actions, and growing of an haughtier mind, he forsook his popular behavior for kingly arro-

gance, odious to the people; to whom in particular the
state which he assumed was hateful.   For he dressed in
scarlet, with the purple-bordered robe over it; he gave
audience on a couch of state, having always about him
some young men called *Celeres*, from their swiftness in
doing commissions; there went before him others with
staves, to make room, with leather thongs tied on their
bodies, to bind on the moment whomever he commanded.
The Latins formerly used *ligare* in the same sense as now
alligare, to bind, whence the name *lictors*, for these officers,
and *bacula*, or staves, for their rods, because staves were
then used.   It is probable, however, they were first called
litores, afterwards, by putting in a *c*, *lictores*, or, in Greek,
lituryi, or people's officers, for *leïtos* is still Greek for the
commons, and *laös* for the people in general.

But when, after the death of his grandfather Numitor
in Alba, the throne devolving upon Romulus, he, to court
the people, put the government into their own hands,
and appointed an annual magistrate over the Albans,
this taught the great men of Rome to seek after a free
and anti-monarchical state, wherein all might in turn be
subjects and rulers.   For neither were the patricians any
longer admitted to state affairs, only had the name and
title left them, convening in council rather for fashion's
sake than advice, where they heard in silence the king's
commands, and so departed, exceeding the commonalty
only in hearing first what was done.   These and the like
were matters of small moment; but when he of his own
accord parted among his soldiers what lands were acquired by war, and restored the Veientes their hostages,
the senate neither consenting nor approving of it, then,
indeed, he seemed to put a great affront upon them; so
that, on his sudden and strange disappearance a short
while after, the senate fell under suspicion and calumny.
He disappeared on the Nones of July, as they now call

the month which was then Quintilis, leaving nothing of
certainty to be related of his death; only the time, as
just mentioned, for on that day many ceremonies are
still performed in representation of what happened.
Neither is this uncertainty to be thought strange, seeing
the manner of the death of Scipio Africanus, who died at
his own home after supper, has been found capable neither
of proof or disproof; for some say he died a natural death,
being of a sickly habit; others, that he poisoned himself;
others again, that his enemies, breaking in upon him in
the night, stifled him. Yet Scipio's dead body lay open
to be seen of all, and any one, from his own observation,
might form his suspicions and conjectures; whereas Romulus, when he vanished, left neither the least part of
his body, nor any remnant of his clothes to be seen. So
that some fancied, the senators, having fallen upon him in
the temple of Vulcan, cut his body into pieces, and took
each a part away in his bosom; others think his disappearance was neither in the temple of Vulcan, nor with
the senators only by, but that, it came to pass that, as he
was haranguing the people without the city, near a place
called the Goat's Marsh, on a sudden strange and unac-
countable disorders and alterations took place in the air;
the face of the sun was darkened, and the day turned
into night, and that, too, no quiet, peaceable night, but
with terrible thunderings, and boisterous winds from all
quarters; during which the common people dispersed
and fled, but the senators kept close together. The tempest being over and the light breaking out, when the
people gathered again, they missed and inquired for their
king; the senators suffered them not to search, or busy
themselves about the matter, but commanded them to
honor and worship Romulus as one taken up to the gods,
and about to be to them, in the place of a good prince,
now a propitious god. The multitude, hearing this, went

away believing and rejoicing in hopes of good things from him; but there were some, who, canvassing the matter in a hostile temper, accused and aspersed the patricians, as men that persuaded the people to believe ridiculous tales, when they themselves were the murderers of the king.

Things being in this disorder, one, they say, of the patricians, of noble family and approved good character, and a faithful and familiar friend of Romulus himself, having come with him from Alba, Julius Proculus by name, presented himself in the forum; and, taking a most sacred oath, protested before them all, that, as he was travelling on the road, he had seen Romulus coming to meet him, looking taller and comelier than ever, dressed in shining and flaming armor; and he, being affrighted at the apparition, said, "Why, O king, or for what purpose have you abandoned us to unjust and wicked surmises, and the whole city to bereavement and endless sorrow?" and that he made answer, "It pleased the gods, O Proculus, that we, who came from them, should remain so long a time amongst men as we did; and, having built a city to be the greatest in the world for empire and glory, should again return to heaven. But farewell; and tell the Romans, that, by the exercise of temperance and fortitude, they shall attain the height of human power; we will be to you the propitious god Quirinus." This seemed credible to the Romans, upon the honesty and oath of the relater, and indeed, too, there mingled with it a certain divine passion, some preternatural influence similar to possession by a divinity; nobody contradicted it, but, laying aside all jealousies and detractions, they prayed to Quirinus and saluted him as a god.

This is like some of the Greek fables of Aristeas the Proconnesian, and Cleomedes the Astypalaean; for they say Aristeas died in a fuller's work-shop, and his friends,

coming to look for him, found his body vanished; and
that some presently after, coming from abroad, said they
met him travelling towards Croton. And that Cleomedes,
being an extraordinarily strong and gigantic man, but
also wild and mad, committed many desperate freaks;
and at last, in a school-house, striking a pillar that sustained the roof with his fist, broke it in the middle, so
that the house fell and destroyed the children in it; and
being pursued, he fled into a great chest, and, shutting to
the lid, held it so fast, that many men, with their united
strength, could not force it open; afterwards, breaking the
chest to pieces, they found no man in it alive or dead; in
astonishment at which, they sent to consult the oracle at
Delphi; to whom the prophetess made this answer,

> Of all the heroes, Cleomede is last.

They say, too, the body of Alcmena, as they were carrying her to her grave, vanished, and a stone was found
lying on the bier. And many such improbabilities do
your fabulous writers relate, deifying creatures naturally
mortal; for though altogether to disown a divine nature
in human virtue were impious and base, so again to mix
heaven with earth is ridiculous. Let us believe with
Pindar, that

> All human bodies yield to Death's decree,
> The soul survives to all eternity.

For that alone is derived from the gods, thence comes,
and thither returns; not with the body, but when most
disengaged and separated from it, and when most entirely
pure and clean and free from the flesh; for the most perfect soul, says Heraclitus, is a dry light, which flies out of
the body as lightning breaks from a cloud; but that
which is clogged and surfeited with body is like gross and

humid incense, slow to kindle and ascend. We must not, therefore, contrary to nature, send the bodies, too, of good men to heaven; but we must really believe that, according to their divine nature and law, their virtue and their souls are translated out of men into heroes, out of heroes into demi-gods, out of demi-gods, after passing, as in the rite of initiation, through a final cleansing and sanctification, and so freeing themselves from all that pertains to mortality and sense, are thus, not by human decree, but really and according to right reason, elevated into gods, admitted thus to the greatest and most blessed perfection.

Romulus's surname Quirinus, some say, is equivalent to Mars; others, that he was so called because the citizens were called Quirites; others, because the ancients called a dart or spear Quiris; thus, the statue of Juno resting on a spear is called Quiritis, and the dart in the Regia is addressed as Mars, and those that were distinguished in war were usually presented with a dart; that, therefore, Romulus, being a martial god, or a god of darts, was called Quirinus. A temple is certainly built to his honor on the mount called from him Quirinalis.

The day he vanished on is called the Flight of the People, and the Nones of the Goats,* because they go then out of the city, and sacrifice at the Goat's Marsh, and, as they go, they shout out some of the Roman names, as Marcus, Lucius, Caius, imitating the way in which they then fled and called upon one another in that fright and hurry. Some, however, say, this was not in imitation of a flight, but of a quick and hasty onset, referring it to the following occasion: after the Gauls who had taken Rome were driven out by Camillus, and the city was scarcely as yet recovering her strength, many of the Latins,

---

* Populifugia, Nonæ Caprotinæ.

under the command of Livius Postumius, took this time
to march against her. Postumius, halting not far from
Rome, sent a herald, signifying that the Latins were
desirous to renew their former alliance and affinity (that
was now almost decayed) by contracting new marriages
between both nations; if, therefore, they would send
forth a good number of their virgins and widows, they
should have peace and friendship, such as the Sabines
had formerly had on the like conditions. The Romans,
hearing this, dreaded a war, yet thought a surrender of
their women little better than mere captivity. Being in
this doubt, a servant-maid called Philotis (or, as some say,
Tutola), advised them to do neither, but, by a stratagem,
avoid both fighting and the giving up of such pledges.
The stratagem was this, that they should send herself,
with other well-looking servant-maids, to the enemy, in
the dress of free-born virgins, and she should in the night
light up a fire-signal, at which the Romans should come
armed and surprise them asleep. The Latins were thus
deceived, and accordingly Philotis set up a torch in a
wild fig-tree, screening it behind with curtains and coverlets from the sight of the enemy, while visible to the
Romans. They, when they saw it, eagerly ran out of the
gates, calling in their haste to each other as they went
out, and so, falling in unexpectedly upon the enemy, they
defeated them, and upon that made a feast of triumph,
called the Nones of the Goats, because of the wild fig-tree,
called by the Romans Caprificus, or the goat-fig. They
feast the women without the city in arbors made of fig-
tree boughs, and the maid-servants gather together and
run about playing; afterwards they fight in sport, and
throw stones one at another, in memory that they then
aided and assisted the Roman men in fight. This only a
few authors admit for true; for the calling upon one another's names by day and the going out to the Goat's

Marsh to do sacrifice seem to agree more with the former story, unless, indeed, we shall say that both the actions might have happened on the same day in different years. It was in the fifty-fourth year of his age and the thirty-eighth of his reign that Romulus, they tell us, left the world.

COMPARISON OF ROMULUS WITH THESEUS.

THIS is what I have learnt of Romulus and Theseus, worthy of memory. It seems, first of all, that Theseus, out of his own free-will, without any compulsion, when he might have reigned in security at Trœzen in the enjoyment of no inglorious empire, of his own motion affected great actions, whereas the other, to escape present servitude and a punishment that threatened him, (according to Plato's phrase) grew valiant purely out of fear, and, dreading the extremest inflictions, attempted great enterprises out of mere necessity. Again, his greatest action was only the killing of one king of Alba; while, as mere by-adventures and preludes, the other can name Sciron, Sinnis, Procrustes, and Corynetes; by reducing and killing of whom, he rid Greece of terrible oppressors, before any of them that were relieved knew who did it; moreover, he might without any trouble as well have gone to Athens by sea, considering he himself never was in the least injured by those robbers; where as Romulus could not but be in trouble whilst Amulius lived. Add to this the fact that Theseus, for no wrong done to himself, but for the sake of others, fell upon these villains; but Romulus and Remus, as long as they themselves suffered no ill by the tyrant, permitted him to oppress all others. And if it be a great thing to have been wounded in battle by the Sabines, to have killed king Acron, and to have conquered many enemies, we may oppose to these actions the battle with the Centaurs and the feats done against the Amazons. But what Theseus adventured, in offering himself voluntarily with young boys and virgins, as part of the tribute unto Crete, either to be a prey to a monster or a victim upon the tomb of Androgeus, or, according to the mildest form of the story, to live vilely and dishonorably in slavery to insulting and cruel men; it is not to be expressed what an act of courage, magnanimity, or justice to the public, or of love for honor and bravery, that was. So that methinks the philosophers did not ill define love to be the provision of the gods for the care and preservation of the young; for the love of Ariadne, above all, seems to have been the proper work and design of some god in order to preserve Theseus; and, indeed, we ought not to blame her for loving him, but rather wonder all men and women were not alike affected towards him; and if she alone were so, truly I dare pronounce her worthy of the love of a god, who was herself so great a lover of virtue and goodness, and the bravest man.

Both Theseus and Romulus were by nature meant for governors; yet neither lived up to the true character of a king, but fell off, and ran, the one into popularity, the other into tyranny, falling both into the same fault out of different passions. For a ruler's first end is to maintain his office, which is done no less by avoiding what is unfit than by observing what is suitable. Whoever is either too remiss or too strict is no more a king or a governor, but either a demagogue or a despot, and so becomes either odious or contemptible to his subjects. Though certainly the one seems to be the fault of easiness and good-nature, the other of pride and severity.

If men's calamities, again, are not to be wholly imputed to fortune, but refer themselves to differences of character, who will acquit either Theseus of rash and unreasonable anger against his son, or Romulus against his brother? Looking at motives, we more easily excuse the anger which a stronger cause, like a severer blow, provoked. Romulus, having disagreed with his brother advisedly and deliberately on public matters, one would think could not on a sudden have been put into so great a passion; but love and jealousy and the complaints of his wife, which few men can avoid being moved by, seduced Theseus to commit that outrage upon his son. And what is more, Romulus, in his anger, committed an action of unfortunate consequence; but that of Theseus ended only in words, some evil speaking, and an old man's curse; the rest of the youth's disasters seem to have proceeded from fortune; so that, so far, a man would give his vote on Theseus's part.

But Romulus has, first of all, one great plea, that his performances proceeded from very small beginnings; for both the brothers being thought servants and the sons of swincherds, before becoming freemen themselves, gave liberty to almost all the Latins, obtaining at once all the most honorable titles, as destroyers of their country's enemies, preservers of their friends and kindred, princes of the people, founders of cities, not removers, like Theseus, who raised and compiled only one house out of many, demolishing many cities bearing the names of ancient kings and heroes. Romulus, indeed, did the same afterwards, forcing his enemies to deface and ruin their own dwellings, and to sojourn with their conquerors; but at first, not by removal, or increase of an existing city, but by foundation of a new one, he obtained himself lands, a country, a kingdom, wives, children, and relations. And, in so doing, he killed or destroyed nobody, but benefited those that wanted houses and homes and were willing to be of a society and become citizens. Robbers and malefactors he slew not; but he subdued nations, he overthrew cities, he triumphed over kings and commanders. As to Remus, it is doubtful by whose hand he fell; it is generally imputed to others. His mother he clearly retrieved from death, and placed his grandfather, who was brought under base and dishonorable vassalage, on the ancient throne of Æneas, to whom he did voluntarily many good offices, but never did him harm even inadvertently. But Theseus, in his forgetfulness and neglect of the command concerning the flag, can scarcely, methinks, by any excuses, or before the most indulgent judges, avoid the imputation of parricide. And, indeed, one of the Attic writers, perceiving it to be very hard to make an excuse for this, feigns that Ægeus, at the approach of the ship, running hastily to the Acropolis to see what news, slipped and fell down, as if he had no servants, or none would attend him on his way to the shore.

And, indeed, the faults committed in the rapes of women admit of no plausible excuse in Theseus. First, because of the often repetition of the crime; for he stole Ariadne, Antiope, Anaxo the Troezenian, at last Helen, when he was an old man, and she not marriageable; she a child, and he at an age past even lawful wedlock. Then, on account of the cause; for the Troezenian, Lacedæmonian, and Amazonian virgins, beside that they were not betrothed to him, were not worthier to raise children by than the Athenian women, derived from Erechtheus and Cecrops; but it is to be suspected these things were done out of wantonness and lust. Romulus, when he had taken near eight hundred women, chose not all, but only Hersilia, as they say, for himself; the rest he divided among the chief of the city; and afterwards, by the respect and tenderness and justice shown towards them, he made it clear that this violence and injury was a commendable and politic exploit to establish a society; by which he intermixed and united both nations, and made it the fountain of after friendship and public stability. And to the reverence and love and constancy he established in matrimony, time can witness; for in two hundred and thirty years, neither any husband deserted his wife, nor any wife her husband ; but, as the curious among the Greeks can name the first case of parricide or matricide, so the Romans all well know that Spurius Carvilius was the first who put away his wife, accusing her of barrenness. The immediate results were similar; for upon those marriages the two princes shared in the dominion, and both nations fell under the same government. But from the marriages of Theseus proceeded nothing of friendship or correspondence for the advantage of commerce, but enmities and wars and the slaughter of citizens, and, at last, the loss of the city Aphidnæ, when only out of the compassion of the enemy, whom they entreated and caressed like gods, they escaped suffering what Troy did by Paris. Theseus's mother, however, was not only in danger, but suffered actually what Hecuba did, deserted and neglected by her son, unless her captivity be not a fiction, as I could wish both that and other things were. The circumstances of the divine intervention, said to have preceded or accompanied their births, are also in contrast; for Romulus was preserved by the special favor of the gods ; but the oracle given to Ægeus, commanding him to abstain, seems to demonstrate that the birth of Theseus was not agreeable to the will of the gods.

LYCURGUS.

THERE is so much uncertainty in the accounts which historians have left us of Lycurgus, the lawgiver of Sparta, that scarcely any thing is asserted by one of them which is not called into question or contradicted by the rest. Their sentiments are quite different as to the family he came of, the voyages he undertook, the place and manner of his death, but most of all when they speak of the laws he made and the commonwealth which he founded. They cannot, by any means, be brought to an agreement as to the very age in which he lived; for some of them say that he flourished in the time of Iphitus, and that they two jointly contrived the ordinance for the cessation of arms during the solemnity of the Olympic games. Of this opinion was Aristotle; and for confirmation of it, he alleges an inscription upon one of the copper quoits used in those sports, upon which the name of Lycurgus continued uneffaced to his time. But Eratosthenes and Apollodorus and other chronologers, computing the time by the successions of the Spartan kings, pretend to demonstrate that he was much more ancient than the institution of the Olympic games. Timæus conjectures that there were two of this name, and in diverse times, but that the one of them being much more famous than the other, men gave to him the glory of the exploits of both; the elder of the

two, according to him, was not long after Homer; and
some are so particular as to say that he had seen him.
But that he was of great antiquity may be gathered from
a passage in Xenophon, where he makes him contemporary with the Heraclidæ. By descent, indeed, the very
last kings of Sparta were Heraclidæ too; but he seems in
that place to speak of the first and more immediate successors of Hercules. But notwithstanding this confusion
and obscurity, we shall endeavor to compose the history
of his life, adhering to those statements which are least
contradicted, and depending upon those authors who are
most worthy of credit.

The poet Simonides will have it that Lycurgus was the
son of Prytanis, and not of Eunomus; but in this opinion
he is singular, for all the rest deduce the genealogy of
them both as follows: —

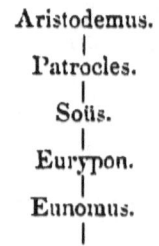

Aristodemus.
|
Patrocles.
|
Soüs.
|
Eurypon.
|
Eunomus.
|

Polydectes by his first wife.   Lycurgus by Dionassa his second.

Dieuchidas says he was the sixth from Patrocles and the
eleventh from Hercules. Be this as it will, Soüs certainly was the most renowned of all his ancestors, under
whose conduct the Spartans made slaves of the Helots,
and added to their dominions, by conquest, a good part
of Arcadia. There goes a story of this king Soüs, that,
being besieged by the Clitorians in a dry and stony place
so that he could come at no water, he was at last constrained to agree with them upon these terms, that he
would restore to them all his conquests, provided that
himself and all his men should drink of the nearest

spring. After the usual oaths and ratifications, he called his soldiers together, and offered to him that would forbear drinking, his kingdom for a reward; and when not a man of them was able to forbear, in short, when they had all drunk their fill, at last comes king Soüs himself to the spring, and, having sprinkled his face only, without swallowing one drop, marches off in the face of his enemies, refusing to yield up his conquests, because himself and all his men had not, according to the articles, drunk of their water.

Although he was justly had in admiration on this account, yet his family was not surnamed from him, but from his son Eurypon (of whom they were called Eurypontids); the reason of which was that Eurypon relaxed the rigor of the monarchy, seeking favor and popularity with the many. They, after this first step, grew bolder; and the succeeding kings partly incurred hatred with their people by trying to use force, or, for popularity's sake and through weakness, gave way; and anarchy and confusion long prevailed in Sparta, causing, moreover, the death of the father of Lycurgus. For as he was endeavoring to quell a riot, he was stabbed with a butcher's knife, and left the title of king to his eldest son Polydectes.

He, too, dying soon after, the right of succession (as every one thought) rested in Lycurgus; and reign he did, until it was found that the queen, his sister-in-law, was with child; upon which he immediately declared that the kingdom belonged to her issue, provided it were male, and that he himself exercised the regal jurisdiction only as his guardian; the Spartan name for which office is *prodicus*. Soon after, an overture was made to him by the queen, that she would herself in some way destroy the infant, upon condition that he would marry her when he came to the crown. Abhorring the woman's wickedness, he nevertheless did not reject her proposal, but, making show of closing with her, despatched the messenger with thanks and expressions of joy, but dissuaded her earnestly from procuring herself to miscarry, which would impair her health, if not endanger her life ; he himself, he said, would see to it, that the child, as soon as born, should be taken out of the way. By such artifices having drawn on the woman to the time of her lying-in, as soon as he heard that she was in labor, he sent persons to be by and observe all that passed, with orders that if it were a girl they should deliver it to the women, but if a boy, should bring it to him whereso-ever he were, and whatsoever doing. It so fell out that when he was at supper with the principal magistrates the queen was brought to bed of a boy, who was soon after presented to him as he was at the table ; he, taking him into his arms, said to those about him, "Men of Sparta, here is a king born unto us ;" this said, he laid him down in the king's place, and named him Charilaus, that is, the joy of the people'; because that all were transported with joy and with wonder at his noble and just spirit. His reign had lasted only eight months, but he was honored on other accounts by the citizens, and there were more who obeyed him because of his eminent virtues, than because he was regent to the king and had the royal power in his hands. Some, however, envied and sought to impede his growing influence while he was still young ; chiefly the kindred and friends of the queen-mother, who pretended to have been dealt with injuri-ously. Her brother Leonidas, in a warm debate which fell out betwixt him and Lycurgus, went so far as to tell him to his face that he was well assured that ere long he should see him king ; suggesting suspicions and preparing the way for an accusation of him, as though he had made away with his nephew, if the child should chance to·fail, though by a natural death. Words of the like import were designedly cast abroad by the queen-mother and her adherents.

Troubled at this, and not knowing what it might come to, he thought it his wisest course to avoid their envy by a voluntary exile, and to travel from place to place until his nephew came to marriageable years, and, by having a son, had secured the succession; setting sail, therefore, with this resolution, he first arrived at Crete, where, having considered their several forms of government, and got an acquaintance with the principal men amongst them, some of their laws he very much approved of, and resolved to make use of them in his own country; a good part he rejected as useless. Amongst the persons there the most renowned for their learning and their wisdom in state matters was one Thales, whom Lycurgus, by importunities and assurances of friendship, persuaded to go over to Lacedæmon; where, though by his outward appearance and his own profession he seemed to be no other than a lyric poet, in reality he performed the part of one of the ablest lawgivers in the world. The very songs which he composed were exhortations to obedience and concord, and the very measure and cadence of the verse, conveying impressions of order and tranquillity, had so great an influence on the minds of the listeners, that they were insensibly softened and civilized, insomuch that they renounced their private feuds and animosities, and were reunited in a common admiration of virtue. So that it may truly be said that Thales prepared the way for the discipline introduced by Lycurgus.

From Crete he sailed to Asia, with design, as is said, to examine the difference betwixt the manners and rules of life of the Cretans, which were very sober and temperate, and those of the Ionians, a people of sumptuous and delicate habits, and so to form a judgment; just as physicians do by comparing healthy and diseased bodies. Here he had the first sight of Homer's works, in the hands, we may suppose, of the posterity of Creophylus; and, having observed that the few loose expressions and actions of ill example which are to be found in his poems were much outweighed by serious lessons of state and rules of morality, he set himself eagerly to transcribe and digest them into order, as thinking they would be of good use in his own country. They had, indeed, already obtained some slight repute amongst the Greeks, and scattered portions, as chance conveyed them, were in the hands of individuals; but Lycurgus first made them really known.

The Egyptians say that he took a voyage into Egypt, and that, being much taken with their way of separating the soldiery from the rest of the nation, he transferred it from them to Sparta, a removal from contact with those employed in low and mechanical occupations giving high refinement and beauty to the state. Some Greek writers also record this. But as for his voyages into Spain, Africa, and the Indies, and his conferences there with the Gymnosophists, the whole relation, as far as I can find, rests on the single credit of the Spartan Aristocrates, the son of Hipparchus.

Lycurgus was much missed at Sparta, and often sent for, " for kings indeed we have," they said, " who wear the marks and assume the titles of royalty, but as for the qualities of their minds, they have nothing by which they are to be distinguished from their subjects;" adding, that in him alone was the true foundation of sovereignty to be seen, a nature made to rule, and a genius to gain obedience. Nor were the kings themselves averse to see him back, for they looked upon his presence as a bulwark against the insolencies of the people.

Things being in this posture at his return, he applied himself, without loss of time, to a thorough reformation.

and resolved to change the whole face of the commonwealth ; for what could a few particular laws and a par-
tial alteration avail ? He must act as wise physicians do,
in the case of one who labors under a complication of
diseases, by force of medicines reduce and exhaust him,
change his whole temperament, and then set him upon a
totally new regimen of diet. Having thus projected
things, away he goes to Delphi to consult Apollo there ;
which having done, and offered his sacrifice, he returned
with that renowned oracle, in which he is called beloved
of God, and rather God than man ; that his prayers were
heard, that his laws should be the best, and the commonwealth which observed them the most famous in the
world. Encouraged by these things, he set himself to
bring over to his side the leading men of Sparta, exhorting them to give him a helping hand in his great undertaking ; he broke it first to his particular friends, and
then by degrees gained others, and animated them all to
put his design in execution. When things were ripe for
action, he gave order to thirty of the principal men of
Sparta to be ready armed at the market-place by break
of day, to the end that he might strike a terror into the
opposite party. Hermippus hath set down the names of
twenty of the most eminent of them ; but the name of
him whom Lycurgus most confided in, and who was of
most use to him, both in making his laws and putting
them in execution, was Arthmiadas. Things growing to
a tumult, king Charilaus, apprehending that it was a conspiracy against his person, took sanctuary in the temple
of Minerva of the Brazen House ; but, being soon after
undeceived, and having taken an oath of them that they
had no designs against him, he quitted his refuge, and
himself also entered into the confederacy with them ; of
so gentle and flexible a disposition he was, to which Ar-
chelaus, his brother-king, alluded, when, hearing him ex-

tolled for his goodness, he said, "Who can say he is any thing but good ? he is so even to the bad."

Amongst the many changes and alterations which Lycurgus made, the first and of greatest importance was the establishment of the senate, which, having a power equal to the kings' in matters of great consequence, and, as Plato expresses it, allaying and qualifying the fiery genius of the royal office, gave steadiness and safety to the commonwealth. For the state, which before had no firm basis to stand upon, but leaned one while towards an absolute monarchy, when the kings had the upper hand, and another while towards a pure democracy, when the people had the better, found in this establishment of the senate a central weight, like ballast in a ship, which always kept things in a just equilibrium; the twenty-eight always adhering to the kings so far as to resist democracy, and, on the other hand, supporting the people against the establishment of absolute monarchy. As for the determinate number of twenty-eight, Aristotle states, that it so fell out because two of the original associates, for want of courage, fell off from the enterprise; but Sphærus assures us that there were but twenty-eight of the confederates at first; perhaps there is some mystery in the number, which consists of seven multiplied by four, and is the first of perfect numbers after six, being, as that is, equal to all its parts.* For my part, I believe Lycurgus fixed upon the number of twenty-eight, that, the two kings being reckoned amongst them, they might be thirty in all. So eagerly set was he upon this establishment, that he took the trouble to obtain an oracle about it from Delphi, the Rhetra, which runs thus : "After that you have built a temple to Jupiter Hellanius, and to Minerva Hellania, and after that you have *phyle'd* the people into *phyles,* and *obe'd* them into *obes,* you shall establish a com-

---

* 14, 2, 7, 4, 1. make by addition 28 ; as 3, 2, 1, make 6.

cil of thirty elders, the leaders included, and shall, from
time to time, *apellazein* the people betwixt Babyca and
Cnacion, there propound and put to the vote. The commons have the final voice and decision." By *phyles* and
obes are meant the divisions of the people; by the *leaders*,
the two kings; *apellazein*, referring to the Pythian Apollo,
signifies to assemble; Babyca and Cnacion they now
call Œnus; Aristotle says Cnacion is a river, and Babyca
a bridge. Betwixt this Babyca and Cnacion, their assemblies were held, for they had no council-house or building
to meet in. Lycurgus was of opinion that ornaments
were so far from advantaging them in their counsels, that
they were rather an hinderance, by diverting their attention from the business before them to statues and pictures, and roofs curiously fretted, the usual embellish-
ments of such places amongst the other Greeks. The
people then being thus assembled in the open air, it was
not allowed to any one of their order to give his advice,
but only either to ratify or reject what should be propounded to them by the king or senate. But because it
fell out afterwards that the people, by adding or omitting
words, distorted and perverted the sense of propositions,
kings Polydorus and Theopompus inserted into the Rhetra, or grand covenant, the following clause: "That if
the people decide crookedly, it should be lawful for the
elders and leaders to dissolve;" that is to say, refuse ratification, and dismiss the people as depravers and pervert-
ers of their counsel. It passed among the people, by
their management, as being equally authentic with the
rest of the Rhetra, as appears by these verses of Tyr-
tæus, —

These oracles they from Apollo heard,
And brought from Pytho home the perfect word:
The heaven-appointed kings, who love the land,
Shall foremost in the nation's council stand;

The elders next to them ; the commons last ;
Let a straight *Rhetra* among all be passed.

Although Lycurgus had, in this manner, used all the
qualifications possible in the constitution of his commonwealth, yet those who succeeded him found the oligarchical element still too strong and dominant, and, to check
its high temper and its violence, put, as Plato says, a bit
in its mouth, which was the power of the ephori, established an hundred and thirty years after the death of
Lycurgus. Elatus and his colleagues were the first who
had this dignity conferred upon them, in the reign of
king Theopompus, who, when his queen upbraided him
one day that he would leave the regal power to his children less than he had received it from his ancestors, said,
in answer, "No, greater; for it will last longer." For,
indeed, their prerogative being thus reduced within reasonable bounds, the Spartan kings were at once freed
from all further jealousies and consequent danger, and
never experienced the calamities of their neighbors at
Messene and Argos, who, by maintaining their prerogative too strictly, for want of yielding a little to the populace, lost it all.

Indeed, whosoever shall look at the sedition and mis-
government which befell these bordering nations to whom
they were as near related in blood as situation, will find
in them the best reason to admire the wisdom and foresight of Lycurgus. For these three states, in their first rise,
were equal, or, if there were any odds, they lay on the
side of the Messenians and Argives, who, in the first allotment, were thought to have been luckier than the Spartans; yet was their happiness but of small continuance,
partly the tyrannical temper of their kings and partly the
ungovernableness of the people quickly bringing upon
them such disorders, and so complete an overthrow of all
existing institutions, as clearly to show how truly divine a

blessing the Spartans had had in that wise lawgiver who gave their government its happy balance and temper. But of this I shall say more in its due place.

After the creation of the thirty senators, his next task, and, indeed, the most hazardous he ever undertook, was the making a new division of their lands. For there was an extreme inequality amongst them, and their state was overloaded with a multitude of indigent and necessitous persons, while its whole wealth had centered upon a very few. To the end, therefore, that he might expel from the state arrogance and envy, luxury and crime, and those yet more inveterate diseases of want and superfluity, he obtained of them to renounce their properties, and to con-sent to a new division of the land, and that they should live all together on an equal footing; merit to be their only road to eminence, and the disgrace of evil, and credit of worthy acts, their one measure of difference between man and man.

Upon their consent to these proposals, proceeding at once to put them into execution, he divided the country of Laconia in general into thirty thousand equal shares, and the part attached to the city of Sparta into nine thousand; these he distributed among the Spartans, as he did the others to the country citizens. Some authors say that he made but six thousand lots for the citizens of Sparta, and that king Polydorus added three thousand more. Others say that Polydorus doubled the number Lycurgus had made, which, according to them, was but four thousand five hundred. A lot was so much as to yield, one year with another, about seventy bushels of grain for the master of the family, and twelve for his wife, with a suitable proportion of oil and wine. And this he thought sufficient to keep their bodies in good health and strength; superfluities they were better without. It is reported, that, as he returned from a journey shortly after the division of the lands, in harvest time, the ground being newly reaped, seeing the stacks all standing equal and alike, he smiled, and said to those about him, "Methinks all Laconia looks like one family estate just divided among a number of brothers."

Not contented with this, he resolved to make a division of their movables too, that there might be no odious distinction or inequality left amongst them; but finding that it would be very dangerous to go about it openly, he took another course, and defeated their avarice by the following stratagem : he commanded that all gold and silver coin should be called in, and that only a sort of money made of iron should be current, a great weight and quantity of which was but very little worth; so that to lay up twenty or thirty pounds there was required a pretty large closet, and, to remove it, nothing less than a yoke of oxen. With the diffusion of this money, at once a number of vices were banished from Lacedæmon ; for who would rob another of such a coin ? Who would unjustly detain or take by force, or accept as a bribe, a thing which it was not easy to hide, nor a credit to have, nor indeed of any use to cut in pieces ? For when it was just red hot, they quenched it in vinegar, and by that means spoilt it, and made it almost incapable of being worked.

In the next place, he declared an outlawry of all needless and superfluous arts; but here he might almost have spared his proclamation; for they of themselves would have gone after the gold and silver, the money which remained being not so proper payment for curious work ; for, being of iron, it was scarcely portable, neither, if they should take the pains to export it. would it pass amongst the other Greeks, who ridiculed it. So there was now no more means of purchasing foreign goods and small wares ; merchants sent no shiploads into Laconian ports ; no rhetoric-master, no itinerant fortune-teller, no harlot-monger, or gold or silversmith, engraver, or jeweller, set foot in a country·which had no money; so that luxury, deprived little by little of that which fed and fomented it, wasted to nothing, and died away of itself. For the rich had no advantage here over the poor, as their wealth and abundance had no road to come abroad by, but were shut up at home doing nothing. And in this way they became excellent artists in common, necessary things; bedsteads, chairs, and tables, and such like staple utensils in a family, were admirably well made there; their cup, particularly, was very much in fashion, and eagerly bought up by soldiers, as Critias reports; for its color was such as to prevent water, drunk upon necessity and disagreeable to look at, from being noticed; and the shape of it was such that the mud stuck to the sides, so that only the purer part came to the drinker's mouth. For this, also, they had to thank their lawgiver, who, by relieving the artisans of the trouble of making useless things, set them to show their skill in giving beauty to those of daily and indispensable use.

The third and most masterly stroke of this great lawgiver, by which he struck a yet more effectual blow against luxury and the desire of riches, was the ordinance he made, that they should all eat in common, of the same bread and same meat, and of kinds that were specified, and should not spend their lives at home, laid on costly couches at splendid tables, delivering themselves up into the hands of their tradesmen and cooks, to fatten them in corners, like greedy brutes, and to ruin not their minds only but their very bodies, which, enfeebled by indulgence and excess, would stand in need of long sleep, warm bathing, freedom from work, and, in a word, of as much care and attendance as if they were continually sick. It was certainly an extraordinary thing to have brought about such a result as this, but a greater yet to have taken away from wealth, as Theophrastus observes, not merely the property of being coveted, but its very nature of being wealth. For the rich, being obliged to go to the same table with the poor, could not make use of or enjoy their abundance, nor so much as please their vanity by looking at or displaying it. So that the common proverb, that Plutus, the god of riches, is blind, was nowhere in all the world literally verified but in Sparta. There, indeed, he was not only blind, but like a picture, without either life or motion. Nor were they allowed to take food at home first, and then attend the public tables, for every one had an eye upon those who did not eat and drink like the rest, and reproached them with being dainty and effeminate.

This last ordinance in particular exasperated the wealthier men. They collected in a body against Lycurgus, and from ill words came to throwing stones, so that at length he was forced to run out of the market-place, and make to sanctuary to save his life; by good-hap he outran all, excepting one Alcander, a young man otherwise not ill accomplished, but hasty and violent, who came up so close to him, that, when he turned to see who was near him, he struck him upon the face with his stick, and put out one of his eyes. Lycurgus, so far from being daunted and discouraged by this accident, stopped short, and showed his disfigured face and eye beat out to his countrymen; they, dismayed and ashamed at the sight, delivered Alcander into his hands to be punished, and escorted him home, with expressions of great concern for his ill usage. Lycurgus, having thanked them for their care of his person, dismissed them all, excepting only Alcander; and, taking him with him into his house, neither did nor said any thing severely to him, but, dismissing those whose place it was, bade Alcander to wait upon him at table. The young man, who was of an ingenuous temper, without murmuring did as he was commanded ; and, being thus admitted to live with Lycurgus, he had an opportunity to observe in him, besides his gentleness and calmness of temper, an extraordinary sobriety and an indefatigable industry, and so, from an enemy, became one of his most zealous admirers, and told his friends and relations that Lycurgus was not that morose and illnatured man they had formerly taken him for, but the one mild and gentle character of the world. And thus did Lycurgus, for chastisement of his fault, make of a wild and passionate young man one of the discreetest citizens of Sparta.

In memory of this accident, Lycurgus built a temple to Minerva, surnamed Optilētis ; *optilus* being the Doric of these parts for *ophthalmus*, the eye. Some authors, however, of whom Dioscorides is one (who wrote a treatise on the commonwealth of Sparta), say that he was wounded, indeed, but did not lose his eye with the blow; and that he built the temple in gratitude for the cure. Be this as it will, certain it is, that, after this misadventure, the Lacedæmonians made it a rule never to carry so much as a staff into their public assemblies.

But to return to their public repasts;—these had several names in Greek ; the Cretans called them *andria,* because the men only came to them. The Lacedæmonians called them *phiditia,* that is, by changing *l* into *d,* the same as *philitia,* love feasts, because that, by eating and drinking together, they had opportunity of making friends. Or perhaps from *phido,* parsimony, because they were so many schools of sobriety ; or perhaps the first letter is an addition, and the word at first was *editia,* from *edode,* eating. They met by companies of fifteen, more or less, and each of them stood bound to bring in monthly a bushel of meal, eight gallons of wine, five pounds of cheese, two pounds and a half of figs, and some very small sum of money to buy flesh or fish with. Besides this, when any of them made sacrifice to the gods, they always sent a dole to the common hall; and, likewise, when any of them had been a hunting, he sent thither a part of the venison he had killed; for these two occasions were the only excuses allowed for supping at home. The custom of eating together was observed strictly for a great while afterwards; insomuch that king Agis himself, after having vanquished the Athenians, sending for his commons at his return home, because he desired to eat privately with his queen, was refused them by the polemarchs; which refusal when he resented so much as to omit next day the sacrifice due for a war happily ended, they made him pay a fine.

They used to send their children to these tables as to schools of temperance; here they were instructed in state affairs by listening to experienced statesmen; here they learnt to converse with pleasantry, to make jests without scurrility, and take them without ill humor. In this point of good breeding, the Lacedæmonians excelled particularly, but if any man were uneasy under it, upon the least hint given there was no more to be said to him. It was customary also for the eldest man in the company to say to each of them, as they came in, "Through this" (pointing to the door), "no words go out." When any one had a desire to be admitted into any of these little societies; he was to go through the following probation, each man in the company took a little ball of soft bread, which they were to throw into a deep basin, which a waiter carried round upon his head; those that liked the person to be chosen dropped their ball into the basin without altering its figure, and those who disliked him pressed it betwixt their fingers, and made it flat; and this signified as much as a negative voice. And if there were but one of these flattened pieces in the basin, the suitor was rejected, so desirous were they that all the members of the company should be agreeable to each other. The basin was called *caddichus*, and the rejected candidate had a name thence derived. Their most famous dish was the black broth, which was so much valued that the elderly men fed only upon that, leaving what flesh there was to the younger.

They say that a certain king of Pontus, having heard much of this black broth of theirs, sent for a Lacedæmonian cook on purpose to make him some, but had no sooner tasted it than he found it extremely bad, which the cook observing, told him, "Sir, to make this broth relish, you should have bathed yourself first in the river Eurotas."

After drinking moderately, every man went to his home without lights, for the use of them was, on all occasions, forbid, to the end that they might accustom themselves to march boldly in the dark. Such was the common fashion of their meals.

Lycurgus would never reduce his laws into writing; nay, there is a Rhetra expressly to forbid it. For he thought that the most material points, and such as most directly tended to the public welfare, being imprinted on the hearts of their youth by a good discipline, would be sure to remain, and would find a stronger security, than any compulsion would be, in the principles of action formed in them by their best lawgiver, education. And as for things of lesser importance, as pecuniary contracts, and such like, the forms of which have to be changed as occasion requires, he thought it the best way to prescribe no positive rule or inviolable usage in such cases, willing that their manner and form should be altered according to the circumstances of time, and determinations of men of sound judgment. Every end and object of law and enactment it was his design education should effect.

One, then, of the Rhetras was, that their laws should
not be written; another is particularly levelled against
luxury and expensiveness, for by it it was ordained that
the ceilings of their houses should only be wrought by
the axe, and their gates and doors smoothed only by the
saw. Epaminondas's famous dictum about his own table,
that "Treason and a dinner like this do not keep company together," may be said to have been anticipated by
Lycurgus. Luxury and a house of this kind could not
well be companions. For a man must have a less than
ordinary share of sense that would furnish such plain and
common rooms with silver-footed couches and purple
coverlets and gold and silver plate. Doubtless he had
good reason to think that they would proportion their
beds to their houses, and their coverlets to their beds, and
the rest of their goods and furniture to these. It is
reported that king Leotychides, the first of that name,
was so little used to the sight of any other kind of
work, that, being entertained at Corinth in a stately
room, he was much surprised to see the timber and ceil-
ing so finely carved and panelled, and asked his host
whether the trees grew so in his country.

A third ordinance or Rhetra was, that they should not
make war often, or long, with the same enemy, lest that
they should train and instruct them in war, by habitua-
ting them to defend themselves. And this is what Agesilaus was much blamed for, a long time after; it being
thought, that, by his continual incursions into Bœotia, he
made the Thebans a match for the Lacedæmonians; and
therefore Antalcidas, seeing him wounded one day, said to
him, that he was very well paid for taking such pains to
make the Thebans good soldiers, whether they would or
no. These laws were called the Rhetras, to intimate that
they were divine sanctions and revelations.

In order to the good education of their youth (which,

as I said before, he thought the most important and
noblest work of a lawgiver), he went so far back as to
take into consideration their very conception and birth,
by regulating their marriages. For Aristotle is wrong in
saying, that, after he had tried all ways to reduce the
women to more modesty and sobriety, he was at last
forced to leave them as they were, because that, in the
absence of their husbands, who spent the best part of
their lives in the wars, their wives, whom they were
obliged to leave absolute mistresses at home, took great
liberties and assumed the superiority; and were treated
with overmuch respect and called by the title of lady or
queen. The truth is, he took in their case, also, all the
care that was possible; he ordered the maidens to exercise themselves with wrestling, running, throwing the
quoit, and casting the dart, to the end that the fruit they
conceived might, in strong and healthy bodies, take firmer
root and find better growth, and withal that they, with
this greater vigor, might be the more able to undergo
the pains of child-bearing. And to the end he might
take away their over-great tenderness and fear of exposure to the air, and all acquired womanishness, he
ordered that the young women should go naked in the
processions, as well as the young men, and dance, too, in
that condition, at certain solemn feasts, singing certain
songs, whilst the young men stood around, seeing and
hearing them. On these occasions, they now and then
made, by jests, a befitting reflection upon those who had
misbehaved themselves in the wars; and again sang enco-
miums upon those who had done any gallant action, and
by these means inspired the younger sort with an emulation of their glory. Those that were thus commended
went away proud, elated, and gratified with their honor
among the maidens; and those who were rallied were as
sensibly touched with it as if they had been formally

reprimanded; and so much the more, because the kings and the elders, as well as the rest of the city, saw and heard all that passed. Nor was there any thing shameful in this nakedness of the young women; modesty attended them, and all wantonness was excluded. It taught them simplicity and a care for good health, and gave them some taste of higher feelings, admitted as they thus were to the field of noble action and glory. Hence it was natural for them to think and speak as Gorgo, for example, the wife of Leonidas, is said to have done, when some foreign lady, as it would seem, told her that the women of Lacedæmon were the only women of the world who could rule men; "With good reason," she said, "for we are the only women who bring forth men."

These public processions of the maidens, and their appearing naked in their exercises and dancings, were incitements to marriage, operating upon the young with the rigor and certainty, as Plato says, of love, if not of mathematics. But besides all this, to promote it yet more effectually, those who continued bachelors were in a degree disfranchised by law; for they were excluded from the sight of those public processions in which the young men and maidens danced naked, and, in winter-time, the officers compelled them to march naked themselves round the market-place, singing as they went a certain song to their own disgrace, that they justly suffered this punishment for disobeying the laws. Moreover, they were denied that respect and observance which the younger men paid their elders; and no man, for example, found fault with what was said to Dercyllidas, though so eminent a commander; upon whose approach one day, a young man, instead of rising, retained his seat, remarking, "No child of yours will make room for me."

In their marriages, the husband carried off his bride by

a sort of force ; nor were their brides ever small and of tender years, but in their full bloom and ripeness. After this, she who superintended the wedding comes and clips the hair of the bride close round her head, dresses her up in man's clothes, and leaves her upon a mattress in the dark ; afterwards comes the bridegroom, in his every-day clothes, sober and composed, as having supped at the common table, and, entering privately into the room where the bride lies, unties her virgin zone, and takes her to himself; and, after staying some time together, he returns composedly to his own apartment, to sleep as usual with the other young men. And so he continues to do, spending his days, and, indeed, his nights with them, visiting his bride in fear and shame, and with circumspection, when he thought he should not be observed ; she, also, on her part, using her wit to help and find favorable opportunities for their meeting, when company was out of the way. In this manner they lived a long time, insomuch that they sometimes had children by their wives before ever they saw their faces by daylight. Their interviews, being thus difficult and rare, served not only for continual exercise of their self-control, but brought them together with their bodies healthy and vigorous, and their affections fresh and lively, unsated and undulled by easy access and long continuance with each other ; while their partings were always early enough to leave behind unextinguished in each of them some remainder fire of longing and mutual delight. After guarding marriage with this modesty and reserve, he was equally careful to banish empty and womanish jealousy. For this object, excluding all licentious disorders, he made it, nevertheless, honorable for men to give the use of their wives to those whom they should think fit, that so they might have children by them ; ridiculing those in whose opinion such favors are so unfit for participation as to fight and shed blood and go to war about it. Lycurgus allowed a man who was advanced in years and had a young wife to recommend some virtuous and approved young man, that she might have a child by him, who might inherit the good qualities of the father, and be a son to himself. On the other side, an honest man who had love for a married woman upon account of her modesty and the well-favoredness of her children, might, without formality, beg her company of her husband, that he might raise, as it were, from this plot of good ground, worthy and well-allied children for himself. And, indeed, Lycurgus was of a persuasion that children were not so much the property of their parents as of the whole commonwealth, and, therefore, would not have his citizens begot by the first comers, but by the best men that could be found; the laws of other nations seemed to him very absurd and inconsistent, where people would be so solicitous for their dogs and horses as to exert interest and pay money to procure fine breeding, and yet kept their wives shut up, to be made mothers only by themselves, who might be foolish, infirm, or diseased; as if it were not apparent that children of a bad breed would prove their bad qualities first upon those who kept and were rearing them, and well-born children, in like manner, their good qualities. These regulations, founded on natural and social grounds, were certainly so far from that scandalous liberty which was afterwards charged upon their women, that they knew not what adultery meant. It is told, for instance, of Geradas, a very ancient Spartan, that, being asked by a stranger what punishment their law had appointed for adulterers, he answered, "There are no adulterers in our country." "But," replied the stranger, "suppose there were?" "Then," answered he, "the offender would have to give the plaintiff a bull with a neck so long as that he might drink from the top of Taygetus of the Eurotas river below it." The man, surprised at this, said, "Why, 't is impossible to find such a bull." Geradas smilingly replied, " 'T is as possible as to find an adulterer in Sparta." So much I had to say of their marriages.

Nor was it in the power of the father to dispose of the child as he thought fit; he was obliged to carry it before certain triers at a place called Lesche ; these were some of the elders of the tribe to which the child belonged; their business it was carefully to view the infant, and, if they found it stout and well made, they gave order for its rearing, and allotted to it one of the nine thousand shares of land above mentioned for its maintenance, but, if they found it puny and ill-shaped, ordered it to be taken to what was called the Apothetæ, a sort of chasm under Taygetus; as thinking it neither for the good of the child itself, nor for the public interest, that it should be brought up, if it did not, from the very outset, appear made to be healthy and vigorous. Upon the same account, the women did not bathe the new-born children with water, as is the custom in all other countries, but with wine, to prove the temper and complexion of their bodies; from a notion they had that epileptic and weakly children faint and waste away upon their being thus bathed, while, on the contrary, those of a strong and vigorous habit acquire firmness and get a temper by it, like steel. There was much care and art, too, used by the nurses; they had no swaddling bands; the children grew up free and unconstrained in limb and form, and not dainty and fanciful about their food; not afraid in the dark, or of being left alone; without any peevishness or ill humor or crying. Upon this account, Spartan nurses were often bought up, or hired by people of other countries; and it is recorded that she who suckled Alcibiades was a Spartan; who, however, if fortunate in his nurse, was not so in his preceptor; his guardian, Pericles, as

Plato tells us, chose a servant for that office called Zopy-rus, no better than any common slave.

Lycurgus was of another mind; he would not have masters bought out of the market for his young Spartans, nor such as should sell their pains; nor was it lawful, indeed, for the father himself to breed up the children after his own fancy; but as soon as they were seven years old they were to be enrolled in certain companies and classes, where they all lived under the same order and discipline, doing their exercises and taking their play to-gether. Of these, he who showed the most conduct and courage was made captain; they had their eyes always upon him, obeyed his orders, and underwent patiently whatsoever punishment he inflicted; so that the whole course of their education was one continued exercise of a ready and perfect obedience. The old men, too, were spec-tators of their performances, and often raised quarrels and disputes among them, to have a good opportunity of find-ing out their different characters, and of seeing which would be valiant, which a coward, when they should come to more dangerous encounters. Reading and writing they gave them, just enough to serve their turn; their chief care was to make them good subjects, and to teach them to endure pain and conquer in battle. To this end, as they grew in years, their discipline was proportionably in-creased; their heads were close-clipped, they were accus-tomed to go bare-foot, and for the most part to play naked.

After they were twelve years old, they were no longer allowed to wear any under-garment; they had one coat to serve them a year;* their bodies were hard and dry, with but little acquaintance of baths and unguents; these human indulgences they were allowed only on some few

* The *chiton* and the *himation*, sponding in use to the Roman tunic one inside and one out, constituted and toga. the ordinary Greek dress : corre-

particular days in the year. They lodged together in little bands upon beds made of the rushes which grew by the banks of the river Eurotas, which they were to break off with their hands without a knife; if it were winter, they mingled some thistle-down with their rushes, which it was thought had the property of giving warmth. By the time they were come to this age, there was not any of the more hopeful boys who had not a lover to bear him company. The old men, too, had an eye upon them, coming often to the grounds to hear and see them contend either in wit or strength with one another, and this as seriously and with as much concern as if they were their fathers, their tutors, or their magistrates; so that there scarcely was any time or place without some one present to put them in mind of their duty, and punish them if they had neglected it.

Besides all this, there was always one of the best and honestest men in the city appointed to undertake the charge and governance of them; he again arranged them into their several bands, and set over each of them for their captain the most temperate and boldest of those they called Irens, who were usually twenty years old, two years out of the boys; and the eldest of the boys, again, were Mell-Irens, as much as to say, who would shortly be men. This young man, therefore, was their captain when they fought, and their master at home, using them for the offices of his house; sending the oldest of them to fetch wood, and the weaker and less able, to gather salads and herbs, and these they must either go without or steal; which they did by creeping into the gardens, or conveying themselves cunningly and closely into the eating-houses; if they were taken in the fact, they were whipped without mercy, for thieving so ill and awkwardly. They stole, too, all other meat they could lay their hands on, looking out and watching all opportunities, when people were asleep or more careless than usual. If they were caught, they were not only punished with whipping, but hunger, too, being reduced to their ordinary allowance, which was but very slender, and so contrived on purpose, that they might set about to help themselves, and be forced to exercise their energy and address. This was the principal design of their hard fare; there was another not inconsiderable, that they might grow taller; for the vital spirits, not being overburdened and oppressed by too great a quantity of nourishment, which necessarily discharges itself into thickness and breadth, do, by their natural lightness, rise; and the body, giving and yielding because it is pliant, grows in height. The same thing seems, also, to conduce to beauty of shape; a dry and lean habit is a better subject for nature's configuration, which the gross and over-fed are too heavy to submit to properly. Just as we find that women who take physic whilst they are with child, bear leaner and smaller but better-shaped and prettier children; the material they come of having been more pliable and easily moulded. The reason, however, I leave others to determine.

To return from whence we have digressed. So seriously did the Lacedæmonian children go about their stealing, that a youth, having stolen a young fox and hid it under his coat, suffered it to tear out his very bowels with its teeth and claws, and died upon the place, rather than let it be seen. What is practised to this very day in Lacedæmon is enough to gain credit to this story, for I myself have seen several of the youths endure whipping to death at the foot of the altar of Diana surnamed Orthia.

The Iren, or under-master, used to stay a little with them after supper, and one of them he bade to sing a song, to another he put a question which required an advised and deliberate answer; for example, Who was the best man in the city? What he thought of such an action of such a man? They used them thus early to pass a right judgment upon persons and things, and to inform themselves of the abilities or defects of their countrymen. If they had not an answer ready to the question Who was a good or who an ill-reputed citizen, they were looked upon as of a dull and careless disposition, and to have little or no sense of virtue and honor; besides this, they were to give a good reason for what they said, and in as few words and as comprehensive as might be; he that failed of this, or answered not to the purpose, had his thumb bit by his master. Sometimes the Iren did this in the presence of the old men and magistrates, that they might see whether he punished them justly and in due measure or not; and when he did amiss, they would not reprove him before the boys, but, when they were gone, he was called to an account and underwent correction, if he had run far into either of the extremes of indulgence or severity.

Their lovers and favorers, too, had a share in the young boy's honor or disgrace; and there goes a story that one of them was fined by the magistrates, because the lad whom he loved cried out effeminately as he was fighting. And though this sort of love was so approved among them, that the most virtuous matrons would make professions of it to young girls, yet rivalry did not exist, and if several men's fancies met in one person, it was rather the beginning of an intimate friendship, whilst they all jointly conspired to render the object of their affection as accomplished as possible.

They taught them, also, to speak with a natural and graceful raillery, and to comprehend much matter of thought in few words. For Lycurgus, who ordered, as we saw, that a great piece of money should be but of an inconsiderable value, on the contrary would allow no discourse to be current which did not contain in few words a great deal of useful and curious sense; children in Sparta, by a habit of long silence, came to give just and sententious answers; for, indeed, as loose and incontinent livers are seldom fathers of many children, so loose and incontinent talkers seldom originate many sensible words. King Agis, when some Athenian laughed at their short swords, and said that the jugglers on the stage swallowed them with ease, answered him, "We find them long enough to reach our enemies with;" and as their swords were short and sharp, so, it seems to me, were their sayings. They reach the point and arrest the attention of the hearers better than any. Lycurgus himself seems to have been short and sententious, if we may trust the anecdotes of him; as appears by his answer to one who by all means would set up democracy in Lacedæmon. "Begin, friend," said he, "and set it up in your family." Another asked him why he allowed of such mean and trivial sacrifices to the gods. He replied, "That we may always have something to offer to them." Being asked what sort of martial exercises or combats he approved of, he answered, "All sorts, except that in which you stretch out your hands." * Similar answers, addressed to his countrymen by letter, are ascribed to him; as, being consulted how they might best oppose an invasion of their enemies, he returned this answer, "By continuing poor, and not coveting each man to be greater than his fellow." Being consulted again whether it were requisite to enclose the city with a wall, he sent them word, "The city is well fortified which hath a wall of men instead of brick." But whether these letters are counterfeit or not is not easy to determine.

Of their dislike to talkativeness, the following apo-

---

* The form of crying quarter among the ancients.

phthegms are evidence. King Leonidas said to one who held him in discourse upon some useful matter, but not in due time and place, "Much to the purpose, Sir, elsewhere." King Charilaus, the nephew of Lycurgus, being asked why his uncle had made so few laws, answered, "Men of few words require but few laws." When one blamed Hecatæus the sophist because that, being invited to the public table, he had not spoken one word all supper-time, Archidamidas answered in his vindication, "He who knows how to speak, knows also when."

The sharp and yet not ungraceful retorts which I mentioned may be instanced as follows. Demaratus, being asked in a troublesome manner by an importunate fellow, Who was the best man in Lacedæmon? answered at last, "He, Sir, that is the least like you." Some, in company where Agis was, much extolled the Eleans for their just and honorable management of the Olympic games; "Indeed," said Agis, "they are highly to be commended if they can do justice one day in five years." Theopompus answered a stranger who talked much of his affection to the Lacedæmonians, and said that his countrymen called him Philolacon (a lover of the Lacedæmonians), that it had been more for his honor if they had called him Philopolites (a lover of his own countrymen). And Plistoanax, the son of Pausanias, when an orator of Athens said the Lacedæmonians had no learning, told him, "You say true, Sir; we alone of all the Greeks have learned none of your bad qualities." One asked Archidamidas what number there might be of the Spartans; he answered, "Enough, Sir, to keep out wicked men."

We may see their character, too, in their very jests. For they did not throw them out at random, but the very wit of them was grounded upon something or other worth thinking about. For instance, one, being asked to go hear a man who exactly counterfeited the voice of a nightingale, answered, "Sir, I have heard the nightingale itself." Another, having read the following inscription upon a tomb,

Seeking to quench a cruel tyranny,
They, at Selinus, did in battle die,

said, it served them right; for instead of trying to quench the tyranny they should have let it burn out. A lad, being offered some game-cocks that would die upon the spot, said that he cared not for cocks that would die, but for such that would live and kill others. Another, seeing people easing themselves on seats, said, "God forbid I should sit where I could not get up to salute my elders." In short, their answers were so sententious and pertinent, that one said well that intellectual much more truly than athletic exercise was the Spartan characteristic.

Nor was their instruction in music and verse less carefully attended to than their habits of grace and good breeding in conversation. And their very songs had a life and spirit in them that inflamed and possessed men's minds with an enthusiasm and ardor for action; the style of them was plain and without affectation; the subject always serious and moral; most usually, it was in praise of such men as had died in defence of their country, or in derision of those that had been cowards; the former they declared happy and glorified; the life of the latter they described as most miserable and abject. There were also vaunts of what they would do, and boasts of what they had done, varying with the various ages, as, for example, they had three choirs in their solemn festivals, the first of the old men, the second of the young men, and the last of the children; the old men began thus:

We once were young, and brave and strong;

the young men answered them, singing,

> And we're so now, come on and try ;

the children came last and said,

> But we'll be strongest by and by.

Indeed, if we will take the pains to consider their compositions, some of which were still extant in our days, and the airs on the flute to which they marched when going to battle, we shall find that Terpander and Pindar had reason to say that music and valor were allied. The first says of Lacedæmon —

> The spear and song in her do meet,
> And Justice walks about her street ;

and Pindar —

> Councils of wise elders here,
> And the young men's conquering spear,
> And dance, and song, and joy appear ;

both describing the Spartans as no less musical than warlike ; in the words of one of their own poets —

> With the iron stern and sharp
> Comes the playing on the harp.

For, indeed, before they engaged in battle, the king first did sacrifice to the Muses, in all likelihood to put them in mind of the manner of their education, and of the judgment that would be passed upon their actions, and thereby to animate them to the performance of exploits that should deserve a record. At such times, too, the Lacedæmonians abated a little the severity of their manners in favor of their young men, suffering them to curl and adorn their hair, and to have costly arms, and fine clothes ;

and were well pleased to see them, like proud horses,
neighing and pressing to the course. And therefore, as
soon as they came to be well-grown, they took a great
deal of care of their hair, to have it parted and trimmed,
especially against a day of battle, pursuant to a saying
recorded of their lawgiver, that a large head of hair added
beauty to a good face, and terror to an ugly one.

When they were in the field, their exercises were generally more moderate, their fare not so hard, nor so strict
a hand held over them by their officers, so that they
were the only people in the world to whom war gave
repose. When their army was drawn up in battle array
and the enemy near, the king sacrificed a goat, commanded the soldiers to set their garlands upon their
heads, and the pipers to play the tune of the hymn to
Castor, and himself began the pæan of advance. It was
at once a magnificent and a terrible sight to see them
march on to the tune of their flutes, without any disorder in their ranks, any discomposure in their minds or
change in their countenance, calmly and cheerfully moving with the music to the deadly fight. Men, in this temper, were not likely to be possessed with fear or any
transport of fury, but with the deliberate valor of hope
and assurance, as if some divinity were attending and
conducting them. The king had always about his person some one who had been crowned in the Olympic
games; and upon this account a Lacedæmonian is said to
have refused a considerable present, which was offered to
him upon condition that he would not come into the
lists; and when he had with much to-do thrown his antagonist, some of the spectators saying to him, "And now,
Sir Lacedæmonian, what are you the better for your victory?" he answered smiling, "I shall fight next the king."
After they had routed an enemy, they pursued him till
they were well assured of the victory, and then they

sounded a retreat, thinking it base and unworthy of a
Grecian people to cut men in pieces, who had given up
and abandoned all resistance. This manner of dealing
with their enemies did not only show magnanimity, but
was politic too ; for, knowing that they killed only those
who made resistance, and gave quarter to the rest, men
generally thought it their best way to consult their safety
by flight.

Hippias the sophist says that Lycurgus himself was a
great soldier and an experienced commander. Philoste-
phanus attributes to him the first division of the cavalry
into troops of fifties in a square body ; but Demetrius the
Phalerian says quite the contrary, and that he made all
his laws in a continued peace. And, indeed, the Olympic
holy truce, or cessation of arms, that was procured by his
means and management, inclines me to think him a kind-
natured man, and one that loved quietness and peace.
Notwithstanding all this, Hermippus tells us that he had
no hand in the ordinance ; that Iphitus made it, and Lycurgus came only as a spectator, and that by mere accident too. Being there, he heard as it were a man's voice
behind him, blaming and wondering at him that he did
not encourage his countrymen to resort to the assembly,
and, turning about and seeing no man, concluded that it
was a voice from heaven, and upon this immediately went
to Iphitus, and assisted him in ordering the ceremonies of
that feast, which, by his means, were better established,
and with more repute than before.

To return to the Lacedæmonians. Their discipline
continued still after they were full-grown men. No one
was allowed to live after his own fancy ; but the city was
a sort of camp, in which every man had his share of provisions and business set out, and looked upon himself
not so much born to serve his own ends as the interest of
his country. Therefore, if they were commanded noth-

ing else, they went to see the boys perform their exercises, to teach them something useful, or to learn it themselves of those who knew better.   And, indeed, one of the
greatest and highest blessings Lycurgus procured his people was the abundance of leisure, which proceeded from
his forbidding to them the exercise of any mean and mechanical trade.   Of the money-making that depends on
troublesome going about and seeing people and doing
business, they had no need at all in a state where wealth
obtained no honor or respect.   The Helots tilled their
ground for them, and paid them yearly in kind the appointed quantity, without any trouble of theirs.   To this
purpose there goes a story of a Lacedæmonian who, happening to be at Athens when the courts were sitting, was
told of a citizen that had been fined for living an idle
life, and was being escorted home in much distress of
mind by his condoling friends; the Lacedæmonian was
much surprised at it, and desired his friend to show him
the man who was condemned for living like a freeman.
So much beneath them did they esteem the frivolous
devotion of time and attention to the mechanical arts
and to money-making.

It need not be said, that, upon the prohibition of gold
and silver, all lawsuits immediately ceased, for there was
now neither avarice nor poverty amongst them, but
equality, where every one's wants were supplied, and
independence, because those wants were so small.   All
their time, except when they were in the field, was taken
up by the choral dances and the festivals, in hunting,
and in attendance on the exercise-grounds and the places
of public conversation.*   Those who were under thirty
years of age were not allowed to go into the market-
place, but had the necessaries of their family supplied by

* Leschæ.

the care of their relations and lovers; nor was it for the
credit of elderly men to be seen too often in the market-
place; it was esteemed more suitable for them to frequent the exercise-grounds and places of conversation,
where they spent their leisure rationally in conversation,
not on money-making and market-prices, but for the
most part in passing judgment on some action worth
considering; extolling the good, and censuring those who
were otherwise, and that in a light and sportive manner,
conveying, without too much gravity, lessons of advice
and improvement. Nor was Lycurgus himself unduly
austere; it was he who dedicated, says Sosibius, the little
statue of Laughter. Mirth, introduced seasonably at their
suppers and places of common entertainment, was to serve
as a sort of sweetmeat to accompany their strict and hard
life. To conclude, he bred up his citizens in such a way
that they neither would nor could live by themselves;
they were to make themselves one with the public good,
and, clustering like bees around their commander, be by
their zeal and public spirit carried all but out of themselves, and devoted wholly to their country. What their
sentiments were will better appear by a few of their sayings. Pædaretus, not being admitted into the list of the
three hundred, returned home with a joyful face, well
pleased to find that there were in Sparta three hundred
better men than himself. And Polycratidas, being sent
with some others ambassador to the lieutenants of the king
of Persia, being asked by them whether they came in a
private or in a public character, answered, " In a public, if
we succeed; if not, in a private character." Argileonis,
asking some who came from Amphipolis if her son Brasidas died courageously and as became a Spartan, on their
beginning to praise him to a high degree, and saying there
was not such another left in Sparta, answered, " Do not

say so; Brasidas was a good and brave man, but there are in Sparta many better than he."

The senate, as I said before, consisted of those who were Lycurgus's chief aiders and assistants in his plans. The vacancies he ordered to be supplied out of the best and most deserving men past sixty years old; and we need not wonder if there was much striving for it; for what more glorious competition could there be amongst men, than one in which it was not contested who was swiftest among the swift or strongest of the strong, but who of many wise and good was wisest and best, and fittest to be intrusted for ever after, as the reward of his merits, with the supreme authority of the commonwealth, and with power over the lives, franchises, and highest interests of all his countrymen? The manner of their election was as follows: the people being called together, some selected persons were locked up in a room near the place of election, so contrived that they could neither see nor be seen, but could only hear the noise of the assembly without; for they decided this, as most other affairs of moment, by the shouts of the people. This done, the competitors were not brought in and presented all together, but one after another by lot, and passed in order through the assembly without speaking a word. Those who were locked up had writing-tables with them, in which they recorded and marked each shout by its loudness, without knowing in favor of which candidate each of them was made, but merely that they came first, second, third, and so forth. He who was found to have the most and loudest acclamations was declared senator duly elected. Upon this he had a garland set upon his head, and went in procession to all the temples to give thanks to the gods; a great number of young men followed him with applauses, and women, also, singing verses in his honor, and extolling the virtue and happiness of his life. As he went round

the city in this manner, each of his relations and friends
set a table before him, saying, " The city honors you with
this banquet;" but he, instead of accepting, passed round
to the common table where he formerly used to eat, and
was served as before, excepting that now he had a second
allowance, which he took and put by. By the time supper was ended, the women who were of kin to him had
come about the door; and he, beckoning to her whom he
most esteemed, presented to her the portion he had saved,
saying, that it had been a mark of esteem to him, and
was so now to her; upon which she was triumphantly
waited upon home by the women.

Touching burials, Lycurgus made very wise regulations;
for, first of all, to cut off all superstition, he allowed them
to bury their dead within the city, and even round about
their temples, to the end that their youth might be accustomed to such spectacles, and not be afraid to see a dead
body, or imagine that to touch a corpse or to tread upon
a grave would defile a man. In the next place, he commanded them to put nothing into the ground with them,
except, if they pleased, a few olive leaves, and the scarlet
cloth that they were wrapped in. He would not suffer the
names to be inscribed, except only of men who fell in the
wars, or women who died in a sacred office. The time,
too, appointed for mourning, was very short, eleven days;
on the twelfth, they were to do sacrifice to Ceres, and
leave it off; so that we may see, that as he cut off all
superfluity, so in things necessary there was nothing so
small and trivial which did not express some homage of
virtue or scorn of vice. He filled Lacedæmon all through
with proofs and examples of good conduct; with the constant sight of which from their youth up, the people
would hardly fail to be gradually formed and advanced
in virtue.

And this was the reason why he forbade them to travel

abroad, and go about acquainting themselves with foreign rules of morality, the habits of ill-educated people, and different views of government. Withal he banished from Lacedæmon all strangers who could not give a very good reason for their coming thither; not because he was afraid lest they should inform themselves of and imitate his manner of government (as Thucydides says), or learn any thing to their good; but rather lest they should introduce something contrary to good manners. With strange people, strange words must be admitted; these novelties produce novelties in thought; and on these follow views and feelings whose discordant character destroys the harmony of the state. He was as careful to save his city from the infection of foreign bad habits, as men usually are to prevent the introduction of a pestilence.

Hitherto I, for my part, see no sign of injustice or want of equity in the laws of Lycurgus, though some who admit them to be well contrived to make good soldiers, pronounce them defective in point of justice. The Cryptia, perhaps (if it were one of Lycurgus's ordinances, as Aristotle says it was), gave both him and Plato, too, this opinion alike of the lawgiver and his government. By this ordinance, the magistrates despatched privately some of the ablest of the young men into the country, from time to time, armed only with their daggers, and taking a little necessary provision with them; in the daytime, they hid themselves in out-of-the-way places, and there lay close, but, in the night, issued out into the highways, and killed all the Helots they could light upon; sometimes they set upon them by day, as they were at work in the fields, and murdered them. As, also, Thucydides, in his history of the Peloponnesian war, tells us, that a good number of them, after being singled out for their bravery by the Spartans, garlanded, as enfranchised persons, and led about to all the temples in token of honors, shortly after disappeared all of a sudden, being about the number of two thousand; and no man either then or since could give an account how they came by their deaths. And Aristotle, in particular, adds, that the ephori, so soon as they were entered into their office, used to declare war against them, that they might be massacred without a breach of religion. It is confessed, on all hands, that the Spartans dealt with them very hardly; for it was a common thing to force them to drink to excess, and to lead them in that condition into their public halls, that the children might see what a sight a drunken man is; they made them to dance low dances, and sing ridiculous songs, forbidding them expressly to meddle with any of a better kind. And, accordingly, when the Thebans made their invasion into Laconia, and took a great number of the Helots, they could by no means persuade them to sing the verses of Terpander, Alcman, or Spendon, "For," said they, "the masters * do not like it." So that it was truly observed by one, that in Sparta he who was free was most so, and he that was a slave there, the greatest slave in the world. For my part, I am of opinion that these outrages and cruelties began to be exercised in Sparta at a later time, especially after the great earthquake, when the Helots made a general insurrection, and, joining with the Messenians, laid the country waste, and brought the greatest danger upon the city. For I cannot persuade myself to ascribe to Lycurgus so wicked and barbarous a course, judging of him from the gentleness of his disposition and justice upon all other occasions; to which the oracle also testified.

When he perceived that his more important institutions had taken root in the minds of his countrymen, that

* Literally, "the lordships," — tas desposynas.

custom had rendered them familiar and easy, that his commonwealth was now grown up and able to go alone,
then, as, Plato somewhere tells us, the Maker of the world,
when first he saw it existing and beginning its motion,
felt joy, even so Lycurgus, viewing with joy and satisfaction the greatness and beauty of his political structure,
now fairly at work and in motion, conceived the thought
to make it immortal too, and, as far as human forecast
could reach, to deliver it down unchangeable to posterity.
He called an extraordinary assembly of all the people,
and told them that he now thought every thing reason-
ably well established, both for the happiness and the virtue of the state; but that there was one thing still behind,
of the greatest importance, which he thought not fit to
impart until he had consulted the oracle; in the mean
time, his desire was that they would observe the laws
without any the least alteration until his return, and then
he would do as the god should direct him.   They all consented readily, and bade him hasten his journey; but, before
he departed, he administered an oath to the two kings,
the senate, and the whole commons, to abide by and maintain the established form of polity until Lycurgus should
be come back.   This done, he set out for Delphi, and, having sacrificed to Apollo, asked him whether the laws he
had established were good, and sufficient for a people's
happiness and virtue.   The oracle answered that the laws
were excellent, and that the people, while it observed
them, should live in the height of renown. Lycurgus took
the oracle in writing, and sent it over to Sparta; and,
having sacrificed the second time to Apollo, and taken
leave of his friends and his son, he resolved that the Spartans should not be released from the oath they had taken,
and that he would, of his own act, close his life where he
was.   He was now about that age in which life was still
tolerable, and yet might be quitted without regret.   Every

thing, morever, about him was in a sufficiently prosperous condition. He, therefore, made an end of himself by a total abstinence from food; thinking it a statesman's duty to make his very death, if possible, an act of service to the state, and even in the end of his life to give some example of virtue and effect some useful purpose. He would, on the one hand, crown and consummate his own happiness by a death suitable to so honorable a life, and, on the other, would secure to his countrymen the enjoyment of the advantages he had spent his life in obtaining for them, since they had solemnly sworn the maintenance of his institutions until his return. Nor was he deceived in his expectations, for the city of Lacedæmon continued the chief city of all Greece for the space of five hundred years, in strict observance of Lycurgus's laws; in all which time there was no manner of alteration made, during the reign of fourteen kings, down to the time of Agis, the son of Archidamus. For the new creation of the ephori, though thought to be in favor of the people, was so far from diminishing, that it very much heightened, the aristocratical character of the government.

In the time of Agis, gold and silver first flowed into Sparta, and with them all those mischiefs which attend the immoderate desire of riches. Lysander promoted this disorder; for, by bringing in rich spoils from the wars, although himself incorrupt, he yet by this means filled his country with avarice and luxury, and subverted the laws and ordinances of Lycurgus; so long as which were in force, the aspect presented by Sparta was rather that of a rule of life followed by one wise and temperate man, than of the political government of a nation. And as the poets feign of Hercules, that, with his lion's skin and his club, he went over the world, punishing lawless and cruel tyrants, so may it be said of the Lacedæmonians, that, with a common staff* and a coarse coat, they gained the willing and joyful obedience of Greece, through whose whole extent they suppressed unjust usurpations and despotisms, arbitrated in war, and composed civil dissensions; and this often without so much as taking down one buckler, but barely by sending some one single deputy, to whose direction all at once submitted, like bees swarming and taking their places around their prince. Such a fund of order and equity, enough and to spare for others, existed in their state.

And therefore I cannot but wonder at those who say that the Spartans were good subjects, but bad governors, and for proof of it allege a saying of king Theopompus, who, when one said that Sparta held up so long because their kings could command so well, replied, "Nay, rather because the people know so well how to obey." For people do not obey, unless rulers know how to command; obedience is a lesson taught by commanders. A true leader himself creates the obedience of his own followers; as it is the last attainment in the art of riding to make a horse gentle and tractable, so is it of the science of government, to inspire men with a willingness to obey. The Lacedæmonians inspired men not with a mere willingness, but with an absolute desire, to be their subjects. For they did not send petitions to them for ships or money, or a supply of armed men, but only for a Spartan commander; and, having obtained one, used him with honor and reverence; so the Sicilians behaved to Gylippus, the Chalcidians to Brasidas, and all the Greeks in Asia to Lysander, Callicratidas, and Agesilaus; they styled them the composers and chasteners of each people or prince they were sent to, and had their eyes always

* The scytale, around which their despatches were rolled.

fixed upon the city of Sparta itself, as the perfect model
of good manners and wise government. The rest seemed
as scholars, they the masters of Greece; and to this Stra-
tonicus pleasantly alluded, when in jest he pretended
to make a law that the Athenians should conduct religious processions and the mysteries, the Eleans should
preside at the Olympic games, and, if either did amiss,
the Lacedæmonians be beaten. Antisthenes, too, one
of the scholars of Socrates, said, in earnest, of the Thebans, when they were elated by their victory at Leuctra,
that they looked like schoolboys who had beaten their
master.

However, it was not the design of Lycurgus that his
city should govern a great many others; he thought
rather that the happiness of a state, as of a private man,
consisted chiefly in the exercise of virtue, and in the concord of the inhabitants; his aim, therefore, in all his
arrangements, was to make and keep them free-minded,
self-dependent, and temperate. And therefore all those
who have written well on politics, as Plato, Diogenes, and
Zeno, have taken Lycurgus for their model, leaving behind them, however, mere projects and words; whereas
Lycurgus was the author, not in writing but in reality, of
a government which none else could so much as copy;
and while men in general have treated the individual
philosophic character as unattainable, he, by the example
of a complete philosophic state, raised himself high above
all other lawgivers of Greece. And so Aristotle says they
did him less honor at Lacedæmon after his death than he
deserved, although he has a temple there, and they offer
sacrifices yearly to him as to a god.

It is reported that when his bones were brought home
to Sparta his tomb was struck with lightning; an accident which befell no eminent person but himself, and
Euripides, who was buried at Arethusa in Macedonia;

and it may serve that poet's admirers as a testimony in his favor, that he had in this the same fate with that holy man and favorite of the gods. Some say Lycurgus died in Cirrha; Apollothemis says, after he had come to Elis; Timæus and Aristoxenus, that he ended his life in Crete; Aristoxenus adds that his tomb is shown by the Cretans in the district of Pergamus, near the strangers' road. He left an only son, Antiorus, on whose death without issue, his family became extinct. But his relations and friends kept up an annual commemoration of him down to a long time after; and the days of the meeting were called Lycurgides. Aristocrates, the son of Hipparchus, says that he died in Crete, and that his Cretan friends, in accordance with his own request, when they had burned his body, scattered the ashes into the sea; for fear lest, if his relics should be transported to Lacedæmon, the people might pretend to be released from their oaths, and make innovations in the government. Thus much may suffice for the life and actions of Lycurgus.

NUMA POMPILIUS.

THOUGH the pedigrees of noble families of Rome go
back in exact form as far as Numa Pompilius, yet there
is great diversity amongst historians concerning the time
in which he reigned; a certain writer called Clodius,* in
a book of his entitled Strictures on Chronology, avers
that the ancient registers of Rome were lost when the
city was sacked by the Gauls, and that those which are
now extant were counterfeited, to flatter and serve the
humor of some men who wished to have themselves
derived from some ancient and noble lineage, though in
reality with no claim to it. And though it be commonly
reported that Numa was a scholar and a familiar acquaintance of Pythagoras, yet it is again contradicted
by others, who affirm, that he was acquainted with neither the Greek language nor learning, and that he was a
person of that natural talent and ability as of himself to
attain to virtue, or else that he found some barbarian in-
structor superior to Pythagoras. Some affirm, also, that
Pythagoras was not contemporary with Numa, but lived at
least five generations after him; and that some other Pythagoras, a native of Sparta, who, in the sixteenth Olympiad, in the third year of which Numa became king, won
a prize at the Olympic race, might, in his travel through

---

* Probably Claudius Quadrigarius.

Italy, have gained acquaintance with Numa, and assisted him in the constitution of his kingdom; whence it comes that many Laconian laws and customs appear amongst the Roman institutions. Yet, in any case, Numa was descended of the Sabines, who declare themselves to be a colony of the Lacedæmonians. And chronology, in general, is uncertain; especially when fixed by the lists of victors in the Olympic games, which were published at a late period by Hippias the Elean, and rest on no positive authority. Commencing, however, at a convenient point, we will proceed to give the most noticeable events that are recorded of the life of Numa.

It was the thirty-seventh year, counted from the foundation of Rome, when Romulus, then reigning, did, on the fifth day of the month of July, called the Caprotine Nones, offer a public sacrifice at the Goat's Marsh, in presence of the senate and people of Rome. Suddenly the sky was darkened, a thick cloud of storm and rain settled on the earth; the common people fled in affright, and were dispersed; and in this whirlwind Romulus disappeared, his body being never found either living or dead. A foul suspicion presently attached to the patricians, and rumors were current among the people as if that they, weary of kingly government, and exasperated of late by the imperious deportment of Romulus towards them, had plotted against his life and made him away, that so they might assume the authority and government into their own hands. This suspicion they sought to turn aside by decreeing divine honors to Romulus, as to one not dead but translated to a higher condition. And Proculus, a man of note, took oath that he saw Romulus caught up into heaven in his arms and vestments, and heard him, as he ascended, cry out that they should hereafter style him by the name of Quirinus.

This trouble, being appeased, was followed by another, about the election of a new king; for the minds of the

original Romans and the new inhabitants were not as yet
grown into that perfect unity of temper, but that there
were diversities of factions amongst the commonalty, and
jealousies and emulations amongst the senators; for
though all agreed that it was necessary to have a king,
yet what person or of which nation, was matter of dispute.
For those who had been builders of the city with Romulus, and had already yielded a share of their lands and
dwellings to the Sabines, were indignant at any pretension on their part to rule over their benefactors. On the
other side, the Sabines could plausibly allege, that, at their
king Tatius's decease, they had peaceably submitted to
the sole command of Romulus; so now their turn was
come to have a king chosen out of their own nation; nor
did they esteem themselves to have combined with the
Romans as inferiors, nor to have contributed less than
they to the increase of Rome, which, without their numbers and association, could scarcely have merited the
name of a city.

Thus did both parties argue and dispute their cause;
but lest meanwhile discord, in the absence of all command, should occasion general confusion, it was agreed
that the hundred and fifty senators should interchangea-
bly execute the office of supreme magistrate, and each in
succession, with the ensigns of royalty, should offer the
solemn sacrifices and despatch public business for the
space of six hours by day and six by night; which vicissitude and equal distribution of power would preclude all
rivalry amongst the senators and envy from the people,
when they should behold one, elevated to the degree of a
king, levelled within the space of a day to the condition
of a private citizen. This form of government is termed,
by the Romans, interregnum. Nor yet could they, by
this plausible and modest way of rule, escape suspicion
and clamor of the vulgar, as though they were changing

the form of government to an oligarchy, and designing to keep the supreme power in a sort of wardship under themselves, without ever proceeding to choose a king. Both parties came at length to the conclusion that the one should choose a king out of the body of the other; the Romans make choice of a Sabine, or the Sabines name a Roman; this was esteemed the best expedient to put an end to all party spirit, and the prince who should be chosen would have an equal affection to the one party as his electors and to the other as his kinsmen. The Sabines remitted the choice to the original Romans, and they, too, on their part, were more inclinable to receive a Sabine king elected by themselves than to see a Roman exalted by the Sabines. Consultations being accordingly held, they named Numa Pompilius, of the Sabine race, a person of that high reputation for excellence, that, though he were not actually residing at Rome, yet he was no sooner nominated than accepted by the Sabines, with acclamation almost greater than that of the electors themselves.

The choice being declared and made known to the people, principal men of both parties were appointed to visit and entreat him, that he would accept the administration of the government. Numa resided at a famous city of the Sabines called Cures, whence the Romans and Sabines gave themselves the joint name of Quirites. Pomponius, an illustrious person, was his father, and he the youngest of his four sons, being (as it had been divinely ordered) born on the twenty-first day of April, the day of the foundation of Rome. He was endued with a soul rarely tempered by nature, and disposed to virtue, which he had yet more subdued by discipline, a severe life, and the study of philosophy; means which had not only succeeded in expelling the baser passions, but also the violent and rapacious temper which barbarians are apt to think highly of; true bravery, in his judgment, was regarded as consisting in the subjugation of our passions by reason.

He banished all luxury and softness from his own home, and, while citizens alike and strangers found in him an incorruptible judge and counsellor, in private he devoted himself not to amusement or lucre, but to the worship of the immortal gods, and the rational contemplation of their divine power and nature. So famous was he, that Tatius, the colleague of Romulus, chose him for his son-in-law, and gave him his only daughter, which, however, did not stimulate his vanity to desire to dwell with his father-in-law at Rome; he rather chose to inhabit with his Sabines, and cherish his own father in his old age; and Tatia, also, preferred the private condition of her husband before the honors and splendor she might have enjoyed with her father. She is said to have died after she had been married thirteen years, and then Numa, leaving the conversation of the town, betook himself to a country life, and in a solitary manner frequented the groves and fields consecrated to the gods, passing his life in desert places. And this in particular gave occasion to the story about the goddess, namely, that Numa did not retire from human society out of any melancholy or disorder of mind, but because he had tasted the joys of more elevated intercourse, and, admitted to celestial wedlock in the love and converse of the goddess Egeria, had attained to blessedness, and to a divine wisdom.

The story evidently resembles those very ancient fables which the Phrygians have received and still recount of Attis, the Bithynians of Herodotus, the Arcadians of Endymion, not to mention several others who were thought blessed and beloved of the gods; nor does it seem strange if God, a lover, not of horses or birds, but men, should not disdain to dwell with the virtuous and converse with the wise and temperate soul, though it be altogether hard, indeed, to believe, that any god or dæmon is capable of a sensual or bodily love and passion for any human form or beauty. Though, indeed, the wise Egyptians do not unplausibly make the distinction, that it may be possible for a divine spirit so to apply itself to the nature of a woman, as to imbreed in her the first beginnings of generation, while on the other side they conclude it impossible for the male kind to have any intercourse or mixture by the body with any divinity, not considering, however, that what takes place on the one side, must also take place on the other; intermixture, by force of terms, is reciprocal. Not that it is otherwise than befitting to suppose that the gods feel towards men affection, and love, in the sense of affection, and in the form of care and solicitude for their virtue and their good dispositions. And, therefore, it was no error of those who feigned, that Phorbas, Hyacinthus, and Admetus were beloved by Apollo; or that Hippolytus the Sicyonian was so much in his favor, that, as often as he sailed from Sicyon to Cirrha, the Pythian prophetess uttered this heroic verse, expressive of the god's attention and joy:

> Now doth Hippolytus return again,
> And venture his dear life upon the main.

It is reported, also, that Pan became enamoured of Pindar for his verses, and the divine power rendered honor to Hesiod and Archilochus after their death for the sake of the Muses; there is a statement, also, that Æsculapius sojourned with Sophocles in his lifetime, of which many proofs still exist, and that, when he was dead, another deity took care for his funeral rites. And so if any credit may be given to these instances, why should we judge it incongruous, that a like spirit of the gods should visit Zaleucus, Minos, Zoroaster, Lycurgus, and Numa, the controllers of kingdoms, and the legislators for commonwealths? Nay, it may be reasonable to believe, that the gods, with a serious purpose, assist at the councils and serious debates of such men, to inspire and direct them; and visit poets and musicians, if at all, in their more sportive moods; but, for difference of opinion here, as Bacchylides said, "the road is broad." For there is no absurdity in the account also given, that Lycurgus and Numa, and other famous lawgivers, having the task of subduing perverse and refractory multitudes, and of introducing great innovations, themselves made this pretension to divine authority, which, if not true, assuredly was expedient for the interests of those it imposed upon.

Numa was about forty years of age when the ambassadors came to make him offers of the kingdom; the speakers were Proculus and Velesus,* one or other of whom it had been thought the people would elect as their new king; the original Romans being for Proculus, and the Sabines for Velesus. Their speech was very short, supposing that, when they came to tender a kingdom, there needed little to persuade to an acceptance; but, contrary to their expectation, they found that they had to use many reasons and entreaties to induce one, that lived in peace and quietness, to accept the government of a city whose foundation and increase had been made, in a manner, in war. In presence of his father and his kinsman Marcius, he returned answer that "Every alteration of a man's life is dangerous to him; but madness only could induce one who needs nothing and is satisfied with every thing to quit a life he is accustomed to; which, whatever else it is deficient in, at any rate has the advantage of certainty over one wholly doubtful and unknown. Though, indeed, the difficulties of this government cannot even be called unknown; Romulus, who first held it, did not escape the suspicion of having plot-

* Or Volesus, founder of the Valerian house.

ted against the life of his colleague Tatius; nor the senate the like accusation, of having treasonably murdered
Romulus. Yet Romulus had the advantage to be thought
divinely born and miraculously preserved and nurtured.
My birth was mortal; I was reared and instructed by
men that are known to you. The very points of my
character that are most commended mark me as unfit to
reign, — love of retirement and of studies inconsistent
with business, a passion that has become inveterate in
me for peace; for unwarlike occupations, and for the society of men whose meetings are but those of worship and
of kindly intercourse, whose lives in general are spent
upon their farms and their pastures. I should but be,
methinks, a laughing-stock, while I should go about to in-
culcate the worship of the gods, and give lessons in the
love of justice and the abhorrence of violence and war, to
a city whose needs are rather for a captain than for a king."

The Romans, perceiving by these words that he was
declining to accept the kingdom, were the more instant
and urgent with him that he would not forsake and desert
them in this condition, and suffer them to relapse, as they
must, into their former sedition and civil discord, there
being no person on whom both parties could accord but
on himself. And, at length, his father and Marcius, taking
him aside, persuaded him to accept a gift so noble in
itself, and tendered to him rather from heaven than from
men. "Though," said they, "you neither desire riches,
being content with what you have, nor court the fame of
authority, as having already the more valuable fame of
virtue, yet you will consider that government itself is a
service of God, who now calls out into action your qualities of justice and wisdom, which were not meant to be
left useless and unemployed. Cease, therefore, to avoid
and turn your back upon an office which, to a wise man,
is a field for great and honorable actions, for the magnifi-

cent worship of the gods, and for the introduction of habits of piety, which authority alone can effect amongst a people. Tatius, though a foreigner, was beloved, and the memory of Romulus has received divine honors; and who knows but that this people, being victorious, may be satiated with war, and, content with the trophies and spoils they have acquired, may be, above all things, desirous to have a pacific and justice-loving prince, to lead them to good order and quiet? But if, indeed, their desires are uncontrollably and madly set on war, were it not better, then, to have the reins held by such a moderating hand as is able to divert the fury another way, and that your native city and the whole Sabine nation should possess in you a bond of good-will and friendship with this young and growing power?"

With these reasons and persuasions several auspicious omens are said to have concurred, and the zeal, also, of his fellow-citizens, who, on understanding what message the Roman ambassadors had brought him, entreated him to accompany them, and to accept the kingdom as a means to unanimity and concord between the nations.

Numa, yielding to these inducements, having first performed divine sacrifice, proceeded to Rome, being met in his way by the senate and people, who, with an impatient desire, came forth to receive him; the women, also, welcomed him with joyful acclamations, and sacrifices were offered for him in all the temples, and so universal was the joy, that they seemed to be receiving, not a new king, but a new kingdom. In this manner he descended into the forum, where Spurius Vettius, whose turn it was to be interrex at that hour, put it to the vote; and all declared him king. Then the regalities and robes of authority were brought to him; but he refused to be invested with them until he had first consulted and been confirmed by the gods; so, being accompanied by the priests and augurs, he ascended the Capitol, which at that time the Romans called the Tarpeian Hill. Then the chief of the augurs covered Numa's head, and turned his face towards the south, and, standing behind him, laid his right hand on his head, and prayed, turning his eyes every way, in expectation of some auspicious signal from the gods. It was wonderful, meantime, with what silence and devotion the multitude stood assembled in the forum, in similar expectation and suspense, till auspicious birds appeared and passed on the right. Then Numa, apparelling himself in his royal robes, descended from the hill to the people, by whom he was received and congratulated with shouts and acclamations of welcome, as a holy king, and beloved of all the gods.

The first thing he did at his entrance into government was to dismiss the band of three hundred men which had been Romulus's life-guard, called by him Celeres, saying, that he would not distrust those who put confidence in him, nor rule over a people that distrusted him. The next thing he did was to add to the two priests of Jupiter and Mars a third in honor of Romulus, whom he called the Flamen Quirinalis. The Romans anciently called their priests Flamines, by corruption of the word Pilamines, from a certain cap which they wore, called Pileus. In those times, Greek words were more mixed with the Latin than at present; thus also the royal robe, which is called Læna, Juba says, is the same as the Greek Chlæna; and that the name of Camillus, given to the boy with both his parents living, who serves in the temple of Jupiter, was taken from the name given by some Greeks to Mercury, denoting his office of attendance on the gods.*

When Numa had, by such measures, won the favor and affection of the people, he set himself, without delay, to the task of bringing the hard and iron Roman temper to

* Cadōlos or Cadoulos.

NUMA.   137

somewhat more of gentleness and equity. Plato's expression of a city in high fever was never more applicable than to Rome at that time; in its origin formed by
daring and warlike spirits, whom bold and desperate adventure brought thither from every quarter, it had found
in perpetual wars and incursions on its neighbors its after
sustenance and means of growth, and in conflict with
danger the source of new strength; like piles, which the
blows of the rammer serve to fix into the ground. Wherefore Numa, judging it no slight undertaking to mollify
and bend to peace the presumptuous and stubborn spirits
of this people, began to operate upon them with the sanctions of religion. He sacrificed often, and used processions and religious dances, in which most commonly he
officiated in person; by such combinations of solemnity
with refined and humanizing pleasures, seeking to win
over and mitigate their fiery and warlike tempers. At
times, also, he filled their imaginations with religious terrors, professing that strange apparitions had been seen,
and dreadful voices heard; thus subduing and humbling
their minds by a sense of supernatural fears.

This method which Numa used made it believed that
he had been much conversant with Pythagoras; for in the
philosophy of the one, as in the policy of the other, man's
relations to the deity occupy a great place. It is said,
also, that the solemnity of his exterior garb and gestures
was adopted by him from the same feeling with Pythagoras. For it is said of Pythagoras, that he had taught an
eagle to come at his call, and stoop down to him in its
flight; and that, as he passed among the people assembled
at the Olympic games, he showed them his golden thigh;
besides many other strange and miraculous seeming practices, on which Timon the Phliasian wrote the distich,—

Who, of the glory of a juggler proud,
With solemn talk imposed upon the crowd.

In like manner Numa spoke of a certain goddess or mountain nymph that was in love with him, and met him in
secret, as before related; and professed that he entertained familiar conversation with the Muses, to whose
teaching he ascribed the greatest part of his revelations;
and amongst them, above all, he recommended to the
veneration of the Romans one in particular, whom he
named Tacita, the Silent; which he did perhaps in imitation and honor of the Pythagorean silence. His opinion,
also, of images is very agreeable to the doctrine of Pythagoras; who conceived of the first principle of being as
transcending sense and passion, invisible and incorrupt,
and only to be apprehended by abstract intelligence. So
Numa forbade the Romans to represent God in the form
of man or beast, nor was there any painted or graven
image of a deity admitted amongst them for the space of
the first hundred and seventy years, all which time their
temples and chapels were kept free and pure from images; to such baser objects they deemed it impious to
liken the highest, and all access to God impossible, except
by the pure act of the intellect. His sacrifices, also, had
great similitude to the ceremonial of Pythagoras, for they
were not celebrated with effusion of blood, but consisted
of flour, wine, and the least costly offerings. Other external proofs, too, are urged to show the connection Numa
had with Pythagoras. The comic writer Epicharmus, an
ancient author, and of the school of Pythagoras, in a book
of his dedicated to Antenor, records that Pythagoras was
made a freeman of Rome. Again, Numa gave to one of
his four sons the name of Mamercus, which was the name
of one of the sons of Pythagoras; from whence, as they
say, sprang that ancient patrician family of the Æmilii,
for that the king gave him in sport the surname of
Æmilius, for his engaging and graceful manner in speaking.* I remember, too, that when I was at Rome, I

* Aimulos, or æmylus, Gr., engaging, or wily.

heard many say, that, when the oracle directed two statues to be raised, one to the wisest, and another to the
most valiant man of Greece, they erected two of brass,
one representing Alcibiades, and the other Pythagoras.

But to pass by these matters, which are full of uncertainty, and not so important as to be worth our time to
insist on them, the original constitution of the priests,
called Pontifices, is ascribed unto Numa, and he himself
was, it is said, the first of them; and that they have the
name of Pontifices from *potens*, powerful, because they
attend the service of the gods, who have power and command over all. Others make the word refer to exceptions of impossible cases; the priests were to perform all
the duties possible to them; if any thing lay beyond
their power, the exception was not to be cavilled at. The
most common opinion is the most absurd, which derives
this word from *pons*, and assigns the priests the title of
bridge-makers. The sacrifices performed on the bridge
were amongst the most sacred and ancient, and the
keeping and repairing of the bridge attached, like any
other public sacred office, to the priesthood. It was accounted not simply unlawful, but a positive sacrilege, to
pull down the wooden bridge; which moreover is said, in
obedience to an oracle, to have been built entirely of timber and fastened with wooden pins, without nails or
cramps of iron. The stone bridge was built a very long
time after, when Æmilius was quæstor, and they do, indeed,
say also that the wooden bridge was not so old as Numa's
time, but was finished by Ancus Marcius, when he was
king, who was the grandson of Numa by his daughter.

The office of Pontifex Maximus, or chief priest, was to
declare and interpret the divine law, or, rather, to preside
over sacred rites; he not only prescribed rules for public
ceremony, but regulated the sacrifices of private persons,
not suffering them to vary from established custom, and

giving information to every one of what was requisite for purposes of worship or supplication. He was also guardian of the vestal virgins, the institution of whom, and of their perpetual fire, was attributed to Numa, who, perhaps, fancied the charge of pure and uncorrupted flames would be fitly intrusted to chaste and unpolluted persons, or that fire, which consumes, but produces nothing, bears an analogy to the virgin estate. In Greece, wherever a perpetual holy fire is kept, as at Delphi and Athens, the charge of it is committed, not to virgins, but widows past the time of marriage. And in case by any accident it should happen that this fire became extinct, as the holy lamp was at Athens under the tyranny of Aristion, and at Delphi, when that temple was burnt by the Medes, as also in the time of the Mithridatic and Roman civil war, when not only the fire was extinguished, but the altar demolished, then, afterwards, in kindling this fire again, it was esteemed an impiety to light it from common sparks or flame, or from any thing but the pure and unpolluted rays of the sun, which they usually effect by concave mirrors, of a figure formed by the revolution of an isosceles rectangular triangle, all the lines from the circumference of which meeting in a centre, by holding it in the light of the sun they can collect and concentrate all its rays at this one point of convergence; where the air will now become rarefied, and any light, dry, combustible matter will kindle as soon as applied, under the effect of the rays, which here acquire the substance and active force of fire. Some are of opinion that these vestals had no other business than the preservation of this fire; but others conceive that they were keepers of other divine secrets, concealed from all but themselves, of which we have told all that may lawfully be asked or told, in the life of Camillus. Gegania and Verenia, it is recorded, were the names of the first two virgins consecrated and ordained by Numa; Canuleia and Tarpeia succeeded; Servius afterwards added two, and the number of four has continued to the present time.

The statutes prescribed by Numa for the vestals were these: that they should take a vow of virginity for the space of thirty years, the first ten of which they were to spend in learning their duties, the second ten in performing them, and the remaining ten in teaching and instructing others. Thus the whole term being completed, it was lawful for them to marry, and, leaving the sacred order, to choose any condition of life that pleased them; but this permission few, as they say, made use of; and in cases where they did so, it was observed that their change was not a happy one, but accompanied ever after with regret and melancholy; so that the greater number, from religious fears and scruples, forbore, and continued to old age and death in the strict observance of a single life.

For this condition he compensated by great privileges and prerogatives; as that they had power to make a will in the lifetime of their father; that they had a free administration of their own affairs without guardian or tutor, which was the privilege of women who were the mothers of three children; when they go abroad, they have the fasces carried before them; and if in their walks they chance to meet a criminal on his way to execution, it saves his life, upon oath made that the meeting was an accidental one, and not concerted or of set purpose. Any one who presses upon the chair on which they are carried, is put to death. If these vestals commit any minor fault, they are punishable by the high-priest only, who scourges the offender, sometimes with her clothes off, in a dark place, with a curtain drawn between; but she that has broken her vow is buried alive

near the gate called Collina, where a little mound of
earth stands, inside the city, reaching some little distance,
called in Latin *agger*; under it a narrow room is constructed, to which a descent is made by stairs; here
they prepare a bed, and light a lamp, and leave a small
quantity of victuals, such as bread, water, a pail of milk,
and some oil; that so that body which had been consecrated and devoted to the most sacred service of religion
might not be said to perish by such a death as famine.
The culprit herself is put in a litter, which they cover
over, and tie her down with cords on it, so that nothing
she utters may be heard.   They then take her to the
forum; all people silently go out of the way as she
passes, and such as follow accompany the bier with
solemn and speechless sorrow; and, indeed, there is not
any spectacle more appalling, nor any day observed by
the city with greater appearance of gloom and sadness.
When they come to the place of execution, the officers
loose the cords, and then the high-priest, lifting his hands
to heaven, pronounces certain prayers to himself before
the act; then he brings out the prisoner, being still
covered, and placing her upon the steps that lead down
to the cell, turns away his face with the rest of the
priests; the stairs are drawn up after she has gone down,
and a quantity of earth is heaped up over the entrance
to the cell, so as to prevent it from being distinguished
from the rest of the mound.   This is the punishment of
those who break their vow of virginity.

It is said, also, that Numa built the temple of Vesta,
which was intended for a repository of the holy fire, of a
circular form, not to represent the figure of the earth,
as if that were the same as Vesta, but that of the general
universe, in the centre of which the Pythagoreans place
the element of fire, and give it the name of Vesta and

the unit; and do not hold that the earth is immovable, or that it is situated in the centre of the globe, but that it keeps a circular motion about the seat of fire, and is not in the number of the primary elements; in this agreeing with the opinion of Plato, who, they say, in his later life, conceived that the earth held a lateral position, and that the central and sovereign space was reserved for some nobler body.

There was yet a farther use of the priests, and that was to give people directions in the national usages at funeral rites. Numa taught them to regard these offices, not as a pollution, but as a duty paid to the gods below, into whose hands the better part of us is transmitted; especially they were to worship the goddess Libitina, who presided over all the ceremonies performed at burials; whether they meant hereby Proserpina, or, as the most learned of the Romans conceive, Venus, not inaptly attributing the beginning and end of man's life to the agency of one and the same deity. Numa also prescribed rules for regulating the days of mourning, according to certain times and ages. As, for example, a child of three years was not to be mourned for at all; one older, up to ten years, for as many months as it was years old; and the longest time of mourning for any person whatsoever was not to exceed the term of ten months; which was the time appointed for women that lost their husbands to continue in widowhood. If any married again before that time, by the laws of Numa she was to sacrifice a cow big with calf.

Numa, also, was founder of several other orders of priests, two of which I shall mention, the Salii and the Feciales, which are among the clearest proofs of the devoutness and sanctity of his character. These Fecials, or guardians of peace, seem to have had their name

from their office,* which was to put a stop to disputes by
conference and speech; for it was not allowable to take
up arms until they had declared all hopes of accommoda-
tion to be at an end, for in Greek, too, we call it peace
when disputes are settled by words, and not by force.
The Romans commonly despatched the Fecials, or heralds,
to those who had offered them injury, requesting satisfaction; and, in case they refused, they then called the gods
to witness, and, with imprecations upon themselves and
their country should they be acting unjustly, so declared
war; against their will, or without their consent, it was
lawful neither for soldier nor king to take up arms; the
war was begun with them, and, when they had first handed
it over to the commander as a just quarrel, then his business was to deliberate of the manner and ways to carry
it on.   It is believed that the slaughter and destruction
which the Gauls made of the Romans was a judgment on
the city for neglect of this religious proceeding; for that
when these barbarians besieged the Clusinians, Fabius
Ambustus was despatched to their camp to negotiate
peace for the besieged; and, on their returning a rude
refusal, Fabius imagined that his office of ambassador was
at an end, and, rashly engaging on the side of the Clusinians, challenged the bravest of the enemy to a single
combat.   It was the fortune of Fabius to kill his adversary, and to take his spoils; but when the Gauls discovered it, they sent a herald to Rome to complain against
him; since, before war was declared, he had, against the
law of nations, made a breach of the peace.   The matter
being debated in the senate, the Fecials were of opinion

---

* The allusion seems to be to the   made, too, in the words that follow,
Greek *phēmi*, to say, with which it   to a derivation of *eirēne*, the Greek
is possible Fecialis may really be   word for peace, from *eirein*, to
connected. Reference, perhaps, is   speak.

that Fabius ought to be consigned into the hands of the Gauls; but he, being forewarned of their judgment, fled to the people, by whose protection and favor he escaped the sentence. On this, the Gauls marched with their army to Rome, where, having taken the Capitol, they sacked the city. The particulars of all which are fully given in the history of Camillus.

The origin of the Salii is this. In the eighth year of the reign of Numa, a terrible pestilence, which traversed all Italy, ravaged likewise the city of Rome; and the citizens being in distress and despondent, a brazen target, they say, fell from heaven into the hands of Numa, who gave them this marvellous account of it: that Egeria and the Muses had assured him it was sent from heaven for the cure and safety of the city, and that, to keep it secure, he was ordered by them to make eleven others, so like in dimension and form to the original that no thief should be able to distinguish the true from the counterfeit. He farther declared, that he was commanded to consecrate to the Muses the place, and the fields about it, where they had been chiefly wont to meet with him, and that the spring which watered the field should be hallowed for the use of the vestal virgins, who were to wash and cleanse the penetralia of their sanctuary with those holy waters. The truth of all which was speedily verified by the cessation of the pestilence. Numa displayed the target to the artificers, and bade them show their skill in making others like it; all despaired, until at length one Mamurius Veturius, an excellent workman, happily hit upon it, and made all so exactly the same that Numa himself was at a loss, and could not distinguish. The keeping of these targets was committed to the charge of certain priests, called Salii, who did not receive their name, as some tell the story, from Salius, a dancing-master, born in Samothrace, or at Mantinea, who taught the way of dancing in arms; but more truly from that jumping dance which the Salii themselves use, when in the month of March they carry the sacred targets through the city; at which procession they are habited in short frocks of purple, girt with a broad belt studded with brass; on their heads they wear a brass helmet, and carry in their hands short daggers, which they clash every now and then against the targets. But the chief thing is the dance itself. They move with much grace, performing, in quick time and close order, various intricate figures, with a great display of strength and agility. The targets were called Ancilia from their form; for they are not made round, nor like proper targets, of a complete circumference, but are cut out into a wavy line, the ends of which are rounded off and turned in at the thickest part towards each other; so that their shape is curvilinear, or, in Greek, *ancylon*; or the name may come from *ancon*, the elbow, on which they are carried. Thus Juba writes, who is eager to make it Greek. But it might be, for that matter, from its having come down *anecathen*, from above; or from its *akesis*, or cure of diseases; or *auchmon lysis*, because it put an end to a drought; or from its *anaschesis*, or relief from calamities, which is the origin of the Athenian name Anaces, given to Castor and Pollux; if we must, that is, reduce it to Greek. The reward which Mamurius received for his art was to be mentioned and commemorated in the verses which the Salii sang, as they danced in their arms through the city; though some will have it that they do not say Veturium Mamurium, but Veterem Memoriam, ancient remembrance.

After Numa had in this manner instituted these several orders of priests, he erected, near the temple of Vesta, what is called to this day Regia, or king's house, where he spent the most part of his time, performing divine service, instructing the priests, or conversing with them on sacred

subjects. He had another house upon the Mount Quiri
nalis, the site of which they show to this day. In all
public processions and solemn prayers, criers were sent
before to give notice to the people that they should forbear their work, and rest. They say that the Pythagoreans did not allow people to worship and pray to their
gods by the way, but would have them go out from their
houses direct, with their minds set upon the duty, and so
Numa, in like manner, wished that his citizens should
neither see nor hear any religious service in a perfunc-
tory and inattentive manner, but, laying aside all other
occupations, should apply their minds to religion as to a
most serious business; and that the streets should be free
from all noises and cries that accompany manual labor,
and clear for the sacred solemnity. Some traces of this
custom remain at Rome to this day, for, when the consul
begins to take auspices or do sacrifice, they call out to
the people, *Hoc age*, Attend to this, whereby the auditors
then present are admonished to compose and recollect
themselves. Many other of his precepts resemble those
of the Pythagoreans. The Pythagoreans said, for example, "Thou shalt not make a peck-measure thy seat to sit
on. Thou shalt not stir the fire with a sword. When
thou goest out upon a journey, look not behind thee.
When thou sacrificest to the celestial gods, let it be with
an odd number, and when to the terrestrial, with even."
The significance of each of which precepts they would
not commonly disclose. So some of Numa's traditions
have no obvious meaning. "Thou shalt not make libation to the gods of wine from an unpruned vine. No
sacrifices shall be performed without meal. Turn round
to pay adoration to the gods; sit after you have worshipped." The first two directions seem to denote the culti-
vation and subduing of the earth as a part of religion;
and as to the turning which the worshippers are to use in

divine adoration, it is said to represent the rotatory motion of the world. But, in my opinion, the meaning
rather is, that the worshipper, since the temples front the
east, enters with his back to the rising sun ; there, faces
round to the east, and so turns back to the god of the
temple, by this circular movement referring the fulfil-
ment of his prayer to both divinities. Unless, indeed,
this change of posture may have a mystical meaning, like
the Egyptian wheels, and signify to us the instability of
human fortune, and that, in whatever way God changes
and turns our lot and condition, we should rest contented,
and accept it as right and fitting. They say, also, that
the sitting after worship was to be by way of omen of
their petitions being granted, and the blessing they asked
assured to them. Again, as different courses of actions
are divided by intervals of rest, they might seat themselves after the completion of what they had done, to
seek favor of the gods for beginning something else.
And this would very well suit with what we had before ;
the lawgiver wants to habituate us to make our petitions
to the deity not by the way, and as it were, in a hurry,
when we have other things to do, but with time and
leisure to attend to it. By such discipline and schooling
in religion, the city passed insensibly into such a submissiveness of temper, and stood in such awe and reverence
of the virtue of Numa, that they received, with an un-
doubted assurance, whatever he delivered, though never
so fabulous, and thought nothing incredible or impossible
from him.

There goes a story that he once invited a great number of citizens to an entertainment, at which the dishes
in which the meat was served were very homely and
plain, and the repast itself poor and ordinary fare ; the
guests seated, he began to tell them that the goddess that
consulted with him was then at that time come to him ;

when on a sudden the room was furnished with all
sorts of costly drinking-vessels, and the tables loaded
with rich meats, and a most sumptuous entertainment.
But the dialogue which is reported to have passed between him and Jupiter surpasses all the fabulous legends
that were ever invented. They say that before Mount
Aventine was inhabited or enclosed within the walls of
the city, two demi-gods, Picus and Faunus, frequented the
springs and thick shades of that place; which might be
two satyrs, or Pans, except that they went about Italy
playing the same sorts of tricks, by skill in drugs and
magic, as are ascribed by the Greeks to the Dactyli of
Mount Ida. Numa contrived one day to surprise these
demi-gods, by mixing wine and honey in the waters of
the spring of which they usually drank. On finding
themselves ensnared, they changed themselves into various shapes, dropping their own form and assuming every
kind of unusual and hideous appearance; but when they
saw they were safely entrapped, and in no possibility of
getting free, they revealed to him many secrets and future events; and particularly a charm for thunder and
lightning, still in use, performed with onions and hair and
pilchards. Some say they did not tell him the charm,
but by their magic brought down Jupiter out of heaven;
and that he then, in an angry manner answering the inquiries, told Numa, that, if he would charm the thunder
and lightning, he must do it with heads. "How," said
Numa, "with the heads of onions?" "No," replied Jupiter,
"of men." But Numa, willing to elude the cruelty of
this receipt, turned it another way, saying, "Your meaning is, the hairs of men's heads." "No," replied Jupiter,
"with living"——"pilchards," said Numa, interrupting
him. These answers he had learnt from Egeria. Jupiter
returned again to heaven, pacified and *ileōs*, or propitious.

The place was, in remembrance of him, called Ilicium,*
from this Greek word; and the spell in this manner
effected.

These stories, laughable as they are, show us the feelings which people then, by force of habit, entertained
towards the deity. And Numa's own thoughts are said
to have been fixed to that degree on divine objects,
that he once, when a message was brought to him that
"Enemies are approaching," answered with a smile, "And
I am sacrificing." It was he, also, that built the temples
of Faith and Terminus, and taught the Romans that the
name of Faith was the most solemn oath that they could
swear. They still use it; and to the god Terminus, or
Boundary, they offer to this day both public and private
sacrifices, upon the borders and stone-marks of their land;
living victims now, though anciently those sacrifices
were solemnized without blood; for Numa reasoned that
the god of boundaries, who watched over peace, and
testified to fair dealing, should have no concern with
blood. It is very clear that it was this king who first
prescribed bounds to the territory of Rome; for Romulus would but have openly betrayed how much he
had encroached on his neighbors' lands, had he ever set
limits to his own; for boundaries are, indeed, a defence
to those who choose to observe them. but are only a
testimony against the dishonesty of those who break
through them. The truth is, the portion of lands which
the Romans possessed at the beginning was very narrow,
until Romulus enlarged them by war; all whose acqui-

* Neither Ilicium nor Elicium
was, so far as appears. the name
of the place; but Elicius the title
of Jupiter, whose presence was
there *elicited*. "Eliciunt cœlo te,
Jupiter, unde minores Nunc quo-
que te celebrant, Eliciumque vo-
cant," says Ovid in the Fasti. iii.
327, where he gives the whole
story.

sitions Numa now divided amongst the indigent commonalty, wishing to do away with that extreme want which
is a compulsion to dishonesty, and, by turning the people
to husbandry, to bring them, as well as their lands, into
better order. For there is no employment that gives so
keen and quick a relish for peace as husbandry and a
country life, which leave in men all that kind of courage that makes them ready to fight in defence of their
own, while it destroys the license that breaks out into acts
of injustice and rapacity. Numa, therefore, hoping agri-
culture would be a sort of charm to captivate the affections of his people to peace, and viewing it rather as a
means to moral than to economical profit, divided all the
lands into several parcels, to which he gave the name of
pagus, or parish, and over every one of them he ordained
chief overseers; and, taking a delight sometimes to inspect
his colonies in person, he formed his judgment of every
man's habits by the results; of which being witness himself,
he preferred those to honors and employments who had
done well, and by rebukes and reproaches incited the
indolent and careless to improvement. But of all his
measures the most commended was his distribution of
the people by their trades into companies or guilds; for
as the city consisted, or rather did not consist of, but was
divided into, two different tribes, the diversity between
which could not be effaced and in the mean time prevented all unity and caused perpetual tumult and ill-
blood, reflecting how hard substances that do not readily
mix when in the lump may, by being beaten into powder, in that minute form be combined, he resolved to
divide the whole population into a number of small divisions, and thus hoped, by introducing other distinctions, to
obliterate the original and great distinction, which would
be lost among the smaller. So, distinguishing the whole
people by the several arts and trades, he formed the com-

panics of musicians, goldsmiths, carpenters, dyers, shoe-
makers, skinners, braziers, and potters; and all other
handicraftsmen he composed and reduced into a single
company, appointing every one their proper courts, councils, and religious observances. In this manner all fac-
tious distinctions began, for the first time, to pass out ot
use, no person any longer being either thought of or
spoken of under the notion of a Sabine or a Roman, a
Romulian or a Tatian; and the new division became a
source of general harmony and intermixture.

He is also much to be commended for the repeal, or
rather amendment, of that law which gives power to
fathers to sell their children; he exempted such as were
married, conditionally that it had been with the liking
and consent of their parents; for it seemed a hard thing
that a woman who had given herself in marriage to a
man whom she judged free should afterwards find herself
living with a slave.

He attempted, also, the formation of a calendar, not
with absolute exactness, yet not without some scientific
knowledge. During the reign of Romulus, they had let
their months run on without any certain or equal term;
some of them contained twenty days, others thirty-five,
others more; they had no sort of knowledge of the
inequality in the motions of the sun and moon; they
only kept to the one rule that the whole course of the
year contained three hundred and sixty days. Numa,
calculating the difference between the lunar and the solar
year at eleven days, for that the moon completed her
anniversary course in three hundred and fifty-four days,
and the sun in three hundred and sixty-five, to remedy
this incongruity doubled the eleven days, and every other
year added an intercalary month, to follow February, consisting of twenty-two days, and called by the Romans the
month Mercedinus. This amendment, however, itself, in

course of time, came to need other amendments. He also altered the order of the months; for March, which was reckoned the first, he put into the third place; and January, which was the eleventh, he made the first; and February, which was the twelfth and last, the second. Many will have it, that it was Numa, also, who added the two months of January and February; for in the beginning they had had a year of ten months; as there are barbarians who count only three; the Arcadians, in Greece, had but four; the Acarnanians, six. The Egyptian year at first, they say, was of one month; afterwards, of four; and so, though they live in the newest of all countries, they have the credit of being a more ancient nation than any, and reckon, in their genealogies, a prodigious number of years, counting months, that is, as years. That the Romans, at first, comprehended the whole year within ten, and not twelve months, plainly appears by the name of the last, December, meaning the tenth month; and that March was the first is likewise evident, for the fifth month after it was called Quintilis, and the sixth Sextilis, and so the rest; whereas, if January and February had, in this account, preceded March, Quintilis would have been fifth in name and seventh in reckoning. It was also natural, that March, dedicated to Mars, should be Romulus's first, and April, named from Venus, or Aphrodite, his second month; in it they sacrifice to Venus, and the women bathe on the calends, or first day of it, with myrtle garlands on their heads. But others, because of its being *p* and not *ph*, will not allow of the derivation of this word from Aphrodite, but say it is called April from *aperio*, Latin for to open, because that this month is high spring, and opens and discloses the buds and flowers. The next is called May, from Maia, the mother of Mercury, to whom it is sacred; then June follows, so called from Juno; some, however, derive them from the two ages, old and young, *majores* being their name for older, and *juniores* for younger men. To the other months they gave denominations according to their order; so the fifth was called Quintilis, Sextilis the sixth, and the rest, September, October, November, and December. Afterwards Quintilis received the name of Julius, from Cæsar who defeated Pompey; as also Sextilis that of Augustus, from the second Cæsar, who had that title. Domitian, also, in imitation, gave the two other following months his own names, of Germanicus and Domitianus; but, on his being slain, they recovered their ancient denominations of September and October. The two last are the only ones that have kept their names throughout without any alteration. Of the months which were added or transposed in their order by Numa, February comes from *februa;* and is as much as Purification month; in it they make offerings to the dead, and celebrate the Lupercalia, which, in most points, resembles a purification. January was so called from Janus, and precedence given to it by Numa before March, which was dedicated to the god Mars; because, as I conceive, he wished to take every opportunity of intimating that the arts and studies of peace are to be preferred before those of war. For this Janus, whether in remote antiquity he were a demi-god or a king, was certainly a great lover of civil and social unity, and one who reclaimed men from brutal and savage living; for which reason they figure him with two faces, to represent the two states and conditions out of the one of which he brought mankind, to lead them into the other. His temple at Rome has two gates, which they call the gates of war, because they stand open in the time of war, and shut in the times of peace; of which latter there was very seldom an example, for, as the Roman empire was enlarged and extended, it was so encompassed with barbarous nations and enemies to be resisted, that it was seldom or never at

peace. Only in the time of Augustus Cæsar, after he
had overcome Antony, this temple was shut; as likewise
once before, when Marcus Atilius and Titus Manlius *
were consuls; but then it was not long before, wars
breaking out, the gates were again opened. But, during
the reign of Numa, those gates were never seen open a
single day, but continued constantly shut for a space of
forty-three years together; such an entire and universal
cessation of war existed. For not only had the people
of Rome itself been softened and charmed into a peaceful
temper by the just and mild rule of a pacific prince, but
even the neighboring cities, as if some salubrious and
gentle air had blown from Rome upon them, began to
experience a change of feeling, and partook in the general longing for the sweets of peace and order, and for
life employed in the quiet tillage of soil, bringing up of
children, and worship of the gods. Festival days and
sports, and the secure and peaceful interchange of friendly
visits and hospitalities prevailed all through the whole of
Italy. The love of virtue and justice flowed from Numa's
wisdom as from a fountain, and the serenity of his spirit
diffused itself, like a calm, on all sides; so that the hyper-
boles of poets were flat and tame to express what then
existed; as that

> Over the iron shield the spiders hang their threads,

or that

> Rust eats the pointed spear and double-edged sword.
> No more is heard the trumpet's brazen roar,
> Sweet sleep is banished from our eyes no more.

For, during the whole reign of Numa, there was neither
war, nor sedition, nor innovation in the state, nor any

* At the close of the first punic war, 519 A. U. C.

envy or ill-will to his person, nor plot or conspiracy from views of ambition. Either fear of the gods that were thought to watch over him, or reverence for his virtue, or a divine felicity of fortune that in his days preserved human innocence, made his reign, by whatever means, a living example and verification of that saying which Plato, long afterwards, ventured to pronounce, that the sole and only hope of respite or remedy for human evils was in some happy conjunction of events, which should unite in a single person the power of a king and the wisdom of a philosopher, so as to elevate virtue to control and mastery over vice. The wise man is blessed in himself, and blessed also are the auditors who can hear and receive those words which flow from his mouth; and perhaps, too, there is no need of compulsion or menaces to affect the multitude, for the mere sight itself of a shining and conspicuous example of virtue in the life of their prince will bring them spontaneously to virtue, and to a conformity with that blameless and blessed life of good will and mutual concord, supported by temperance and justice, which is the highest benefit that human means can confer; and he is the truest ruler who can best introduce it into the hearts and practice of his subjects. It is the praise of Numa that no one seems ever to have discerned this so clearly as he.

As to his children and wives, there is a diversity of reports by several authors; some will have it that he never had any other wife than Tatia, nor more children than one daughter called Pompilia; others will have it that he left also four sons, namely, Pompo, Pinus, Calpus, and Mamercus, every one of whom had issue, and from them descended the noble and illustrious families of Pomponii, Pinarii, Calpurnii, and Mamerci, which for this reason took also the surname of Rex, or King. But there is a third set of writers who say that these pedigrees are but a piece of flattery used by writers, who, to gain favor with these great families, made them fictitious genealogies from the lineage of Numa; and that Pompilia was not the daughter of Tatia, but Lucretia, another wife whom he married after he came to his kingdom; however, all of them agree in opinion that she was married to the son of that Marcius who persuaded him to accept the government, and accompanied him to Rome, where, as a mark of honor, he was chosen into the senate, and, after the death of Numa, standing in competition with Tullus Hostilius for the kingdom, and being disappointed of the election, in discontent killed himself; his son Marcius, however, who had married Pompilia, continuing at Rome, was the father of Ancus Marcius, who succeeded Tullus Hostilius in the kingdom, and was but five years of age when Numa died.

Numa lived something above eighty years, and then, as Piso writes, was not taken out of the world by a sudden or acute disease, but died of old age and by a gradual and gentle decline. At his funeral all the glories of his life were consummated, when all the neighboring states in alliance and amity with Rome met to honor and grace the rites of his interment with garlands and public presents; the senators carried the bier on which his corpse was laid, and the priests followed and accompanied the solemn procession; while a general crowd, in which women and children took part, followed with such cries and weeping as if they had bewailed the death and loss of some most dear relation taken away in the flower of age, and not of an old and worn-out king. It is said that his body, by his particular command, was not burnt, but that they made, in conformity with his order, two stone coffins, and buried both under the hill Janiculum, in one of which his body was laid, and in the other his sacred books, which, as the Greek legislators their tables, he had

written out for himself, but had so long inculcated the
contents of them, whilst he lived, into the minds and
hearts of the priests, that their understandings became
fully possessed with the whole spirit and purpose of
them; and he, therefore, bade that they should be buried
with his body, as though such holy precepts could not
without irreverence be left to circulate in mere lifeless
writings. For this very reason, they say, the Pythagoreans bade that their precepts should not be committed to
paper, but rather preserved in the living memories of
those who were worthy to receive them; and when some
of their out-of-the-way and abstruse geometrical processes had been divulged to an unworthy person, they
said the gods threatened to punish this wickedness and
profanity by a signal and wide-spreading calamity. With
these several instances, concurring to show a similarity in
the lives of Numa and Pythagoras, we may easily pardon
those who seek to establish the fact of a real acquaintance
between them.

Valerius Antias writes that the books which were
buried in the aforesaid chest or coffin of stone were
twelve volumes of holy writ and twelve others of Greek
philosophy, and that about four hundred years afterwards,
when P. Cornelius and M. Bæbius were consuls, in a time
of heavy rains, a violent torrent washed away the earth,
and dislodged the chests of stone; and, their covers falling off, one of them was found wholly empty, without
the least relic of any human body; in the other were
the books before mentioned, which the prætor Petilius
having read and perused, made oath in the senate, that,
in his opinion, it was not fit for their contents to be made
public to the people; whereupon the volumes were all
carried to the Comitium, and there burnt.

It is the fortune of all good men that their virtue rises
in glory after their deaths, and that the envy which evil

men conceive against them never outlives them long; some have the happiness even to see it die before them; but in Numa's case, also, the fortunes of the succeeding kings served as foils to set off the brightness of his reputation. For after him there were five kings, the last of whom ended his old age in banishment, being deposed from his crown; of the other four, three were assassinated and murdered by treason; the other, who was Tullus Hostilius, that immediately succeeded Numa, derided his virtues, and especially his devotion to religious worship, as a cowardly and mean-spirited occupation, and diverted the minds of the people to war; but was checked in these youthful insolences, and was himself driven by an acute and tormenting disease into superstitions wholly different from Numa's piety, and left others also to participate in these terrors when he died by the stroke of a thunderbolt.

COMPARISON OF NUMA WITH LYCURGUS.

HAVING thus finished the lives of Lycurgus and Numa, we shall now, though the work be difficult, put together their points of difference as they lie here before our view. Their points of likeness are obvious; their moderation, their religion, their capacity of government and discipline, their both deriving their laws and constitutions from the gods. Yet in their common glories there are circumstances of diversity; for, first, Numa accepted and Lycurgus resigned a kingdom; Numa received without desiring it, Lycurgus had it and gave it up; the one from a private person and a stranger was raised by others to be their king, the other from the condition of a prince voluntarily descended to the state of privacy. It was glorious to acquire a throne by justice, yet more glorious to prefer justice before a throne; the same virtue which made the one appear worthy of regal power exalted the other to the disregard of it. Lastly, as musicians tune their harps, so the one let down the high-flown spirits of the people at Rome to a lower key, as the other screwed them up at Sparta to a higher note, when they were sunken low by dissoluteness and riot. The harder task was that of Lycurgus; for it was not so much his business to persuade his citizens to put off their armor or ungird their swords, as to cast away their gold or silver, and abandon costly furniture and rich tables; nor was it necessary to preach to them, that, laying aside their arms, they should observe the festivals, and sacrifice to the gods, but rather,

that, giving up feasting and drinking, they should employ
their time in laborious and martial exercises; so that
while the one effected all by persuasions and his people's
love for him, the other, with danger and hazard of his
person, scarcely in the end succeeded. Numa's muse was
a gentle and loving inspiration, fitting him well to turn
and soothe his people into peace and justice out of their
violent and fiery tempers; whereas, if we must admit the
treatment of the Helots to be a part of Lycurgus's legislation, a most cruel and iniquitous proceeding, we must
own that Numa was by a great deal the more humane
and Greek-like legislator, granting even to actual slaves
a license to sit at meat with their masters at the feast of
Saturn, that they, also, might have some taste and relish
of the sweets of liberty. For this custom, too, is ascribed
to Numa, whose wish was, they conceive, to give a place
in the enjoyment of the yearly fruits of the soil to those
who had helped to produce them. Others will have it
to be in remembrance of the age of Saturn, when there
was no distinction between master and slave, but all lived
as brothers and as equals in a condition of equality.

In general, it seems that both aimed at the same design
and intent, which was to bring their people to moderation and frugality; but, of other virtues, the one set
his affection most on fortitude, and the other on justice;
unless we will attribute their different ways to the different habits and temperaments which they had to work
upon by their enactments; for Numa did not out of cowardice or fear affect peace, but because he would not be
guilty of injustice; nor did Lycurgus promote a spirit of
war in his people that they might do injustice to others,
but that they might protect themselves by it.

In bringing the habits they formed in their people to
a just and happy mean, mitigating them where they ex-

ceeded, and strengthening them where they were deficient, both were compelled to make great innovations.
The frame of government which Numa formed was democratic and popular to the last extreme, goldsmiths and
flute-players and shoemakers constituting his promiscuous,
many-colored commonalty. Lycurgus was rigid and aristocratical, banishing all the base and mechanic arts to the
company of servants and strangers, and allowing the
true citizens no implements but the spear and shield,
the trade of war only, and the service of Mars, and no
other knowledge or study but that of obedience to their
commanding officers, and victory over their enemies.
Every sort of money-making was forbid them as freemen;
and to make them thoroughly so and to keep them so
through their whole lives, every conceivable concern
with money was handed over, with the cooking and the
waiting at table, to slaves and helots. But Numa made
none of these distinctions; he only suppressed military
rapacity, allowing free scope to every other means of
obtaining wealth; nor did he endeavor to do away with
inequality in this respect, but permitted riches to be
amassed to any extent, and paid no attention to the gradual and continual augmentation and influx of poverty;
which it was his business at the outset, whilst there
was as yet no great disparity in the estates of men,
and whilst people still lived much in one manner, to
obviate, as Lycurgus did, and take measures of pre-
caution against the mischiefs of avarice, mischiefs not of
small importance, but the real seed and first beginning of
all the great and extensive evils of after times. The
re-division of estates, Lycurgus is not, it seems to me, to
be blamed for making, nor Numa for omitting; this
equality was the basis and foundation of the one commonwealth; but at Rome, where the lands had been

lately divided, there was nothing to urge any re-division or any disturbance of the first arrangement, which was probably still in existence.

With respect to wives and children, and that community which both, with a sound policy, appointed, to prevent all jealousy, their methods, however, were different. For when a Roman thought himself to have a sufficient number of children, in case his neighbor who had none should come and request his wife of him, he had a lawful power to give her up to him who desired her, either for a certain time, or for good. The Lacedæmonian husband on the other hand, might allow the use of his wife to any other that desired to have children by her, and yet still keep her in his house, the original marriage obligation still subsisting as at first. Nay, many husbands, as we have said, would invite men whom they thought likely to procure them fine and good-looking children into their houses. What is the difference, then, between the two customs? Shall we say that the Lacedæmonian system is one of an extreme and entire unconcern about their wives, and would cause most people endless disquiet and annoyance with pangs and jealousies? the Roman course wears an air of a more delicate acquiescence, draws the veil of a new contract over the change, and concedes the general insupportableness of mere community? Numa's directions, too, for the care of young women are better adapted to the female sex and to propriety; Lycurgus's are altogether unreserved and unfeminine, and have given a great handle to the poets, who call them (Ibycus, for example) *Phænomerides*, bare-thighed; and give them the character (as does Euripides) of being wild after husbands;·

These with the young men from the house go out,
With thighs that show, and robes that fly about.

For in fact the skirts of the frock worn by unmarried

girls were not sewn together at the lower part, but used to fly back and show the whole thigh bare as they walked. The thing is most distinctly given by Sophocles.

> — She, also, the young maid,
> Whose frock, no robe yet o'er it laid,*
> Folding back, leaves her bare thigh free,
> Hermione.

And so their women, it is said, were bold and masculine, overbearing to their husbands in the first place, absolute mistresses in their houses, giving their opinions about public matters freely, and speaking openly even on the most important subjects. But the matrons, under the government of Numa, still indeed received from their husbands all that high respect and honor which had been paid them under Romulus as a sort of atonement for the violence done to them; nevertheless, great modesty was enjoined upon them; all busy intermeddling forbidden, sobriety insisted on, and silence made habitual. Wine they were not to touch at all, nor to speak, except in their husband's company, even on the most ordinary subjects. So that once when a woman had the confidence to plead her own cause in a court of judicature, the senate, it is said, sent to inquire of the oracle what the prodigy did portend; and, indeed, their general good behavior and submissiveness is justly proved by the record of those that were otherwise; for as the Greek historians record in their annals the names of those who first unsheathed the sword of civil war, or murdered their brothers, or were parricides, or killed their mothers, so the Roman writers report it as the first example, that Spurius Carvilius divorced his wife, being a case that

---

* *Astūlos chitōn*, the under garment, frock, or tunic, without any thing, either *himation* or *peplus*, over it.

never before happened, in the space of two hundred and thirty years from the foundation of the city; and that one Thalæa, the wife of Pinarius, had a quarrel (the first instance of the kind) with her mother-in-law, Gegania, in the reign of Tarquinius Superbus; so successful was the legislator in securing order and good conduct in the marriage relation. Their respective regulations for marrying the young women are in accordance with those for their education. Lycurgus made them brides when they were of full age and inclination for it. Intercourse, where nature was thus consulted, would produce, he thought, love and tenderness, instead of the dislike and fear attending an unnatural compulsion; and their bodies, also, would be better able to bear the trials of breeding and of bearing children, in his judgment the one end of marriage.

The Romans, on the other hand, gave their daughters in marriage as early as twelve years old, or even under; thus they thought their bodies alike and minds would be delivered to the future husband pure and undefiled. The way of Lycurgus seems the more natural with a view to the birth of children; the other, looking to a life to be spent together, is more moral. However, the rules which Lycurgus drew up for superintendence of children, their collection into companies, their discipline and association, as also his exact regulations for their meals, exercises, and sports, argue Numa no more than an ordinary law-giver. Numa left the whole matter simply to be decided by the parent's wishes or necessities; he might, if he pleased, make his son a husbandman or carpenter, copper-smith or musician; as if it were of no importance for them to be directed and trained up from the beginning to one and the same common end, or as though it would do for them to be like passengers on shipboard, brought thither each for his own ends and by his own choice, uniting to act for the common good only in time of danger upon occasion of their private fears, in general looking simply to their own interest.

We may forbear, indeed, to blame common legislators, who may be deficient in power or knowledge. But when a wise man like Numa had received the sovereignty over a new and docile people, was there any thing that would better deserve his attention than the education of children, and the training up of the young, not to contrariety and discordance of character, but to the unity of the common model of virtue, to which from their cradle they should have been formed and moulded? One benefit among many that Lycurgus obtained by his course was the permanence which it secured to his laws. The obligation of oaths to preserve them would have availed but little, if he had not, by discipline and education, infused them into the children's characters, and imbued their whole early life with a love of his government. The result was that the main points and fundamentals of his legislation continued for above five hundred years, like some deep and thoroughly ingrained tincture, retaining their hold upon the nation. But Numa's whole design and aim, the continuance of peace and good-will, on his death vanished with him; no sooner did he expire his last breath than the gates of Janus's temple flew wide open, and, as if war had, indeed, been kept and caged up within those walls, it rushed forth to fill all Italy with blood and slaughter; and thus that best and justest fabric of things was of no long continuance, because it wanted that cement which should have kept all together, education. What, then, some may say, has not Rome been advanced and bettered by her wars? A question that will need a long answer, if it is to be one to satisfy men who take the *better* to consist in riches, luxury, and dominion, rather than in security, gentleness, and that independence which is accompanied by justice. However, it makes much for

Lycurgus, that, after the Romans deserted the doctrine and discipline of Numa, their empire grew and their power increased so much; whereas so soon as the Lacedæmonians fell from the institutions of Lycurgus, they sank from the highest to the lowest state, and, after forfeiting their supremacy over the rest of Greece, were themselves in danger of absolute extirpation. Thus much, meantime, was peculiarly signal and almost divine in the circumstances of Numa, that he was an alien, and yet courted to come and accept a kingdom, the frame of which though he entirely altered, yet he performed it by mere persuasion, and ruled a city that as yet had scarce become one city, without recurring to arms or any violence (such as Lycurgus used, supporting himself by the aid of the nobler citizens against the commonalty), but, by mere force of wisdom and justice, established union and harmony amongst all.

SOLON.

DIDYMUS. the grammarian, in his answer to Asclepiades concerning Solon's Tables of Law, mentions a passage of one Philocles, who states that Solon's father's name was Euphorion, contrary to the opinion of all others who have written concerning him; for they generally agree that he was the son of Exccestides, a man of moderate wealth and power in the city, but of a most noble stock, being descended from Codrus; his mother, as Heraclides Ponticus affirms, was cousin to Pisistratus's mother, and the two at first were great friends, partly because they were akin, and partly because of Pisistratus's noble qualities and beauty. And they say Solon loved him; and that is the reason, I suppose, that when afterwards they differed about the government, their enmity never produced any hot and violent passion, they remembered their old kindnesses, and retained —

Still in its embers living the strong fire

of their love and dear affection. For that Solon was not proof against beauty, nor of courage to stand up to passion and meet it,

Hand to hand as in the ring —

we may conjecture by his poems, and one of his laws, in which there are practices forbidden to slaves, which

he would appear, therefore, to recommend to freemen.
Pisistratus, it is stated, was similarly attached to one
Charinus; he it was who dedicated the figure of Love
in the Academy, where the runners in the sacred torch-
race light their torches. Solon, as Hermippus writes,
when his father had ruined his estate in doing benefits
and kindnesses to other men, though he had friends
enough that were willing to contribute to his relief, yet
was ashamed to be beholden to others, since he was descended from a family who were accustomed to do kindnesses rather than receive them; and therefore applied
himself to merchandise in his youth; though others
assure us that he travelled rather to get learning and experience than to make money. It is certain that he was
a lover of knowledge, for when he was old he would say,
that he

> Each day grew older, and learnt something new;

and yet no admirer of riches, esteeming as equally
wealthy the man, —

> Who hath both gold and silver in his hand,
> Horses and mules, and acres of wheat-land,
> And him whose all is decent food to eat,
> Clothes to his back and shoes upon his feet,
> And a young wife and child, since so 't will be,
> And no more years than will with that agree ; —

and in another place, —

> Wealth I would have, but wealth by wrong procure
> I would not ; justice, e'en if slow, is sure.

And it is perfectly possible for a good man and a statesman, without being solicitous for superfluities, to show
some concern for competent necessaries. In his time, as

Hesiod says, — "Work was a shame to none," nor was any distinction made with respect to trade, but merchandise was a noble calling, which brought home the good things which the barbarous nations enjoyed, was the occasion of friendship with their kings, and a great source of experience. Some merchants have built great cities, as Protis, the founder of Massilia, to whom the Gauls near the Rhone were much attached. Some report also that Thales and Hippocrates the mathematician traded; and that Plato defrayed the charges of his travels by selling oil in Egypt. Solon's softness and profuseness, his popular rather than philosophical tone about pleasure in his poems, have been ascribed to his trading life; for, having suffered a thousand dangers, it was natural they should be recompensed with some gratifications and enjoyments; but that he accounted himself rather poor than rich is evident from the lines,

> Some wicked men are rich, some good are poor,
> We will not change our virtue for their store ;
> Virtue's a thing that none can take away,
> But money changes owners all the day.

At first he used his poetry only in trifles, not for any serious purpose, but simply to pass away his idle hours; but afterwards he introduced moral sentences and state matters, which he did, not to record them merely as an historian, but to justify his own actions, and sometimes to correct, chastise, and stir up the Athenians to noble performances. Some report that he designed to put his laws into heroic verse, and that they began thus, —

> We humbly beg a blessing on our laws
> From mighty Jove, and honor, and applause.

In philosophy, as most of the wise men then, he chiefly

esteemed the political part of morals; in physics, he was very plain and antiquated, as appears by this, —

It is the clouds that make the snow and hail,
And thunder comes from lightning without fail;
The sea is stormy when the winds have blown,
But it deals fairly when 't is left alone.

And, indeed, it is probable that at that time Thales alone had raised philosophy above mere practice into speculation; and the rest of the wise men were so called from prudence in political concerns. It is said, that they had an interview at Delphi, and another at Corinth, by the procurement of Periander, who made a meeting for them, and a supper. But their reputation was chiefly raised by sending the tripod to them all, by their modest refusal, and complaisant yielding to one another. For, as the story goes, some of the Coans fishing with a net, some strangers, Milesians, bought the draught at a venture; the net brought up a golden tripod, which, they say, Helen, at her return from Troy, upon the remembrance of an old prophecy, threw in there. Now, the strangers at first contesting with the fishers about the tripod, and the cities espousing the quarrel so far as to engage themselves in a war, Apollo decided the controversy by commanding to present it to the wisest man; and first it was sent to Miletus to Thales, the Coans freely presenting him with that for which they fought against the whole body of the Milesians; but, Thales declaring Bias the wiser person, it was sent to him; from him to another; and so, going round them all, it came to Thales a second time; and, at last, being carried from Miletus to Thebes, was there dedicated to Apollo Ismenius. Theophrastus writes that it was first presented to Bias at Priene; and next to Thales at Miletus, and so through all it returned to Bias, and was afterwards sent to Delphi. This is the gene-

ral report, only some, instead of a tripod, say this present
was a cup sent by Crœsus; others, a piece of plate that
one Bathycles had left. It is stated, that Anacharsis and
Solon, and Solon and Thales, were familiarly acquainted,
and some have delivered parts of their discourse; for, they
say, Anacharsis, coming to Athens, knocked at Solon's
door, and told him, that he, being a stranger, was come to
be his guest, and contract a friendship with him; and
Solon replying, "It is better to make friends at home,"
Anacharsis replied, "Then you that are at home make
friendship with me." Solon, somewhat surprised at the
readiness of the repartee, received him kindly, and kept
him some time with him, being already engaged in public business and the compilation of his laws; which when
Anacharsis understood, he laughed at him for imagining
the dishonesty and covetousness of his countrymen could
be restrained by written laws, which were like spiders'
webs, and would catch, it is true, the weak and poor, but
easily be broken by the mighty and rich. To this Solon
rejoined that men keep their promises when neither side
can get any thing by the breaking of them; and he would
so fit his laws to the citizens, that all should understand
it was more eligible to be just than to break the laws.
But the event rather agreed with the conjecture of Anacharsis than Solon's hope. Anacharsis, being once at the
assembly, expressed his wonder at the fact that in Greece
wise men spoke and fools decided.

Solon went, they say, to Thales at Miletus, and wondered that Thales took no care to get him a wife and
children. To this, Thales made no answer for the present;
but, a few days after, procured a stranger to pretend that
he had left Athens ten days ago; and Solon inquiring
what news there, the man, according to his instructions,
replied, "None but a young man's funeral, which the
whole city attended; for he was the son, they said, of an

honorable man, the most virtuous of the citizens, who was not then at home, but had been travelling a long time." Solon replied, "What a miserable man is he! But what was his name?" "I have heard it," says the man, "but have now forgotten it, only there was great talk of his wisdom and his justice." Thus Solon was drawn on by every answer, and his fears heightened, till at last, being extremely concerned, he mentioned his own name, and asked the stranger if that young man was called Solon's son; and the stranger assenting, he began to beat his head, and to do and say all that is usual with men in transports of grief. But Thales took his hand, and, with a smile, said, "These things, Solon, keep me from marriage and rearing children, which are too great for even your constancy to support; however, be not concerned at the report, for it is a fiction." This Hermippus relates, from Pataecus, who boasted that he had Æsop's soul.

However, it is irrational and poor-spirited not to seek conveniences for fear of losing them, for upon the same account we should not allow ourselves to like wealth, glory, or wisdom, since we may fear to be deprived of all these; nay, even virtue itself, than which there is no greater nor more desirable possession, is often suspended by sickness or drugs. Now Thales, though unmarried, could not be free from solicitude, unless he likewise felt no care for his friends, his kinsmen, or his country; yet we are told he adopted Cybisthus, his sister's son. For the soul, having a principle of kindness in itself, and being born to love, as well as perceive, think, or remember, inclines and fixes upon some stranger, when a man has none of his own to embrace. And alien or illegitimate objects insinuate themselves into his affections, as into some estate that lacks lawful heirs; and with affection come anxiety and care; insomuch that you may see men that use the strongest language against the marriage-bed and the fruit of it, when some servant's or concubine's child is sick or dies, almost killed with grief, and abjectly lamenting. Some have given way to shameful and desperate sorrow at the loss of a dog or horse; others have borne the deaths of virtuous children without any extravagant or unbecoming grief, have passed the rest of their lives like men, and according to the principles of reason. It is not affection, it is weakness, that brings men, unarmed against fortune by reason, into these endless pains and terrors; and they indeed have not even the present enjoyment of what they doat upon, the possibility of the future loss causing them continual pangs, tremors, and distresses. We must not provide against the loss of wealth by poverty, or of friends by refusing all acquaintance, or of children by having none, but by morality and reason. But of this too much.

Now, when the Athenians were tired with a tedious and difficult war that they conducted against the Megarians for the island Salamis, and made a law that it should be death for any man, by writing or speaking, to assert that the city ought to endeavor to recover it, Solon, vexed at the disgrace, and perceiving thousands of the youth wished for somebody to begin, but did not dare to stir first for fear of the law, counterfeited a distraction, and by his own family it was spread about the city that he was mad. He then secretly composed some elegiac verses, and getting them by heart, that it might seem extempore, ran out into the market-place with a cap upon his head, and, the people gathering about him, got upon the herald's stand, and sang that elegy which begins thus : —

I am a herald come from Salamis the fair,
My news from thence my verses shall declare.

The poem is called Salamis, it contains an hundred

verses, very elegantly written; when it had been sung,
his friends commended it, and especially Pisistratus exhorted the citizens to obey his directions; insomuch that
they recalled the law, and renewed the war under Solon's
conduct. The popular tale is, that with Pisistratus he
sailed to Colias, and, finding the women, according to the
custom of the country there, sacrificing to Ceres, he sent
a trusty friend to Salamis, who should pretend himself a
renegade, and advise them, if they desired to seize the
chief Athenian women, to come with him at once to
Colias; the Megarians presently sent off men in the
vessel with him; and Solon, seeing it put off from the
island, commanded the women to be gone, and some
beardless youths, dressed in their clothes, their shoes, and
caps, and privately armed with daggers, to dance and
play near the shore till the enemies had landed and the
vessel was in their power. Things being thus ordered,
the Megarians were allured with the appearance, and,
coming to the shore, jumped out, eager who should first
seize a prize, so that not one of them escaped; and the
Athenians set sail for the island and took it.

Others say that it was not taken this way, but that he
first received this oracle from Delphi:

> Those heroes that in fair Asopia rest,
> All buried with their faces to the west,
> Go and appease with offerings of the best;

and that Solon, sailing by night to the island, sacrificed
to the heroes Periphemus and Cychreus, and then, taking
five hundred Athenian volunteers (a law having passed
that those that took the island should be highest in the
government), with a number of fisher-boats and one
thirty-oared ship, anchored in a bay of Salamis that looks
towards Nisæa; and the Megarians that were then in the
island, hearing only an uncertain report, hurried to their

arms, and sent a ship to reconnoitre the enemies. This
ship Solon took, and, securing the Megarians, manned it
with Athenians, and gave them orders to sail to the island
with as much privacy as possible; meantime he, with the
other soldiers, marched against the Megarians by land,
and whilst they were fighting, those from the ship took
the city. And this narrative is confirmed by the following solemnity, that was afterwards observed: an Athenian
ship used to sail silently at first to the island, then, with
noise and a great shout, one leapt out armed, and with a
loud cry ran to the promontory Sciradium to meet those
that approached upon the land. And just by there stands
a temple which Solon dedicated to Mars. For he beat
the Megarians, and as many as were not killed in the
battle he sent away upon conditions.

The Megarians, however, still contending, and both
sides having received considerable losses, they chose the
Spartans for arbitrators. Now, many affirm that Homer's
authority did Solon a considerable kindness, and that,
introducing a line into the Catalogue of Ships, when the
matter was to be determined, he read the passage as
follows:

> Twelve ships from Salamis stout Ajax brought,
> And ranked his men where the Athenians fought.

The Athenians, however, call this but an idle story, and
report, that Solon made it appear to the judges, that Philæus and Eurysaces, the sons of Ajax, being made citizens
of Athens, gave them the island, and that one of them
dwelt at Brauron in Attica, the other at Melite; and
they have a township of Philaidæ, to which Pisistratus
belonged, deriving its name from this Philæus. Solon
took a farther argument against the Megarians from the
dead bodies, which, he said, were not buried after their
fashion, but according to the Athenian; for the Mega-

rians turn the corpse to the east, the Athenians to the
west. But Hereas the Megarian denies this, and affirms
that they likewise turn the body to the west, and also
that the Athenians have a separate tomb for everybody,
but the Megarians put two or three into one. However,
some of Apollo's oracles, where he calls Salamis Ionian,
made much for Solon. This matter was determined by
five Spartans, Critolaidas, Amompharetus, Hypsechidas,
Anaxilas, and Cleomenes.

For this, Solon grew famed and powerful; but his advice in favor of defending the oracle at Delphi, to give
aid, and not to suffer the Cirrhæans to profane it, but to
maintain the honor of the god, got him most repute
among the Greeks: for upon his persuasion the Amphic-
tyons undertook the war, as, amongst others, Aristotle affirms, in his enumeration of the victors at the Pythian
games, where he makes Solon the author of this counsel.
Solon, however, was not general in that expedition, as
Hermippus states, out of Evanthes the Samian; for
Æschines the orator says no such thing, and, in the Del-
phian register, Alcmæon, not Solon, is named as commander of the Athenians.

Now the Cylonian pollution had a long while disturbed
the commonwealth, ever since the time when Megacles
the archon persuaded the conspirators with Cylon that
took sanctuary in Minerva's temple to come down and
stand to a fair trial. And they, tying a thread to the
image, and holding one end of it, went down to the tribunal; but when they came to the temple of the Furies,
the thread broke of its own accord, upon which, as if the
goddess had refused them protection, they were seized by
Megacles and the other magistrates; as many as were
without the temples were stoned, those that fled for sanctuary were butchered at the altar, and only those escaped
who made supplication to the wives of the magistrates.

But they from that time were considered under pollution, and regarded with hatred. The remainder of the faction of Cylon grew strong again, and had continual quarrels with the family of Megacles; and now the quarrel being at its height, and the people divided, Solon, being in reputation, interposed with the chiefest of the Athenians, and by entreaty and admonition persuaded the polluted to submit to a trial and the decision of three hundred noble citizens. And Myron of Phlya being their accuser, they were found guilty, and as many as were then alive were banished, and the bodies of the dead were dug up, and scattered beyond the confines of the country. In the midst of these distractions, the Megarians falling upon them, they lost Nisæa and Salamis again; besides, the city was disturbed with superstitious fears and strange appearances, and the priests declared that the sacrifices intimated some villanies and pollutions that were to be expiated. Upon this, they sent for Epimenides the Phæstian from Crete, who is counted the seventh wise man by those that will not admit Periander into the number. He seems to have been thought a favorite of heaven, possessed of knowledge in all the supernatural and ritual parts of religion; and, therefore, the men of his age called him a new Cures,* and son of a nymph named Balte. When he came to Athens, and grew acquainted with Solon, he served him in many instances, and prepared the way for his legislation. He made them moderate in their forms of worship, and abated their mourning by ordering some sacrifices presently after the funeral, and taking off those severe and barbarous ceremonies which the women usually practised; but the greatest benefit was his purifying and sanctifying the city, by certain propitiatory and expiatory lustrations, and foundation of sacred buildings;

* One of the old Curetes. who   upon his birth in Crete, come, as it
took charge of the infant Jupiter   were, to life again.

by that means making them more submissive to justice, and more inclined to harmony. It is reported that, looking upon Munychia, and considering a long while, he said to those that stood by, "How blind is man in future things! for did the Athenians foresee what mischief this would do their city, they would even eat it with their own teeth to be rid of it." A similar anticipation is ascribed to Thales; they say he commanded his friends to bury him in an obscure and contemned quarter of the territory of Miletus, saying that it should some day be the market-place of the Milesians. Epimenides, being much honored, and receiving from the city rich offers of large gifts and privileges, requested but one branch of the sacred olive, and, on that being granted, returned.

The Athenians, now the Cylonian sedition was over and the polluted gone into banishment, fell into their old quarrels about the government, there being as many different parties as there were diversities in the country.* The Hill quarter favored democracy, the Plain, oligarchy, and those that lived by the Sea-side stood for a mixed sort of government, and so hindered either of the other parties from prevailing. And the disparity of fortune between the rich and the poor, at that time, also reached its height; so that the city seemed to be in a truly dangerous condition, and no other means for freeing it from disturbances and settling it, to be possible but a despotic power. All the people were indebted to the rich; and either they tilled their land for their creditors, paying them a sixth part of the increase, and were, therefore, called Hectemorii and Thetes, or else they engaged their body for the debt, and might be seized, and either sent into slavery at home, or sold to strangers; some (for no law forbade it) were forced to sell their children, or fly

* The Diacrii, Pedicis, and Parali.

their country to avoid the cruelty of their creditors; but
the most part and the bravest of them began to combine
together and encourage one another to stand to it, to
choose a leader, to liberate the condemned debtors, divide
the land, and change the government.

Then the wisest of the Athenians, perceiving Solon was
of all men the only one not implicated in the troubles,
that he had not joined in the exactions of the rich, and
was not involved in the necessities of the poor, pressed
him to succor the commonwealth and compose the differences.   Though Phanias the Lesbian affirms, that Solon,
to save his country, put a trick upon both parties, and
privately promised the poor a division of the lands, and
the rich, security for their debts.   Solon, however, himself, says that it was reluctantly at first that he engaged
in state affairs, being afraid of the pride of one party
and the greediness of the other; he was chosen archon,
however, after Philombrotus, and empowered to be an
arbitrator and lawgiver; the rich consenting because he
was wealthy, the poor because he was honest.   There was
a saying of his current before the election, that when
things are *even* there never can be war, and this pleased
both parties, the wealthy and the poor; the one conceiving him to mean, when all have their fair proportion;
the others, when all are absolutely equal.   Thus, there
being great hopes on both sides, the chief men pressed
Solon to take the government into his own hands, and,
when he was once settled, manage the business freely and
according to his pleasure; and many of the commons,
perceiving it would be a difficult change to be effected
by law and reason, were willing to have one wise and
just man set over the affairs; and some say that Solon
had this oracle from Apollo —

> Take the mid-seat, and be the vessel's guide;
> Many in Athens are upon your side.

But chiefly his familiar friends chid him for disaffecting monarchy only because of the name, as if the virtue of the ruler could not make it a lawful form; Eubœa had made this experiment when it chose Tynnondas, and Mitylene, which had made Pittacus its prince; yet this could not shake Solon's resolution; but, as they say, he replied to his friends, that it was true a tyranny was a very fair spot, but it had no way down from it; and in a copy of verses to Phocus he writes, —

           — that I spared my land,
And withheld from usurpation and from violence my hand,
And forbore to fix a stain and a disgrace on my good name,
I regret not; I believe that it will be my chiefest fame.

From which it is manifest that he was a man of great reputation before he gave his laws. The several mocks that were put upon him for refusing the power, he records in these words, —

Solon surely was a dreamer, and a man of simple mind;
When the gods would give him fortune, he of his own will declined;
When the net was full of fishes, over-heavy thinking it,
He declined to haul it up, through want of heart and want of wit.
Had but I that chance of riches and of kingship, for one day,
I would give my skin for flaying, and my house to die away.

Thus he makes the many and the low people speak of him. Yet, though he refused the government, he was not too mild in the affair; he did not show himself mean and submissive to the powerful, nor make his laws to pleasure those that chose him. For where it was well before, he applied no remedy, nor altered any thing, for fear lest,

       Overthrowing altogether and disordering the state,

he should be too weak to new-model and recompose it to a tolerable condition; but what he thought he could effect by persuasion upon the pliable, and by force upon the stubborn, this he did, as he himself says,

With force and justice working both in one.

And, therefore, when he was afterwards asked if he had left the Athenians the best laws that could be given, he replied, "The best they could receive." The way which, the moderns say, the Athenians have of softening the badness of a thing, by ingeniously giving it some pretty and innocent appellation, calling harlots, for example, mistresses, tributes customs, a garrison a guard, and the jail the chamber, seems originally to have been Solon's contrivance, who called cancelling debts Seisacthea, a relief, or disencumbrance. For the first thing which he settled was, that what debts remained should be forgiven, and no man, for the future, should engage the body of his debtor for security. Though some, as Androtion, affirm that the debts were not cancelled, but the interest only lessened, which sufficiently pleased the people; so that they named this benefit the Seisacthea, together with the enlarging their measures, and raising the value of their money; for he made a pound, which before passed * for seventy-three drachmas, go for a hundred; so that, though the number of pieces in the payment was equal, the value was less; which proved a considerable benefit to those that were to discharge great debts, and no loss to the creditors. But most agree that it was the taking off the debts that was called Seisacthea, which is confirmed by some places in his poem, where he takes honor to himself, that

The mortgage-stones that covered her, by me
Removed, — the land that was a slave is free;

---

* That is to say, if a man owed three hundred drachmas, his debt would now be discharged upon payment of three minas, or pounds; whereas before, he would have paid something more than four. The drachma was reduced twenty-seven per cent.

that some who had been seized for their debts he had
brought back from other countries, where

> — so far their lot to roam,
> They had forgot the language of their home ;

and some he had set at liberty, —

> Who here in shameful servitude were held.

While he was designing this, a most vexatious thing happened ; for when he had resolved to take off the debts,
and was considering the proper form and fit beginning
for it, he told some of his friends, Conon, Clinias, and
Hipponicus, in whom he had a great deal of confidence,
that he would not meddle with the lands, but only free
the people from their debts ; upon which, they, using
their advantage, made haste and borrowed some considerable sums of money, and purchased some large farms ;
and when the law was enacted, they kept the possessions,
and would not return the money ; which brought Solon
into great suspicion and dislike, as if he himself had not
been abused, but was concerned in the contrivance.   But
he presently stopped this suspicion, by releasing his
debtors of five talents (for he had lent so much), according to the law ; others, as Polyzelus the Rhodian, say
fifteen ; his friends, however, were ever afterward called
Chreocopidæ, repudiators.

In this he pleased neither party, for the rich were
angry for their money, and the poor that the land was
not divided, and, as Lycurgus ordered in his commonwealth, all men reduced to equality. He, it is true,
being the eleventh from Hercules, and having reigned
many years in Lacedæmon, had got a great reputation
and friends and power, which he could use in modelling
his state ; and, applying force more than persuasion, inso-

much that he lost his eye in the scuffle, was able to employ the most effectual means for the safety and harmony of a state, by not permitting any to be poor or rich in his commonwealth. Solon could not rise to that in his polity, being but a citizen of the middle classes; yet he acted fully up to the height of his power, having nothing but the good-will and good opinion of his citizens to rely on; and that he offended the most part, who looked for another result, he declares in the words,

> Formerly they boasted of me vainly; with averted eyes
> Now they look askance upon me; friends no more, but enemies.

And yet had any other man, he says, received the same power,

> He would not have forborne, nor let alone,
> But made the fattest of the milk his own.

Soon, however, becoming sensible of the good that was done, they laid by their grudges, made a public sacrifice, calling it Seisacthea, and chose Solon to new-model and make laws for the commonwealth, giving him the entire power over every thing, their magistracies, their assemblies, courts, and councils; that he should appoint the number, times of meeting, and what estate they must have that could be capable of these, and dissolve or continue any of the present constitutions, according to his pleasure.

First, then, he repealed all Draco's laws, except those concerning homicide, because they were too severe, and the punishments too great; for death was appointed for almost all offences, insomuch that those that were convicted of idleness were to die, and those that stole a cabbage or an apple to suffer even as villains that committed sacrilege or murder. So that Demades, in after time, was thought to have said very happily, that Draco's laws were written not with ink, but blood; and he himself, being once asked why he made death the punishment of most offences, replied, "Small ones deserve that, and I have no higher for the greater crimes."

Next, Solon, being willing to continue the magistracies in the hands of the rich men, and yet receive the people into the other part of the government, took an account of the citizens' estates, and those that were worth five hundred measures of fruits, dry and liquid, he placed in the first rank, calling them Pentacosiomedimni; those that could keep an horse, or were worth three hundred measures, were named Hippada Teluntes, and made the second class; the Zeugitæ, that had two hundred measures, were in the third; and all the others were called Thetes, who were not admitted to any office, but could come to the assembly, and act as jurors; which at first seemed nothing, but afterwards was found an enormous privilege, as almost every matter of dispute came before them in this latter capacity. Even in the cases which he assigned to the archons' cognizance, he allowed an appeal to the courts. Besides, it is said that he was obscure and ambiguous in the wording of his laws, on purpose to increase the honor of his courts; for since their differences could not be adjusted by the letter, they would have to bring all their causes to the judges, who thus were in a manner masters of the laws. Of this equalization he himself makes mention in this manner:

> Such power I gave the people as might do,
> Abridged not what they had, now lavished new.
> Those that were great in wealth and high in place,
> My counsel likewise kept from all disgrace.
> Before them both I held my shield of might,
> And let not either touch the other's right.

And for the greater security of the weak commons, he gave general liberty of indicting for an act of injury; if any one was beaten, maimed, or suffered any violence, any man that would and was able, might prosecute the wrongdoer; intending by this to accustom the citizens, like members of the same body, to resent and be sensible of one another's injuries. And there is a saying of his agreeable to this law, for, being asked what city was best modelled, "That," said he, "where those that are not injured try and punish the unjust as much as those that are."

When he had constituted the Areopagus of those who had been yearly archons, of which he himself was a member therefore, observing that the people, now free from their debts, were unsettled and imperious, he formed another council of four hundred, a hundred out of each of the four tribes, which was to inspect all matters before they were propounded to the people, and to take care that nothing but what had been first examined should be brought before the general assembly. The upper council, or Areopagus, he made inspectors and keepers of the laws, conceiving that the commonwealth, held by these two councils, like anchors, would be less liable to be tossed by tumults, and the people be more at quiet. Such is the general statement, that Solon instituted the Areopagus; which seems to be confirmed, because Draco makes no mention of the Areopagites, but in all causes of blood refers to the Ephetæ; yet Solon's thirteenth table contains the eighth law set down in these very words: "Whoever before Solon's archonship were disfranchised, let them be restored, except those that, being condemned by the Areopagus, Ephetæ, or in the Prytaneum by the kings,* for homicide, murder, or designs against the government, were in banishment when this law was made;" and these words seem to show that the Areopagus existed before Solon's laws, for who could be condemned by that council before his time, if he was the first that instituted the court? unless, which is probable, there is some ellipsis,

* That is, the king-archons.

or want of precision, in the language, and it should run thus, — "Those that are convicted of such offences as belong to the cognizance of the Areopagites, Ephetæ, or the Prytanes, when this law was made," shall remain still in disgrace, whilst others are restored; of this the reader must judge.

Amongst his other laws, one is very peculiar and surprising, which disfranchises all who stand neuter in a sedition; for it seems he would not have any one remain insensible and regardless of the public good, and, securing his private affairs, glory that he has no feeling of the distempers of his country; but at once join with the good party and those that have the right upon their side, assist and venture with them, rather than keep out of harm's way and watch who would get the better. It seems an absurd and foolish law which permits an heiress, if her lawful husband fail her, to take his nearest kinsman; yet some say this law was well contrived against those, who, conscious of their own unfitness, yet, for the sake of the portion, would match with heiresses, and make use of law to put a violence upon nature; for now, since she can quit him for whom she pleases, they would either abstain from such marriages, or continue them with disgrace, and suffer for their covetousness and designed affront; it is well done, moreover, to confine her to her husband's nearest kinsman, that the children may be of the same family. Agreeable to this is the law that the bride and bridegroom shall be shut into a chamber, and eat a quince together; and that the husband of an heiress shall consort with her thrice a month; for though there be no children, yet it is an honor and due affection which an husband ought to pay to a virtuous, chaste wife; it takes off all petty differences, and will not permit their little quarrels to proceed to a rupture.

In all other marriages he forbade dowries to be given;

the wife was to have three suits of clothes, a little inconsiderable household stuff, and that was all; for he would not have marriages contracted for gain or an estate, but for pure love, kind affection, and birth of children. When the mother of Dionysius desired him to marry her to one of his citizens, "Indeed," said he, "by my tyranny I have broken my country's laws, but cannot put a violence upon those of nature by an unseasonable marriage." Such disorder is never to be suffered in a commonwealth, nor such unseasonable and unloving and unperforming marriages, which attain no due end or fruit; any provident governor or lawgiver might say to an old man that takes a young wife what is said to Philoctetes in the tragedy,—

> Truly, in a fit state thou to marry!

and if he finds a young man, with a rich and elderly wife, growing fat in his place, like the partridges, remove him to a young woman of proper age. And of this enough.

Another commendable law of Solon's is that which forbids men to speak evil of the dead; for it is pious to think the deceased sacred, and just, not to meddle with those that are gone, and politic, to prevent the perpetuity of discord. He likewise forbade them to speak evil of the living in the temples, the courts of justice, the public offices, or at the games, or else to pay three drachmas to the person, and two to the public. For never to be able to control passion shows a weak nature and ill-breeding; and always to moderate it is very hard, and to some impossible. And laws must look to possibilities, if the maker designs to punish few in order to their amendment, and not many to no purpose.

He is likewise much commended for his law concerning wills; for before him none could be made, but all the wealth and estate of the deceased belonged to his family;

but he, by permitting them, if they had no children, to bestow it on whom they pleased, showed that he esteemed
friendship a stronger tie than kindred, and affection than
necessity; and made every man's estate truly his own.
Yet he allowed not all sorts of legacies, but those only
which were not extorted by the frenzy of a disease,
charms, imprisonment, force, or the persuasions of a wife;
with good reason thinking that being seduced into wrong
was as bad as being forced, and that between deceit and
necessity, flattery and compulsion, there was little difference, since both may equally suspend the exercise of
reason.

He regulated the walks, feasts, and mourning of the
women, and took away every thing that was either unbecoming or immodest; when they walked abroad, no more
than three articles * of dress were allowed them; an obol's
worth of meat and drink; and no basket above a cubit
high; and at night they were not to go about unless in a
chariot with a torch before them. Mourners tearing themselves to raise pity, and set wailings, and at one man's
funeral to lament for another, he forbade. To offer an
ox at the grave was not permitted, nor to bury above
three pieces of dress with the body, or visit the tombs of
any besides their own family, unless at the very funeral;
most of which are likewise forbidden by our laws,† but
this is further added in ours, that those that are convicted
of extravagance in their mournings, are to be punished
as soft and effeminate by the censors of women.

Observing the city to be filled with persons that flocked
from all parts into Attica for security of living, and that
most of the country was barren and unfruitful, and that

---

* For example, the *chitōn* or tunic, *himation* or pallium, and *peplus*,
i. e., the frock with two shawls, or
one and a scarf; or perhaps an inner and an outer frock, with one
shawl or scarf over them.

† In Bœotia, or perhaps at Chæronea.

traders at sea import nothing to those that could give
them nothing in exchange, he turned his citizens to
trade, and made a law that no son should be obliged to
relieve a father who had not bred him up to any calling.
It is true, Lycurgus, having a city free from all strangers,
and land, according to Euripides,

Large for large hosts, for twice their number much,

and, above all, an abundance of laborers about Sparta,
who should not be left idle, but be kept down with continual toil and work, did well to take off his citizens from
laborious and mechanical occupations, and keep them to
their arms, and teach them only the art of war. But
Solon, fitting his laws to the state of things, and not making things to suit his laws, and finding the ground scarce
rich enough to maintain the husbandmen, and altogether
incapable of feeding an unoccupied and leisurely multitude, brought trades into credit, and ordered the Areopagites to examine how every man got his living, and
chastise the idle. But that law was yet more rigid which,
as Heraclides Ponticus delivers, declared the sons of unmarried mothers not obliged to relieve their fathers; for
he that avoids the honorable form of union shows that he
does not take a woman for children, but for pleasure, and
thus gets his just reward, and has taken away from himself every title to upbraid his children, to whom he has
made their very birth a scandal and reproach.

Solon's laws in general about women are his strangest;
for he permitted any one to kill an adulterer that found
him in the act; but if any one forced a free woman, a
hundred drachmas was the fine; if he enticed her, twenty;
except those that sell themselves openly, that is, harlots,
who go openly to those that hire them. He made it
unlawful to sell a daughter or a sister, unless, being yet

unmarried, she was found wanton. Now it is irrational
to punish the same crime sometimes very severely and
without remorse, and sometimes very lightly, and, as it
were, in sport, with a trivial fine; unless, there being
little money then in Athens, scarcity made those mulcts
the more grievous punishment. In the valuation for
sacrifices, a sheep and a bushel were both estimated at a
drachma;* the victor in the Isthmian games was to have
for reward an hundred drachmas; the conqueror in the
Olympian, five hundred; he that brought a wolf, five
drachmas; for a whelp, one; the former sum, as Demetrius the Phalerian asserts, was the value of an ox, the
latter, of a sheep. The prices which Solon, in his sixteenth
table, sets on choice victims, were naturally far greater;
yet they, too, are very low in comparison of the present.
The Athenians were, from the beginning, great enemies
to wolves, their fields being better for pasture than corn.
Some affirm their tribes did not take their names from
the sons of Ion, but from the different sorts of occupation
that they followed; the soldiers were called Hoplitæ, the
craftsmen Ergades, and, of the remaining two, the farmers
Gedeontes, and the shepherds and graziers Ægicores.

Since the country has but few rivers, lakes, or large
springs, and many used wells which they had dug, there
was a law made, that, where there was a public well within a *hippicon*, that is, four furlongs, all should draw at that;
but, when it was farther off, they should try and procure
a well of their own; and, if they had dug ten fathom
deep and could find no water, they had liberty to fetch
a pitcherful of four gallons and a half in a day from their
neighbors'; for he thought it prudent to make provision

* The Attic drachma, it is convenient to remember, is just about
equivalent to a French franc; the
obol, six of which went to the
drachma, was, therefore, worth
about three half-pence, or three
cents.

against want, but not to supply laziness. He showed skill in his orders about planting, for any one that would plant another tree was not to set it within five feet of his neighbor's field; but if a fig or an olive, not within nine; for their roots spread farther, nor can they be planted near all sorts of trees without damage, for they draw away the nourishment, and in some cases are noxious by their effluvia. He that would dig a pit or a ditch was to dig it at the distance of its own depth from his neighbor's ground; and he that would raise stocks of bees was not to place them within three hundred feet of those which another had already raised.

He permitted only oil to be exported, and those that exported any other fruit, the archon was solemnly to curse, or else pay an hundred drachmas himself; and this law was written in his first table, and, therefore, let none think it incredible, as some affirm, that the exportation of figs was once unlawful, and the informer against the delinquents called a sycophant. He made a law, also, concerning hurts and injuries from beasts, in which he commands the master of any dog that bit a man to deliver him up with a log about his neck, four and a half feet long; a happy device for men's security. The law concerning naturalizing strangers is of doubtful character; he permitted only those to be made free of Athens who were in perpetual exile from their own country, or came with their whole family to trade there; this he did, not to discourage strangers, but rather to invite them to a permanent participation in the privileges of the government; and, besides, he thought those would prove the more faithful citizens who had been forced from their own country, or voluntarily forsook it. The law of public entertainment (*parasitein* is his name for it) is, also, peculiarly Solon's, for if any man came often, or if he that was invited refused, they were punished, for he concluded that one was greedy, the other a contemner of the state.

All his laws he established for an hundred years, and wrote them on wooden tables or rollers, named axones, which might be turned round in oblong cases; some of their relics were in my time still to be seen in the Prytaneum, or common hall, at Athens. These, as Aristotle states, were called cyrbes, and there is a passage of Cratinus the comedian,

> By Solon, and by Draco, if you please,
> Whose Cyrbes make the fires that parch our peas.

But some say those are properly cyrbes, which contain laws concerning sacrifices and the rites of religion, and all the others axones. The council all jointly swore to confirm the laws, and every one of the Thesmothetæ vowed for himself at the stone in the market-place, that, if he broke any of the statutes, he would dedicate a golden statue, as big as himself, at Delphi.

Observing the irregularity of the months, and that the moon does not always rise and set with the sun, but often in the same day overtakes and gets before him, he ordered the day should be named the Old and New,* attributing that part of it which was before the conjunction to the old moon, and the rest to the new, he being the first, it seems, that understood that verse of Homer,

> The end and the beginning of the month,

and the following day he called the new moon. After the twentieth he did not count by addition, but, like the moon itself in its wane, by subtraction; thus up to the thirtieth.

Now when these laws were enacted, and some came to

* Enē cai nea.

Solon every day, to commend or dispraise them, and
to advise, if possible, to leave out, or put in something,
and many criticized, and desired him to explain, and tell
the meaning of such and such a passage, he, knowing
that to do it was useless, and not to do it would get him
ill-will, and desirous to bring himself out of all straits,
and to escape all displeasure and exceptions, it being a
hard thing, as he himself says,

> In great affairs to satisfy all sides,

as an excuse for travelling, bought a trading vessel,
and, having obtained leave for ten years' absence, departed, hoping that by that time his laws would have
become familiar.

His first voyage was for Egypt, and he lived, as he
himself says,

> Near Nilus' mouth, by fair Canopus' shore,

and spent some time in study with Psenophis of Helio-
polis, and Sonchis the Saite, the most learned of all the
priests; from whom, as Plato says, getting knowledge of
the Atlantic story, he put it into a poem, and proposed
to bring it to the knowledge of the Greeks. From thence
he sailed to Cyprus, where he was made much of by Philocyprus, one of the kings there, who had a small city
built by Demophon, Theseus's son, near the river Cla-
rius, in a strong situation, but incommodious and uneasy
of access. Solon persuaded him, since there lay a fair
plain below, to remove, and build there a pleasanter and
more spacious city. And he stayed himself, and assisted in
gathering inhabitants, and in fitting it both for defence and
convenience of living; insomuch that many flocked to
Philocyprus, and the other kings imitated the design;
and, therefore, to honor Solon, he called the city Soli,
which was formerly named Æpea. And Solon himself,

in his Elegies, addressing Philocyprus, mentions this foundation in these words —

> Long may you live, and fill the Solian throne,
> Succeeded still by children of your own ;
> And from your happy island while I sail,
> Let Cyprus * send for me a favoring gale ;
> May she advance, and bless your new command,
> Prosper your town, and send me safe to land.

That Solon should discourse with Crœsus, some think not agreeable with chronology; but I cannot reject so famous and well-attested a narrative, and, what is more, so agreeable to Solon's temper, and so worthy his wisdom and greatness of mind, because, forsooth, it does not agree with some chronological canons, which thousands have endeavored to regulate, and yet, to this day, could never bring their differing opinions to any agreement. They say, therefore, that Solon, coming to Crœsus at his request, was in the same condition as an inland man when first he goes to see the sea; for as he fancies every river he meets with to be the ocean, so Solon, as he passed through the court, and saw a great many nobles richly dressed, and proudly attended with a multitude of guards and footboys, thought every one had been the king, till he was brought to Crœsus, who was decked with every possible rarity and curiosity, in ornaments of jewels, purple, and gold, that could make a grand and gorgeous spectacle of him. Now when Solon came before him, and seemed not at all surprised, nor gave Crœsus those compliments he expected, but showed himself to all discerning eyes to be a man that despised the gaudiness and petty ostentation of it, he commanded them to open all his treasure houses, and carry him to see his sumptuous furniture and luxuries, though he did not wish it; Solon could judge of

* The Cyprian Venus.

him well enough by the first sight of him; and, when he returned from viewing all, Crœsus asked him if ever he had known a happier man than he. And when Solon answered that he had known one Tellus, a fellow-citizen of his own, and told him that this Tellus had been an honest man, had had good children, a competent estate, and died bravely in battle for his country, Crœsus took him for an ill-bred fellow and a fool, for not measuring happiness by the abundance of gold and silver, and preferring the life and death of a private and mean man before so much power and empire. He asked him, however, again, if, besides Tellus, he knew any other man more happy. And Solon replying, Yes, Cleobis and Biton, who were loving brothers, and extremely dutiful sons to their mother, and, when the oxen delayed her, harnessed themselves to the wagon, and drew her to Juno's temple, her neighbors all calling her happy, and she herself rejoicing; then, after sacrificing and feasting, they went to rest, and never rose again, but died in the midst of their honor a painless and tranquil death, "What," said Crœsus, angrily, "and dost not thou reckon us amongst the happy men at all?" Solon, unwilling either to flatter or exasperate him more, replied, "The gods, O king, have given the Greeks all other gifts in moderate degree; and so our wisdom, too, is a cheerful and a homely, not a noble and kingly wisdom; and this, observing the numerous misfortunes that attend all conditions, forbids us to grow insolent upon our present enjoyments, or to admire any man's happiness that may yet, in course of time, suffer change. For the uncertain future has yet to come, with every possible variety of fortune; and him only to whom the divinity has continued happiness unto the end, we call happy; to salute as happy one that is still in the midst of life and hazard, we think as little safe and conclusive as to crown and proclaim as victorious the wrestler that is yet in the ring." After this, he was dismissed, having given Crœsus some pain, but no instruction.

Æsop, who wrote the fables, being then at Sardis upon Crœsus's invitation, and very much esteemed, was concerned that Solon was so ill-received, and gave him this advice: "Solon, let your converse with kings be either short or seasonable." "Nay, rather," replied Solon, "either short or reasonable." So at this time Crœsus despised Solon; but when he was overcome by Cyrus, had lost his city, was taken alive, condemned to be burnt, and laid bound upon the pile before all the Persians and Cyrus himself, he cried out as loud as possibly he could three times, "O Solon!" and Cyrus being surprised, and sending some to inquire what man or god this Solon was, whom alone he invoked in this extremity, Crœsus told him the whole story, saying, "He was one of the wise men of Greece, whom I sent for, not to be instructed, or to learn any thing that I wanted, but that he should see and be a witness of my happiness; the loss of which was, it seems, to be a greater evil than the enjoyment was a good; for when I had them they were goods only in opinion, but now the loss of them has brought upon me intolerable and real evils. And he, conjecturing from what then was, this that now is, bade me look to the end of my life, and not rely and grow proud upon uncertainties." When this was told Cyrus, who was a wiser man than Crœsus, and saw in the present example Solon's maxim confirmed, he not only freed Crœsus from punishment, but honored him as long as he lived; and Solon had the glory, by the same saying, to save one king and instruct another.

When Solon was gone, the citizens began to quarrel; Lycurgus headed the Plain; Megacles, the son of Alcmæon, those to the Sea-side; and Pisistratus the Hill-party, in which were the poorest people, the Thetes, and greatest enemies to the rich; insomuch that, though the city still used the new laws, yet all looked for and desired a change of government, hoping severally that the change would be better for them, and put them above the contrary faction.   Affairs standing thus, Solon returned, and was reverenced by all, and honored; but his old age would not permit him to be as active, and to speak in public, as formerly; yet, by privately conferring with the heads of the factions, he endeavored to compose the differences, Pisistratus appearing the most tractable; for he was extremely smooth and engaging in his language, a great friend to the poor, and moderate in his resentments; and what nature had not given him, he had the skill to imitate; so that he was trusted more than the others, being accounted a prudent and orderly man, one that loved equality, and would be an enemy to any that moved against the present settlement. Thus he deceived the majority of people; but Solon quickly discovered his character, and found out his design before any one else; yet did not hate him upon this, but endeavored to humble him, and bring him off from his ambition, and often told him and others, that if any one could banish the passion for preëminence from his mind, and cure him of his desire of absolute power, none would make a more virtuous man or a more excellent citizen. Thespis, at this time, beginning to act tragedies, and the thing, because it was new, taking very much with the multitude, though it was not yet made a matter of competition, Solon, being by nature fond of hearing and learning something new, and now, in his old age, living idly, and enjoying himself, indeed, with music and with wine, went to see Thespis himself, as the ancient custom was, act; and after the play was done, he addressed him, and asked him if he was not ashamed to tell so many lies before such a number of people; and Thespis replying that it was no harm

to say or do so in play, Solon vehemently struck his staff
against the ground: "Ay," said he, "if we honor and
commend such play as this, we shall find it some day in
our business."

Now when Pisistratus, having wounded himself, was
brought into the market-place in a chariot, and stirred
up the people, as if he had been thus treated by his opponents because of his political conduct, and a great
many were enraged and cried out, Solon, coming close to
him, said, "This, O son of Hippocrates, is a bad copy of
Homer's Ulysses; you do, to trick your countrymen, what
he did to deceive his enemies." After this, the people
were eager to protect Pisistratus, and met in an assembly, where one Ariston making a motion that they should
allow Pisistratus fifty clubmen for a guard to his person,
Solon opposed it, and said, much to the same purport as
what he has left us in his poems,

> You doat upon his words and taking phrase;

and again, —

> True, you are singly each a crafty soul,
> But all together make one empty fool.

But observing the poor men bent to gratify Pisistratus,
and tumultuous, and the rich fearful and getting out of
harm's way, he departed, saying he was wiser than some
and stouter than others; wiser than those that did not
understand the design, stouter than those that, though
they understood it, were afraid to oppose the tyranny.
Now, the people, having passed the law, were not nice
with Pisistratus about the number of his clubmen, but
took no notice of it, though he enlisted and kept as
many as he would, until he seized the Acropolis. When
that was done, and the city in an uproar, Megacles, with
all his family, at once fled; but Solon, though he was

now very old, and had none to back him, yet came into
the market-place and made a speech to the citizens,
partly blaming their inadvertency and meanness of spirit,
and in part urging and exhorting them not thus tamely
to lose their liberty; and likewise then spoke that
memorable saying, that, before, it was an easier task
to stop the rising tyranny, but now the greater and
more glorious action to destroy it, when it was begun
already, and had gathered strength. But all being afraid
to side with him, he returned home, and, taking his arms,
he brought them out and laid them in the porch before
his door, with these words: "I have done my part to
maintain my country and my laws," and then he busied
himself no more. His friends advising him to fly, he
refused, but wrote poems, and thus reproached the Athenians in them, —

> If now you suffer, do not blame the Powers,
> For they are good, and all the fault was ours.
> All the strongholds you put into his hands,
> And now his slaves must do what he commands.

And many telling him that the tyrant would take his
life for this, and asking what he trusted to, that he ventured to speak so boldly, he replied, "To my old age." But
Pisistratus, having got the command, so extremely courted
Solon, so honored him, obliged him, and sent to see him,
that Solon gave him his advice, and approved many of
his actions; for he retained most of Solon's laws, observed them himself, and compelled his friends to obey.
And he himself, though already absolute ruler, being
accused of murder before the Areopagus, came quietly to
clear himself; but his accuser did not appear. And he
added other laws, one of which is that the maimed in
the wars should be maintained at the public charge; this
Heraclides Ponticus records, and that Pisistratus followed

Solon's example in this, who had decreed it in the case of one Thersippus, that was maimed; and Theophrastus asserts that it was Pisistratus, not Solon, that made that law against laziness, which was the reason that the country was more productive, and the city tranquiller.

Now Solon, having begun the great work in verse, the history or fable of the Atlantic Island, which he had learned from the wise men in Sais, and thought convenient for the Athenians to know, abandoned it; not, as Plato says, by reason of want of time, but because of his age, and being discouraged at the greatness of the task; for that he had leisure enough, such verses testify, as

Each day grow older, and learn something new;

and again, —

But now the Powers of Beauty, Song, and Wine,
Which are most men's delights, are also mine.

Plato, willing to improve the story of the Atlantic Island, as if it were a fair estate that wanted an heir and came with some title to him, formed, indeed, stately entrances, noble enclosures, large courts, such as never yet introduced any story, fable, or poetic fiction; but, beginning it late, ended his life before his work; and the reader's regret for the unfinished part is the greater, as the satisfaction he takes in that which is complete is extraordinary. For as the city of Athens left only the temple of Jupiter Olympius unfinished, so Plato, amongst all his excellent works, left this only piece about the Atlantic Island imperfect. Solon lived after Pisistratus seized the government, as Heraclides Ponticus asserts, a long time; but Phanias the Eresian says not two full years; for Pisistratus began his tyranny when Comias was archon, and Phanias says Solon died under Hegestratus, who succeeded

Comias. The story that his ashes were scattered about the island Salamis is too strange to be easily believed, or be thought any thing but a mere fable; and yet it is given, amongst other good authors, by Aristotle, the philosopher.

POPLICOLA.

Such was Solon. To him we compare Poplicola, who received this later title from the Roman people for his merit,
as a noble accession to his former name, Publius Valerius.
He descended from Valerius, a man amongst the early
citizens, reputed the principal reconciler of the differences
betwixt the Romans and Sabines, and one that was most
instrumental in persuading their kings to assent to peace
and union. Thus descended, Publius Valerius, as it is said,
whilst Rome remained under its kingly government, obtained as great a name from his eloquence as from his
riches, charitably employing the one in liberal aid to the
poor, the other with integrity and freedom in the service of justice; thereby giving assurance, that, should the
government fall into a republic, he would become a chief
man in the community. The illegal and wicked accession
of Tarquinius Superbus to the crown, with his making it,
instead of kingly rule, the instrument of insolence and
tyranny, having inspired the people with a hatred to his
reign, upon the death of Lucretia (she killing herself
after violence had been done to her), they took an occasion of revolt; and Lucius Brutus, engaging in the change,
came to Valerius before all others, and, with his zealous
assistance, deposed the kings. And whilst the people
inclined towards the electing one leader instead of their
king, Valerius acquiesced, that to rule was rather Bru-

tus's due, as the author of the democracy. But when the
name of monarchy was odious to the people, and a divided.
power appeared more grateful in the prospect, and two
were chosen to hold it, Valerius, entertaining hopes that
he might be elected consul with Brutus, was disappointed;
for, instead of Valerius, notwithstanding the endeavors of
Brutus, Tarquinius Collatinus was chosen, the husband
of Lucretia, a man noways his superior in merit. But
the nobles, dreading the return of their kings, who still
used all endeavors abroad and solicitations at home, were
resolved upon a chieftain of an intense hatred to them,
and noways likely to yield.

Now Valerius was troubled, that his desire to serve
his country should be doubted, because he had sustained
no private injury from the insolence of the tyrants.
He withdrew from the senate and practice of the bar,
quitting all public concerns; which gave an occasion of
discourse, and fear, too, lest his anger should reconcile him
to the king's side, and he should prove the ruin of the
state, tottering as yet under the uncertainties of a change.
But Brutus being doubtful of some others, and determin-
ing to give the test to the senate upon the altars, upon
the day appointed Valerius came with cheerfulness into
the forum, and was the first man that took the oath, in
no way to submit or yield to Tarquin's propositions, but
rigorously to maintain liberty; which gave great satisfaction to the senate and assurance to the consuls, his
actions soon after showing the sincerity of his oath. For
ambassadors came from Tarquin, with popular and specious proposals, whereby they thought to seduce the people, as though the king had cast off all insolence, and
made moderation the only measure of his desires. To this
embassy the consuls thought fit to give public audience,
but Valerius opposed it, and would not permit that the
poorer people, who entertained more fear of war than of

tyranny, should have any occasion offered them, or any temptations to new designs. Afterwards other ambassadors arrived, who declared their king would recede from his crown, and lay down his arms, only capitulating for a restitution to himself, his friends, and allies, of their moneys and estates to support them in their banishment. Now, several inclining to the request, and Collatinus in particular favoring it, Brutus, a man of vehement and unbending nature, rushed into the forum, there proclaiming his fellow-consul to be a traitor, in granting subsidies to tyranny, and supplies for a war to those to whom it was monstrous to allow so much as subsistence in exile. This caused an assembly of the citizens, amongst whom the first that spake was Caius Minucius, a private man, who advised Brutus, and urged the Romans, to keep the property, and employ it against the tyrants, rather than to remit it to the tyrants, to be used against themselves. The Romans, however, decided that whilst they enjoyed the liberty they had fought for, they should not sacrifice peace for the sake of money, but send out the tyrants' property after them. This question, however, of his property, was the least part of Tarquin's design; the demand sounded the feelings of the people, and was preparatory to a conspiracy which the ambassadors endeavored to excite, delaying their return, under pretence of selling some of the goods and reserving others to be sent away, till, in fine, they corrupted two of the most eminent families in Rome, the Aquillian, which had three, and the Vitellian, which had two senators. These all were, by the mother's side, nephews to Collatinus; besides which Brutus had a special alliance to the Vitellii from his marriage with their sister, by whom he had several children; two of whom, of their own age, their near relations and daily companions, the Vitellii seduced to join in the plot, to ally themselves to the great house and royal hopes of the Tarquins, and gain emancipation from the violence and imbecility united of their father, whose austerity to offenders they termed violence, while the imbecility which he had long feigned, to protect himself from the tyrants, still, it appears, was, in name at least, ascribed to him. When upon these inducements the youths came to confer with the Aquillii, all thought it convenient to bind themselves in a solemn and dreadful oath, by tasting the blood of a murdered man, and touching his entrails. For which design they met at the house of the Aquillii. The building chosen for the transaction was, as was natural, dark and unfrequented, and a slave named Vindicius had, as it chanced, concealed himself there, not out of design or any intelligence of the affair, but, accidentally being within, seeing with how much haste and concern they came in, he was afraid to be discovered, and placed himself behind a chest, where he was able to observe their actions and overhear their debates. Their resolutions were to kill the consuls, and they wrote letters to Tarquin to this effect, and gave them to the ambassadors, who were lodging upon the spot with the Aquillii, and were present at the consultation.

Upon their departure, Vindicius secretly quitted the house, but was at a loss what to do in the matter, for to arraign the sons before the father Brutus, or the nephews before the uncle Collatinus, seemed equally (as indeed it was) shocking; yet he knew no private Roman to whom he could intrust secrets of such importance. Unable, however, to keep silence, and burdened with his knowledge, he went and addressed himself to Valerius, whose known freedom and kindness of temper were an inducement; as he was a person to whom the needy had easy access, and who never shut his gates against the petitions or indigences of humble people. But when Vindicius came and made a complete discovery to him, his brother Marcus

and his own wife being present, Valerius was struck with
amazement, and by no means would dismiss the discov-
erer, but confined him to the room, and placed his wife
as a guard to the door, sending his brother in the interim
to beset the king's palace, and seize, if possible, the writings there, and secure the domestics, whilst he, with his
constant attendance of clients and friends, and a great
retinue of attendants, repaired to the house of the Aquillii, who were, as it chanced, absent from home; and so,
forcing an entrance through the gates, they lit upon the
letters then lying in the lodgings of the ambassadors.
Meantime the Aquillii returned in all haste, and, coming
to blows about the gate, endeavored a recovery of the
letters.   The other party made a resistance, and, throwing
their gowns round their opponents' necks, at last, after
much struggling on both sides, made their way with their
prisoners through the streets into the forum. The like engagement happened about the king's palace, where Marcus seized some other letters which it was designed should
be conveyed away in the goods, and, laying hands on such
of the king's people as he could find, dragged them also
into the forum. When the consuls had quieted the
tumult, Vindicius was brought out by the orders of Valerius, and the accusation stated, and the letters were
opened, to which the traitors could make no plea. Most
of the people standing mute and sorrowful, some only,
out of kindness to Brutus, mentioning banishment, the
tears of Collatinus, attended with Valerius's silence, gave
some hopes of mercy. But Brutus, calling his two sons
by their names, "Canst not thou," said he, "O Titus, or
thou, Tiberius, make any defence against the indictment?"
The question being thrice proposed, and no reply made,
he turned himself to the lictors, and cried, "What remains
is your duty." They immediately seized the youths, and,
stripping them of their clothes, bound their hands behind

them, and scourged their bodies with their rods; too tra·
gical a scene for others to look at; Brutus, however, is
said not to have turned aside his face, nor allowed the
least glance of pity to soften and smoothe his aspect of
rigor and austerity; but sternly watched his children
suffer, even till the lictors, extending them on the ground,
cut off their heads with an axe; then departed, commit-
ting the rest to the judgment of his colleague. An action
truly open alike to the highest commendation and the
strongest censure; for either, the greatness of his virtue
raised him above the impressions of sorrow, or the ex·
travagance of his misery took away all sense of it; but
neither seemed common, or the result of humanity, but
either divine or brutish. Yet it is more reasonable that
our judgment should yield to his reputation, than that
his merit should suffer detraction by the weakness of our
judgment; in the Romans' opinion, Brutus did a greater
work in the establishment of the government than Romulus in the foundation of the city.

Upon Brutus's departure out of the forum, consternation, horror, and silence for some time possessed all that
reflected on what was done; the easiness and tardiness,
however, of Collatinus, gave confidence to the Aquillii to
request some time to answer their charge, and that Vindicius, their servant, should be remitted into their hands,
and no longer harbored amongst their accusers. The
consul seemed inclined to their proposal, and was proceeding to dissolve the assembly; but Valerius would not
suffer Vindicius, who was surrounded by his people, to be
surrendered, nor the meeting to withdraw without punishing the traitors; and at length laid violent hands upon
the Aquillii, and, calling Brutus to his assistance, ex-
claimed against the unreasonable course of Collatinus, to
impose upon his colleague the necessity of taking away
the lives of his own sons, and yet have thoughts of grati-

fying some women with the lives of traitors and public
enemies. Collatinus, displeased at this, and commanding
Vindicius to be taken away, the lictors made their way
through the crowd and seized their man, and struck all
who endeavored a rescue. Valerius's friends headed the
resistance, and the people cried out for Brutus, who, returning, on silence being made, told them he had been competent to pass sentence by himself upon his own sons, but left
the rest to the suffrages of the free citizens: "Let every
man speak that wishes, and persuade whom he can."
But there was no need of oratory, for, it being referred to
the vote, they were returned condemned by all the suffrages, and were accordingly beheaded.

Collatinus's relationship to the kings had, indeed, already rendered him suspicious, and his second name, too,
had made him obnoxious to the people, who were loth
to hear the very sound of Tarquin; but after this had
happened, perceiving himself an offence to every one, he
relinquished his charge and departed from the city. At
the new elections in his room, Valerius obtained, with
high honor, the consulship, as a just reward of his zeal;
of which he thought Vindicius deserved a share, whom
he made, first of all freedmen, a citizen of Rome, and
gave him the privilege of voting in what tribe soever he
was pleased to be enrolled; other freedmen received the
right of suffrage a long time after from Appius, who thus
courted popularity; and from this Vindicius, a perfect
manumission is called to this day *vindicta.* This done,
the goods of the kings were exposed to plunder, and the
palace to ruin.

The pleasantest part of the field of Mars, which Tarquin had owned, was devoted to the service of that
god; but, it happening to be harvest season, and the
sheaves yet being on the ground, they thought it not
proper to commit them to the flail, or unsanctify them

with any use; and, therefore, carrying them to the river-side, and trees withal that were cut down, they cast all into the water, dedicating the soil, free from all occupation, to the deity. Now, these thrown in, one upon another, and closing together, the stream did not bear them far, but where the first were carried down and came to a bottom, the remainder, finding no farther conveyance, were stopped and interwoven one with another; the stream working the mass into a firmness, and washing down fresh mud. This, settling there, became an accession of matter, as well as cement, to the rubbish, insomuch that the violence of the waters could not remove it, but forced and compressed it all together. Thus its bulk and solidity gained it new subsidies, which gave it extension enough to stop on its way most of what the stream brought down. This is now a sacred island, lying by the city, adorned with temples of the gods, and walks, and is called in the Latin tongue *inter duos pontes*. Though some say this did not happen at the dedication of Tarquin's field, but in after-times, when Tarquinia, a vestal priestess, gave an adjacent field to the public, and obtained great honors in consequence, as, amongst the rest, that of all women her testimony alone should be received; she had also the liberty to marry, but refused it; thus some tell the story.

Tarquin, despairing of a return to his kingdom by the conspiracy, found a kind reception amongst the Tuscans, who, with a great army, proceeded to restore him. The consuls headed the Romans against them, and made their rendezvous in certain holy places, the one called the Arsian grove, the other the Æsuvian meadow. When they came into action, Aruns, the son of Tarquin, and Brutus, the Roman consul, not accidentally encountering each other, but out of hatred and rage, the one to avenge tyranny and enmity to his country, the other his banish-

ment, set spurs to their horses, and, engaging with more
fury than forethought, disregarding their own security,
fell together in the combat. This dreadful onset hardly
was followed by a more favorable end; both armies,
doing and receiving equal damage, were separated by a
storm. Valerius was much concerned, not knowing what
the result of the day was, and seeing his men as well dismayed at the sight of their own dead, as rejoiced at the
loss of the enemy; so apparently equal in the number
was the slaughter on either side. Each party, however,
felt surer of defeat from the actual sight of their own
dead, than they could feel of victory from conjecture
about those of their adversaries. The night being come
(and such as one may presume must follow such a battle), and the armies laid to rest, they say that the grove
shook, and uttered a voice, saying that the Tuscans had
lost one man more than the Romans; clearly a divine an-
nouncement; and the Romans at once received it with
shouts and expressions of joy; whilst the Tuscans, through
fear and amazement, deserted their tents, and were for
the most part dispersed. The Romans, falling upon the
remainder, amounting to nearly five thousand, took them
prisoners, and plundered the camp; when they numbered
the dead, they found on the Tuscans' side eleven thousand
and three hundred, exceeding their own loss but by one
man. This fight happened upon the last day of February, and Valerius triumphed in honor of it, being
the first consul that drove in with a four-horse chariot;
which sight both appeared magnificent, and was received
with an admiration free from envy or offence (as some
suggest) on the part of the spectators; it would not
otherwise have been continued with so much eagerness
and emulation through all the after ages. The people
applauded likewise the honors he did to his colleague, in
adding to his obsequies a funeral oration; which was so

much liked by the Romans, and found so good a reception, that it became customary for the best men to celebrate the funerals of great citizens with speeches in their commendation; and their antiquity in Rome is affirmed to be greater than in Greece, unless, with the orator Anaximenes, we make Solon the first author.

Yet some part of Valerius's behavior did give offence and disgust to the people, because Brutus, whom they esteemed the father of their liberty, had not presumed to rule without a colleague, but united one and then another to him in his commission; while Valerius, they said, centering all authority in himself, seemed not in any sense a successor to Brutus in the consulship, but to Tarquin in the tyranny; he might make verbal harangues to Brutus's memory, yet, when he was attended with all the rods and axes, proceeding down from a house than which the king's house that he had demolished had not been statelier, those actions showed him an imitator of Tarquin. For, indeed, his dwelling-house on the Velia was somewhat imposing in appearance, hanging over the forum, and overlooking all transactions there; the access to it was hard, and to see him far off coming down, a stately and royal spectacle. But Valerius showed how well it were for men in power and great offices to have ears that give admittance to truth before flattery; for upon his friends telling him that he displeased the people, he contended not, neither resented it, but while it was still night, sending for a number of workpeople, pulled down his house and levelled it with the ground; so that in the morning the people, seeing and flocking together, expressed their wonder and their respect for his magnanimity, and their sorrow, as though it had been a human being, for the large and beautiful house which was thus lost to them by an unfounded jealousy, while its owner, their consul, without a roof of his own, had to beg a lodging with his friends. For his friends received him, till a place the people gave him was furnished with a house, though less stately than his own, where now stands the temple, as it is called, of Vica Pota.

He resolved to render the government, as well as himself, instead of terrible, familiar and pleasant to the people, and parted the axes from the rods, and always, upon his entrance into the assembly, lowered these also to the people, to show, in the strongest way, the republican foundation of the government; and this the consuls observe to this day. But the humility of the man was but a means, not, as they thought, of lessening himself, but merely to abate their envy by this moderation; for whatever he detracted from his authority he added to his real power, the people still submitting with satisfaction, which they expressed by calling him Poplicola, or people-lover, which name had the preëminence of the rest, and, therefore, in the sequel of this narrative we shall use no other.

He gave free leave to any to sue for the consulship; but before the admittance of a colleague, mistrusting the chances, lest emulation or ignorance should cross his designs, by his sole authority enacted his best and most important measures. First, he supplied the vacancies of the senators, whom either Tarquin long before had put to death, or the war lately cut off; those that he enrolled, they write, amounted to a hundred and sixty-four; afterwards he made several laws which added much to the people's liberty, in particular one granting offenders the liberty of appealing to the people from the judgment of the consuls; a second, that made it death to usurp any magistracy without the people's consent; a third, for the relief of poor citizens, which, taking off their taxes, encouraged their labors; another, against disobedience to the consuls, which was no less popular than the rest, and rather to the benefit of the commonalty than to the advantage of the nobles, for it imposed upon disobedience the penalty of ten oxen and two sheep; the price of a sheep being ten obols, of an ox, an hundred. For the use of money was then infrequent amongst the Romans, but their wealth in cattle great; even now pieces of property are called *peculia*, from *pecus*, cattle; and they had stamped upon their most ancient money an ox, a sheep, or a hog; and surnamed their sons Suillii, Bubulci, Caprarii, and Porcii, from *capræ*, goats, and *porci*, hogs.

Amidst this mildness and moderation, for one excessive fault he instituted one excessive punishment; for he made it lawful without trial to take away any man's life that aspired to a tyranny, and acquitted the slayer, if he produced evidence of the crime; for though it was not probable for a man, whose designs were so great, to escape all notice; yet because it was possible he might, although observed, by force anticipate judgment, which the usurpation itself would then preclude, he gave a license to any to anticipate the usurper. He was honored likewise for the law touching the treasury; for because it was necessary for the citizens to contribute out of their estates to the maintenance of wars, and he was unwilling himself to be concerned in the care of it, or to permit his friends, or indeed to let the public money pass into any private house, he allotted the temple of Saturn for the treasury, in which to this day they deposit the tribute-money, and granted the people the liberty of choosing two young men as quæstors, or treasurers. The first were Publius Veturius and Marcus Minucius; and a large sum was collected, for they assessed one hundred and thirty thousand, excusing orphans and widows from the payment. After these dispositions, he admitted Lucretius, the father of Lucretia, as his colleague, and gave him the precedence in the government, by resigning the fasces to him, as due to his years, which privilege of seniority continued to our time. But within a few days Lucretius died, and in a new election Marcus Horatius succeeded in that honor, and continued consul for the remainder of the year.

Now, whilst Tarquin was making preparations in Tuscany for a second war against the Romans, it is said a great portent occurred. When Tarquin was king, and had all but completed the buildings of the Capitol, designing, whether from oracular advice or his own pleasure, to erect an earthen chariot upon the top, he intrusted the workmanship to Tuscans of the city Veii, but soon after lost his kingdom. The work thus modelled, the Tuscans set in a furnace, but the clay showed not those passive qualities which usually attend its nature, to subside and be condensed upon the evaporation of the moisture, but rose and swelled out to that bulk, that, when solid and firm, notwithstanding the removal of the roof and opening the walls of the furnace, it could not be taken out without much difficulty. The soothsayers looked upon this as a divine prognostic of success and power to those that should possess it; and the Tuscans resolved not to deliver it to the Romans, who demanded it, but answered that it rather belonged to Tarquin than to those who had sent him into exile. A few days after, they had a horse-race there, with the usual shows and solemnities, and as the charioteer, with his garland on his head, was quietly driving the victorious chariot out of the ring, the horses, upon no apparent occasion, taking fright, either by divine instigation or by accident, hurried away their driver at full speed to Rome; neither did his holding them in prevail, nor his voice, but he was forced along with violence till, coming to the Capitol, he was thrown out by the gate called Ratumena. This occurrence raised wonder and fear in the Veientines, who now permitted the delivery of the chariot.

The building of the temple of the Capitoline Jupiter

had been vowed by Tarquin, the son of Demaratus, when
warring with the Sabines; Tarquinius Superbus, his son or
grandson, built, but could not dedicate it, because he lost
his kingdom before it was quite finished. And now that
it was completed with all its ornaments, Poplicola was
ambitious to dedicate it; but the nobility envied him that
honor, as, indeed, also, in some degree, those his prudence
in making laws and conduct in wars entitled him to
Grudging him, at any rate, the addition of this, they urged
Horatius to sue for the dedication, and, whilst Poplicola
was engaged in some military expedition, voted it to
Horatius, and conducted him to the Capitol, as though,
were Poplicola present, they could not have carried it.
Yet, some write, Poplicola was by lot destined against his
will to the expedition, the other to the dedication; and
what happened in the performance seems to intimate
some ground for this conjecture; for, upon the Ides of
September, which happens about the full moon of the
month Metagitnion, the people having assembled at the
Capitol and silence being enjoined, Horatius, after the
performance of other ceremonies, holding the doors, according to custom, was proceeding to pronounce the
words of dedication, when Marcus, the brother of Poplicola, who had got a place on purpose beforehand near the
door, observing his opportunity, cried, "O consul, thy son
lies dead in the camp;" which made a great impression
upon all others who heard it, yet in nowise discomposed
Horatius, who returned merely the reply, "Cast the dead
out whither you please; I am not a mourner;" and so
completed the dedication. The news was not true, but
Marcus thought the lie might avert him from his performance; but it argues him a man of wonderful self-pos-
session, whether he at once saw through the cheat, or,
believing it as true, showed no discomposure.

The same fortune attended the dedication of the second

temple; the first, as has been said, was built by Tarquin, and dedicated by Horatius; it was burnt down in the civil wars. The second, Sylla built, and, dying before the dedication, left that honor to Catulus; and when this was demolished in the Vitellian sedition, Vespasian, with the same success that attended him in other things, began a third, and lived to see it finished, but did not live to see it again destroyed, as it presently was; but was as fortunate in dying before its destruction, as Sylla was the reverse in dying before the dedication of his. For immediately after Vespasian's death it was consumed by fire. The fourth, which now exists, was both built and dedicated by Domitian. It is said Tarquin expended forty thousand pounds of silver in the very foundations; but the whole wealth of the richest private man in Rome would not discharge the cost of the gilding of this temple in our days, it amounting to above twelve thousand talents; the pillars were cut out of Pentelican marble, of a length most happily proportioned to their thickness; these we saw at Athens; but when they were cut anew at Rome and polished, they did not gain so much in embellishment, as they lost in symmetry, being rendered too taper and slender. Should any one who wonders at the costliness of the Capitol visit any one gallery in Domitian's palace, or hall, or bath, or the apartments of his concubines, Epicharmus's remark upon the prodigal, that

> 'T is not beneficence, but, truth to say,
> A mere disease of giving things away,

would be in his mouth in application to Domitian. It is neither piety, he would say, nor magnificence, but, indeed, a mere disease of building, and a desire, like Midas, of converting every thing into gold or stone. And thus much for this matter.

Tarquin, after the great battle wherein he lost his son

in combat with Brutus, fled to Clusium, and sought aid
from Lars Porsenna, then one of the most powerful
princes of Italy, and a man of worth and generosity;
who assured him of assistance, immediately sending his
commands to Rome that they should receive Tarquin as
their king, and, upon the Romans' refusal, proclaimed
war, and, having signified the time and place where he
intended his attack, approached with a great army. Poplicola was, in his absence, chosen consul a second time,
and Titus Lucretius his colleague, and, returning to Rome,
to show a spirit yet loftier than Porsenna's, built the city
Sigliuria * when Porsenna was already in the neighborhood; and, walling it at great expense, there placed a
colony of seven hundred men, as being little concerned
at the war. Nevertheless, Porsenna, making a sharp
assault, obliged the defendants to retire to Rome, who
had almost in their entrance admitted the enemy into
the city with them; only Poplicola by sallying out at
the gate prevented them, and, joining battle by Tiber
side, opposed the enemy, that pressed on with their multitude, but at last, sinking under desperate wounds, was
carried out of the fight. The same fortune fell upon
Lucretius, so that the Romans, being dismayed, retreated
into the city for their security, and Rome was in great
hazard of being taken, the enemy forcing their way on
to the wooden bridge, where Horatius Cocles, seconded
by two of the first men in Rome, Herminius and Lartius,
made head against them. Horatius obtained this name
from the loss of one of his eyes in the wars, or, as others
write, from the depressure of his nose, which, leaving
nothing in the middle to separate them, made both eyes
appear but as one; and hence, intending to say Cyclops,

---

* No such city is heard of in   to Livy, was founded earlier in
any other author. Possibly it   the reign of the last Tarquin.
should be Signia, which, according

POPLICOLA.

POPLICOLA. 219

by a mispronunciation they called him Cocles. This Cocles kept the bridge, and held back the enemy, till his own party broke it down behind, and then with his armor dropped into the river, and swam to the hither side, with a wound in his hip from a Tuscan spear. Poplicola, admiring his courage, proposed at once that the Romans should every one make him a present of a day's provisions, and afterwards gave him as much land as he could plough round in one day, and besides erected a brazen statue to his honor in the temple of Vulcan, as a requital for the lameness caused by his wound.

But Porsenna laying close siege to the city, and a famine raging amongst the Romans, also a new army of the Tuscans making incursions into the country, Poplicola, a third time chosen consul, designed to make, without sallying out, his defence against Porsenna, but, privately stealing forth against the new army of the Tuscans, put them to flight, and slew five thousand. The story of Mucius is variously given; we, like others, must follow the commonly received statement. He was a man endowed with every virtue, but most eminent in war; and, resolving to kill Porsenna, attired himself in the Tuscan habit, and, using the Tuscan language, came to the camp, and approaching the seat where the king sat amongst his nobles, but not certainly knowing the king, and fearful to inquire, drew out his sword, and stabbed one who he thought had most the appearance of king. Mucius was taken in the act, and whilst he was under examination, a pan of fire was brought to the king, who intended to sacrifice; Mucius thrust his right hand into the flame, and whilst it burnt stood looking at Porsenna with a steadfast and undaunted countenance; Porsenna at last in admiration dismissed him, and returned his sword, reaching it from his seat; Mucius received it in his left hand, which occasioned the name of Scævola, left-handed, and said, " I have

overcome the terrors of Porsenna, yet am vanquished by
his generosity, and gratitude obliges me to disclose what
no punishment could extort;" and assured him then,
that three hundred Romans, all of the same resolution,
lurked about his camp, only waiting for an opportunity;
he, by lot appointed to the enterprise, was not sorry that
he had miscarried in it, because so brave and good a man
deserved rather to be a friend to the Romans than an
enemy. To this Porsenna gave credit, and thereupon
expressed an inclination to a truce, not, I presume, so
much out of fear of the three hundred Romans, as in admiration of the Roman courage. All other writers call
this man Mucius Scævola, yet Athenodorus, son of San-
don, in a book addressed to Octavia, Cæsar's sister, avers
he was also called Postumus.

Poplicola, not so much esteeming Porsenna's enmity
dangerous to Rome as his friendship and alliance serviceable, was induced to refer the controversy with Tarquin to
his arbitration, and several times undertook to prove
Tarquin the worst of men, and justly deprived of his
kingdom. But Tarquin proudly replied he would admit
no judge, much less Porsenna, that had fallen away from
his engagements; and Porsenna, resenting this answer,
and mistrusting the equity of his cause, moved also by
the solicitations of his son Aruns, who was earnest for the
Roman interest, made a peace on these conditions, that
they should resign the land they had taken from the
Tuscans, and restore all prisoners and receive back their
deserters. To confirm the peace, the Romans gave as
hostages ten sons of patrician parents, and as many
daughters, amongst whom was Valeria, the daughter of
Poplicola.

Upon these assurances, Porsenna ceased from all acts
of hostility, and the young girls went down to the river
to bathe, at that part where the winding of the bank

formed a bay and made the waters stiller and quieter; and, seeing no guard, nor any one coming or going over, they were encouraged to swim over, notwithstanding the depth and violence of the stream. Some affirm that one of them, by name Clœlia, passing over on horseback, persuaded the rest to swim after; but, upon their safe arrival, presenting themselves to Poplicola, he neither praised nor approved their return, but was concerned lest he should appear less faithful than Porsenna, and this boldness in the maidens should argue treachery in the Romans; so that, apprehending them, he sent them back to Porsenna. But Tarquin's men, having intelligence of this, laid a strong ambuscade on the other side for those that conducted them; and while these were skirmishing together, Valeria, the daughter of Poplicola, rushed through the enemy and fled, and with the assistance of three of her attendants made good her escape, whilst the rest were dangerously hedged in by the soldiers; but Aruns, Porsenna's son, upon tidings of it, hastened to their rescue, and, putting the enemy to flight, delivered the Romans. When Porsenna saw the maidens returned, demanding who was the author and adviser of the act, and understanding Clœlia to be the person, he looked on her with a cheerful and benignant countenance, and, commanding one of his horses to be brought, sumptuously adorned, made her a present of it. This is produced as evidence by those who affirm that only Clœlia passed the river on horseback; those who deny it call it only the honor the Tuscan did to her courage; a figure, however, on horseback stands in the Via Sacra, as you go to the Palatium, which some say is the statue of Clœlia, others of Valeria. Porsenna, thus reconciled to the Romans, gave them a fresh instance of his generosity, and commanded his soldiers to quit the camp merely with their arms, leaving their tents, full of corn and other stores, as a gift to the Romans. Hence, even down to our time, when there is a public sale of goods, they cry Porsenna's first, by way of perpetual commemoration of his kindness. There stood, also, by the senate-house, a brazen statue of him, of plain and antique workmanship.

Afterwards, the Sabines making incursions upon the Romans, Marcus Valerius, brother to Poplicola, was made consul, and with him Postumius Tubertus. Marcus, through the management of affairs by the conduct and direct assistance of Poplicola, obtained two great victories, in the latter of which he slew thirteen thousand Sabines without the loss of one Roman, and was honored, as an accession to his triumph, with an house built in the Palatium at the public charge; and whereas the doors of other houses opened inward into the house, they made this to open outward into the street, to intimate their perpetual public recognition of his merit by thus continually making way for him. The same fashion in their doors the Greeks, they say, had of old universally, which appears from their comedies, where those that are going out make a noise at the door within, to give notice to those that pass by or stand near the door, that the opening the door into the street might occasion no surprisal.

The year after, Poplicola was made consul the fourth time, when a confederacy of the Sabines and Latins threatened a war; a superstitious fear also overran the city on the occasion of general miscarriages of their women, no single birth coming to its due time. Poplicola, upon consultation of the Sibylline books, sacrificing to Pluto, and renewing certain games commanded by Apollo, restored the city to more cheerful assurance in the gods, and then prepared against the menaces of men. There were appearances of great preparation, and of a formidable confederacy. Amongst the Sabines there was

one Appius Clausus, a man of a great wealth and strength
of body, but most eminent for his high character and for
his eloquence; yet, as is usually the fate of great men, he
could not escape the envy of others, which was much
occasioned by his dissuading the war, and seeming to promote the Roman interest, with a view, it was thought, to
obtaining absolute power in his own country for himself.
Knowing how welcome these reports would be to the
multitude, and how offensive to the army and the abet-
tors of the war, he was afraid to stand a trial, but, having a considerable body of friends and allies to assist
him, raised a tumult amongst the Sabines, which delayed
the war. Neither was Poplicola wanting, not only to understand the grounds of the sedition, but to promote and
increase it, and he despatched emissaries with instructions
to Clausus, that Poplicola was assured of his goodness
and justice, and thought it indeed unworthy in any man,
however injured, to seek revenge upon his fellow-citizens; yet if he pleased, for his own security, to leave his
enemies and come to Rome, he should be received, both
in public and private, with the honor his merit deserved,
and their own glory required. Appius, seriously weigh-
ing the matter, came to the conclusion that it was the
best resource which necessity left him, and advising
with his friends, and they inviting again others in the
same manner, he came to Rome, bringing five thousand
families, with their wives and children; people of the
quietest and steadiest temper of all the Sabines. Poplicola, informed of their approach, received them with all
the kind offices of a friend, and admitted them at once to
the franchise, allotting to every one two acres of land by
the river Anio, but to Clausus twenty-five acres, and gave
him a place in the senate; a commencement of political power which he used so wisely, that he rose to the

highest reputation, was very influential, and left the Claudian house behind him, inferior to none in Rome.

The departure of these men rendered things quiet amongst the Sabines; yet the chief of the community would not suffer them to settle into peace, but resented that Clausus now, by turning deserter, should disappoint that revenge upon the Romans, which, while at home, he had unsuccessfully opposed. Coming with a great army, they sat down before Fidenæ, and placed an ambuscade of two thousand men near Rome, in wooded and hollow spots, with a design that some few horsemen, as soon as it was day, should go out and ravage the country, commanding them upon their approach to the town so to retreat as to draw the enemy into the ambush. Poplicola, however, soon advertised of these designs by deserters, disposed his forces to their respective charges. Postumius Balbus, his son-in-law, going out with three thousand men in the evening, was ordered to take the hills, under which the ambush lay, there to observe their motions; his colleague, Lucretius, attended with a body of the lightest and boldest men, was appointed to meet the Sabine horse; whilst he, with the rest of the army, encompassed the enemy. And a thick mist rising accidentally, Postumius, early in the morning, with shouts from the hills, assailed the ambuscade, Lucretius charged the light-horse, and Poplicola besieged the camp; so that on all sides defeat and ruin came upon the Sabines, and without any resistance the Romans killed them in their flight, their very hopes leading them to their death, for each division, presuming that the other was safe, gave up all thought of fighting or keeping their ground; and these quitting the camp to retire to the ambuscade, and the ambuscade flying to the camp, fugitives thus met fugitives, and found those from whom they expected succor

as much in need of succor from themselves. The nearness, however, of the city Fidenæ was the preservation
of the Sabines, especially those that fled from the camp;
those that could not gain the city either perished in the
field, or were taken prisoners. This victory, the Romans,
though usually ascribing such success to some god, attributed to the conduct of one captain; and it was observed
to be heard amongst the soldiers, that Poplicola had delivered their enemies lame and blind, and only not in
chains, to be despatched by their swords. From the spoil
and prisoners great wealth accrued to the people.

Poplicola, having completed his triumph, and bequeathed
the city to the care of the succeeding consuls, died; thus
closing a life which, so far as human life may be, had
been full of all that is good and honorable. The people,
as though they had not duly rewarded his deserts when
alive, but still were in his debt, decreed him a public
interment, every one contributing his *quadrans* towards the
charge; the women, besides, by private consent, mourned
a whole year, a signal mark of honor to his memory.
He was buried, by the people's desire, within the city, in
the part called Velia, where his posterity had likewise
privilege of burial; now, however, none of the family are
interred there, but the body is carried thither and set
down, and some one places a burning torch under it, and
immediately takes it away, as an attestation of the deceased's privilege, and his receding from his honor; after
which the body is removed.

COMPARISON OF POPLICOLA WITH SOLON.

THERE is something singular in the present parallel which has not occurred in any other of the lives; that the one should be the imitator of the other, and the other his best evidence. Upon the survey of Solon's sentence to Crœsus in favor of Tellus's happiness, it seems more applicable to Poplicola; for Tellus, whose virtuous life and dying well had gained him the name of the happiest man, yet was never celebrated in Solon's poems for a good man, nor have his children or any magistracy of his deserved a memorial; but Poplicola's life was the most eminent amongst the Romans, as well for the greatness of his virtue as his power, and also since his death many amongst the distinguished families, even in our days, the Poplicolæ, Messalæ, and Valerii, after a lapse of six hundred years, acknowledge him as the fountain of their honor. Besides, Tellus, though keeping his post and fighting like a valiant soldier, was yet slain by his enemies; but Poplicola, the better fortune, slew his, and saw his country victorious under his command. And his honors and triumphs brought him, which was Solon's ambition, to a happy end; the ejaculation which, in his verses against Mimnermus about the continuance of man's life, he himself made,

> Mourned let me die; and may I, when life ends,
> Occasion sighs and sorrows to my friends,

is evidence to Poplicola's happiness; his death did not

only draw tears from his friends and acquaintance, but was the object of universal regret and sorrow through the whole city; the women deplored his loss as that of a son, brother, or common father. "Wealth I would have," said Solon, "but wealth by wrong procure would not," because punishment would follow. But Poplicola's riches were not only justly his, but he spent them nobly in doing good to the distressed. So that if Solon was reputed the wisest man, we must allow Poplicola to be the happiest; for what Solon wished for as the greatest and most perfect good, this Poplicola had, and used and enjoyed to his death.

And as Solon may thus be said to have contributed to Poplicola's glory, so did also Poplicola to his, by his choice of him as his model in the formation of republican institutions; in reducing, for example, the excessive powers and assumption of the consulship. Several of his laws, indeed, he actually transferred to Rome, as his empowering the people to elect their officers, and allowing offenders the liberty of appealing to the people, as Solon did to the jurors. He did not, indeed, create a new senate, as Solon did, but augmented the old to almost double its number. The appointment of treasurers again, the quæstors, has a like origin; with the intent that the chief magistrate should not, if of good character, be withdrawn from greater matters; or, if bad, have the greater temptation to injustice, by holding both the government and treasury in his hands. The aversion to tyranny was stronger in Poplicola; any one who attempted usurpation could, by Solon's law, only be punished upon conviction; but Poplicola made it death before a trial. And though Solon justly gloried, that, when arbitrary power was absolutely offered to him by circumstances, and when his countrymen would have willingly seen him accept it, he yet declined it; still Poplicola merited no less, who, re-

ceiving a despotic command, converted it to a popular
office, and did not employ the whole legal power which
he held. We must allow, indeed, that Solon was before
Poplicola in observing that

> A people always minds its rulers best
> When it is neither humored nor oppressed.

The remission of debts was peculiar to Solon; it was
his great means for confirming the citizens' liberty; for a
mere law to give all men equal rights is but useless, if
the poor must sacrifice those rights to their debts, and,
in the very seats and sanctuaries of equality, the courts
of justice, the offices of state, and the public discussions,
be more than anywhere at the beck and bidding of the
rich. A yet more extraordinary success was, that, although
usually civil violence is caused by any remission of debts,
upon this one occasion this dangerous but powerful
remedy actually put an end to civil violence already existing, Solon's own private worth and reputation over-
balancing all the ordinary ill-repute and discredit of the
change. The beginning of his government was more
glorious, for he was entirely original, and followed no
man's example, and, without the aid of any ally, achieved
his most important measures by his own conduct; yet
the close of Poplicola's life was more happy and desirable,
for Solon saw the dissolution of his own commonwealth,
Poplicola's maintained the state in good order down to
the civil wars. Solon, leaving his laws, as soon as he had
made them, engraven in wood, but destitute of a defender,
departed from Athens; whilst Poplicola, remaining, both
in and out of office, labored to establish the government.
Solon, though he actually knew of Pisistratus's ambition,
yet was not able to suppress it, but had to yield to usurpation in its infancy; whereas Poplicola utterly sub-

verted and dissolved a potent monarchy, strongly settled
by long continuance; uniting thus to virtues equal to
those, and purposes identical with those of Solon, the good
fortune and the power that alone could make them effec-
tive.

In military exploits, Daimachus of Platæa will not even
allow Solon the conduct of the war against the Megarians, as was before intimated; but Poplicola was victorious
in the most important conflicts, both as a private soldier
and commander. In domestic politics, also, Solon, in play,
as it were, and by counterfeiting madness, induced the
enterprise against Salamis; whereas Poplicola, in the very
beginning, exposed himself to the greatest risk, took
arms against Tarquin, detected the conspiracy, and, being
principally concerned both in preventing the escape of and
afterwards punishing the traitors, not only expelled the
tyrants from the city, but extirpated their very hopes.
And as, in cases calling for contest and resistance and
manful opposition, he behaved with courage and resolution, so, in instances where peaceable language, persuasion, and concession were requisite, he was yet more to
be commended; and succeeded in gaining happily to reconciliation and friendship, Porsenna, a terrible and
invincible enemy. Some may, perhaps, object, that Solon
recovered Salamis, which they had lost, for the Athenians;
whereas Poplicola receded from part of what the Romans
were at that time possessed of; but judgment is to be
made of actions according to the times in which they
were performed. The conduct of a wise politician is ever
suited to the present posture of affairs; often by forego-
ing a part he saves the whole, and by yielding in a small
matter secures a greater; and so Poplicola, by restoring
what the Romans had lately usurped, saved their un-
doubted patrimony, and procured, moreover, the stores
of the enemy for those who were only too thankful to

secure their city. Permitting the decision of the controversy to his adversary, he not only got the victory, but
likewise what he himself would willingly have given to
purchase the victory, Porsenna putting an end to the
war, and leaving them all the provision of his camp, from
the sense of the virtue and gallant disposition of the
Romans which their consul had impressed upon him.

THEMISTOCLES.

THE birth of Themistocles was somewhat too obscure to do him honor. His father, Neocles, was not of the distinguished people of Athens, but of the township of Phrearrhi, and of the tribe Leontis; and by his mother's side, as it is reported, he was base-born.

> I am not of the noble Grecian race,
> I'm poor Abrotonon, and born in Thrace;
> Let the Greek women scorn me, if they please,
> I was the mother of Themistocles.

Yet Phanias writes that the mother of Themistocles was not of Thrace, but of Caria, and that her name was not Abrotonon, but Euterpe; and Neanthes adds farther that she was of Halicarnassus in Caria. And, as illegitimate children, including those that were of the half-blood or had but one parent an Athenian, had to attend at the Cynosarges (a wrestling-place outside the gates, dedicated to Hercules, who was also of half-blood amongst the gods, having had a mortal woman for his mother), Themistocles persuaded several of the young men of high birth to accompany him to anoint and exercise themselves together at Cynosarges; an ingenious device for destroying the distinction between the noble and the base-born, and between those of the whole and those of the half-

blood of Athens.   However, it is certain that he was related to the house of the Lycomedæ; for Simonides
records, that he rebuilt the chapel of Phlya, belonging to
that family, and beautified it with pictures and other
ornaments, after it had been burnt by the Persians.

It is confessed by all that from his youth he was of a
vehement and impetuous nature, of a quick apprehension, and a strong and aspiring bent for action and great
affairs.   The holidays and intervals in his studies he did
not spend in play or idleness, as other children, but would
be always inventing or arranging some oration or declama-
tion to himself, the subject of which was generally the
excusing or accusing his companions, so that his master
would often say to him, "You, my boy, will be nothing
small, but great one way or other, for good or else for
bad."   He received reluctantly and carelessly instructions
given him to improve his manners and behavior, or to
teach him any pleasing or graceful accomplishment, but
whatever was said to improve him in sagacity, or in
management of affairs, he would give attention to, beyond one of his years, from confidence in his natural
capacities for such things.   And thus afterwards, when
in company where people engaged themselves in what
are commonly thought the liberal and elegant amuse-
ments, he was obliged to defend himself against the
observations of those who considered themselves highly
accomplished, by the somewhat arrogant retort, that he
certainly could not make use of any stringed instrument,
could only, were a small and obscure city put into his
hands, make it great and glorious.   Notwithstanding
this, Stesimbrotus says that Themistocles was a hearer of
Anaxagoras, and that he studied natural philosophy under Melissus, contrary to chronology; for Melissus commanded the Samians in their siege by Pericles, who was
much Themistocles's junior; and with Pericles, also, Anaxa-

goras was intimate. They, therefore, might rather be credited, who report, that Themistocles was an admirer of Mnesiphilus the Phrearrhian, who was neither rhetorician nor natural philosopher, but a professor of that which was then called wisdom, consisting in a sort of political shrewdness and practical sagacity, which had begun and continued, almost like a sect of philosophy, from Solon; but those who came afterwards, and mixed it with pleadings and legal artifices, and transformed the practical part of it into a mere art of speaking and an exercise of words, were generally called sophists. Themistocles resorted to Mnesiphilus when he had already embarked in politics.

In the first essays of his youth he was not regular nor happily balanced; he allowed himself to follow mere natural character, which, without the control of reason and instruction, is apt to hurry, upon either side, into sudden and violent courses, and very often to break away and determine upon the worst; as he afterwards owned himself, saying, that the wildest colts make the best horses, if they only get properly trained and broken in. But those who upon this fasten stories of their own invention, as of his being disowned by his father, and that his mother died for grief of her son's ill fame, certainly calumniate him; and there are others who relate, on the contrary, how that to deter him from public business, and to let him see how the vulgar behave themselves towards their leaders when they have at last no farther use of them, his father showed him the old galleys as they lay forsaken and cast about upon the sea-shore.

Yet it is evident that his mind was early imbued with the keenest interest in public affairs, and the most passionate ambition for distinction. Eager from the first to obtain the highest place, he unhesitatingly accepted the hatred of the most powerful and influential leaders in the city, but more especially of Aristides, the son of Lysimachus, who always opposed him.   And yet all this great enmity between them arose, it appears, from a very boyish occasion, both being attached to the beautiful Stesilaus of Ceos, as Ariston the philosopher tells us; ever after which, they took opposite sides, and were rivals in politics.   Not but that the incompatibility of their lives and manners may seem to have increased the difference, for Aristides was of a mild nature, and of a nobler sort of character, and, in public matters, acting always with a view, not to glory or popularity, but to the best interests of the state consistently with safety and honesty, he was often forced to oppose Themistocles, and interfere against the increase of his influence, seeing him stirring up the people to all kinds of enterprises, and introducing various innovations.   For it is said that Themistocles was so transported with the thoughts of glory, and so inflamed with the passion for great actions, that, though he was still young when the battle of Marathon was fought against the Persians, upon the skilful conduct of the general, Miltiades, being everywhere talked about, he was observed to be thoughtful, and reserved, alone by himself; he passed the nights without sleep, and avoided all his usual places of recreation, and to those who wondered at the change, and inquired the reason of it, he gave the answer, that "the trophy of Miltiades would not let him sleep."   And when others were of opinion that the battle of Marathon would be an end to the war, Themistocles thought that it was but the beginning of far greater conflicts, and for these, to the benefit of all Greece, he kept himself in continual readiness, and his city also in proper training, foreseeing from far before what would happen.

And, first of all, the Athenians being accustomed to divide amongst themselves the revenue proceeding

from the silver mines at Laurium, he was the only man
that durst propose to the people that this distribution
should cease, and that with the money ships should be
built to make war against the Æginetans, who were the
most flourishing people in all Greece, and by the number of their ships held the sovereignty of the sea; and
Themistocles thus was more easily able to persuade them,
avoiding all mention of danger from Darius or the Persians, who were at a great distance, and their coming very
uncertain, and at that time not much to be feared; but,
by a seasonable employment of the emulation and anger
felt by the Athenians against the Æginetans, he induced
them to preparation. So that with this money an hundred ships were built, with which they afterwards fought
against Xerxes. And, henceforward, little by little, turning and drawing the city down towards the sea, in the
belief, that, whereas by land they were not a fit match
for their next neighbors, with their ships they might be
able to repel the Persians and command Greece, thus, as
Plato says, from steady soldiers he turned them into mariners and seamen tossed about the sea, and gave occasion
for the reproach against him, that he took away from the
Athenians the spear and the shield, and bound them to
the bench and the oar. These measures he carried in the
assembly, against the opposition, as Stesimbrotus relates,
of Miltiades; and whether or no he hereby injured the
purity and true balance of government, may be a question for philosophers, but that the deliverance of Greece
came at that time from the sea, and that these galleys
restored Athens again after it was destroyed, were others
wanting, Xerxes himself would be sufficient evidence,
who, though his land-forces were still entire, after his defeat at sea, fled away, and thought himself no longer able
to encounter the Greeks; and, as it seems to me, left Mar-

donius behind him, not out of any hopes he could have to
bring them into subjection, but to hinder them from pursuing him.

Themistocles is said to have been eager in the acquisi-
tion of riches, according to some, that he might be the
more liberal ; for loving to sacrifice often, and to be
splendid in his entertainment of strangers, he required a
plentiful revenue ; yet he is accused by others of having
been parsimonious and sordid to that degree that he
would sell provisions which were sent to him as a present.
He desired Diphilides, who was a breeder of horses, to
give him a colt, and when he refused it, threatened that
in a short time he would turn his house into a wooden *
horse, intimating that he would stir up dispute and litiga-
tion between him and some of his relations.

He went beyond all men in the passion for distinction.
When he was still young and unknown in the world, he
entreated Epicles of Hermione, who had a good hand at
the lute and was much sought after by the Athenians, to
come and practise at home with him, being ambitious of
having people inquire after his house and frequent his
company. When he came to the Olympic games, and
was so splendid in his equipage and entertainments, in his
rich tents and furniture, that he strove to outdo Cimon,
he displeased the Greeks, who thought that such magnificence might be allowed in one who was a young man and
of a great family but was a great piece of insolence in
one as yet undistinguished, and without title or means for
making any such display. In a dramatic contest, the play
he paid for won the prize, which was then a matter that
excited much emulation ; he put up a tablet in record of
it, with the inscription, " Themistocles of Phrearrhi was
at the charge of it; Phrynichus made it ; Adimantus was

* Full of people ready for fighting, like the Trojan horse.

archon." He was well liked by the common people, would salute every particular citizen by his own name, and always show himself a just judge in questions of business between private men; he said to Simonides, the poet of Ceos, who desired something of him, when he was commander of the army, that was not reasonable, " Simonides, you would be no good poet if you wrote false measure, nor should I be a good magistrate if for favor I made false law." And at another time, laughing at Simonides, he said, that he was a man of little judgment to speak against the Corinthians, who were inhabitants of a great city, and to have his own picture drawn so often, having so ill-looking a face.

Gradually growing to be great, and winning the favor of the people, he at last gained the day with his faction over that of Aristides, and procured his banishment by ostracism. When the king of Persia was now advancing against Greece, and the Athenians were in consultation who should be general, and many withdrew themselves of their own accord, being terrified with the greatness of the danger, there was one Epicydes, a popular speaker, son to Euphemides, a man of an eloquent tongue, but of a faint heart, and a slave to riches, who was desirous of the command, and was looked upon to be in a fair way to carry it by the number of votes; but Themistocles, fearing that, if the command should fall into such hands, all would be lost, bought off Epicydes and his pretensions, it is said, for a sum of money.

When the king of Persia sent messengers into Greece, with an interpreter, to demand earth and water, as an acknowledgment of subjection, Themistocles, by the consent of the people, seized upon the interpreter, and put him to death, for presuming to publish the barbarian orders and decrees in the Greek language; this is one of the actions he is commended for, as also for what he did to Arth-

mius of Zelea, who brought gold from the king of Persia
to corrupt the Greeks, and was, by an order from Themistocles, degraded and disfranchised, he and his children
and his posterity; but that which most of all redounded
to his credit was, that he put an end to all the civil wars
of Greece, composed their differences, and persuaded
them to lay aside all enmity during the war with the
Persians; and in this great work, Chileus the Arcadian
was, it is said, of great assistance to him.

Having taken upon himself the command of the Athenian forces, he immediately endeavored to persuade the
citizens to leave the city, and to embark upon their galleys, and meet with the Persians at a great distance from
Greece; but many being against this, he led a large
force, together with the Lacedæmonians, into Tempe, that
in this pass they might maintain the safety of Thessaly,
which had not as yet declared for the king; but when
they returned without performing any thing, and it was
known that not only the Thessalians, but all as far as
Bœotia, was going over to Xerxes, then the Athenians
more willingly hearkened to the advice of Themistocles
to fight by sea, and sent him with a fleet to guard the
straits of Artemisium.

When the contingents met here, the Greeks would
have the Lacedæmonians to command, and Eurybiades to
be their admiral; but the Athenians, who surpassed all
the rest together in number of vessels, would not submit
to come after any other, till Themistocles, perceiving the
danger of this contest, yielded his own command to Eurybiades, and got the Athenians to submit, extenuating
the loss by persuading them, that if in this war they behaved themselves like men, he would answer for it after
that, that the Greeks, of their own will, would submit to
their command.   And by this moderation of his, it is evident that he was the chief means of the deliverance of

Greece, and gained the Athenians the glory of alike sur-
passing their enemies in valor, and their confederates in
wisdom.

As soon as the Persian armada arrived at Aphetæ, Eurybiades was astonished to see such a vast number of
vessels before him, and, being informed that two hundred
more were sailing round behind the island of Sciathus, he
immediately determined to retire farther into Greece, and
to sail back into some part of Peloponnesus, where their
land army and their fleet might join, for he looked upon
the Persian forces to be altogether unassailable by sea.
But the Eubœans, fearing that the Greeks would forsake
them, and leave them to the mercy of the enemy, sent
Pelagon to confer privately with Themistocles, taking
with him a good sum of money, which, as Herodotus
reports, he accepted and gave to Eurybiades. In this
affair none of his own countrymen opposed him so much
as Architeles, captain of the sacred galley, who, having no
money to supply his seamen, was eager to go home; but
Themistocles so incensed the Athenians against him, that
they set upon him and left him not so much as his supper, at which Architeles was much surprised, and took it
very ill; but Themistocles immediately sent him in a
chest a service of provisions, and at the bottom of it a
talent of silver, desiring him to sup to-night, and to-mor-
row provide for his seamen; if not, he would report it
amongst the Athenians that he had received money from
the enemy. So Phanias the Lesbian tells the story.

Though the fights between the Greeks and Persians in
the straits of Eubœa were not so important as to make
any final decision of the war, yet the experience which
the Greeks obtained in them was of great advantage;
for thus, by actual trial and in real danger, they found
out, that neither number of ships, nor riches and ornaments, nor boasting shouts, nor barbarous songs of vic-

tory, were any way terrible to men that knew how to
fight, and were resolved to come hand to hand with their
enemies; these things they were to despise, and to come
up close and grapple with their foes. This, Pindar appears to have seen, and says justly enough of the fight at
Artemisium, that

> There the sons of Athens set
> The stone that freedom stands on yet.

For the first step towards victory undoubtedly is to gain
courage. Artemisium is in Eubœa, beyond the city of
Histiæa, a sea-beach open to the north; most nearly opposite to it stands Olizon, in the country which formerly
was under Philoctetes; there is a small temple there,
dedicated to Diana, surnamed of the Dawn, and trees
about it, around which again stand pillars of white marble; and if you rub them with your hand, they send forth
both the smell and color of saffron. On one of the pillars these verses are engraved, —

> With numerous tribes from Asia's regions brought
> The sons of Athens on these waters fought;
> Erecting. after they had quelled the Mede,
> To Artemis this record of the deed.

There is a place still to be seen upon this shore, where, in
the middle of a great heap of sand, they take out from
the bottom a dark powder like ashes, or something that
has passed the fire; and here, it is supposed, the shipwrecks and bodies of the dead were burnt.

But when news came from Thermopylæ to Artemisium,
informing them that king Leonidas was slain, and that
Xerxes had made himself master of all the passages by
land, they returned back to the interior of Greece, the
Athenians having the command of the rear, the place of

honor and danger, and much elated by what had been done.

As Themistocles sailed along the coast, he took notice of the harbors and fit places for the enemies' ships to come to land at, and engraved large letters in such stones as he found there by chance, as also in others which he set up on purpose near to the landing-places, or where they were to water; in which inscriptions he called upon the Ionians to forsake the Medes, if it were possible, and come over to the Greeks, who were their proper founders and fathers, and were now hazarding all for their liberties; but, if this could not be done, at any rate to impede and disturb the Persians in all engagements. He hoped that these writings would prevail with the Ionians to revolt, or raise some trouble by making their fidelity doubtful to the Persians.

Now, though Xerxes had already passed through Doris and invaded the country of Phocis, and was burning and destroying the cities of the Phocians, yet the Greeks sent them no relief; and, though the Athenians earnestly desired them to meet the Persians in Bœotia, before they could come into Attica, as they themselves had come forward by sea at Artemisium, they gave no ear to their request, being wholly intent upon Peloponnesus, and resolved to gather all their forces together within the Isthmus, and to build a wall from sea to sea in that narrow neck of land; so that the Athenians were enraged to see themselves betrayed, and at the same time afflicted and dejected at their own destitution. For to fight alone against such a numerous army was to no purpose, and the only expedient now left them was to leave their city and cling to their ships; which the people were very unwilling to submit to, imagining that it would signify little now to gain a victory, and not understanding how there could be deliverance any longer after they had once forsaken the temples of their gods and exposed the tombs and monuments of their ancestors to the fury of their enemies.

Themistocles, being at a loss, and not able to draw the people over to his opinion by any human reason, set his machines to work, as in a theatre, and employed prodigies and oracles. The serpent of Minerva, kept in the inner part of her temple, disappeared; the priests gave it out to the people that the offerings which were set for it were found untouched, and declared, by the suggestion of Themistocles, that the goddess had left the city, and taken her flight before them towards the sea. And he often urged them with the oracle* which bade them trust to walls of wood, showing them that walls of wood could signify nothing else but ships; and that the island of Salamis was termed in it, not miserable or unhappy, but had the epithet of divine, for that it should one day be associated with a great good fortune of the Greeks. At length his opinion prevailed, and he obtained a decree that the city should be committed to the protection of Minerva, "queen of Athens;" that they who were of age to bear arms should embark, and that each should see to sending away his children, women, and slaves where he could. This decree being confirmed, most of the Athenians removed their parents, wives, and children to Trœzen, where they were received with eager good-will by the Trœzenians, who passed a vote that they should be maintained at the public charge, by a daily payment of two obols to every one,

---

* "While all things else are taken," said the oracle, "within the boundary of Cecrops and the covert of divine Cithaeron, Zeus grants to Athena that the wall of wood alone shall remain uncaptured; that shall help thee and thy children. Stay not for horsemen and an host of men on foot, coming from the mainland; retire turning thy back; one day yet thou shalt show thy face. O divine Salamis, but thou shalt slay children of women, either at the scattering of Demeter or at the gathering."

and leave be given to the children to gather fruit where they pleased, and schoolmasters paid to instruct them. This vote was proposed by Nicagoras.

There was no public treasure at that time in Athens; but the council of Areopagus, as Aristotle says, distributed to every one that served, eight drachmas, which was a great help to the manning of the fleet; but Clidemus ascribes this also to the art of Themistocles. When the Athenians were on their way down to the haven of Piræus, the shield with the head of Medusa was missing; and he, under the pretext of searching for it, ransacked all places, and found among their goods considerable sums of money concealed, which he applied to the public use; and with this the soldiers and seamen were well provided for their voyage.

When the whole city of Athens were going on board, it afforded a spectacle worthy of pity alike and admiration, to see them thus send away their fathers and children before them, and, unmoved with their cries and tears, pass over into the island. But that which stirred compassion most of all was, that many old men, by reason of their great age, were left behind; and even the tame domestic animals could not be seen without some pity, running about the town and howling, as desirous to be carried along with their masters that had kept them; among which it is reported that Xanthippus, the father of Pericles, had a dog that would not endure to stay behind, but leaped into the sea, and swam along by the galley's side till he came to the island of Salamis, where he fainted away and died, and that spot in the island, which is still called the Dog's Grave, is said to be his.

Among the great actions of Themistocles at this crisis, the recall of Aristides was not the least, for, before the war, he had been ostracized by the party which Themistocles headed, and was in banishment; but now, percei-

ving that the people regretted his absence, and were fearful that he might go over to the Persians to revenge himself, and thereby ruin the affairs of Greece, Themistocles
proposed a decree that those who were banished for a
time might return again, to give assistance by word and
deed to the cause of Greece with the rest of their fellow-
citizens.

Eurybiades, by reason of the greatness of Sparta, was
admiral of the Greek fleet, but yet was faint-hearted in
time of danger, and willing to weigh anchor and set sail
for the isthmus of Corinth, near which the land army lay
encamped ; which Themistocles resisted ; and this was the
occasion of the well-known words, when Eurybiades, to
check his impatience, told him that at the Olympic
games they that start up before the rest are lashed ;
"And they," replied Themistocles, "that are left behind
are not crowned." Again, Eurybiades lifting up his staff
as if he were going to strike, Themistocles said, "Strike
if you will, but hear ;" Eurybiades, wondering much at
his moderation, desired him to speak, and Themistocles
now brought him to a better understanding. And when
one who stood by him told him that it did not become
those who had neither city nor house to lose, to persuade
others to relinquish their habitations and forsake their
countries, Themistocles gave this reply: "We have indeed left our houses and our walls, base fellow, not
thinking it fit to become slaves for the sake of things
that have no life nor soul; and yet our city is the
greatest of all Greece, consisting of two hundred galleys,
which are here to defend you, if you please; but if you
run away and betray us, as you did once before, the
Greeks shall soon hear news of the Athenians possessing
as fair a country, and as large and free a city, as that they
have lost." These expressions of Themistocles made Eurybiades suspect that if he retreated the Athenians would

fall off from him. When one of Eretria began to oppose him, he said, "Have you any thing to say of war, that are like an ink-fish? you have a sword, but no heart." * Some say that while Themistocles was thus speaking things upon the deck, an owl was seen flying to the right hand of the fleet, which came and sate upon the top of the mast; and this happy omen so far disposed the Greeks to follow his advice, that they presently prepared to fight. Yet, when the enemy's fleet was arrived at the haven of Phalerum, upon the coast of Attica, and with the number of their ships concealed all the shore, and when they saw the king himself in person come down with his land army to the sea-side, with all his forces united, then the good counsel of Themistocles was soon forgotten, and the Peloponnesians cast their eyes again towards the isthmus, and took it very ill if any one spoke against their returning home; and, resolving to depart that night, the pilots had order what course to steer.

Themistocles, in great distress that the Greeks should retire, and lose the advantage of the narrow seas and strait passage, and slip home every one to his own city, considered with himself, and contrived that stratagem that was carried out by Sicinnus. This Sicinnus was a Persian captive, but a great lover of Themistocles, and the attendant of his children. Upon this occasion, he sent him privately to Xerxes, commanding him to tell the king, that Themistocles, the admiral of the Athenians, having espoused his interest, wished to be the first to inform him that the Greeks were ready to make their escape, and that he counselled him to hinder their flight, to set upon them while they were in this confusion and at a distance from their land army, and hereby destroy all their forces by sea. Xerxes was very joyful at this

---

* The *Teuthis*, loligo, or cuttle-fish, is said to have a bone or carti- lage shaped like a sword, and was conceived to have no heart.

message, and received it as from one who wished him all
that was good, and immediately issued instructions to the
commanders of his ships. that they should instantly set
out with two hundred galleys to encompass all the islands,
and enclose all the straits and passages, that none of the
Greeks might escape, and that they should afterwards
follow with the rest of their fleet at leisure. This being
done, Aristides, the son of Lysimachus, was the first man
that perceived it, and went to the tent of Themistocles,
not out of any friendship, for he had been formerly banished by his means, as has been related, but to inform
him how they were encompassed by their enemies. Themistocles, knowing the generosity of Aristides, and much
struck by his visit at that time, imparted to him all that
he had transacted by Sicinnus, and entreated him, that, as
he would be more readily believed among the Greeks, he
would make use of his credit to help to induce them to
stay and fight their enemies in the narrow seas. Aristides applauded Themistocles, and went to the other commanders and captains of the galleys, and encouraged
them to engage ; yet they did not perfectly assent to
him, till a galley of Tenos, which deserted from the Persians, of which Panætius was commander, came in, while
they were still doubting, and confirmed the news that
all the straits and passages were beset ; and then their
rage and fury, as well as their necessity. provoked them
all to fight.

As soon as it was day, Xerxes placed himself high up,
to view his fleet, and how it was set in order. Phano-
demus says, he sat upon a promontory above the temple
of Hercules. where the coast of Attica is separated from
the island by a narrow channel ; but Acestodorus writes,
that it was in the confines of Megara, upon those hills
which are called the Horns, where he sat in a chair of
gold. with many secretaries about him to write down all
that was done in the fight.

When Themistocles was about to sacrifice, close to the admiral's galley, there were three prisoners brought to him, fine looking men, and richly dressed in ornamented clothing and gold, said to be the children of Artayctes and Sandauce, sister to Xerxes. As soon as the prophet Euphrantides saw them, and observed that at the same time the fire blazed out from the offerings with a more than ordinary flame, and that a man sneezed on the right, which was an intimation of a fortunate event, he took Themistocles by the hand, and bade him consecrate the three young men for sacrifice, and offer them up with prayers for victory to Bacchus the Devourer: so should the Greeks not only save themselves, but also obtain victory. Themistocles was much disturbed at this strange and terrible prophecy, but the common people, who, in any difficult crisis and great exigency, ever look for relief rather to strange and extravagant than to reasonable means, calling upon Bacchus with one voice, led the captives to the altar, and compelled the execution of the sacrifice as the prophet had commanded. This is reported by Phanias the Lesbian, a philosopher well read in history.

The number of the enemy's ships the poet Æschylus gives in his tragedy called the Persians, as on his certain knowledge, in the following words —

> Xerxes, I know, did into battle lead
> One thousand ships; of more than usual speed
> Seven and two hundred. So is it agreed.

The Athenians had a hundred and eighty; in every ship eighteen men fought upon the deck, four of whom were archers and the rest men-at-arms.

As Themistocles had fixed upon the most advantageous place, so, with no less sagacity, he chose the best time of fighting; for he would not run the prows of his galleys against the Persians, nor begin the fight till the time of

day was come, when there regularly blows in a fresh
breeze from the open sea, and brings in with it a strong
swell into the channel; which was no inconvenience to
the Greek ships, which were low-built, and little above the
water, but did much hurt to the Persians, which had high
sterns and lofty decks, and were heavy and cumbrous in
their movements, as it presented them broadside to the
quick charges of the Greeks, who kept their eyes upon
the motions of Themistocles, as their best example, and
more particularly because, opposed to his ship, Ariamenes,
admiral to Xerxes, a brave man, and by far the best and
worthiest of the king's brothers, was seen throwing darts
and shooting arrows from his huge galley, as from the
walls of a castle. Aminias the Decelean and Sosicles the
Pedian, who sailed in the same vessel, upon the ships meeting stem to stem, and transfixing each the other with their
brazen prows, so that they were fastened together, when
Ariamenes attempted to board theirs, ran at him with their
pikes, and thrust him into the sea; his body, as it floated
amongst other shipwrecks, was known to Artemisia, and
carried to Xerxes.

It is reported, that, in the middle of the fight, a great
flame rose into the air above the city of Eleusis, and that
sounds and voices were heard through all the Thriasian
plain, as far as the sea, sounding like a number of men
accompanying and escorting the mystic Iacchus, and that
a mist seemed to form and rise from the place from whence
the sounds came, and, passing forward, fell upon the galleys. Others believed that they saw apparitions, in the
shape of armed men, reaching out their hands from the
island of Ægina before the Grecian galleys; and supposed
they were the Æacidæ, whom they had invoked to their
aid before the battle. The first man that took a ship was
Lycomedes the Athenian, captain of a galley, who cut
down its ensign, and dedicated it to Apollo the Laurel-
crowned. And as the Persians fought in a narrow arm

of the sea, and could bring but part of their fleet to fight, and fell foul of one another, the Greeks thus equalled them in strength, and fought with them till the evening, forced them back, and obtained, as says Simonides, that noble and famous victory, than which neither amongst the Greeks nor barbarians was ever known more glorious exploit on the seas; by the joint valor, indeed, and zeal of all who fought, but by the wisdom and sagacity of Themistocles.

After this sea-fight, Xerxes, enraged at his ill-fortune, attempted, by casting great heaps of earth and stones into the sea, to stop up the channel and to make a dam, upon which he might lead his land-forces over into the island of Salamis.

Themistocles, being desirous to try the opinion of Aristides, told him that he proposed to set sail for the Hellespont, to break the bridge of ships, so as to shut up, he said, Asia a prisoner within Europe; but Aristides, disliking the design, said, "We have hitherto fought with an enemy who has regarded little else but his pleasure and luxury; but if we shut him up within Greece, and drive him to necessity, he that is master of such great forces will no longer sit quietly with an umbrella of gold over his head, looking upon the fight for his pleasure; but in such a strait will attempt all things; he will be resolute, and appear himself in person upon all occasions, he will soon correct his errors, and supply what he has formerly omitted through remissness, and will be better advised in all things. Therefore, it is noways our interest, Themistocles," he said, "to take away the bridge that is already made, but rather to build another, if it were possible, that he might make his retreat with the more expedition." To which Themistocles answered, "If this be requisite, we must immediately use all diligence, art, and industry, to rid ourselves of him as soon as may be;" and to this pur-

pose he found out among the captives one of the king of
Persia's eunuchs, named Arnaces, whom he sent to the
king, to inform him that the Greeks, being now victorious
by sea, had decreed to sail to the Hellespont, where the
boats were fastened together, and destroy the bridge;
but that Themistocles, being concerned for the king, revealed this to him, that he might hasten towards the
Asiatic seas, and pass over into his own dominions; and
in the mean time would cause delays, and hinder the confederates from pursuing him. Xerxes no sooner heard
this, but, being very much terrified, he proceeded to retreat out of Greece with all speed. The prudence of
Themistocles and Aristides in this was afterwards more
fully understood at the battle of Platæa, where Mardo-
nius, with a very small fraction of the forces of Xerxes,
put the Greeks in danger of losing all.

Herodotus writes, that, of all the cities of Greece,
Ægina was held to have performed the best service in
the war; while all single men yielded to Themistocles,
though, out of envy, unwillingly; and when they returned to the entrance of Peloponnesus, where the several commanders delivered their suffrages at the altar, to
determine who was most worthy, every one gave the
first vote for himself and the second for Themistocles.
The Lacedæmonians carried him with them to Sparta,
where, giving the rewards of valor to Eurybiades, and of
wisdom and conduct to Themistocles, they crowned him
with olive, presented him with the best chariot in the
city, and sent three hundred young men to accompany
him to the confines of their country. And at the next
Olympic games, when Themistocles entered the course,
the spectators took no farther notice of those who were
contesting the prizes, but spent the whole day in looking
upon him, showing him to the strangers, admiring him,
and applauding him by clapping their hands, and other

expressions of joy, so that he himself, much gratified, confessed to his friends that he then reaped the fruit of all his labors for the Greeks.

He was, indeed, by nature, a great lover of honor, as is evident from the anecdotes recorded of him. When chosen admiral by the Athenians, he would not quite conclude any single matter of business, either public or private, but deferred all till the day they were to set sail, that, by despatching a great quantity of business all at once, and having to meet a great variety of people, he might make an appearance of greatness and power. Viewing the dead bodies cast up by the sea, he perceived bracelets and necklaces of gold about them, yet passed on, only showing them to a friend that followed him, saying, "Take you these things, for you are not Themistocles." He said to Antiphates, a handsome young man, who had formerly avoided, but now in his glory courted him, "Time, young man, has taught us both a lesson." He said that the Athenians did not honor him or admire him, but made, as it were, a sort of plane-tree of him; sheltered themselves under him in bad weather, and, as soon as it was fine, plucked his leaves and cut his branches. When the Seriphian told him that he had not obtained this honor by himself, but by the greatness of his city, he replied, "You speak truth; I should never have been famous if I had been of Seriphus; nor you, had you been of Athens." When another of the generals, who thought he had performed considerable service for the Athenians, boastingly compared his actions with those of Themistocles, he told him that once upon a time the Day after the Festival found fault with the Festival: "On you there is nothing but hurry and trouble and preparation, but, when I come, everybody sits down quietly and enjoys himself;" which the Festival admitted was true, but "if I had not come first, you would not have come at

all." "Even so," he said, "if Themistocles had not come
before, where had you been now?" Laughing at his
own son, who got his mother, and, by his mother's means,
his father also, to indulge him, he told him that he had
the most power of any one in Greece: "For the Athenians
command the rest of Greece, I command the Athenians,
your mother commands me, and you command your
mother." Loving to be singular in all things, when he
had land to sell, he ordered the crier to give notice that
there were good neighbors near it. Of two who made
love to his daughter, he preferred the man of worth to
the one who was rich, saying he desired a man without
riches, rather than riches without a man. Such was the
character of his sayings.

After these things, he began to rebuild and fortify the
city of Athens, bribing, as Theopompus reports, the Lacedæmonian ephors not to be against it, but, as most relate
it, overreaching and deceiving them. For, under pretext of an embassy, he went to Sparta, where, upon the
Lacedæmonians charging him with rebuilding the walls,
and Poliarchus coming on purpose from Ægina to de-
nounce it, he denied the fact, bidding them to send people to Athens to see whether it were so or no; by which
delay he got time for the building of the wall, and also
placed these ambassadors in the hands of his countrymen
as hostages for him; and so, when the Lacedæmonians
knew the truth, they did him no hurt, but, suppressing
all display of their anger for the present, sent him
away.

Next he proceeded to establish the harbor of Piræus,
observing the great natural advantages of the locality,
and desirous to unite the whole city with the sea, and to
reverse, in a manner, the policy of ancient Athenian
kings, who, endeavoring to withdraw their subjects from
the sea, and to accustom them to live, not by sailing

about, but by planting and tilling the earth, spread the
story of the dispute between Minerva and Neptune for
the sovereignty of Athens, in which Minerva, by producing to the judges an olive tree, was declared to have
won; whereas Themistocles did not only knead up, as
Aristophanes says, the port and the city into one, but
made the city absolutely the dependant and the adjunct
of the port, and the land of the sea, which increased the
power and confidence of the people against the nobility;
the authority coming into the hands of sailors and boat-
swains and pilots. Thus it was one of the orders of the
thirty tyrants, that the hustings in the assembly, which
had faced towards the sea, should be turned round towards the land; implying their opinion that the empire
by sea had been the origin of the democracy, and that
the farming population were not so much opposed to
oligarchy.

Themistocles, however, formed yet higher designs with
a view to naval supremacy. For, after the departure of
Xerxes, when the Grecian fleet was arrived at Pagasæ,
where they wintered, Themistocles, in a public oration
to the people of Athens, told them that he had a design to perform something that would tend greatly to
their interests and safety, but was of such a nature, that
it could not be made generally public. The Athenians
ordered him to impart it to Aristides only; and, if he
approved of it, to put it in practice. And when Themistocles had discovered to him that his design was to burn
the Grecian fleet in the haven of Pagasæ, Aristides, coming out to the people, gave this report of the stratagem
contrived by Themistocles, that no proposal could be
more politic, or more dishonorable; on which the Athenians commanded Themistocles to think no farther of it.

When the Lacedæmonians proposed, at the general

council of the Amphictyonians, that the representatives
of those cities which were not in the league, nor had
fought against the Persians, should be excluded, Themistocles, fearing that, the Thessalians, with those of
Thebes, Argos, and others, being thrown out of the council, the Lacedæmonians would become wholly masters of
the votes, and do what they pleased, supported the deputies of the cities, and prevailed with the members then
sitting to alter their opinion in this point, showing them
that there were but one and thirty cities which had par-
taken in the war, and that most of these, also, were very
small; how intolerable would it be, if the rest of Greece
should be excluded, and the general council should
come to be ruled by two or three great cities. By this,
chiefly, he incurred the displeasure of the Lacedæmonians,
whose honors and favors were now shown to Cimon, with
a view to making him the opponent of the state policy
of Themistocles.

He was also burdensome to the confederates, sailing
about the islands and collecting money from them. Herodotus says, that, requiring money of those of the island
of Andros, he told them that he had brought with him
two goddesses, Persuasion and Force; and they answered
him that they had also two great goddesses, which prohi-
bited them from giving him any money, Poverty and
Impossibility. Timocreon, the Rhodian poet, reprehends
him somewhat bitterly for being wrought upon by money
to let some who were banished return, while abandoning
himself, who was his guest and friend. The verses are
these: —

Pausanias you may praise, and Xanthippus he be for,
For Leutychidas, a third; Aristides, I proclaim,
From the sacred Athens came,
The one true man of all; for Themistocles Latona doth abhor,

The liar, traitor, cheat, who, to gain his filthy pay,
Timocreon, his friend, neglected to restore
To his native Rhodian shore ;
Three silver talents took, and departed (curses with him) on his way,

Restoring people here, expelling there, and killing here,
Filling evermore his purse : and at the Isthmus gave a treat,
To be laughed at, of cold meat,
Which they ate, and prayed the gods some one else might give the
    feast another year.

But after the sentence and banishment of Themistocles,
Timocreon reviles him yet more immoderately and wildly
in a poem which begins thus : —

    Unto all the Greeks repair
    O Muse, and tell these verses there,
    As is fitting and is fair.

The story is, that it was put to the question whether
Timocreon should be banished for siding with the Persians, and Themistocles gave his vote against him. So
when Themistocles was accused of intriguing with the
Medes, Timocreon made these lines upon him : —

So now Timocreon, indeed, is not the sole friend of the Mede,
There are some knaves besides ; nor is it only mine that fails,
But other foxes have lost tails. —

When the citizens of Athens began to listen willingly to
those who traduced and reproached him, he was forced,
with somewhat obnoxious frequency, to put them in mind
of the great services he had performed, and ask those
who were offended with him whether they were weary
with receiving benefits often from the same person, so
rendering himself more odious. And he yet more provoked the people by building a temple to Diana with
the epithet of Aristobule, or Diana of Best Counsel ;
intimating thereby, that he had given the best counsel,

not only to the Athenians, but to all Greece.   He built
this temple near his own house, in the district called
Melite, where now the public officers carry out the bodies
of such as are executed, and throw the halters and
clothes of those that are strangled or otherwise put to
death.   There is to this day a small figure of Themistocles in the temple of Diana of Best Counsel, which
represents him to be a person, not only of a noble mind,
but also of a most heroic aspect.   At length the Athenians banished him, making use of the ostracism to humble his eminence and authority, as they ordinarily did with
all whom they thought too powerful, or, by their greatness,
disproportionable to the equality thought requisite in a
popular government.   For the ostracism was instituted,
not so much to punish the offender, as to mitigate and
pacify the violence of the envious, who delighted to humble eminent men, and who, by fixing this disgrace upon
them, might vent some part of their rancor.

Themistocles being banished from Athens, while he
stayed at Argos the detection of Pausanias happened,
which gave such advantage to his enemies, that Leobotes
of Agraule, son of Alcmæon, indicted him of treason, the
Spartans supporting him in the accusation.

When Pausanias went about this treasonable design,
he concealed it at first from Themistocles, though he were
his intimate friend ; but when he saw him expelled out of
the commonwealth, and how impatiently he took his banishment, he ventured to communicate it to him, and
desired his assistance, showing him the king of Persia's
letters, and exasperating him against the Greeks, as a
villanous, ungrateful people.   However, Themistocles
immediately rejected the proposals of Pausanias, and
wholly refused to be a party in the enterprise, though he
never revealed his communications, nor disclosed the conspiracy to any man, either hoping that Pausanias would

desist from his intentions, or expecting that so inconsiderate an attempt after such chimerical objects would be discovered by other means.

After that Pausanias was put to death, letters and writings being found concerning this matter, which rendered Themistocles suspected, the Lacedæmonians were clamorous against him, and his enemies among the Athenians accused him; when, being absent from Athens, he made his defence by letters, especially against the points that had been previously alleged against him. In answer to the malicious detractions of his enemies, he merely wrote to the citizens, urging that he who was always ambitious to govern, and not of a character or a disposition to serve, would never sell himself and his country into slavery to a barbarous and hostile nation.

Notwithstanding this, the people, being persuaded by his accusers, sent officers to take him and bring him away to be tried before a council of the Greeks, but, having timely notice of it, he passed over into the island of Corcyra, where the state was under obligations to him; for, being chosen as arbitrator in a difference between them and the Corinthians, he decided the controversy by ordering the Corinthians to pay down twenty talents, and declaring the town and island of Leucas a joint colony from both cities. From thence he fled into Epirus, and, the Athenians and Lacedæmonians still pursuing him, he threw himself upon chances of safety that seemed all but desperate. For he fled for refuge to Admetus, king of the Molossians, who had formerly made some request to the Athenians, when Themistocles was in the height of his authority, and had been disdainfully used and insulted by him, and had let it appear plain enough, that, could he lay hold of him, he would take his revenge. Yet in this misfortune, Themistocles, fearing the recent hatred of his neighbors and fellow-citizens more than

the old displeasure of the king, put himself at his mercy,
and became an humble suppliant to Admetus, after a peculiar manner, different from the custom of other countries.   For taking the king's son, who was then a child,
in his arms, he laid himself down at his hearth, this being
the most sacred and only manner of supplication, among
the Molossians, which was not to be refused.   And some
say that his wife, Phthia, intimated to Themistocles this
way of petitioning, and placed her young son with him
before the hearth ; others, that king Admetus, that he
might be under a religious obligation not to deliver him
up to his pursuers, prepared and enacted with him a sort
of stage-play to this effect.   At this time, Epicrates of
Acharnæ privately conveyed his wife and children out of
Athens, and sent them hither, for which afterwards
Cimon condemned him and put him to death ; as Stesimbrotus reports, and yet somehow, either forgetting this
himself, or making Themistocles to be little mindful of it,
says presently that he sailed into Sicily, and desired in
marriage the daughter of Hiero, tyrant of Syracuse,
promising to bring the Greeks under his power ; and, on
Hiero refusing him, departed thence into Asia ; but this
is not probable.

For Theophrastus writes, in his work on Monarchy,
that when Hiero sent race-horses to the Olympian games,
and erected a pavilion sumptuously furnished, Themistocles made an oration to the Greeks, inciting them to
pull down the tyrant's tent, and not to suffer his horses
to run.   Thucydides says, that, passing over land to the
Ægæan Sea, he took ship at Pydna in the bay of Therme,
not being known to any one in the ship, till, being terrified to see the vessel driven by the winds near to Naxos,
which was then besieged by the Athenians, he made himself known to the master and pilot, and, partly entreating
them, partly threatening that if they went on shore he

would accuse them, and make the Athenians to believe that they did not take him in out of ignorance, but that he had corrupted them with money from the beginning, he compelled them to bear off and stand out to sea, and sail forward towards the coast of Asia.

A great part of his estate was privately conveyed away by his friends, and sent after him by sea into Asia; besides which, there was discovered and confiscated to the value of fourscore talents, as Theophrastus writes; Theopompus says an hundred; though Themistocles was never worth three talents before he was concerned in public affairs.

When he arrived at Cyme, and understood that all along the coast there were many laid wait for him, and particularly Ergoteles and Pythodorus (for the game was worth the hunting for such as were thankful to make money by any means, the king of Persia having offered by public proclamation two hundred talents to him that should take him), he fled to Ægæ, a small city of the Æolians, where no one knew him but only his host Nicogenes, who was the richest man in Æolia, and well known to the great men of Inner Asia. While Themistocles lay hid for some days in his house, one night, after a sacrifice and supper ensuing, Olbius, the attendant upon Nicogenes's children, fell into a sort of frenzy and fit of inspiration, and cried out in verse, —

> Night shall speak, and night instruct thee,
> By the voice of night conduct thee.

After this, Themistocles, going to bed, dreamed that he saw a snake coil itself up upon his belly, and so creep to his neck; then, as soon as it touched his face, it turned into an eagle, which spread its wings over him, and took him up and flew away with him a great distance; then there appeared a herald's golden wand, and upon this at last it set him down securely, after infinite terror and disturbance.

His departure was effected by Nicogenes by the following artifice; the barbarous nations, and amongst them the Persians especially, are extremely jealous, severe, and suspicious about their women, not only their wives, but also their bought slaves and concubines, whom they keep so strictly that no one ever sees them abroad; they spend their lives shut up within doors, and, when they take a journey, are carried in close tents, curtained in on all sides, and set upon a wagon. Such a travelling carriage being prepared for Themistocles, they hid him in it, and carried him on his journey, and told those whom they met or spoke with upon the road that they were conveying a young Greek woman out of Ionia to a nobleman at court.

Thucydides and Charon of Lampsacus say that Xerxes was dead, and that Themistocles had an interview with his son; but Ephorus, Dinon, Clitarchus, Heraclides, and many others, write that he came to Xerxes. The chronological tables better agree with the account of Thucydides, and yet neither can their statements be said to be quite set at rest.

When Themistocles was come to the critical point, he applied himself first to Artabanus, commander of a thousand men, telling him that he was a Greek, and desired to speak with the king about important affairs concerning which the king was extremely solicitous. Artabanus answered him, "O stranger, the laws of men are different, and one thing is honorable to one man, and to others another; but it is honorable for all to honor and observe their own laws. It is the habit of the Greeks, we are told, to honor, above all things, liberty and equality; but amongst our many excellent laws, we account this the most excellent, to honor the king, and to worship him, as the image of the great preserver of the universe; if, then, you shall consent to our laws, and fall down before the king and worship him, you may both see him and speak to him; but if your mind be otherwise, you must make use of others to intercede for you, for it is not the national custom here for the king to give audience to any one that doth not fall down before him." Themistocles, hearing this, replied, "Artabanus, I that come hither to increase the power and glory of the king, will not only submit myself to his laws, since so it hath pleased the god who exalteth the Persian empire to this greatness, but will also cause many more to be worshippers and adorers of the king. Let not this, therefore, be an impediment why I should not communicate to the king what I have to impart." Artabanus asking him, "Who must we tell him that you are? for your words signify you to be no ordinary person," Themistocles answered, "No man, O Artabanus, must be informed of this before the king himself." Thus Phanias relates; to which Eratosthenes, in his treatise on Riches, adds, that it was by the means of a woman of Eretria, who was kept by Artabanus, that he obtained this audience and interview with him.

When he was introduced to the king, and had paid his reverence to him, he stood silent, till the king commanding the interpreter to ask him who he was, he replied, "O king, I am Themistocles the Athenian, driven into banishment by the Greeks. The evils that I have done to the Persians are numerous; but my benefits to them yet greater, in withholding the Greeks from pursuit, so soon as the deliverance of my own country allowed me to show kindness also to you. I come with a mind suited to my present calamities; prepared alike for favors and for anger; to welcome your gracious reconciliation, and to deprecate your wrath. Take my own countrymen for witnesses of the services I have done for Persia, and make use of this occasion to show the world your virtue, rather than to satisfy your indignation. If you save me, you will save your suppliant; if otherwise, will destroy an enemy of the Greeks." He talked also of divine admonitions, such as the vision which he saw at Nicogenes's house, and the direction given him by the oracle of Dodona, where Jupiter commanded him to go to him that had a name like his, by which he understood that he was sent from Jupiter to him, seeing that they both were great, and had the name of kings.

The king heard him attentively, and, though he admired his temper and courage, gave him no answer at that time; but, when he was with his intimate friends, rejoiced in his great good fortune, and esteemed himself very happy in this, and prayed to his god Arimanius, that all his enemies might be ever of the same mind with the Greeks, to abuse and expel the bravest men amongst them. Then he sacrificed to the gods, and presently fell to drinking, and was so well pleased, that in the night, in the middle of his sleep, he cried out for joy three times, " I have Themistocles the Athenian."

In the morning, calling together the chief of his court, he had Themistocles brought before him, who expected no good of it, when he saw, for example, the guards fiercely set against him as soon as they learnt his name, and giving him ill language. As he came forward towards the king, who was seated, the rest keeping silence, passing by Roxanes, a commander of a thousand men, he heard him, with a slight groan, say, without stirring out of his place, " You subtle Greek serpent, the king's good genius hath brought thee hither." Yet, when he came into the presence, and again fell down, the king saluted him, and spake to him kindly, telling him he was now indebted to him two hundred talents; for it was just and reasonable that he should receive the reward which was proposed to whosoever should bring Themistocles; and promising much more, and encouraging him, he commanded him to speak freely what he would concerning the affairs of Greece. Themistocles replied, that a man's discourse was like to a rich Persian carpet, the beautiful figures and patterns of which can only be shown by spreading and extending it out; when it is contracted and folded up, they are obscured and lost; and, therefore, he desired time. The king being pleased with the comparison, and bidding him take what time he would, he desired a year; in which time, having learnt the Persian language sufficiently, he spoke with the king by himself without the help of an interpreter, it being supposed that he discoursed only about the affairs of Greece; but there happening, at the same time, great alterations at court, and removals of the king's favorites, he drew upon himself the envy of the great people, who imagined that he had taken the boldness to speak concerning them. For the favors shown to other strangers were nothing in comparison with the honors conferred on him; the king invited him to partake of his own pastimes and recreations both at home and abroad, carrying him with him a-hunting, and made him his intimate so far that he permitted him to see the queen-mother, and converse frequently with her. By the king's command, he also was made acquainted with the Magian learning.

When Demaratus the Lacedæmonian, being ordered by the king to ask whatsoever he pleased, and it should immediately be granted him, desired that he might make his public entrance, and be carried in state through the city of Sardis, with the tiara set in the royal manner upon his head, Mithropaustes, cousin to the king, touched him on the head, and told him that he had no brains for the royal tiara to cover, and if Jupiter should give him his lightning and thunder, he would not any the more be Jupiter for that; the king also repulsed him with anger, resolving never to be reconciled to him, but to be inexorable to all supplications on his behalf. Yet Themistocles pacified him, and prevailed with him to forgive him. And it is reported, that the succeeding kings, in whose reigns there was a greater communication between the Greeks and Persians, when they invited any considerable Greek into their service, to encourage him, would write, and promise him that he should be as great with them as Themistocles had been. They relate, also, how Themistocles, when he was in great prosperity, and courted by many, seeing himself splendidly served at his table, turned to his children and said, "Children, we had been undone if we had not been undone." Most writers say that he had three cities given him, Magnesia, Myus, and Lampsacus, to maintain him in bread, meat, and wine. Neanthes of Cyzicus, and Phanias, add two more, the city of Palæscepsis, to provide him with clothes, and Percote, with bedding and furniture for his house.

As he was going down towards the sea-coast to take measures against Greece, a Persian whose name was Epixyes, governor of the upper Phrygia, laid wait to kill him, having for that purpose provided a long time before a number of Pisidians, who were to set upon him when he should stop to rest at a city that is called Lion's-head. But Themistocles, sleeping in the middle of the day, saw the Mother of the gods appear to him in a dream and say unto him, "Themistocles, keep back from the Lion's-head, for fear you fall into the lion's jaws; for this advice I expect that your daughter Mnesiptolema should be my servant." Themistocles was much astonished, and, when he had made his vows to the goddess, left the broad road, and, making a circuit, went another way, changing his intended station to avoid that place, and at night took up his rest in the fields. But one of the sumpter-horses, which carried the furniture for his tent, having fallen that day into the river, his servants spread out the tapestry, which was wet, and hung it up to dry; in the mean time the Pisidians made towards them with their swords drawn, and, not discerning exactly by the moon what it was that was stretched out, thought it to be the tent of Themistocles, and that they should find him resting himself within it; but when they came near, and lifted up the hangings, those who watched there fell upon them and took them. Themistocles, having escaped this great danger, in admiration of the goodness of the goddess that appeared to him, built, in memory of it, a temple in the city of Magnesia, which he dedicated to Dindymene, Mother of the gods, in which he consecrated and devoted his daughter Mnesiptolema to her service.

When he came to Sardis, he visited the temples of the gods, and observing, at his leisure, their buildings, ornaments, and the number of their offerings, he saw in the temple of the Mother of the gods, the statue of a virgin in brass, two cubits high, called the water-bringer. Themistocles had caused this to be made and set up when he was surveyor of waters at Athens, out of the fines of those whom he detected in drawing off and diverting the public water by pipes for their private use; and whether he had some regret to see this image in captivity, or was desirous to let the Athenians see in what great credit and authority he was with the king, he entered into a treaty with the governor of Lydia to persuade him to send this statue back to Athens, which so enraged the Persian officer, that he told him he would write the king word of it. Themistocles, being affrighted hereat, got access to his wives and concubines, by presents of money to whom, he appeased the fury of the governor; and afterwards behaved with more reserve and circumspection, fearing the envy of the Persians, and did not, as Theopompus writes, continue to travel about Asia, but lived quietly in his own house in Magnesia, where for a long time he passed his days in great security, being courted by all, and enjoying rich presents, and honored equally with the greatest persons in the Persian empire; the king, at that time, not minding his concerns with Greece, being taken up with the affairs of Inner Asia.

But when Egypt revolted, being assisted by the Athenians, and the Greek galleys roved about as far as Cyprus and Cilicia, and Cimon had made himself master of the seas, the king turned his thoughts thither, and, bending his mind chiefly to resist the Greeks, and to check the growth of their power against him, began to raise forces, and send out commanders, and to despatch messengers to Themistocles at Magnesia, to put him in mind of his promise, and to summon him to act against the Greeks. Yet this did not increase his hatred nor exasperate him against the Athenians, neither was he any way elevated with the thoughts of the honor and powerful command he was to have in this war; but judging, perhaps, that the object would not be attained, the Greeks having at that time, beside other great commanders, Cimon, in particular, who was gaining wonderful military successes; but chiefly, being ashamed to sully the glory of his former great actions, and of his many victories and trophies, he determined to put a conclusion to his life, agreeable to its previous course. He sacrificed to the gods, and invited his friends; and, having entertained them and shaken hands with them, drank bull's blood, as is the usual story; as others state, a poison producing instant death; and ended his days in the city of Magnesia, having lived sixty-five years, most of which he had spent in politics and in the wars, in government and command. The king, being informed of the cause and manner of his death, admired him more than ever, and continued to show kindness to his friends and relations.

Themistocles left three sons by Archippe, daughter to Lysander of Alopece,—Archeptolis, Polyeuctus, and Cleophantus. Plato the philosopher mentions the last as a most excellent horseman, but otherwise insignificant person; of two sons yet older than these, Neocles and Diocles, Neocles died when he was young by the bite of a horse, and Diocles was adopted by his grandfather, Lysander. He had many daughters, of whom Mnesiptolema, whom he had by a second marriage, was wife to Archeptolis, her brother by another mother; Italia was married to Panthoides, of the island of Chios; Sybaris to Nicomedes the Athenian. After the death of Themistocles, his nephew, Phrasicles, went to Magnesia, and married, with her brothers' consent, another daughter, Nicomache, and took charge of her sister Asia, the youngest of all the children.

The Magnesians possess a splendid sepulchre of Themistocles, placed in the middle of their market-place. It is not worth while taking notice of what Andocides states in his Address to his Friends concerning his remains, how the Athenians robbed his tomb, and threw his ashes into the air; for he feigns this, to exasperate the oligarchical faction against the people; and there is no man living but knows that Phylarchus simply invents in his history, where he all but uses an actual stage machine, and brings in Neocles and Demopolis as the sons of Themistocles, to incite or move compassion, as if he were writing a tragedy. Diodorus the cosmographer says, in his work on Tombs, but by conjecture rather than of certain knowledge, that near to the haven of Piræus, where the land runs out like an elbow from the promontory of Alcimus, when you have doubled the cape and passed inward where the sea is always calm, there is a large piece of masonry, and upon this the tomb of Themistocles, in the shape of an altar; and Plato the comedian confirms this, he believes, in these verses, —

Thy tomb is fairly placed upon the strand,
Where merchants still shall greet it with the land;
Still in and out 't will see them come and go,
And watch the galleys as they race below.

Various honors also and privileges were granted to the kindred of Themistocles at Magnesia, which were observed down to our times, and were enjoyed by another Themistocles of Athens, with whom I had an intimate acquaintance and friendship in the house of Ammonius the philosopher.

CAMILLUS.

Among the many remarkable things that are related of Furius Camillus, it seems singular and strange above all, that he, who continually was in the highest commands, and obtained the greatest successes, was five times chosen dictator, triumphed four times, and was styled a second founder of Rome, yet never was so much as once consul. The reason of which was the state and temper of the commonwealth at that time; for the people, being at dissension with the senate, refused to return consuls, but in their stead elected other magistrates, called military tribunes, who acted, indeed, with full consular power, but were thought to exercise a less obnoxious amount of authority, because it was divided among a larger number; for to have the management of affairs intrusted in the hands of six persons rather than two was some satisfaction to the opponents of oligarchy. This was the condition of the times when Camillus was in the height of his actions and glory, and, although the government in the meantime had often proceeded to consular elections, yet he could never persuade himself to be consul against the inclination of the people. In all his other administrations, which were many and various, he so behaved himself, that, when alone in authority, he exercised his power as in common, but the honor of all

actions redounded entirely to himself, even when in joint
commission with others; the reason of the former was his
moderation in command; of the latter, his great judgment and wisdom, which gave him without controversy
the first place.

The house of the Furii was not, at that time, of any
considerable distinction; he, by his own acts, first raised
himself to honor, serving under Postumius Tubertus,
dictator, in the great battle against the Æquians and
Volscians. For riding out from the rest of the army, and
in the charge receiving a wound in his thigh, he for all
that did not quit the fight, but, letting the dart drag in
the wound, and engaging with the bravest of the enemy,
put them to flight; for which action, among other rewards bestowed on him, he was created censor, an office
in those days of great repute and authority. During
his censorship one very good act of his is recorded, that,
whereas the wars had made many widows, he obliged
such as had no wives, some by fair persuasion, others by
threatening to set fines on their heads, to take them in
marriage; another necessary one, in causing orphans to
be rated, who before were exempted from taxes, the frequent wars requiring more than ordinary expenses to
maintain them. What, however, pressed them most was
the siege of Veii. Some call this people Veientani. This
was the head city of Tuscany, not inferior to Rome,
either in number of arms or multitude of soldiers, insomuch that, presuming on her wealth and luxury, and priding herself upon her refinement and sumptuousness, she
engaged in many honorable contests with the Romans
for glory and empire. But now they had abandoned
their former ambitious hopes, having been weakened by
great defeats, so that, having fortified themselves with
high and strong walls, and furnished the city with all
sorts of weapons offensive and defensive, as likewise with

corn and all manner of provisions, they cheerfully endured a siege, which, though tedious to them, was no less
troublesome and distressing to the besiegers. For the
Romans, having never been accustomed to stay away from
home, except in summer, and for no great length of time,
and constantly to winter at home, were then first compelled by the tribunes to build forts in the enemy's
country, and, raising strong works about their camp, to
join winter and summer together. And now, the seventh
year of the war drawing to an end, the commanders
began to be suspected as too slow and remiss in driving
on the siege, insomuch that they were discharged and
others chosen for the war, among whom was Camillus,
then second time tribune. But at present he had no
hand in the siege, the duties that fell by lot to him being
to make war upon the Faliscans and Capenates, who,
taking advantage of the Romans being occupied on all
hands, had carried ravages into their country, and, through
all the Tuscan war, given them much annoyance, but
were now reduced by Camillus, and with great loss shut
up within their walls.

And now, in the very heat of the war, a strange phe-
nomenon in the Alban lake, which, in the absence of any
known cause and explanation by natural reasons, seemed
as great a prodigy as the most incredible that are reported, occasioned great alarm. It was the beginning of
autumn, and the summer now ending had, to all observation, been neither rainy nor much troubled with southern
winds; and of the many lakes, brooks, and springs of
all sorts with which Italy abounds, some were wholly
dried up, others drew very little water with them; all
the rivers, as is usual in summer, ran in a very low and
hollow channel. But the Alban lake, that is fed by
no other waters but its own, and is on all sides encircled

with fruitful mountains, without any cause, unless it were
divine, began visibly to rise and swell, increasing to the
feet of the mountains, and by degrees reaching the level
of the very tops of them, and all this without any waves
or agitation. At first it was the wonder of shepherds
and herdsmen; but when the earth, which, like a great
dam, held up the lake from falling into the lower grounds,
through the quantity and weight of water was broken
down, and in a violent stream it ran through the
ploughed fields and plantations to discharge itself in the
sea, it not only struck terror into the Romans, but was
thought by all the inhabitants of Italy to portend some
extraordinary event. But the greatest talk of it was in
the camp that besieged Veii, so that in the town itself,
also, the occurrence became known.

As in long sieges it commonly happens that parties on
both sides meet often and converse with one another, so
it chanced that a Roman had gained much confidence
and familiarity with one of the besieged, a man versed
in ancient prophecies, and of repute for more than ordinary skill in divination. The Roman, observing him to
be overjoyed at the story of the lake, and to mock at the
siege, told him that this was not the only prodigy that of
late had happened to the Romans; others more wonderful yet than this had befallen them, which he was willing
to communicate to him, that he might the better provide
for his private interests in these public distempers. The
man greedily embraced the proposal, expecting to hear
some wonderful secrets; but when, by little and little, he
had led him on in conversation, and insensibly drawn
him a good way from the gates of the city, he snatched
him up by the middle, being stronger than he, and, by
the assistance of others that came running from the
camp, seized and delivered him to the commanders. The

man, reduced to this necessity, and sensible now that destiny was not to be avoided, discovered to them the secret oracles of Veii; that it was not possible the city should be taken, until the Alban lake, which now broke forth and had found out new passages, was drawn back from that course, and so diverted that it could not mingle with the sea. The senate, having heard and satisfied themselves about the matter, decreed to send to Delphi, to ask counsel of the god. The messengers were persons of the highest repute, Licinius Cossus, Valerius Potitus, and Fabius Ambustus; who, having made their voyage by sea and consulted the god, returned with other answers, particularly that there had been a neglect of some of their national rites relating to the Latin feasts; but the Alban water the oracle commanded, if it were possible, they should keep from the sea, and shut it up in its ancient bounds; but if that was not to be done, then they should carry it off by ditches and trenches into the lower grounds, and so dry it up; which message being delivered, the priests performed what related to the sacrifices, and the people went to work and turned the water.

And now the senate, in the tenth year of the war, taking away all other commands, created Camillus dictator, who chose Cornelius Scipio for his general of horse. And in the first place he made vows unto the gods, that, if they would grant a happy conclusion of the war, he would celebrate to their honor the great games, and dedicate a temple to the goddess whom the Romans call Matuta the Mother, though, from the ceremonies which are used, one would think she was Leucothea. For they take a servant-maid into the secret part of the temple, and there cuff her, and drive her out again, and they embrace their brothers' children in place of their own; and, in general, the ceremonies of the sacrifice remind one of the nursing of Bacchus by Ino, and the calamities occasioned by her husband's concubine.*   Camillus, having made these vows, marched into the country of the Faliscans, and in a great battle overthrew them and the Capenates, their confederates; afterwards he turned to the siege of Veii, and, finding that to take it by assault would prove a difficult and hazardous attempt, proceeded to cut mines under ground, the earth about the city being easy to break up, and allowing such depth for the works as would prevent their being discovered by the enemy. This design going on in a hopeful way, he openly gave assaults to the enemy, to keep them to the walls, whilst they that worked underground in the mines were, without being perceived, arrived within the citadel, close to the temple of Juno, which was the greatest and most honored in all the city.   It is said that the prince of the Tuscans was at that very time at sacrifice, and that the priest, after he had looked into the entrails of the beast, cried out with a loud voice that the gods would give the victory to those that should complete those offerings; and that the Romans who were in the mines, hearing the words, immediately pulled down the floor, and, ascending with noise and clashing of weapons, frighted away the enemy, and, snatching up the entrails, carried them to Camillus.   But this may look like a fable.   The city, however, being taken by storm, and the soldiers busied in pillaging and gathering an infinite quantity of riches and spoil, Camillus, from the high tower, viewing what was done, at first wept for pity; and when they that were by congratulated his good success, he lifted up his hands to heaven, and broke out into this prayer: " O most mighty

* Ino, daughter of Cadmus and Harmonia, nursed her sister Semele's child, the infant Bacchus, and afterwards, according to the story followed by Plutarch both here and in his Roman Questions, in a fit of frantic jealousy of her husband's concubine, an Ætolian servant-maid, killed her own child.

Jupiter, and ye gods that are judges of good and evil actions, ye know that not without just cause, but constrained by necessity, we have been forced to revenge ourselves on the city of our unrighteous and wicked enemies. But if, in the vicissitude of things, there be any calamity due. to counterbalance this great felicity, I beg that it may be diverted from the city and army of the Romans, and fall, with as little hurt as may be, upon my own head." Having said these words, and just turning about (as the custom of the Romans is to turn to the right after adoration or prayer), he stumbled and fell, to the astonishment of all that were present. But, recovering himself presently from the fall, he told them that he had received what he had prayed for, a small mischance, in compensation for the greatest good fortune.

Having sacked the city, he resolved, according as he had vowed, to carry Juno's image to Rome; and, the workmen being ready for that purpose, he sacrificed to the goddess, and made his supplications that she would be pleased to accept of their devotion toward her, and graciously vouchsafe to accept of a place among the gods that presided at Rome; and the statue, they say, answered in a low voice that she was ready and willing to go. Livy writes, that, in praying, Camillus touched the goddess, and invited her, and that some of the standers-by cried out that she was willing and would come. They who stand up for the miracle and endeavor to maintain it have one great advocate on their side in the wonderful fortune of the city, which, from a small and contemptible beginning, could never have attained to that greatness and power without many signal manifestations of the divine presence and coöperation. Other wonders of the like nature, drops of sweat seen to stand on statues, groans heard from them, the figures seen to turn round and to close their eyes, are recorded by many ancient

historians; and we ourselves could relate divers wonderful things, which we have been told by men of our own
time, that are not lightly to be rejected; but to give too
easy credit to such things, or wholly to disbelieve them,
is equally dangerous, so incapable is human infirmity of
keeping any bounds, or exercising command over itself,
running off sometimes to superstition and dotage, at
other times to the contempt and neglect of all that is
supernatural. But moderation is best, and to avoid all
extremes.

Camillus, however, whether puffed up with the greatness of his achievement in conquering a city that was the
rival of Rome, and had held out a ten years' siege, or
exalted with the felicitations of those that were about
him, assumed to himself more than became a civil and
legal magistrate; among other things, in the pride and
haughtiness of his triumph, driving through Rome in a
chariot drawn with four white horses, which no general
either before or since ever did; for the Romans consider
such a mode of conveyance to be sacred, and specially set
apart to the king and father of the gods. This alienated
the hearts of his fellow-citizens, who were not accustomed
to such pomp and display.

The second pique they had against him was his opposing the law by which the city was to be divided; for the
tribunes of the people brought forward a motion that the
people and senate should be divided into two parts, one
of which should remain at home, the other, as the lot
should decide, remove to the new-taken city. By which
means they should not only have much more room, but,
by the advantage of two great and magnificent cities, be
better able to maintain their territories and their fortunes
in general. The people, therefore, who were numerous
and indigent, greedily embraced it, and crowded continually to the forum, with tumultuous demands to have it

put to the vote. But the senate and the noblest citizens, judging the proceedings of the tribunes to tend rather to a destruction than a division of Rome, greatly averse to it, went to Camillus for assistance, who, fearing the result if it came to a direct contest, contrived to occupy the people with other business, and so staved it off. He thus became unpopular. But the greatest and most apparent cause of their dislike against him arose from the tenths of the spoil; the multitude having here, if not a just, yet a plausible case against him. For it seems, as he went to the siege of Veii, he had vowed to Apollo that if he took the city he would dedicate to him the tenth of the spoil. The city being taken and sacked, whether he was loath to trouble the soldiers at that time, or that through the multitude of business he had forgotten his vow, he suffered them to enjoy that part of the spoils also. Some time afterwards, when his authority was laid down, he brought the matter before the senate, and the priests, at the same time, reported, out of the sacrifices, that there were intimations of divine anger, requiring propitiations and offerings. The senate decreed the obligation to be in force.

But seeing it was difficult for every one to produce the very same things they had taken, to be divided anew, they ordained that every one upon oath should bring into the public the tenth part of his gains. This occasioned many annoyances and hardships to the soldiers, who were poor men, and had endured much in the war, and now were forced, out of what they had gained and spent, to bring in so great a proportion. Camillus, being assaulted by their clamor and tumults, for want of a better excuse, betook himself to the poorest of defences, confessing he had forgotten his vow; they in turn complained that he had vowed the tenth of the enemy's goods, and now levied it out of the tenths of the citizens. Nevertheless, every

one having brought in his due proportion, it was decreed
that out of it a bowl of massy gold should be made, and
sent to Delphi. And when there was great scarcity of
gold in the city, and the magistrates were considering
where to get it, the Roman ladies, meeting together and
consulting among themselves, out of the golden ornaments
they wore contributed as much as went to the making the
offering, which in weight came to eight talents of gold.
The senate, to give them the honor they had deserved,
ordained that funeral orations should be used at the obsequies of women as well as men, it having never before
been a custom that any woman after death should receive
any public eulogy. Choosing out, therefore, three of the
noblest citizens as a deputation, they sent them in a vessel of war, well manned and sumptuously adorned. Storm
and calm at sea may both, they say, alike be dangerous;
as they at this time experienced, being brought almost
to the very brink of destruction, and, beyond all expectation, escaping. For near the isles of Æolus the wind
slacking, galleys of the Lipareans came upon them, taking
them for pirates; and, when they held up their hands as
suppliants, forbore indeed from violence, but took their
ship in tow, and carried her into the harbor, where they
exposed to sale their goods and persons as lawful prize,
they being pirates; and scarcely, at last, by the virtue
and interest of one man, Timesitheus by name, who was
in office as general, and used his utmost persuasion, they
were, with much ado, dismissed. He, however, himself
sent out some of his own vessels with them, to accompany them in their voyage and assist them at the dedication; for which he received honors at Rome, as he had
deserved.

And now the tribunes of the people again resuming
their motion for the division of the city, the war against
the Faliscans luckily broke out, giving liberty to the chief

citizens to choose what magistrates they pleased, and to appoint Camillus military tribune, with five colleagues; affairs then requiring a commander of authority and reputation, as well as experience. And when the people had ratified the election, he marched with his forces into the territories of the Faliscans, and laid siege to Falerii, a well-fortified city, and plentifully stored with all necessaries of war. And although he perceived it would be no small work to take it, and no little time would be required for it, yet he was willing to exercise the citizens and keep them abroad, that they might have no leisure, idling at home, to follow the tribunes in factions and seditions; a very common remedy, indeed, with the Romans, who thus carried off, like good physicians, the ill humors of their commonwealth. The Falerians,* trusting in the strength of their city, which was well fortified on all sides, made so little account of the siege, that all, with the exception of those that guarded the walls, as in times of peace, walked about the streets in their common dress; the boys went to school, and were led by their master to play and exercise about the town walls; for the Falerians, like the Greeks, used to have a single teacher for many pupils, wishing their children to live and be brought up from the beginning in each other's company.

This schoolmaster, designing to betray the Falerians by their children, led them out every day under the town wall, at first but a little way, and, when they had exercised, brought them home again. Afterwards by degrees he drew them farther and farther, till by practice he had made them bold and fearless, as if no danger was about them; and at last, having got them all together, he brought them to the outposts of the Romans, and delivered them up, demanding to be led to Camillus.

* The Falerians, in this narra- the Faliscans, the nation in gentive, are the people of the town; eral.

Where being come, and standing in the middle, he said
that he was the master and teacher of these children,
but, preferring his favor before all other obligations, he
was come to deliver up his charge to him, and, in that,
the whole city. When Camillus had heard him out, he
was astounded at the treachery of the act, and, turning
to the standers-by, observed, that "war, indeed, is of
necessity attended with much injustice and violence!
Certain laws, however, all good men observe even in war
itself, nor is victory so great an object as to induce us to
incur for its sake obligations for base and impious acts.
A great general should rely on his own virtue, and not
on other men's vices." Which said, he commanded the
officers to tear off the man's clothes, and bind his hands
behind him, and give the boys rods and scourges, to punish
the traitor and drive him back to the city. By this time
the Falerians had discovered the treachery of the schoolmaster, and the city, as was likely, was full of lamentations and cries for their calamity, men and women of
worth running in distraction about the walls and gates;
when, behold, the boys came whipping their master on,
naked and bound, calling Camillus their preserver and
god and father. Insomuch that it struck not only into
the parents, but the rest of the citizens that saw what
was done, such admiration and love of Camillus's justice,
that, immediately meeting in assembly, they sent ambassadors to him, to resign whatever they had to his disposal.
Camillus sent them to Rome, where, being brought into
the senate, they spoke to this purpose : that the Romans,
preferring justice before victory, had taught them rather
to embrace submission than liberty; they did not so much
confess themselves to be inferior in strength, as they
must acknowledge them to be superior in virtue. The
senate remitted the whole matter to Camillus, to judge
and order as he thought fit; who, taking a sum of money

of the Falerians, and, making a peace with the whole nation of the Faliscans, returned home.

But the soldiers, who had expected to have the pillage of the city, when they came to Rome empty-handed, railed against Camillus among their fellow-citizens, as a hater of the people, and one that grudged all advantage to the poor. Afterwards, when the tribunes of the people again brought their motion for dividing the city to the vote, Camillus appeared openly against it, shrinking from no unpopularity, and inveighing boldly against the promoters of it, and so urging and constraining the multitude, that, contrary to their inclinations, they rejected the proposal; but yet hated Camillus. Insomuch that, though a great misfortune befell him in his family (one of his two sons dying of a disease), commiseration for this could not in the least make them abate of their malice. And, indeed, he took this loss with immoderate sorrow, being a man naturally of a mild and tender disposition, and, when the accusation was preferred against him, kept his house, and mourned amongst the women of his family.

His accuser was Lucius Apuleius; the charge, appropriation of the Tuscan spoils; certain brass gates, part of those spoils, were said to be in his possession. The people were exasperated against him, and it was plain they would take hold of any occasion to condemn him. Gathering, therefore, together his friends and fellow-soldiers, and such as had borne command with him, a considerable number in all, he besought them that they would not suffer him to be unjustly overborne by shameful accusations, and left the mock and scorn of his enemies. His friends, having advised and consulted among themselves, made answer, that, as to the sentence, they did not see how they could help him, but that they would contribute to whatsoever fine should be set upon him. Not able to

endure so great an indignity, he resolved in his anger to
leave the city and go into exile; and so, having taken
leave of his wife and his son, he went silently to the
gate of the city, and, there stopping and turning round,
stretched out his hands to the Capitol, and prayed to the
gods, that if, without any fault of his own, but merely
through the malice and violence of the people, he was
driven out into banishment, the Romans might quickly
repent of it; and that all mankind might witness their
need for the assistance, and desire for the return of Camillus.

Thus, like Achilles, having left his imprecations on the
citizens, he went into banishment; so that, neither appearing nor making defence, he was condemned in the
sum of fifteen thousand asses, which, reduced to silver,
makes one thousand five hundred drachmas; for the
as was the money of the time, ten of such copper
pieces making the denarius, or piece of ten. And there
is not a Roman but believes that immediately upon the
prayers of Camillus a sudden judgment followed, and
that he received a revenge for the injustice done unto
him; which though we cannot think was pleasant, but
rather grievous and bitter to him, yet was very remarkable, and noised over the whole world; such a punishment visited the city of Rome, an era of such loss and
danger and disgrace so quickly succeeded; whether it
thus fell out by fortune, or it be the office of some god
not to see injured virtue go unavenged.

The first token that seemed to threaten some mischief
to ensue was the death of the censor Julius; for the
Romans have a religious reverence for the office of a
censor, and esteem it sacred. The second was, that, just
before Camillus went into exile, Marcus Cædicius, a person
of no great distinction, nor of the rank of senator, but
esteemed a good and respectable man, reported to the

military tribunes a thing worthy their consideration: that, going along the night before in the street called the New Way, and being called by somebody in a loud voice, he turned about, but could see no one, but heard a voice greater than human, which said these words, " Go, Marcus Cædicius, and early in the morning tell the military tribunes that they are shortly to expect the Gauls." But the tribunes made a mock and sport with the story, and a little after came Camillus's banishment.

The Gauls are of the Celtic race, and are reported to have been compelled by their numbers to leave their country, which was insufficient to sustain them all, and to have gone in search of other homes. And being, many thousands of them, young men and able to bear arms, and carrying with them a still greater number of women and young children, some of them, passing the Riphæan mountains, fell upon the Northern Ocean, and possessed themselves of the farthest parts of Europe; others, seating themselves between the Pyrenean mountains and the Alps, lived there a considerable time, near to the Senones and Celtorii ; but, afterwards tasting wine which was then first brought them out of Italy, they were all so much taken with the liquor, and transported with the hitherto unknown delight, that, snatching up their arms and taking their families along with them, they marched directly to the Alps, to find out the country which yielded such fruit, pronouncing all others barren and useless. He that first brought wine among them and was the chief instigator of their coming into Italy is said to have been one Aruns, a Tuscan, a man of noble extraction, and not of bad natural character, but involved in the following misfortune. He was guardian to an orphan, one of the richest of the country, and much admired for his beauty, whose name was Lucumo. From his childhood he had been bred up with Aruns in his family, and when now grown up did not leave his house, professing to wish for the enjoyment of his society. And thus for a great while he secretly enjoyed Aruns's wife, corrupting her, and himself corrupted by her. But when they were both so far gone in their passion that they could neither refrain their lust nor conceal it, the young man seized the woman and openly sought to carry her away. The husband, going to law, and finding himself overpowered by the interest and money of his opponent, left his country, and, hearing of the state of the Gauls, went to them, and was the conductor of their expedition into Italy.

At their first coming they at once possessed themselves of all that country which anciently the Tuscans inhabited, reaching from the Alps to both the seas, as the names themselves testify; for the North or Adriatic Sea is named from the Tuscan city Adria, and that to the south the Tuscan Sea simply. The whole country is rich in fruit trees, has excellent pasture, and is well watered with rivers. It had eighteen large and beautiful cities, well provided with all the means for industry and wealth, and all the enjoyments and pleasures of life. The Gauls cast out the Tuscans, and seated themselves in them. But this was long before.

The Gauls at this time were besieging Clusium, a Tuscan city. The Clusinians sent to the Romans for succor, desiring them to interpose with the barbarians by letters and ambassadors. There were sent three of the family of the Fabii, persons of high rank and distinction in the city. The Gauls received them courteously, from respect to the name of Rome, and, giving over the assault which was then making upon the walls, came to conference with them; when the ambassadors asking what injury they had received of the Clusinians that they thus invaded their city, Brennus, king of the Gauls, laughed and made answer, "The Clusinians do us injury, in that, being able

only to till a small parcel of ground, they must needs
possess a great territory, and will not yield any part to
us who are strangers, many in number, and poor. In the
same nature, O Romans, formerly the Albans, Fidenates,
and Ardeates, and now lately the Veientines and Capenates, and many of the Faliscans and Volscians, did you
injury; upon whom ye make war if they do not yield
you part of what they possess, make slaves of them,
waste and spoil their country, and ruin their cities; neither
in so doing are cruel or unjust, but follow that most
ancient of all laws, which gives the possessions of the fee-
ble to the strong; which begins with God and ends in the
beasts; since all these, by nature, seek, the stronger to
have advantage over the weaker. Cease, therefore, to
pity the Clusinians whom we besiege, lest ye teach the
Gauls to be kind and compassionate to those that are oppressed by you." By this answer the Romans, perceiving
that Brennus was not to be treated with, went into Clusium, and encouraged and stirred up the inhabitants to
make a sally with them upon the barbarians, which they
did either to try their strength or to show their own.
The sally being made, and the fight growing hot about
the walls, one of the Fabii, Quintus Ambustus, being well
mounted, and setting spurs to his horse, made full against
a Gaul, a man of huge bulk and stature, whom he saw
riding out at a distance from the rest. At the first he
was not recognized, through the quickness of the conflict
and the glittering of his armor, that precluded any view
of him; but when he had overthrown the Gaul, and was
going to gather the spoils, Brennus knew him; and, in-
voking the gods to be witnesses, that, contrary to the
known and common law of nations, which is holily observed by all mankind, he who had come as an ambassador
had now engaged in hostility against him, he drew off
his men, and, bidding Clusium farewell, led his army

directly to Rome. But not wishing that it should look as if they took advantage of that injury, and were ready to embrace any occasion of quarrel, he sent a herald to demand the man in punishment, and in the mean time marched leisurely on.

The senate being met at Rome, among many others that spoke against the Fabii, the priests called fecials were the most decided, who, on the religious ground, urged the senate that they should lay the whole guilt and penalty of the fact upon him that committed it, and so exonerate the rest. These fecials Numa Pompilius, the mildest and justest of kings, constituted guardians of peace, and the judges and determiners of all causes by which war may justifiably be made. The senate referring the whole matter to the people, and the priests there, as well as in the senate, pleading against Fabius, the multitude, however, so little regarded their authority, that in scorn and contempt of it they chose Fabius and the rest of his brothers military tribunes. The Gauls, on hearing this, in great rage threw aside every delay, and hastened on with all the speed they could make. The places through which they marched, terrified with their numbers and the splendor of their preparations for war, and in alarm at their violence and fierceness, began to give up their territories as already lost, with little doubt but their cities would quickly follow; contrary, however, to expectation. they did no injury as they passed, nor took any thing from the fields; and, as they went by any city, cried out that they were going to Rome; that the Romans only were their enemies, and that they took all others for their friends.

Whilst the barbarians were thus hastening with all speed, the military tribunes brought the Romans into the field to be ready to engage them, being not inferior to the Gauls in number (for they were no less than forty thousand foot), but most of them raw soldiers, and such as had never handled a weapon before. Besides, they had wholly neglected all religious usages, had not obtained favorable sacrifices, nor made inquiries of the prophets, natural in danger and before battle. No less did the multitude of commanders distract and confound their proceedings; frequently before, upon less occasions, they had chosen a single leader, with the title of dictator, being sensible of what great importance it is in critical times to have the soldiers united under one general with the entire and absolute control placed in his hands. Add to all, the remembrance of Camillus's treatment, which made it now seem a dangerous thing for officers to command without humoring their soldiers. In this condition they left the city, and encamped by the river Allia, about ten miles from Rome, and not far from the place where it falls into the Tiber; and here the Gauls came upon them, and, after a disgraceful resistance, devoid of order and discipline, they were miserably defeated. The left wing was immediately driven into the river, and there destroyed; the right had less damage by declining the shock, and from the low grounds getting to the tops of the hills, from whence most of them afterwards dropped into the city; the rest, as many as escaped, the enemy being weary of the slaughter, stole by night to Veii, giving up Rome and all that was in it for lost.

This battle was fought about the summer solstice, the moon being at full, the very same day in which the sad disaster of the Fabii had happened, when three hundred of that name were at one time cut off by the Tuscans. But from this second loss and defeat the day got the name of Alliensis, from the river Allia, and still retains it. The question of unlucky days, whether we should consider any to be so, and whether Heraclitus did well in upbraiding Hesiod for distinguishing them into fortunate

and unfortunate, as ignorant that the nature of every
day is the same; I have examined in another place; but
upon occasion of the present subject, I think it will not
be amiss to annex a few examples relating to this matter.
On the fifth of their month Hippodromius, which corre-
sponds to the Athenian Hecatombæon, the Bœotians
gained two signal victories, the one at Leuctra, the other
at Ceressus, about three hundred years before, when they
overcame Lattamyas and the Thessalians, both which
asserted the liberty of Greece. Again, on the sixth of
Boëdromion, the Persians were worsted by the Greeks at
Marathon; on the third, at Platæa, as also at Mycale; on
the twenty-fifth, at Arbela. The Athenians, about the
full moon in Boëdromion, gained their sea-victory at
Naxos under the conduct of Chabrias; on the twentieth,
at Salamis, as we have shown in our treatise on Days.
Thargelion was a very unfortunate month to the barbarians, for in it Alexander overcame Darius's generals on
the Granicus; and the Carthaginians, on the twenty-
fourth, were beaten by Timoleon in Sicily, on which
same day and month Troy seems to have been taken, as
Ephorus, Callisthenes, Damastes, and Phylarchus state.
On the other hand, the month Metagitnion, which in
Bœotia is called Panemus, was not very lucky to the
Greeks; for on its seventh day they were defeated by
Antipater, at the battle in Cranon, and utterly ruined;
and before, at Chæronea, were defeated by Philip; and
on the very same day, same month, and same year, those
that went with Archidamus into Italy were there cut off by
the barbarians. The Carthaginians also observe the twenty-
first of the same month, as bringing with it the largest
number and the severest of their losses. I am not ignorant, that, about the Feast of Mysteries, Thebes was destroyed the second time by Alexander; and after that,
upon the very twentieth of Boëdromion, on which day

they lead forth the mystic Iacchus, the Athenians received a garrison of the Macedonians. On the selfsame day the Romans lost their army under Cæpio by the Cimbrians, and in a subsequent year, under the conduct of Lucullus, overcame the Armenians and Tigranes. King Attalus and Pompey died both on their birthdays. One could reckon up several that have had variety of fortune on the same day. This day, meantime, is one of the unfortunate ones to the Romans, and for its sake two others * in every month ; fear and superstition, as the custom of it is, more and more prevailing. But I have discussed this more accurately in my Roman Questions.

And now, after the battle, had the Gauls immediately pursued those that fled, there had been no remedy but Rome must have wholly been ruined, and all those who remained in it utterly destroyed ; such was the terror that those who escaped the battle brought with them into the city, and with such distraction and confusion were themselves in turn infected. But the Gauls, not imagining their victory to be so considerable, and overtaken with the present joy, fell to feasting and dividing the spoil, by which means they gave leisure to those who were for leaving the city to make their escape, and to those that remained, to anticipate and prepare for their coming. For they who resolved to stay at Rome, abandoning the rest of the city, betook themselves to the Capitol, which they fortified with the help of missiles and new works. One of their principal cares was of their holy things, most of which they conveyed into the Capitol. But the consecrated fire the vestal virgins took, and

---

* The day after the Ides, on which, in the month of July, the army marched out, and also the day after the Calends, and the day after the Nones, were in every month accounted unlucky. The Allian day itself was the third after the Ides, July 18.

fled with it, as likewise their other sacred things. Some write that they have nothing in their charge but the ever-living fire which Numa had ordained to be worshipped as the principle of all things; for fire is the most active thing in nature, and all production is either motion, or attended with motion; all the other parts of matter, so long as they are without warmth, lie sluggish and dead, and require the accession of a sort of soul or vitality in the principle of heat; and upon that accession, in whatever way, immediately receive a capacity either of acting or being acted upon. And thus Numa, a man curious in such things, and whose wisdom made it thought that he conversed with the Muses, consecrated fire, and ordained it to be kept ever burning, as an image of that eternal power which orders and actuates all things. Others say that this fire was kept burning in front of the holy things, as in Greece, for purification, and that there were other things hid in the most secret part of the temple, which were kept from the view of all, except those virgins whom they call vestals. The most common opinion was, that the image of Pallas, brought into Italy by Æneas, was laid up there; others say that the Samothracian images lay there, telling a story how that Dardanus carried them to Troy, and, when he had built the city, celebrated those rites, and dedicated those images there; that after Troy was taken, Æneas stole them away, and kept them till his coming into Italy. But they who profess to know more of the matter affirm that there are two barrels, not of any great size, one of which stands open and has nothing in it, the other full and sealed up; but that neither of them may be seen but by the most holy virgins. Others think that they who say this are misled by the fact that the virgins put most of their holy things into two barrels at this time of the Gaulish invasion, and hid them underground in the temple of Quiri-

nus; and that from hence that place to this day bears the
name of Barrels.

However it be, taking the most precious and important
things they had, they fled away with them, shaping their
course along the river side, where Lucius Albinius, a simple citizen of Rome, who among others was making his
escape, overtook them, having his wife, children, and
goods in a cart; and, seeing the virgins dragging along
in their arms the holy things of the gods, in a helpless
and weary condition, he caused his wife and children to get
down, and, taking out his goods, put the virgins in the
cart, that they might make their escape to some of the
Greek cities. This devout act of Albinius, and the respect
he showed thus signally to the gods at a time of such extremity, deserved not to be passed over in silence. But
the priests that belonged to other gods, and the most
elderly of the senators, men who had been consuls and
had enjoyed triumphs, could not endure to leave the
city; but, putting on their sacred and splendid robes, Fabius the high-priest performing the office, they made
their prayers to the gods, and, devoting themselves, as it
were, for their country, sate themselves down in their
ivory chairs in the forum, and in that posture expected
the event.

On the third day after the battle, Brennus appeared
with his army at the city, and, finding the gates wide
open and no guards upon the walls, first began to suspect
it was some design or stratagem, never dreaming that the
Romans were in so desperate a condition. But when he
found it to be so indeed, he entered at the Colline gate,
and took Rome, in the three hundred and sixtieth year,
or a little more, after it was built; if, indeed, it can be supposed probable that an exact chronological statement has
been preserved of events which were themselves the
cause of chronological difficulties about things of later

date; of the calamity itself, however, and of the fact of
the capture, some faint rumors seem to have passed at
the time into Greece. Heraclides Ponticus, who lived
not long after these times, in his book upon the Soul,
relates that a certain report came from the west, that an
army, proceeding from the Hyperboreans, had taken a
Greek city called Rome, seated somewhere upon the great
sea. But I do not wonder that so fabulous and high-
flown an author as Heraclides should embellish the truth
of the story with expressions about Hyperboreans and
the great sea. Aristotle the philosopher appears to have
heard a correct statement of the taking of the city by
the Gauls, but he calls its deliverer Lucius; whereas Camillus's surname was not Lucius, but Marcus. But this is a
matter of conjecture.

Brennus, having taken possession of Rome, set a strong
guard about the Capitol, and, going himself down into the
forum, was there struck with amazement at the sight of
so many men sitting in that order and silence, observing
that they neither rose at his coming, nor so much as
changed color or countenance, but remained without fear
or concern, leaning upon their staves, and sitting quietly,
looking at each other. The Gauls, for a great while, stood
wondering at the strangeness of the sight, not daring to
approach or touch them, taking them for an assembly of
superior beings. But when one, bolder than the rest, drew
near to Marcus Papirius, and, putting forth his hand,
gently touched his chin and stroked his long beard, Papirius with his staff struck him a severe blow on the head;
upon which the barbarian drew his sword and slew him.
This was the introduction to the slaughter; for the rest,
following his example, set upon them all and killed them,
and despatched all others that came in their way; and so
went on to the sacking and pillaging the houses, which
they continued for many days ensuing. Afterwards, they

burnt them down to the ground and demolished them, being incensed at those who kept the Capitol, because they would not yield to summons; but, on the contrary, when assailed, had repelled them, with some loss, from their defences. This provoked them to ruin the whole city, and to put to the sword all that came to their hands, young and old, men, women, and children.

And now, the siege of the Capitol having lasted a good while, the Gauls began to be in want of provision; and dividing their forces, part of them stayed with their king at the siege, the rest went to forage the country, ravaging the towns and villages where they came, but not all together in a body, but in different squadrons and parties; and to such a confidence had success raised them, that they carelessly rambled about without the least fear or apprehension of danger. But the greatest and best ordered body of their forces went to the city of Ardea, where Camillus then sojourned, having, ever since his leaving Rome, sequestered himself from all business, and taken to a private life; but now he began to rouse up himself, and consider not how to avoid or escape the enemy, but to find out an opportunity to be revenged upon them. And perceiving that the Ardeatians wanted not men, but rather enterprise, through the inexperience and timidity of their officers, he began to speak with the young men, first, to the effect that they ought not to ascribe the misfortune of the Romans to the courage of their enemy, nor attribute the losses they sustained by rash counsel to the conduct of men who had no title to victory; the event had been only an evidence of the power of fortune; that it was a brave thing even with danger to repel a foreign and barbarous invader, whose end in conquering was, like fire, to lay waste and destroy, but if they would be courageous and resolute, he was ready to put an opportunity into their hands to gain a victory,

without hazard at all. When he found the young men
embraced the thing, he went to the magistrates and council of the city, and, having persuaded them also, he mus-
tered all that could bear arms, and drew them up within
the walls, that they might not be perceived by the enemy,
who was near; who, having scoured the country, and now
returned heavy-laden with booty, lay encamped in the
plains in a careless and negligent posture, so that, with
the night ensuing upon debauch and drunkenness, silence
prevailed through all the camp. When Camillus learned
this from his scouts, he drew out the Ardeatians, and in
the dead of the night, passing in silence over the ground
that lay between, came up to their works, and, commanding his trumpets to sound and his men to shout and hal-
loo, he struck terror into them from all quarters; while
drunkenness impeded and sleep retarded their movements.
A few, whom fear had sobered, getting into some order,
for awhile resisted; and so died with their weapons in
their hands. But the greatest part of them, buried in
wine and sleep, were surprised without their arms, and
despatched; and as many of them as by the advantage
of the night got out of the camp were the next day
found scattered abroad and wandering in the fields, and
were picked up by the horse that pursued them.

The fame of this action soon flew through the neighboring cities, and stirred up the young men from various
quarters to come and join themselves with him. But
none were so much concerned as those Romans who
escaped in the battle of Allia, and were now at Veii, thus
lamenting with themselves, "O heavens, what a commander has Providence bereaved Rome of, to honor Ardea
with his actions! And that city, which brought forth
and nursed so great a man, is lost and gone, and we, destitute of a leader and shut up within strange walls, sit
idle, and see Italy ruined before our eyes. Come, let us

send to the Ardeatians to have back our general, or else, with weapons in our hands, let us go thither to him; for he is no longer a banished man, nor we citizens, having no country but what is in the possession of the enemy." To this they all agreed, and sent to Camillus to desire him to take the command; but he answered, that he would not, until they that were in the Capitol should legally appoint him; for he esteemed them, as long as they were in being, to be his country; that if they should command him, he would readily obey; but against their consent he would intermeddle with nothing. When this answer was returned, they admired the modesty and temper of Camillus; but they could not tell how to find a messenger to carry the intelligence to the Capitol, or rather, indeed, it seemed altogether impossible for any one to get to the citadel whilst the enemy was in full possession of the city. But among the young men there was one Pontius Cominius, of ordinary birth, but ambitious of honor, who proffered himself to run the hazard, and took no letters with him to those in the Capitol, lest, if he were intercepted, the enemy might learn the intentions of Camillus; but, putting on a poor dress and carrying corks under it, he boldly travelled the greatest part of the way by day, and came to the city when it was dark; the bridge he could not pass, as it was guarded by the barbarians; so that taking his clothes, which were neither many nor heavy, and binding them about his head, he laid his body upon the corks, and, swimming with them, got over to the city. And avoiding those quarters where he perceived the enemy was awake, which he guessed at by the lights and noise, he went to the Carmental gate, where there was greatest silence, and where the hill of the Capitol is steepest, and rises with craggy and broken rock. By this way he got up, though with much difficulty, by the hollow of the cliff, and presented himself to the

guards, saluting them, and telling them his name; he was
taken in, and carried to the commanders. And a senate
being immediately called, he related to them in order the
victory of Camillus, which they had not heard of before,
and the proceedings of the soldiers, urging them to
confirm Camillus in the command, as on him alone all
their fellow-countrymen outside the city would rely
Having heard and consulted of the matter, the senate
declared Camillus dictator, and sent back Pontius the
same way that he came, who, with the same success as
before, got through the enemy without being discovered,
and delivered to the Romans outside the decision of the
senate, who joyfully received it. Camillus, on his arrival,
found twenty thousand of them ready in arms; with
which forces, and those confederates he brought along
with him, he prepared to set upon the enemy.

But at Rome some of the barbarians, passing by chance
near the place at which Pontius by night had got into
the Capitol, spied in several places marks of feet and
hands, where he had laid hold and clambered, and places
where the plants that grew to the rock had been rubbed
off, and the earth had slipped, and went accordingly and
reported it to the king, who, coming in person, and viewing it, for the present said nothing, but in the evening,
picking out such of the Gauls as were nimblest of body,
and by living in the mountains were accustomed to climb,
he said to them, " The enemy themselves have shown us
a way how to come at them, which we knew not of
before, and have taught us that it is not so difficult and
impossible but that men may overcome it. It would be
a great shame, having begun well, to fail in the end, and
to give up a place as impregnable, when the enemy himself lets us see the way by which it may be taken; for
where it was easy for one man to get up, it will not be
hard for many, one after another; nay, when many

shall undertake it, they will be aid and strength to each other. Rewards and honors shall be bestowed on every man as he shall acquit himself."

When the king had thus spoken, the Gauls cheerfully undertook to perform it, and in the dead of night a good party of them together, with great silence, began to climb the rock, clinging to the precipitous and difficult ascent, which yet upon trial offered a way to them, and proved less difficult than they had expected. So that the foremost of them having gained the top of all, and put themselves into order, they all but surprised the outworks, and mastered the watch, who were fast asleep; for neither man nor dog perceived their coming. But there were sacred geese kept near the temple of Juno, which at other times were plentifully fed, but now, by reason that corn and all other provisions were grown scarce for all, were but in a poor condition. The creature is by nature of quick sense, and apprehensive of the least noise, so that these, being moreover watchful through hunger, and restless, immediately discovered the coming of the Gauls, and, running up and down with their noise and cackling, they raised the whole camp, while the barbarians on the other side, perceiving themselves discovered, no longer endeavored to conceal their attempt, but with shouting and violence advanced to the assault. The Romans, every one in haste snatching up the next weapon that came to hand, did what they could on the sudden occasion. Manlius, a man of consular dignity, of strong body and great spirit, was the first that made head against them, and, engaging with two of the enemy at once, with his sword cut off the right arm of one just as he was lifting up his blade to strike, and, running his target full in the face of the other, tumbled him headlong down the steep rock; then mounting the rampart, and there standing with others that came running to his assistance, drove down the rest of them, who, indeed, to begin, had not been many, and did nothing worthy of so bold an attempt. The Romans, having thus escaped this danger, early in the morning took the captain of the watch and flung him down the rock upon the heads of their enemies, and to Manlius for his victory voted a reward, intended more for honor than advantage, bringing him, each man of them, as much as he received for his daily allowance, which was half a pound of bread, and one eighth of a pint of wine.

Henceforward, the affairs of the Gauls were daily in a worse and worse condition; they wanted provisions, being withheld from foraging through fear of Camillus, and sickness also was amongst them, occasioned by the number of carcasses that lay in heaps unburied. Being lodged among the ruins, the ashes, which were very deep, blown about with the winds and combining with the sultry heats, breathed up, so to say, a dry and searching air, the inhalation of which was destructive to their health. But the chief cause was the change from their natural climate, coming as they did out of shady and hilly countries, abounding in means of shelter from the heat, to lodge in low, and, in the autumn season, very unhealthy ground; added to which was the length and tediousness of the siege, as they had now sate seven months before the Capitol. There was, therefore, a great destruction among them, and the number of the dead grew so great, that the living gave up burying them. Neither, indeed, were things on that account any better with the besieged, for famine increased upon them, and despondency with not hearing any thing of Camillus, it being impossible to send any one to him, the city was so guarded by the barbarians. Things being in this sad condition on both sides, a motion of treaty was made at first by some of the outposts, as they happened to speak

with one another; which being embraced by the leading
men, Sulpicius, tribune of the Romans, came to a parley
with Brennus, in which it was agreed, that the Romans
laying down a thousand weight of gold, the Gauls upon
the receipt of it should immediately quit the city and
territories. The agreement being confirmed by oath on
both sides, and the gold brought forth, the Gauls used
false dealing in the weights, secretly at first, but afterwards openly pulled back and disturbed the balance; at
which the Romans indignantly complaining, Brennus in
a scoffing and insulting manner pulled off his sword and
belt, and threw them both into the scales; and when
Sulpicius asked what that meant, "What should it mean,"
says he, "but woe to the conquered?" which afterwards
became a proverbial saying. As for the Romans, some
were so incensed that they were for taking their gold
back again, and returning to endure the siege. Others
were for passing by and dissembling a petty injury, and
not to account that the indignity of the thing lay in paying more than was due, since the paying any thing at all
was itself a dishonor only submitted to as a necessity of
the times.

Whilst this difference remained still unsettled, both
amongst themselves and with the Gauls, Camillus was at
the gates with his army; and, having learned what was
going on, commanded the main body of his forces to follow
slowly after him in good order, and himself with the
choicest of his men hastening on, went at once to the
Romans; where all giving way to him, and receiving him
as their sole magistrate, with profound silence and order,
he took the gold out of the scales, and delivered it to his
officers, and commanded the Gauls to take their weights
and scales and depart; saying that it was customary
with the Romans to deliver their country with iron, not
with gold. And when Brennus began to rage, and say that

he was unjustly dealt with in such a breach of contract,
Camillus answered that it was never legally made, and
the agreement of no force or obligation; for that himself
being declared dictator, and there being no other magistrate by law, the engagement had been made with men
who had no power to enter into it; but now they might
say any thing they had to urge, for he was come with
full power by law to grant pardon to such as should ask
it, or inflict punishment on the guilty, if they did not
repent. At this, Brennus broke into violent anger, and
an immediate quarrel ensued; both sides drew their swords
and attacked, but in confusion, as could not otherwise
be amongst houses, and in narrow lanes and places where
it was impossible to form in any order. But Brennus,
presently recollecting himself, called off his men, and, with
the loss of a few only, brought them to their camp; and,
rising in the night with all his forces, left the city, and,
advancing about eight miles, encamped upon the way to
Gabii. As soon as day appeared, Camillus came up with
him, splendidly armed himself, and his soldiers full of
courage and confidence; and there engaging with him in
a sharp conflict, which lasted a long while, overthrew his
army with great slaughter, and took their camp. Of
those that fled, some were presently cut off by the pursuers; others, and these were the greatest number, dispersed hither and thither, and were despatched by the
people that came sallying out from the neighboring towns
and villages.

Thus Rome was strangely taken, and more strangely
recovered, having been seven whole months in the possession of the barbarians, who entered her a little after the
Ides of July, and were driven out about the Ides of February following. Camillus triumphed, as he deserved,
having saved his country that was lost, and brought the
city, so to say, back again to itself. For those that had

fled abroad, together with their wives and children, accompanied him as he rode in; and those who had been shut up in the Capitol, and were reduced almost to the point of perishing with hunger, went out to meet him, embracing each other as they met, and weeping for joy, and, through the excess of the present pleasure, scarce believing in its truth. And when the priests and ministers of the gods appeared, bearing the sacred things, which in their flight they had either hid on the spot, or conveyed away with them, and now openly showed in safety, the citizens who saw the blessed sight felt as if with these the gods themselves were again returned unto Rome. After Camillus had sacrificed to the gods, and purified the city according to the direction of those properly instructed, he restored the existing temples, and erected a new one to Rumour, or Voice,* informing himself of the spot in which that voice from heaven came by night to Marcus Cædicius, foretelling the coming of the barbarian army.

It was a matter of difficulty, and a hard task, amidst so much rubbish, to discover and re-determine the consecrated places; but by the zeal of Camillus, and the incessant labor of the priests, it was at last accomplished. But when it came also to rebuilding the city, which was wholly demolished, despondency seized the multitude, and a backwardness to engage in a work for which they had no materials; at a time, too, when they rather needed relief and repose from their past labors, than any new demands upon their exhausted strength and impaired fortunes. Thus insensibly they turned their thoughts again towards Veii, a city ready-built and well-provided, and gave an opening to the arts of flatterers eager to gratify

---

* Aius Loquens, in Cicero, Aius   cause "aiebat et loquebatur."
Loculius, in Livy, so entitled be-

their desires, and lent their ears to seditious language flung out against Camillus; as that, out of ambition and self-glory, he withheld them from a city fit to receive them, forcing them to live in the midst of ruins, and to re-erect a pile of burnt rubbish, that he might be esteemed not the chief magistrate only and general of Rome, but, to the exclusion of Romulus, its founder, also. The senate, therefore, fearing a sedition, would not suffer Camillus, though desirous, to lay down his authority within the year, though no other dictator had ever held it above six months.

They themselves, meantime, used their best endeavors, by kind persuasions and familiar addresses, to encourage and to appease the people, showing them the shrines and tombs of their ancestors, calling to their remembrance the sacred spots and holy places which Romulus and Numa or any other of their kings had consecrated and left to their keeping; and among the strongest religious arguments, urged the head, newly separated from the body, which was found in laying the foundation of the Capitol, marking it as a place destined by fate to be the head of all Italy; and the holy fire which had just been rekindled again, since the end of the war, by the vestal virgins; "What a disgrace would it be to them to lose and extinguish this, leaving the city it belonged to, to be either inhabited by strangers and new-comers, or left a wild pasture for cattle to graze on?" Such reasons as these, urged with complaint and expostulation, sometimes in private upon individuals, and sometimes in their public assemblies, were met, on the other hand, by laments and protestations of distress and helplessness; entreaties, that, re-united as they just were, after a sort of shipwreck, naked and destitute, they would not constrain them to patch up the pieces of a ruined and shattered city, when they had another at hand ready-built and prepared.

Camillus thought good to refer it to general deliberation, and himself spoke largely and earnestly in behalf of
his country, as also many others. At last, calling to Lucius Lucretius, whose place it was to speak first, he commanded him to give his sentence, and the rest as they followed, in order. Silence being made, and Lucretius just
about to begin, by chance a centurion, passing by outside
with his company of the day-guard, called out with a loud
voice to the ensign-bearer to halt and fix his standard, for
this was the best place to stay in. This voice, coming in that
moment of time, and at that crisis of uncertainty and anxiety for the future, was taken as a direction what was to be
done; so that Lucretius, assuming an attitude of devotion, gave sentence in concurrence with the gods, as he
said, as likewise did all that followed. Even among the
common people it created a wonderful change of feeling;
every one now cheered and encouraged his neighbor, and
set himself to the work, proceeding in it, however, not by
any regular lines or divisions, but every one pitching upon
that plot of ground which came next to hand, or best
pleased his fancy; by which haste and hurry in building,
they constructed their city in narrow and ill-designed
lanes, and with houses huddled together one upon another; for it is said that within the compass of the year
the whole city was raised up anew, both in its public
walls and private buildings. The persons, however, appointed by Camillus to resume and mark out, in this
general confusion, all consecrated places, coming, in their
way round the Palatium, to the chapel of Mars, found the
chapel itself indeed destroyed and burnt to the ground,
like every thing else, by the barbarians; but whilst they
were clearing the place, and carrying away the rubbish,
lit upon Romulus's augural staff, buried under a great
heap of ashes. This sort of staff is crooked at one end,
and is called *lituus;* they make use of it in quartering

out the regions of the heavens when engaged in divination from the flight of birds; Romulus, who was himself
a great diviner, made use of it. But when he disappeared
from the earth, the priests took his staff and kept it, as
other holy things, from the touch of man; and when
they now found that, whereas all other things were consumed, this staff had altogether escaped the flames, they
began to conceive happier hopes of Rome, and to augur
from this token its future everlasting safety.

And now they had scarcely got a breathing time from
their trouble, when a new war came upon them; and the
Æquians, Volscians, and Latins all at once invaded their
territories, and the Tuscans besieged Sutrium, their con-
federate city. The military tribunes who commanded the
army, and were encamped about the hill Mæcius, being
closely besieged by the Latins, and the camp in danger to be
lost, sent to Rome, where Camillus was a third time chosen
dictator. Of this war two different accounts are given; I
shall begin with the more fabulous. They say that the
Latins (whether out of pretence, or a real design to revive
the ancient relationship of the two nations) sent to desire of the Romans some free-born maidens in marriage;
that when the Romans were at a loss how to determine
(for on one hand they dreaded a war, having scarcely yet
settled and recovered themselves, and on the other side
suspected that this asking of wives was, in plain terms,
nothing else but a demand for hostages, though covered
over with the specious name of intermarriage and alliance), a certain handmaid, by name Tutula, or, as some
call her, Philotis, persuaded the magistrates to send with
her some of the most youthful and best-looking maid-servants, in the bridal dress of noble virgins, and leave the
rest to her care and management; that the magistrates,
consenting, chose out as many as she thought necessary
for her purpose, and, adorning them with gold and rich

clothes, delivered them to the Latins, who were encamped not far from the city; that at night the rest stole
away the enemy's swords, but Tutula or Philotis, getting
to the top of a wild fig-tree, and spreading out a thick
woollen cloth behind her, held out a torch towards Rome,
which was the signal concerted between her and the
commanders, without the knowledge, however, of any
other of the citizens, which was the reason that their
issuing out from the city was tumultuous, the officers
pushing their men on, and they calling upon one another's names, and scarce able to bring themselves into
order; that setting upon the enemy's works, who either
were asleep or expected no such matter, they took the
camp, and destroyed most of them; and that this was done
on the nones of July, which was then called Quintilis, and
that the feast that is observed on that day is a commemoration of what was then done. For in it, first, they run
out of the city in great crowds, and call out aloud several
familiar and common names, Caius, Marcus, Lucius, and
the like, in representation of the way in which they
called to one another when they went out in such haste.
In the next place, the maid-servants, gaily dressed, run
about, playing and jesting upon all they meet, and
amongst themselves, also, use a kind of skirmishing, to
show they helped in the conflict against the Latins; and
while eating and drinking, they sit shaded over with
boughs of wild fig-tree, and the day they call Nonæ
Caprotinæ, as some think from that wild fig-tree on which
the maid-servant held up her torch, the Roman name for
a wild fig-tree being *caprificus*. Others refer most of
what is said or done at this feast to the fate of Romulus,
for, on this day, he vanished outside the gates in a sudden darkness and storm (some think it an eclipse of the
sun), and from this, the day was called Nonæ Caprotinæ,

the Latin for a goat being *capra*, and the place where he disappeared having the name of Goat's Marsh, as is stated in his life.

But the general stream of writers prefer the other account of this war, which they thus relate. Camillus, being the third time chosen dictator, and learning that the army under the tribunes was besieged by the Latins and Volscians, was constrained to arm, not only those under, but also those over the age of service; and taking a large circuit round the mountain Mæcius, undiscovered by the enemy, lodged his army on their rear, and then by many fires gave notice of his arrival. The besieged, encouraged by this, prepared to sally forth and join battle; but the Latins and Volscians, fearing this exposure to an enemy on both sides, drew themselves within their works, and fortified their camp with a strong palisade of trees on every side, resolving to wait for more supplies from home, and expecting, also, the assistance of the Tuscans, their confederates. Camillus, detecting their object, and fearing to be reduced to the same position to which he had brought them, namely, to be besieged himself, resolved to lose no time; and finding their rampart was all of timber, and observing that a strong wind constantly at sun-rising blew off from the mountains, after having prepared a quantity of combustibles, about break of day he drew forth his forces, commanding a part with their missiles to assault the enemy with noise and shouting on the other quarter, whilst he, with those that were to fling in the fire, went to that side of the enemy's camp to which the wind usually blew, and there waited his opportunity. When the skirmish was begun, and the sun risen, and a strong wind set in from the mountains, he gave the signal of onset; and, heaping in an infinite quantity of fiery matter, filled all their rampart with it, so that the flame, being fed by the close timber and wooden palisades, went on and spread into all quarters. The Latins, having nothing ready to keep it off or extinguish it, when the camp was now almost full of fire, were driven back within a very small compass, and at last forced by necessity to come into their enemy's hands, who stood before the works ready armed and prepared to receive them; of these very few escaped, while those that stayed in the camp were all a prey to the fire, until the Romans, to gain the pillage, extinguished it.

These things performed, Camillus, leaving his son Lucius in the camp to guard the prisoners and secure the booty, passed into the enemy's country, where, having taken the city of the Æquians and reduced the Volscians to obedience, he then immediately led his army to Sutrium, not having heard what had befallen the Sutrians, but making haste to assist them, as if they were still in danger and besieged by the Tuscans. They, however, had already surrendered their city to their enemies, and destitute of all things, with nothing left but their clothes, met Camillus on the way, leading their wives and children, and bewailing their misfortune. Camillus himself was struck with compassion, and perceiving the soldiers weeping, and commiserating their case, while the Sutrians hung about and clung to them, resolved not to defer revenge, but that very day to lead his army to Sutrium; conjecturing that the enemy, having just taken a rich and plentiful city, without an enemy left within it, nor any from without to be expected, would be found abandoned to enjoyment and unguarded. Neither did his opinion fail him; he not only passed through their country without discovery, but came up to their very gates and possessed himself of the walls, not a man being left to guard them, but their whole army scattered about in the houses, drinking and making merry. Nay, when at last they did

perceive that the enemy had seized the city, they were
so overloaded with meat and wine, that few were able so
much as to endeavor to escape, but either waited shame-
fully for their death within doors, or surrendered themselves to the conqueror. Thus the city of the Sutrians
was twice taken in one day; and they who were in possession lost it, and they who had lost regained it, alike by
the means of Camillus. For all which actions he received
a triumph, which brought him no less honor and reputation than the two former ones; for those citizens who
before most regarded him with an evil eye, and ascribed
his successes to a certain luck rather than real merit, were
compelled by these last acts of his to allow the whole
honor to his great abilities and energy.

Of all the adversaries and enviers of his glory, Marcus
Manlius was the most distinguished, he who first drove
back the Gauls when they made their night attack upon
the Capitol, and who for that reason had been named
Capitolinus. This man, affecting the first place in the
commonwealth, and not able by noble ways to outdo
Camillus's reputation, took that ordinary course towards
usurpation of absolute power, namely, to gain the multitude, those of them especially that were in debt; defending some by pleading their causes against their creditors,
rescuing others by force, and not suffering the law to proceed against them; insomuch that in a short time he
got great numbers of indigent people about him, whose
tumults and uproars in the forum struck terror into the
principal citizens. After that Quintius Capitolinus, who
was made dictator to suppress these disorders, had committed Manlius to prison, the people immediately changed
their apparel, a thing never done but in great and public
calamities, and the senate, fearing some tumult, ordered
him to be released. He, however, when set at liberty,
changed not his course, but was rather the more insolent

in his proceedings, filling the whole city with faction and sedition. They chose, therefore, Camillus again military tribune ; and a day being appointed for Manlius to answer to his charge, the prospect from the place where his trial was held proved a great impediment to his accusers; for the very spot where Manlius by night fought with the Gauls overlooked the forum from the Capitol, so that, stretching forth his hands that way, and weeping, he called to their remembrance his past actions, raising compassion in all that beheld him. Insomuch that the judges were at a loss what to do, and several times adjourned the trial, unwilling to acquit him of the crime, which was sufficiently proved, and yet unable to execute the law while his noble action remained, as it were, before their eyes. Camillus, considering this, transferred the court outside the gates to the Peteline Grove, from whence there is no prospect of the Capitol. Here his accuser went on with his charge, and his judges were capable of remembering and duly resenting his guilty deeds. He was convicted, carried to the Capitol, and flung headlong from the rock; so that one and the same spot was thus the witness of his greatest glory, and monument of his most unfortunate end. The Romans, besides, razed his house, and built there a temple to the goddess they call Moneta, ordaining for the future that none of the patrician order should ever dwell on the Capitoline.

And now Camillus, being called to his sixth tribuneship, desired to be excused, as being aged, and perhaps not unfearful of the malice of fortune, and those reverses which seem to ensue upon great prosperity. But the most apparent pretence was the weakness of his body, for he happened at that time to be sick; the people, however, would admit of no excuses, but, crying that they wanted not his strength for horse or for foot service, but only his counsel and conduct, constrained him to undertake the command, and with one of his fellow-tribunes to lead the army immediately against the enemy. These were the Prænestines and Volscians, who, with large forces, were laying waste the territory of the Roman confederates. Having marched out with his army, he sat down and encamped near the enemy, meaning himself to protract the war, or if there should come any necessity or occasion of fighting, in the mean time to regain his strength. But Lucius Furius, his colleague, carried away with the desire of glory, was not to be held in, but, impatient to give battle, inflamed the inferior officers of the army with the same eagerness; so that Camillus, fearing he might seem out of envy to be wishing to rob the young men of the glory of a noble exploit, consented, though unwillingly, that he should draw out the forces, whilst himself, by reason of weakness, stayed behind with a few in the camp. Lucius, engaging rashly, was discomfited, when Camillus, perceiving the Romans to give ground and fly, could not contain himself, but, leaping from his bed, with those he had about him ran to meet them at the gates of the camp, making his way through the flyers to oppose the pursuers; so that those who had got within the camp turned back at once and followed him, and those that came flying from without made head again and gathered about him, exhorting one another not to forsake their general. Thus the enemy, for that time, was stopped in his pursuit. The next day Camillus, drawing out his forces and joining battle with them, overthrew them by main force, and, following close upon them, entered pell-mell with them into their camp, and took it, slaying the greatest part of them. Afterwards, having heard that the city Satricum was taken by the Tuscans, and the inhabitants, all Romans, put to the sword, he sent home to Rome the main body of his forces and heaviest-armed, and, taking with him the lightest and

most vigorous soldiers, set suddenly upon the Tuscans,
who were in the possession of the city, and mastered
them, slaying some and expelling the rest; and so, returning to Rome with great spoils, gave signal evidence of
their superior wisdom, who, not mistrusting the weakness
and age of a commander endued with courage and conduct, had rather chosen him who was sickly and desirous
to be excused, than younger men who were forward and
ambitious to command.

When, therefore, the revolt of the Tusculans was reported, they gave Camillus the charge of reducing them,
choosing one of his five colleagues to go with him. And
when every one was eager for the place, contrary to the
expectation of all, he passed by the rest and chose Lucius
Furius, the very same man who lately, against the judgment of Camillus, had rashly hazarded and nearly lost a
battle; willing, as it should seem, to dissemble that miscarriage, and free him from the shame of it. The Tusculans, hearing of Camillus's coming against them, made a
cunning attempt at revoking their act of revolt; their
fields, as in times of highest peace, were full of ploughmen
and shepherds; their gates stood wide open, and their
children were being taught in the schools; of the people,
such as were tradesmen, he found in their workshops,
busied about their several employments, and the better
sort of citizens walking in the public places in their ordinary dress; the magistrates hurried about to provide
quarters for the Romans, as if they stood in fear of no
danger and were conscious of no fault. Which arts,
though they could not dispossess Camillus of the conviction he had of their treason, yet induced some compassion
for their repentance; he commanded them to go to the
senate and deprecate their anger, and joined himself as
an intercessor in their behalf, so that their city was
acquitted of all guilt and admitted to Roman citizenship.

These were the most memorable actions of his sixth tribuneship.

After these things, Licinius Stolo raised a great sedition
in the city, and brought the people to dissension with the
senate, contending, that of two consuls one should be
chosen out of the commons, and not both out of the
patricians. Tribunes of the people were chosen, but the
election of consuls was interrupted and prevented by the
people. And as this absence of any supreme magistrate
was leading to yet further confusion, Camillus was the
fourth time created dictator by the senate, sorely against
the people's will, and not altogether in accordance with
his own; he had little desire for a conflict with men
whose past services entitled them to tell him that he had
achieved far greater actions in war along with them than
in politics with the patricians, who, indeed, had only put
him forward now out of envy; that, if successful, he might
crush the people, or, failing, be crushed himself. However, to provide as good a remedy as he could for the present, knowing the day on which the tribunes of the people
intended to prefer the law, he appointed it by proclamation for a general muster, and called the people from the
forum into the Campus, threatening to set heavy fines
upon such as should not obey. On the other side, the
tribunes of the people met his threats by solemnly pro-
testing they would fine him in fifty thousand drachmas
of silver, if he persisted in obstructing the people from
giving their suffrages for the law. Whether it were, then,
that he feared another banishment or condemnation,
which would ill become his age and past great actions, or
found himself unable to stem the current of the multitude,
which ran strong and violent, he betook himself, for the
present, to his house, and afterwards, for some days together, professing sickness, finally laid down his dictatorship. The senate created another dictator; who, choosing

Stolo, leader of the sedition, to be his general of horse, suffered that law to be enacted and ratified, which was most grievous to the patricians, namely, that no person whatsoever should possess above five hundred acres of land. Stolo was much distinguished by the victory he had gained; but, not long after, was found himself to possess more than he had allowed to others, and suffered the penalties of his own law.

And now the contention about election of consuls coming on (which was the main point and original cause of the dissension, and had throughout furnished most matter of division between the senate and the people), certain intelligence arrived, that the Gauls again, proceeding from the Adriatic Sea, were marching in vast numbers upon Rome. On the very heels of the report followed manifest acts also of hostility; the country through which they marched was all wasted, and such as by flight could not make their escape to Rome were dispersing and scattering among the mountains. The terror of this war quieted the sedition; nobles and commons, senate and people together, unanimously chose Camillus the fifth time dictator; who, though very aged, not wanting much of fourscore years, yet, considering the danger and necessity of his country, did not, as before, pretend sickness, or depreciate his own capacity, but at once undertook the charge, and enrolled soldiers. And, knowing that the great force of the barbarians lay chiefly in their swords, with which they laid about them in a rude and inartificial manner, hacking and hewing the head and shoulders, he caused head-pieces entire of iron to be made for most of his men, smoothing and polishing the outside, that the enemy's swords, lighting upon them, might either slide off or be broken; and fitted also their shields with a little rim of brass, the wood itself not being sufficient to bear off the blows. Besides, he taught his soldiers to use their long javelins in close encounter, and, by bringing them under their enemy's swords, to receive their strokes upon them.

When the Gauls drew near, about the river Anio, dragging a heavy camp after them, and loaded with infinite spoil, Camillus drew forth his forces, and planted himself upon a hill of easy ascent, and which had many dips in it, with the object that the greatest part of his army might lie concealed, and those who appeared might be thought to have betaken themselves, through fear, to those upper grounds. And the more to increase this opinion in them, he suffered them, without any disturbance, to spoil and pillage even to his very trenches, keeping himself quiet within his works, which were well fortified; till, at last, perceiving that part of the enemy were scattered about the country foraging, and that those that were in the camp did nothing day and night but drink and revel, in the night time he drew up his lightest-armed men, and sent them out before to impede the enemy while forming into order, and to harass them when they should first issue out of their camp; and early in the morning brought down his main body, and set them in battle array in the lower grounds, a numerous and courageous army, not, as the barbarians had supposed, an inconsiderable and fearful division. The first thing that shook the courage of the Gauls was, that their enemies had, contrary to their expectation, the honor of being aggressors. In the next place, the light-armed men, falling upon them before they could get into their usual order or range themselves in their proper squadrons, so disturbed and pressed upon them, that they were obliged to fight at random, without any order at all. But at last, when Camillus brought on his heavy-armed legions, the barbarians, with their swords drawn, went vigorously to engage them; the Romans, however, opposing their javelins, and receiving the force of their blows on those parts of their defences which were well guarded with steel, turned the edge of their weapons, being made of a soft and ill-tempered metal, so that their swords bent and doubled up in their hands; and their shields were pierced through and through, and grew heavy with the javelins that stuck upon them. And thus forced to quit their own weapons, they endeavored to take advantage of those of their enemies, laid hold of the javelins with their hands, and tried to pluck them away. But the Romans, perceiving them now naked and defenceless, betook themselves to their swords, which they so well used, that in a little time great slaughter was made in the foremost ranks, while the rest fled over all parts of the level country; the hills and upper grounds Camillus had secured beforehand, and their camp they knew it would not be difficult for the enemy to take, as, through confidence of victory, they had left it unguarded. This fight, it is stated, was thirteen years after the sacking of Rome; and from henceforward the Romans took courage, and surmounted the apprehensions they had hitherto entertained of the barbarians, whose previous defeat they had attributed rather to pestilence and a concurrence of mischances than to their own superior valor. And, indeed, this fear had been formerly so great, that they made a law, that priests should be excused from service in war, unless in an invasion from the Gauls.

This was the last military action that ever Camillus performed; for the voluntary surrender of the city of the Velitrani was but a mere accessory to it. But the greatest of all civil contests, and the hardest to be managed, was still to be fought out against the people; who, returning home full of victory and success, insisted, contrary to established law, to have one of the consuls chosen out of their own body. The senate strongly opposed it, and would not suffer Camillus to lay down his dictatorship, thinking, that, under the shelter of his great name and authority, they should be better able to contend for the power of the aristocracy.   But when Camillus was sitting upon the tribunal, despatching public affairs, an officer, sent by the tribunes of the people, commanded him to rise and follow him, laying his hand upon him, as ready to seize and carry him away; upon which, such a noise and tumult as was never heard before, filled the whole forum; some that were about Camillus thrusting the officer from the bench, and the multitude below calling out to him to bring Camillus down.   Being at a loss what to do in these difficulties, he yet laid not down his authority, but, taking the senators along with him, he went to the senate-house; but before he entered, besought the gods that they would bring these troubles to a happy conclusion, solemnly vowing, when the tumult was ended, to build a temple to Concord.   A great conflict of opposite opinions arose in the senate; but, at last, the most moderate and most acceptable to the people prevailed, and consent was given, that of two consuls, one should be chosen from the commonalty.   When the dictator proclaimed this determination of the senate to the people, at the moment, pleased and reconciled with the senate, as indeed could not otherwise be, they accompanied Camillus home, with all expressions and acclamations of joy; and the next day, assembling together, they voted a temple of Concord to be built, according to Camillus's vow, facing the assembly and the forum; and to the feasts, called the Latin holidays, they added one day more, making four in all; and ordained that, on the present occasion, the whole people of Rome should sacrifice with garlands on their heads.

In the election of consuls held by Camillus, Marcus Æmilius was chosen of the patricians, and Lucius Sextius the first of the commonalty; and this was the last of all

Camillus's actions. In the year following, a pestilential sickness infected Rome, which, besides an infinite number of the common people, swept away most of the magistrates, among whom was Camillus; whose death cannot be called immature, if we consider his great age, or greater actions, yet was he more lamented than all the rest put together that then died of that distemper.

PERICLES.

CÆSAR * once, seeing some wealthy strangers at Rome, carrying up and down with them in their arms and bosoms young puppy-dogs and monkeys, embracing and making much of them, took occasion not unnaturally to ask whether the women in their country were not used to bear children; by that prince-like reprimand gravely reflecting upon persons who spend and lavish upon brute beasts that affection and kindness which nature has implanted in us to be bestowed on those of our own kind. With like reason may we blame those who misuse that love of inquiry and observation which nature has implanted in our souls, by expending it on objects unworthy of the attention either of their eyes or their ears, while they disregard such as are excellent in themselves, and would do them good.

The mere outward sense, being passive in responding to the impression of the objects that come in its way and strike upon it, perhaps cannot help entertaining and taking notice of every thing that addresses it, be it what it will, useful or unuseful; but, in the exercise of his mental perception, every man, if he chooses, has a natural power to turn himself upon all occasions, and to change and shift with the greatest ease to what he shall himself judge de-

* Probably Augustus.

sirable. So that it becomes a man's duty to pursue and make after the best and choicest of every thing, that he may not only employ his contemplation, but may also be improved by it. For as that color is most suitable to the eye whose freshness and pleasantness stimulates and strengthens the sight, so a man ought to apply his intellectual perception to such objects as, with the sense of delight, are apt to call it forth, and allure it to its own proper good and advantage.

Such objects we find in the acts of virtue, which also produce in the minds of mere readers about them, an emulation and eagerness that may lead them on to imitation. In other things there does not immediately follow upon the admiration and liking of the thing done, any strong desire of doing the like. Nay, many times, on the very contrary, when we are pleased with the work, we slight and set little by the workman or artist himself, as, for instance, in perfumes and purple dyes, we are taken with the things themselves well enough, but do not think dyers and perfumers otherwise than low and sordid people. It was not said amiss by Antisthenes, when people told him that one Ismenias was an excellent piper, "It may be so," said he, "but he is but a wretched human being, otherwise he would not have been an excellent piper." And king Philip, to the same purpose, told his son Alexander, who once at a merry-meeting played a piece of music charmingly and skilfully, "Are you not ashamed, son, to play so well?" For it is enough for a king or prince to find leisure sometimes to hear others sing, and he does the muses quite honor enough when he pleases to be but present, while others engage in such exercises and trials of skill.

He who busies himself in mean occupations produces, in the very pains he takes about things of little or no use, an evidence against himself of his negligence and indis-

position to what is really good. Nor did any generous
and ingenuous young man, at the sight of the statue of
Jupiter at Pisa, ever desire to be a Phidias, or, on seeing
that of Juno at Argos, long to be a Polycletus, or feel
induced by his pleasure in their poems to wish to be an
Anacreon or Philetas or Archilochus. For it does not
necessarily follow, that, if a piece of work please for its
gracefulness, therefore he that wrought it deserves our
admiration. Whence it is that neither do such things
really profit or advantage the beholders, upon the sight
of which no zeal arises for the imitation of them, nor any
impulse or inclination, which may prompt any desire or
endeavor of doing the like. But virtue, by the bare
statement of its actions, can so affect men's minds as to
create at once both admiration of the things done and
desire to imitate the doers of them. The goods of fortune we would possess and would enjoy; those of virtue
we long to practise and exercise; we are content to
receive the former from others, the latter we wish others
to experience from us. Moral good is a practical
stimulus; it is no sooner seen, than it inspires an impulse to practise; and influences the mind and character
not by a mere imitation which we look at, but, by the
statement of the fact, creates a moral purpose which we
form.

And so we have thought fit to spend our time and
pains in writing of the lives of famous persons; and
have composed this tenth book upon that subject, containing the life of Pericles, and that of Fabius Maximus, who
carried on the war against Hannibal, men alike, as in
their other virtues and good parts, so especially in
their mild and upright temper and demeanor, and in
that capacity to bear the cross-grained humors of their
fellow-citizens and colleagues in office which made them
both most useful and serviceable to the interests of their

countries. Whether we take a right aim at our intended purpose, it is left to the reader to judge by what he shall here find.

Pericles was of the tribe Acamantis, and the township Cholargus, of the noblest birth both on his father's and mother's side. Xanthippus, his father, who defeated the king of Persia's generals in the battle at Mycale, took to wife Agariste, the grandchild of Clisthenes, who drove out the sons of Pisistratus, and nobly put an end to their tyrannical usurpation, and moreover made a body of laws, and settled a model of government admirably tempered and suited for the harmony and safety of the people.

His mother, being near her time, fancied in a dream that she was brought to bed of a lion, and a few days after was delivered of Pericles, in other respects perfectly formed, only his head was somewhat longish and out of proportion. For which reason almost all the images and statues that were made of him have the head covered with a helmet, the workmen apparently being willing not to expose him. The poets of Athens called him *Schino-cephalos*, or squill-head, from *schinos*, a squill, or sea-onion. One of the comic poets, Cratinus, in the Chirons, tells us that —

> Old Chronos once took queen Sedition to wife;
> Which two brought to life
> That tyrant far-famed,
> Whom the gods the supreme skull-compeller* have named.

And, in the Nemesis, addresses him —

> Come, Jove, thou *head* of gods.

* Kephalegeretes, a play on Nephelegeretes, the cloud-compeller.

And a second, Teleclides, says, that now, in embarrassment with political difficulties, he sits in the city, —

> Fainting underneath the load
> Of his own head ; and now abroad,
> From his huge gallery of a pate,
> Sends forth trouble to the state.

And a third, Eupolis, in the comedy called the Demi, in a series of questions about each of the demagogues, whom he makes in the play to come up from hell, upon Pericles being named last, exclaims, —

> And here by way of summary, now we 've done,
> Behold, in brief, the heads of all in one.

The master that taught him music, most authors are agreed, was Damon (whose name, they say, ought to be pronounced with the first syllable short). Though Aristotle tells us that he was thoroughly practised in all accomplishments of this kind by Pythoclides. Damon, it is not unlikely, being a sophist, out of policy, sheltered himself under the profession of music to conceal from people in general his skill in other things, and under this pretence attended Pericles, the young athlete of politics, so to say, as his training-master in these exercises. Damon's lyre, however, did not prove altogether a successful blind ; he was banished the country by ostracism for ten years, as a dangerous intermeddler and a favorer of arbitrary power, and, by this means, gave the stage occasion to play upon him. As, for instance, Plato, the comic poet, introduces a character, who questions him —

> Tell me, if you please,
> Since you 're the Chiron who taught Pericles.

Pericles, also, was a hearer of Zeno, the Eleatic, who

treated of natural philosophy in the same manner as Par-
menides did, but had also perfected himself in an art of
his own for refuting and silencing opponents in argument;
as Timon of Phlius describes it, —

Also the two-edged tongue of mighty Zeno, who,
Say what one would, could argue it untrue.

But he that saw most of Pericles, and furnished him
most especially with a weight and grandeur of sense,
superior to all arts of popularity, and in general gave him
his elevation and sublimity of purpose and of character,
was Anaxagoras of Clazomenæ; whom the men of those
times called by the name of Nous, that is, mind, or intelligence, whether in admiration of the great and extraordinary gift he displayed for the science of nature, or because that he was the first of the philosophers who did not
refer the first ordering of the world to fortune or chance,
nor to necessity or compulsion, but to a pure, unadulte-
rated intelligence, which in all other existing mixed and
compound things acts as a principle of discrimination, and
of combination of like with like.

For this man, Pericles entertained an extraordinary
esteem and admiration, and, filling himself with this lofty,
and, as they call it, up-in-the-air sort of thought, derived
hence not merely, as was natural, elevation of purpose and
dignity of language, raised far above the base and dis-
honest buffooneries of mob-eloquence, but, besides this,
a composure of countenance, and a serenity and calmness
in all his movements, which no occurrence whilst he was
speaking could disturb, a sustained and even tone of
voice, and various other advantages of a similar kind,
which produced the greatest effect on his hearers. Once,
after being reviled and ill-spoken of all day long in
his own hearing by some vile and abandoned fellow in

the open market-place, where he was engaged in the
despatch of some urgent affair, he continued his business
in perfect silence, and in the evening returned home
composedly, the man still dogging him at the heels, and
pelting him all the way with abuse and foul language;
and stepping into his house, it being by this time dark, he
ordered one of his servants to take a light, and to go along
with the man and see him safe home.　Ion, it is true, the
dramatic poet, says that Pericles's manner in company
was somewhat over-assuming and pompous; and that
into his high bearing there entered a good deal of slight-
ingness and scorn of others; he reserves his commendation for Cimon's ease and pliancy and natural grace in
society.　Ion, however, who must needs make virtue, like
a show of tragedies, include some comic scenes,* we shall
not altogether rely upon; Zeno used to bid those who
called Pericles's gravity the affectation of a charlatan, to
go and affect the like themselves; inasmuch as this mere
counterfeiting might in time insensibly instil into them
a real love and knowledge of those noble qualities.

Nor were these the only advantages which Pericles
derived from Anaxagoras's acquaintance; he seems also
to have become, by his instructions, superior to that
superstition with which an ignorant wonder at appearances, for example, in the heavens possesses the minds of
people unacquainted with their causes, eager for the supernatural, and excitable through an inexperience which
the knowledge of natural causes removes, replacing wild
and timid superstition by the good hope and assurance
of an intelligent piety.

There is a story, that once Pericles had brought to him

* Three tragedies represented in succession were followed by a burlesque, the so-called *satyric* drama, which has no connection, it must be remembered, with the moral satire of the Romans, but takes its name from the grotesque satyrs of the Greek woods.

from a country farm of his, a ram's head with one horn, and that Lampon, the diviner, upon seeing the horn grow strong and solid out of the midst of the forehead, gave it as his judgment, that, there being at that time two potent factions, parties, or interests in the city, the one of Thucydides and the other of Pericles, the government would come about to that one of them in whose ground or estate this token or indication of fate had shown itself. But that Anaxagoras, cleaving the skull in sunder, showed to the bystanders that the brain had not filled up its natural place, but being oblong, like an egg, had collected from all parts of the vessel which contained it, in a point to that place from whence the root of the horn took its rise. And that, for that time, Anaxagoras was much admired for his explanation by those that were present; and Lampon no less a little while after, when Thucydides was overpowered, and the whole affairs of the state and government came into the hands of Pericles.

And yet, in my opinion, it is no absurdity to say that they were both in the right, both natural philosopher and diviner, one justly detecting the cause of this event, by which it was produced, the other the end for which it was designed. For it was the business of the one to find out and give an account of what it was made, and in what manner and by what means it grew as it did; and of the other to foretell to what end and purpose it was so made, and what it might mean or portend. Those who say that to find out the cause of a prodigy is in effect to destroy its supposed signification as such, do not take notice that, at the same time, together with divine prodigies, they also do away with signs and signals of human art and concert, as, for instance, the clashings of quoits, fire-beacons, and the shadows on sun-dials, every one of which things has its cause, and by that cause and contrivance is a sign of something else. But these are subjects, perhaps, that would better befit another place.

Pericles, while yet but a young man, stood in considerable apprehension of the people, as he was thought in face and figure to be very like the tyrant Pisistratus, and those of great age remarked upon the sweetness of his voice, and his volubility and rapidity in speaking, and were struck with amazement at the resemblance. Reflecting, too, that he had a considerable estate, and was descended of a noble family, and had friends of great influence, he was fearful all this might bring him to be banished as a dangerous person; and for this reason meddled not at all with state affairs, but in military service showed himself of a brave and intrepid nature. But when Aristides was now dead, and Themistocles driven out, and Cimon was for the most part kept abroad by the expeditions he made in parts out of Greece, Pericles, seeing things in this posture, now advanced and took his side, not with the rich and few, but with the many and poor, contrary to his natural bent, which was far from democratical; but, most likely, fearing he might fall under suspicion of aiming at arbitrary power, and seeing Cimon on the side of the aristocracy, and much beloved by the better and more distinguished people, he joined the party of the people, with a view at once both to secure himself and procure means against Cimon.

He immediately entered, also, on quite a new course of life and management of his time. For he was never seen to walk in any street but that which led to the market-place and the council-hall, and he avoided invitations of friends to supper, and all friendly visiting and intercourse whatever; in all the time he had to do with the public, which was not a little, he was never known to have gone to any of his friends to a supper, except that once when his near kinsman Euryptolemus married, he remained present till the ceremony of the drink-offering,* and then immediately rose from table and went his way. For these friendly meetings are very quick to defeat any assumed superiority, and in intimate familiarity an exterior of gravity is hard to maintain. Real excellence, indeed, is most recognized when most openly looked into; and in really good men, nothing which meets the eyes of external observers so truly deserves their admiration, as their daily common life does that of their nearer friends. Pericles, however, to avoid any feeling of commonness, or any satiety on the part of the people, presented himself at intervals only, not speaking to every business, nor at all times coming into the assembly, but, as Critolaus says, reserving himself, like the Salaminian galley,† for great occasions, while matters of lesser importance were despatched by friends or other speakers under his direction. And of this number we are told Ephialtes made one, who broke the power of the council of Areopagus, giving the people, according to Plato's expression, so copious and so strong a draught of liberty, that, growing wild and unruly, like an unmanageable horse, it, as the comic poets say, —

> " —— got beyond all keeping in,
> Champing at Euboea, and among the islands leaping in."

The style of speaking most consonant to his form of life and the dignity of his views he found, so to say, in the tones of that instrument with which Anaxagoras had furnished him; of his teaching he continually availed himself, and deepened the colors of rhetoric with the dye

* The *spondai*, or libations, which, like the modern grace, concluded the meal, and were followed by the dessert.

† The Salaminia and the Paralus were the two sacred state-galleys of Athens, used only on special missions.

of natural science. For having, in addition to his great natural genius, attained, by the study of nature, to use the words of the divine Plato, this height of intelligence, and this universal consummating power, and drawing hence whatever might be of advantage to him in the art of speaking, he showed himself far superior to all others. Upon which account, they say, he had his nickname given him, though some are of opinion he was named the Olympian from the public buildings with which he adorned the city; and others again, from his great power in public affairs, whether of war or peace. Nor is it unlikely that the confluence of many attributes may have conferred it on him. However, the comedies represented at the time, which, both in good earnest and in merriment, let fly many hard words at him, plainly show that he got that appellation especially from his speaking; they speak of his "thundering and lightning" when he harangued the people, and of his wielding a dreadful thunderbolt in his tongue.

A saying also of Thucydides, the son of Melesias, stands on record, spoken by him by way of pleasantry upon Pericles's dexterity. Thucydides was one of the noble and distinguished citizens, and had been his greatest opponent; and, when Archidamus, the king of the Lacedæmonians, asked him whether he or Pericles were the better wrestler, he made this answer: "When I," said he, "have thrown him and given him a fair fall, by persisting that he had no fall, he gets the better of me, and makes the bystanders, in spite of their own eyes, believe him." The truth, however, is, that Pericles himself was very careful what and how he was to speak, insomuch that, whenever he went up to the hustings, he prayed the gods that no one word might unawares slip from him unsuitable to the matter and the occasion.

He has left nothing in writing behind him, except some

decrees; and there are but very few of his sayings
recorded; one, for example, is, that he said Ægina
must, like a gathering in a man's eye, be removed from
Piræus; and another, that he said he saw already war
moving on its way towards them out of Peloponnesus.
Again, when on a time Sophocles, who was his fellow-com-
missioner in the generalship, was going on board with
him, and praised the beauty of a youth they met with in
the way to the ship, "Sophocles," said he, "a general
ought not only to have clean hands, but also clean eyes."
And Stesimbrotus tells us, that, in his encomium on those
who fell in battle at Samos, he said they were become
immortal, as the gods were. "For," said he, "we do not
see them themselves, but only by the honors we pay
them, and by the benefits they do us, attribute to them
immortality; and the like attributes belong also to those
that die in the service of their country."

Since Thucydides describes the rule of Pericles as an
aristocratical government, that went by the name of a
democracy, but was, indeed, the supremacy of a single
great man, while many others say, on the contrary, that
by him the common people were first encouraged and led
on to such evils as appropriations of subject territory;
allowances for attending theatres, payments for performing public duties, and by these bad habits were, under the
influence of his public measures, changed from a sober,
thrifty people, that maintained themselves by their own
labors, to lovers of expense, intemperance, and license,
let us examine the cause of this change by the actual
matters of fact.

At the first, as has been said, when he set himself
against Cimon's great authority, he did caress the people.
Finding himself come short of his competitor in wealth
and money, by which advantages the other was enabled
to take care of the poor, inviting every day some one or

other of the citizens that was in want to supper, and bestowing clothes on the aged people, and breaking down the hedges and enclosures of his grounds, that all that would might freely gather what fruit they pleased, Pericles, thus outdone in popular arts, by the advice of one Damonides of Œa, as Aristotle states, turned to the distribution of the public moneys; and in a short time having bought the people over, what with moneys allowed for shows and for service on juries, and what with other forms of pay and largess, he made use of them against the council of Areopagus, of which he himself was no member, as having never been appointed by lot either chief archon, or lawgiver, or king, or captain.* For from of old these offices were conferred on persons by lot, and they who had acquitted themselves duly in the discharge of them were advanced to the court of Areopagus. And so Pericles, having secured his power and interest with the populace, directed the exertions of his party against this council with such success, that most of those causes and matters which had been used to be tried there, were, by the agency of Ephialtes, removed from its cognizance; Cimon, also, was banished by ostracism as a favorer of the Lacedæmonians and a hater of the people, though in wealth and noble birth he was among the first, and had won several most glorious victories over the barbarians, and had filled the city with money and spoils of war; as is recorded in the history of his life. So vast an authority had Pericles obtained among the people.

The ostracism was limited by law to ten years; but the Lacedæmonians, in the mean time, entering with a

---

* Eponymus, Thesmothetes, Basileus, Polemarchus; titles of the different archons, the chief civic dignitaries, who, after the period of the Persian wars, were appointed, not by election, but simply by lot, from the whole body of citizens. Hence, at this time, the importance of the board of the ten *strategi*, or generals, who were elected, and were always persons of real or supposed capacity.

great army into the territory of Tanagra, and the Athenians going out against them, Cimon, coming from his banishment before his time was out, put himself in arms and array with those of his fellow-citizens that were of his own tribe, and desired by his deeds to wipe off the suspicion of his favoring the Lacedæmonians, by venturing his own person along with his countrymen. But Pericles's friends, gathering in a body, forced him to retire as a banished man. For which cause also Pericles seems to have exerted himself more in that than in any battle, and to have been conspicuous above all for his exposure of himself to danger. All Cimon's friends, also, to a man, fell together side by side, whom Pericles had accused with him of taking part with the Lacedæmonians. Defeated in this battle on their own frontiers, and expecting a new and perilous attack with return of spring, the Athenians now felt regret and sorrow for the loss of Cimon, and repentance for their expulsion of him. Pericles, being sensible of their feelings, did not hesitate or delay to gratify it, and himself made the motion for recalling him home. He, upon his return, concluded a peace betwixt the two cities; for the Lacedæmonians entertained as kindly feelings towards him as they did the reverse towards Pericles and the other popular leaders.

Yet some there are who say that Pericles did not propose the order for Cimon's return till some private articles of agreement had been made between them, and this by means of Elpinice, Cimon's sister; that Cimon, namely, should go out to sea with a fleet of two hundred ships, and be commander-in-chief abroad, with a design to reduce the king of Persia's territories, and that Pericles should have the power at home.

This Elpinice, it was thought, had before this time procured some favor for her brother Cimon at Pericles's hands, and induced him to be more remiss and gentle in urging the charge when Cimon was tried for his life; for Pericles was one of the committee appointed by the commons to plead against him. And when Elpinice came and besought him in her brother's behalf, he answered, with a smile, "O Elpinice, you are too old a woman to undertake such business as this." But, when he appeared to impeach him, he stood up but once to speak, merely to acquit himself of his commission, and went out of court, having done Cimon the least prejudice of any of his accusers.

How, then, can one believe Idomeneus, who charges Pericles as if he had by treachery procured the murder of Ephialtes, the popular statesman, one who was his friend, and of his own party in all his political course, out of jealousy, forsooth, and envy of his great reputation? This historian, it seems, having raked up these stories, I know not whence, has befouled with them a man who, perchance, was not altogether free from fault or blame, but yet had a noble spirit, and a soul that was bent on honor; and where such qualities are, there can no such cruel and brutal passion find harbor or gain admittance. As to Ephialtes, the truth of the story, as Aristotle has told it, is this: that having made himself formidable to the oligarchical party, by being an uncompromising asserter of the people's rights in calling to account and prosecuting those who any way wronged them, his enemies, lying in wait for him, by the means of Aristodicus the Tanagræan, privately despatched him.

Cimon, while he was admiral, ended his days in the Isle of Cyprus. And the aristocratical party, seeing that Pericles was already before this grown to be the greatest and foremost man of all the city, but nevertheless wishing there should be somebody set up against him, to blunt and turn the edge of his power, that it might not altogether prove a monarchy, put forward Thucydides of

Alopece, a discreet person, and a near kinsman of Cimon's, to conduct the opposition against him; who, indeed, though less skilled in warlike affairs than Cimon was, yet was better versed in speaking and political business, and keeping close guard in the city, and engaging with Pericles on the hustings, in a short time brought the government to an equality of parties. For he would not suffer those who were called the honest and good (persons of worth and distinction) to be scattered up and down and mix themselves and be lost among the populace, as formerly, diminishing and obscuring their superiority amongst the masses;' but taking them apart by themselves and uniting them in one body, by their combined weight he was able, as it were upon the balance, to make a counterpoise to the other party.

For, indeed, there was from the beginning a sort of concealed split, or seam, as it might be in a piece of iron, marking the different popular and aristocratical tendencies; but the open rivalry and contention of these two opponents made the gash deep, and severed the city into the two parties of the people and the few. And so Pericles, at that time more than at any other, let loose the reins to the people, and made his policy subservient to their pleasure, contriving continually to have some great public show or solemnity, some banquet, or some procession or other in the town to please them, coaxing his countrymen like children, with such delights and pleasures as were not, however, unedifying. Besides that every year he sent out threescore galleys, on board of which there went numbers of the citizens, who were in pay eight months, learning at the same time and practising the art of seamanship.

He sent, moreover, a thousand of them into the Chersonese as planters, to share the land among them by lot, and five hundred more into the isle of Naxos, and half

that number to Andros, a thousand into Thrace to dwell
among the Bisaltæ, and others into Italy, when the city
Sybaris, which now was called Thurii, was to be repeopled.
And this he did to ease and discharge the city of an idle,
and, by reason of their idleness, a busy, meddling crowd
of people; and at the same time to meet the necessities
and restore the fortunes of the poor townsmen, and to
intimidate, also, and check their allies from attempting
any change, by posting such garrisons, as it were, in the
midst of them.

That which gave most pleasure and ornament to the
city of Athens, and the greatest admiration and even astonishment to all strangers, and that which now is Greece's
only evidence that the power she boasts of and her
ancient wealth are no romance or idle story, was his con-
struction of the public and sacred buildings. Yet this
was that of all his actions in the government which his
enemies most looked askance upon and cavilled at in the
popular assemblies, crying out how that the commonwealth of Athens had lost its reputation and was ill-
spoken of abroad for removing the common treasure of
the Greeks from the isle of Delos into their own custody;
and how that their fairest excuse for so doing, namely,
that they took it away for fear the barbarians should
seize it, and on purpose to secure it in a safe place, this
Pericles had made unavailable, and how that "Greece
cannot but resent it as an insufferable affront, and consider herself to be tyrannized over openly, when she sees
the treasure, which was contributed by her upon a necessity for the war, wantonly lavished out by us upon our
city, to gild her all over, and to adorn and set her forth,
as it were some vain woman, hung round with precious
stones and figures and temples, which cost a world of
money."

Pericles, on the other hand, informed the people, that

they were in no way obliged to give any account of those moneys to their allies, so long as they maintained their defence, and kept off the barbarians from attacking them; while in the mean time they did not so much as supply one horse or man or ship, but only found money for the service; "which money," said he, "is not theirs that give it, but theirs that receive it, if so be they perform the conditions upon which they receive it." And that it was good reason, that, now the city was sufficiently provided and stored with all things necessary for the war, they should convert the overplus of its wealth to such undertakings, as would hereafter, when completed, give them eternal honor, and, for the present, while in process, freely supply all the inhabitants with plenty. With their variety of workmanship and of occasions for service, which summon all arts and trades and require all hands to be employed about them, they do actually put the whole city, in a manner, into state-pay; while at the same time she is both beautified and maintained by herself. For as those who are of age and strength for war are provided for and maintained in the armaments abroad by their pay out of the public stock, so, it being his desire and design that the undisciplined mechanic multitude that stayed at home should not go without their share of public salaries, and yet should not have them given them for sitting still and doing nothing, to that end he thought fit to bring in among them, with the approbation of the people, these vast projects of buildings and designs of works, that would be of some continuance before they were finished, and would give employment to numerous arts, so that the part of the people that stayed at home might, no less than those that were at sea or in garrisons or on expeditions, have a fair and just occasion of receiving the benefit and having their share of the public moneys.

The materials were stone, brass, ivory, gold, ebony, cypress-wood; and the arts or trades that wrought and fashioned them were smiths and carpenters, moulders, founders and braziers, stone-cutters, dyers, goldsmiths, ivory-workers, painters, embroiderers, turners; those again that conveyed them to the town for use, merchants and mariners and ship-masters by sea, and by land, cartwrights, cattle-breeders, waggoners, rope-makers, flax-workers, shoe-makers and leather-dressers, road-makers, miners. And every trade in the same nature, as a captain in an army has his particular company of soldiers under him, had its own hired company of journeymen and laborers belonging to it banded together as in array, to be as it were the instrument and body for the performance of the service. Thus, to say all in a word, the occasions and services of these public works distributed plenty through every age and condition.

As then grew the works up, no less stately in size than exquisite in form, the workmen striving to outvie the material and the design with the beauty of their workmanship, yet the most wonderful thing of all was the rapidity of their execution. Undertakings, any one of which singly might have required, they thought, for their completion, several successions and ages of men, were every one of them accomplished in the height and prime of one man's political service. Although they say, too, that Zeuxis once, having heard Agatharchus the painter boast of despatching his work with speed and ease, replied, "I take a long time." For ease and speed in doing a thing do not give the work lasting solidity or exactness of beauty; the expenditure of time allowed to a man's pains beforehand for the production of a thing is repaid by way of interest with a vital force for its preservation when once produced. For which reason Pericles's works are especially admired, as having been made quickly, to last long. For every particular piece of his work was immediately, even at that time, for its beauty and elegance, antique; and yet in its vigor and freshness looks to this day as if it were just executed. There is a sort of bloom of newness upon those works of his, preserving them from the touch of time, as if they had some perennial spirit and undying vitality mingled in the composition of them.

Phidias had the oversight of all the works, and was surveyor-general, though upon the various portions other great masters and workmen were employed. For Callicrates and Ictinus built the Parthenon; the chapel at Eleusis, where the mysteries were celebrated, was begun by Corœbus, who erected the pillars that stand upon the floor or pavement, and joined them to the architraves; and after his death Metagenes of Xypete added the frieze and the upper line of columns; Xenocles of Cholargus roofed or arched the lantern on the top of the temple of Castor and Pollux; and the long wall, which Socrates says he himself heard Pericles propose to the people, was undertaken by Callicrates. This work Cratinus ridicules, as long in finishing, —

'T is long since Pericles, if words would do it,
Talk'd up the wall; yet adds not one mite to it.

The Odeum, or music-room, which in its interior was full of seats and ranges of pillars, and outside had its roof made to slope and descend from one single point at the top, was constructed, we are told, in imitation of the king of Persia's Pavilion; this likewise by Pericles's order; which Cratinus again, in his comedy called The Thracian Women, made an occasion of raillery, —

So, we see here,
Jupiter Long-pate Pericles appear.
Since ostracism time, he's laid aside his head,
And wears the new Odeum in its stead.

Pericles, also, eager for distinction, then first obtained
the decree for a contest in musical skill to be held yearly
at the Panathenæa, and he himself, being chosen judge,
arranged the order and method in which the competitors
should sing and play on the flute and on the harp. And
both at that time, and at other times also, they sat in this
music-room to see and hear all such trials of skill.

The propylæa, or entrances to the Acropolis, were finished in five years' time, Mnesicles being the principal
architect. A strange accident happened in the course of
building, which showed that the goddess was not averse
to the work, but was aiding and coöperating to bring it
to perfection. One of the artificers, the quickest and the
handiest workman among them all, with a slip of his foot
fell down from a great height, and lay in a miserable condition, the physicians having no hopes of his recovery.
When Pericles was in distress about this, Minerva appeared to him at night in a dream, and ordered a course
of treatment, which he applied, and in a short time and
with great ease cured the man. And upon this occasion
it was that he set up a brass statue of Minerva, surnamed
Health, in the citadel near the altar, which they say was
there before. But it was Phidias who wrought the goddess's image in gold, and he has his name inscribed on the
pedestal as the workman of it; and indeed the whole
work in a manner was under his charge, and he had, as
we have said already, the oversight over all the artists
and workmen, through Pericles's friendship for him; and
this, indeed, made him much envied, and his patron shame-
fully slandered with stories, as if Phidias were in the

habit of receiving, for Pericles's use, freeborn women that
came to see the works. The comic writers of the town,
when they had got hold of this story, made much of it,
and bespattered him with all the ribaldry they could
invent, charging him falsely with the wife of Menippus,
one who was his friend and served as lieutenant under
him in the wars; and with the birds kept by Pyrilampes,
an acquaintance of Pericles, who, they pretended, used to
give presents of peacocks to Pericles's female friends.
And how can one wonder at any number of strange
assertions from men whose whole lives were devoted to
mockery, and who were ready at any time to sacrifice the
reputation of their superiors to vulgar envy and spite, as
to some evil genius, when even Stesimbrotus the Thasian
has dared to lay to the charge of Pericles a monstrous and
fabulous piece of criminality with his son's wife? So very
difficult a matter is it to trace and find out the truth of any
thing by history, when, on the one hand, those who afterwards write it find long periods of time intercepting their
view, and, on the other hand, the contemporary records of
any actions and lives, partly through envy and ill-will,
partly through favor and flattery, pervert and distort
truth.

When the orators, who sided with Thucydides and his
party, were at one time crying out, as their custom was,
against Pericles, as one who squandered away the public
money, and made havoc of the state revenues, he rose in
the open assembly and put the question to the people,
whether they thought that he had laid out much; and
they saying, "Too much, a great deal," "Then," said he,
"since it is so, let the cost not go to your account, but to
mine; and let the inscription upon the buildings stand in
my name." When they heard him say thus, whether it
were out of a surprise to see the greatness of his spirit,
or out of emulation of the glory of the works, they cried

aloud, bidding him to spend on, and lay out what he thought fit from the public purse, and to spare no cost, till all were finished.

At length, coming to a final contest with Thucydides, which of the two should ostracize the other out of the country, and having gone through this peril, he threw his antagonist out, and broke up the confederacy that had been organized against him. So that now all schism and division being at an end, and the city brought to evenness and unity, he got all Athens and all affairs that pertained to the Athenians into his own hands, their tributes, their armies, and their galleys, the islands, the sea, and their wide-extended power, partly over other Greeks and partly over barbarians, and all that empire, which they possessed, founded and fortified upon subject nations and royal friendships and alliances.

After this he was no longer the same man he had been before, nor as tame and gentle and familiar as formerly with the populace, so as readily to yield to their pleasures and to comply with the desires of the multitude, as a steersman shifts with the winds. Quitting that loose, remiss, and, in some cases, licentious court of the popular will, he turned those soft and flowery modulations to the austerity of aristocratical and regal rule; and employing this uprightly and undeviatingly for the country's best interests, he was able generally to lead the people along, with their own wills and consents, by persuading and showing them what was to be done; and sometimes, too, urging and pressing them forward extremely against their will, he made them, whether they would or no, yield submission to what was for their advantage. In which, to say the truth, he did but like a skilful physician, who, in a complicated and chronic disease, as he sees occasion, at one while allows his patient the moderate use of such things as please him, at another while gives him keen pains and drugs to work the cure. For there arising and growing up, as was natural, all manner of distempered feelings among a people which had so vast a command and dominion, he alone, as a great master, knowing how to handle and deal fitly with each one of them, and, in an especial manner, making that use of hopes and fears, as his two chief rudders, with the one to check the career of their confidence at any time, with the other to raise them up and cheer them when under any discouragement, plainly showed by this, that rhetoric, or the art of speaking, is, in Plato's language, the government of the souls of men, and that her chief business is to address the affections and passions, which are as it were the strings and keys to the soul, and require a skilful and careful touch to be played on as they should be. The source of this predominance was not barely his power of language, but, as Thucydides assures us, the reputation of his life, and the confidence felt in his character; his manifest freedom from every kind of corruption, and superiority to all considerations of money. Notwithstanding he had made the city Athens, which was great of itself, as great and rich as can be imagined, and though he were himself in power and interest more than equal to many kings and absolute rulers, who some of them also bequeathed by will their power to their children, he, for his part, did not make the patrimony his father left him greater than it was by one drachma.

Thucydides, indeed, gives a plain statement of the greatness of his power; and the comic poets, in their spiteful manner, more than hint at it, styling his companions and friends the new Pisistratidæ, and calling on him to abjure any intention of usurpation, as one whose eminence was too great to be any longer proportionable to and compatible with a democracy or popular government. And

Teleclides says the Athenians had surrendered up to
him —

The tribute of the cities, and with them, the cities too, to do with them
    as he pleases, and undo ;
To build up, if he likes, stone walls around a town ; and again, if so he
    likes, to pull them down ;
Their treaties and alliances, power, empire, peace, and war, their wealth
    and their success forevermore.

Nor was all this the luck of some happy occasion ; nor
was it the mere bloom and grace of a policy that flourished
for a season ; but having for forty years together maintained the first place among statesmen such as Ephialtes
and Leocrates and Myronides and Cimon and Tolmides
and Thucydides were, after the defeat and banishment
of Thucydides, for no less than fifteen years longer, in the
exercise of one continuous unintermitted command in the
office, to which he was annually reëlected, of General, he
preserved his integrity unspotted ; though otherwise he
was not altogether idle or careless in looking after his
pecuniary advantage ; his paternal estate, which of right
belonged to him, he so ordered that it might neither
through negligence be wasted or lessened, nor yet,
being so full of business as he was, cost him any great
trouble or time with taking care of it ; and put it into such
a way of management as he thought to be the most easy
for himself, and the most exact. All his yearly products
and profits he sold together in a lump, and supplied his
household needs afterward by buying every thing that
he or his family wanted out of the market. Upon which
account, his children, when they grew to age, were not
well pleased with his management, and the women that
lived with him were treated with little cost, and complained of this way of housekeeping, where every thing

was ordered and set down from day to day, and reduced
to the greatest exactness; since there was not there, as
is usual in a great family and a plentiful estate, any thing
to spare, or over and above; but all that went out or
came in, all disbursements and all receipts, proceeded as it
were by number and measure. His manager in all this
was a single servant, Evangelus by name, a man either
naturally gifted or instructed by Pericles so as to excel
every one in this art of domestic economy.

All this, in truth, was very little in harmony with
Anaxagoras's wisdom; if, indeed, it be true that he, by a
kind of divine impulse and greatness of spirit, voluntarily
quitted his house, and left his land to lie fallow and to be
grazed by sheep like a common. But the life of a contem-
plative philosopher and that of an active statesman are, I
presume, not the same thing; for the one merely employs,
upon great and good objects of thought, an intelligence
that requires no aid of instruments nor supply of any
external materials; whereas the other, who tempers and
applies his virtue to human uses, may have occasion for
affluence, not as a matter of mere necessity, but as a
noble thing; which was Pericles's case, who relieved numerous poor citizens.

However, there is a story, that Anaxagoras himself,
while Pericles was taken up with public affairs, lay neglected, and that, now being grown old, he wrapped himself up with a resolution to die for want of food; which
being by chance brought to Pericles's ear, he was horror-
struck, and instantly ran thither, and used all the arguments and entreaties he could to him, lamenting not so
much Anaxagoras's condition as his own, should he lose
such a counsellor as he had found him to be; and that,
upon this, Anaxagoras unfolded his robe, and showing
himself, made answer: "Pericles," said he, "even those
who have occasion for a lamp supply it with oil."

The Lacedæmonians beginning to show themselves troubled at the growth of the Athenian power, Pericles, on the other hand, to elevate the people's spirit yet more, and to raise them to the thought of great actions, proposed a decree, to summon all the Greeks in what part soever, whether of Europe or Asia, every city, little as well as great, to send their deputies to Athens to a general assembly, or convention, there to consult and advise concerning the Greek temples which the barbarians had burnt down, and the sacrifices which were due from them upon vows they had made to their gods for the safety of Greece when they fought against the barbarians; and also concerning the navigation of the sea, that they might henceforward all of them pass to and fro and trade securely, and be at peace among themselves.

Upon this errand, there were twenty men, of such as were above fifty years of age, sent by commission; five to summon the Ionians and Dorians in Asia, and the islanders as far as Lesbos and Rhodes; five to visit all the places in the Hellespont and Thrace, up to Byzantium; and other five besides these to go to Bœotia and Phocis and Peloponnesus, and from hence to pass through the Locrians over to the neighboring continent, as far as Acarnania and Ambracia; and the rest to take their course through Eubœa to the Œtæans and the Malian Gulf, and to the Achæans of Phthiotis and the Thessalians; all of them to treat with the people as they passed, and to persuade them to come and take their part in the debates for settling the peace and jointly regulating the affairs of Greece.

Nothing was effected, nor did the cities meet by their deputies, as was desired; the Lacedæmonians, as it is said, crossing the design underhand, and the attempt being disappointed and baffled first in Peloponnesus. I thought fit, however, to introduce the mention of it, to show the spirit of the man and the greatness of his thoughts.

In his military conduct, he gained a great reputation for wariness; he would not by his good-will engage in any fight which had much uncertainty or hazard; he did not envy the glory of generals whose rash adventures fortune favored with brilliant success, however they were admired by others; nor did he think them worthy his imitation, but always used to say to his citizens that, so far as lay in his power, they should continue immortal, and live forever. Seeing Tolmides, the son of Tolmæus, upon the confidence of his former successes, and flushed with the honor his military actions had procured him, making preparation to attack the Bœotians in their own country, when there was no likely opportunity, and that he had prevailed with the bravest and most enterprising of the youth to enlist themselves as volunteers in the service, who besides his other force made up a thousand, he endeavored to withhold him and to advise him from it in the public assembly, telling him in a memorable saying of his, which still goes about, that, if he would not take Pericles's advice, yet he would not do amiss to wait and be ruled by time, the wisest counsellor of all. This saying, at that time, was but slightly commended; but within a few days after, when news was brought that Tolmides himself had been defeated and slain in battle near Coronea, and that many brave citizens had fallen with him, it gained him great repute as well as good-will among the people, for wisdom and for love of his countrymen.

But of all his expeditions, that to the Chersonese gave most satisfaction and pleasure, having proved the safety of the Greeks who inhabited there. For not only by carrying along with him a thousand fresh citizens of Athens he gave new strength and vigor to the cities, but also by belting the neck of land, which joins the peninsula to the

continent, with bulwarks and forts from sea to sea, he put
a stop to the inroads of the Thracians, who lay all about
the Chersonese, and closed the door against a continual
and grievous war, with which that country had been
long harassed, lying exposed to the encroachments and
influx of barbarous neighbors, and groaning under the
evils of a predatory population both upon and within its
borders.

Nor was he less admired and talked of abroad for his
sailing round the Peloponnesus, having set out from Pegæ,
or The Fountains, the port of Megara, with a hundred galleys. For he not only laid waste the sea-coast, as Tolmides had done before, but also, advancing far up into
main land with the soldiers he had on board, by the
terror of his appearance drove many within their walls;
and at Nemea, with main force, routed and raised a trophy
over the Sicyonians, who stood their ground and joined
battle with him. And having taken on board a supply
of soldiers into the galleys, out of Achaia, then in league
with Athens, he crossed with the fleet to the opposite
continent, and, sailing along by the mouth of the river
Achelous, overran Acarnania, and shut up the Œniadæ
within their city walls, and having ravaged and wasted
their country, weighed anchor for home with the double
advantage of having shown himself formidable to his
enemies, and at the same time safe and energetic to his
fellow-citizens; for there was not so much as any chance-
miscarriage that happened, the whole voyage through,
to those who were under his charge.

Entering also the Euxine Sea with a large and finely
equipped fleet, he obtained for the Greek cities any new
arrangements they wanted, and entered into friendly relations with them; and to the barbarous nations, and
kings and chiefs round about them, displayed the greatness
of the power of the Athenians, their perfect ability and con-

fidence to sail wherever they had a mind, and to bring the whole sea under their control. He left the Sinopians thirteen ships of war, with soldiers under the command of Lamachus, to assist them against Timesileus the tyrant; and when he and his accomplices had been thrown out, obtained a decree that six hundred of the Athenians that were willing should sail to Sinope and plant themselves there with the Sinopians, sharing among them the houses and land which the tyrant and his party had previously held.

But in other things he did not comply with the giddy impulses of the citizens, nor quit his own resolutions to follow their fancies, when, carried away with the thought of their strength and great success, they were eager to interfere again in Egypt, and to disturb the king of Persia's maritime dominions. Nay, there were a good many who were, even then, possessed with that unblest and inauspicious passion for Sicily, which afterward the orators of Alcibiades's party blew up into a flame. There were some also who dreamt of Tuscany and of Carthage, and not without plausible reason in their present large dominion and the prosperous course of their affairs.

But Pericles curbed this passion for foreign conquest, and unsparingly pruned and cut down their ever busy fancies for a multitude of undertakings; and directed their power for the most part to securing and consolidating what they had already got, supposing it would be quite enough for them to do, if they could keep the Lacedæmonians in check; to whom he entertained all along a sense of opposition; which, as upon many other occasions, so he particularly showed by what he did in the time of the holy war. The Lacedæmonians, having gone with an army to Delphi, restored Apollo's temple, which the Phocians had got into their possession, to the Delphians; immediately after their departure, Pericles, with another army, came and restored the Phocians. And the Lacedæmonians having engraven the record of their privilege of consulting the oracle before others, which the Delphians gave them, upon the forehead of the brazen wolf which stands there, he, also, having received from the Phocians the like privilege for the Athenians, had it cut upon the same wolf of brass on his right side.

That he did well and wisely in thus restraining the exertions of the Athenians within the compass of Greece, the events themselves that happened afterward bore sufficient witness. For, in the first place, the Eubœans revolted, against whom he passed over with forces; and then, immediately after, news came that the Megarians were turned their enemies, and a hostile army was upon the borders of Attica, under the conduct of Plistoanax, king of the Lacedæmonians. Wherefore Pericles came with his army back again in all haste out of Eubœa, to meet the war which threatened at home; and did not venture to engage a numerous and brave army eager for battle; but perceiving that Plistoanax was a very young man, and governed himself mostly by the counsel and advice of Cleandrides, whom the ephors had sent with him, by reason of his youth, to be a kind of guardian and assistant to him, he privately made trial of this man's integrity, and, in a short time, having corrupted him with money, prevailed with him to withdraw the Peloponnesians out of Attica. When the army had retired and dispersed into their several states, the Lacedæmonians in anger fined their king in so large a sum of money, that, unable to pay it, he quitted Lacedæmon; while Cleandrides fled, and had sentence of death passed upon him in his absence. This was the father of Gylippus, who overpowered the Athenians in Sicily. And it seems that this covetousness was an hereditary disease transmitted from father to son; for Gylippus also afterwards was caught in foul practices, and expelled from Sparta for it. But this we have told at large in the account of Lysander.

When Pericles, in giving up his accounts of this expedition, stated a disbursement of ten talents, as laid out upon fit occasion, the people, without any question, nor troubling themselves to investigate the mystery, freely allowed of it. And some historians, in which number is Theophrastus the philosopher, have given it as a truth that Pericles every year used to send privately the sum of ten talents to Sparta, with which he complimented those in office, to keep off the war; not to purchase peace neither, but time, that he might prepare at leisure, and be the better able to carry on war hereafter.

Immediately after this, turning his forces against the revolters, and passing over into the island of Euboea with fifty sail of ships and five thousand men in arms, he reduced their cities, and drove out the citizens of the Chalcidians, called Hippobotæ, horse-feeders, the chief persons for wealth and reputation among them; and removing all the Histiæans out of the country, brought in a plantation of Athenians in their room; making them his one example of severity, because they had captured an Attic ship and killed all on board.

After this, having made a truce between the Athenians and Lacedæmonians for thirty years, he ordered, by public decree, the expedition against the Isle of Samos, on the ground, that, when they were bid to leave off their war with the Milesians, they had not complied. And as these measures against the Samians are thought to have been taken to please Aspasia, this may be a fit point for inquiry about the woman, what art or charming faculty she had that enabled her to captivate, as she did, the greatest statesmen, and to give the philosophers occasion to speak so much about her, and that, too, not to her disparagement. That she was a Milesian by birth, the daughter

of Axiochus, is a thing acknowledged. And they say it
was in emulation of Thargelia, a courtesan of the old
Ionian times, that she made her addresses to men of great
power. Thargelia was a great beauty, extremely charming, and at the same time sagacious; she had numerous
suitors among the Greeks, and brought all who had to do
with her over to the Persian interest, and by their means,
being men of the greatest power and station, sowed the
seeds of the Median faction up and down in several cities.*
Aspasia, some say, was courted and caressed by Pericles
upon account of her knowledge and skill in politics.
Socrates himself would sometimes go to visit her, and
some of his acquaintance with him; and those who frequented her company would carry their wives with them
to listen to her. Her occupation was any thing but cred-
itable, her house being a home for young courtesans.
Æschines tells us also, that Lysicles, a sheep-dealer, a
man of low birth and character, by keeping Aspasia company after Pericles's death, came to be a chief man in
Athens. And in Plato's Menexenus, though we do not
take the introduction as quite serious, still thus much
seems to be historical, that she had the repute of being
resorted to by many of the Athenians for instruction in
the art of speaking. Pericles's inclination for her seems,
however, to have rather proceeded from the passion of
love. He had a wife that was near of kin to him, who
had been married first to Hipponicus, by whom she had
Callias, surnamed the Rich; and also she brought Pericles, while she lived with him, two sons, Xanthippus and
Paralus. Afterwards, when they did not well agree nor
like to live together, he parted with her, with her own
consent, to another man, and himself took Aspasia, and

* She was married, says Athenæus, to fourteen husbands; a woman
of great beauty and intellect.

loved her with wonderful affection; every day, both as
he went out and as he came in from the market-place,
he saluted and kissed her.

In the comedies she goes by the nicknames of the new
Omphale and Deianira, and again is styled Juno. Cratinus, in downright terms, calls her a harlot.

> To find him a Juno the goddess of lust
> Bore that harlot past shame,
> Aspasia by name.

It should seem, also, that he had a son by her; Eupolis,
in his Demi, introduced Pericles asking after his safety,
and Myronides replying,

> "My son?" "He lives; a man he had been long,
> But that the harlot-mother did him wrong."

Aspasia, they say, became so celebrated and renowned,
that Cyrus also, who made war against Artaxerxes for the
Persian monarchy, gave her whom he loved the best of
all his concubines the name of Aspasia, who before that
was called Milto. She was a Phocæan by birth, the
daughter of one Hermotimus, and, when Cyrus fell in
battle, was carried to the king, and had great influence at
court. These things coming into my memory as I am
writing this story, it would be unnatural for me to omit
them.

Pericles, however, was particularly charged with having
proposed to the assembly the war against the Samians,
from favor to the Milesians, upon the entreaty of Aspasia.
For the two states were at war for the possession of
Priene; and the Samians, getting the better, refused to
lay down their arms and to have the controversy betwixt
them decided by arbitration before the Athenians. Pericles, therefore, fitting out a fleet, went and broke up

the oligarchical government at Samos, and, taking fifty of the principal men of the town as hostages, and as many of their children, sent them to the isle of Lemnos, there to be kept, though he had offers, as some relate, of a talent a piece for himself from each one of the hostages, and of many other presents from those who were anxious not to have a democracy. Moreover, Pissuthnes the Persian, one of the king's lieutenants, bearing some good-will to the Samians, sent him ten thousand pieces of gold to excuse the city. Pericles, however, would receive none of all this; but after he had taken that course with the Samians which he thought fit, and set up a democracy among them, sailed back to Athens.

But they, however, immediately revolted, Pissuthnes having privily got away their hostages for them, and provided them with means for the war. Whereupon Pericles came out with a fleet a second time against them, and found them not idle nor slinking away, but manfully resolved to try for the dominion of the sea. The issue was, that, after a sharp sea-fight about the island called Tragia, Pericles obtained a decisive victory, having with forty-four ships routed seventy of the enemy's, twenty of which were carrying soldiers.

Together with his victory and pursuit, having made himself master of the port, he laid siege to the Samians, and blocked them up, who yet, one way or other, still ventured to make sallies, and fight under the city walls. But after that another greater fleet from Athens was arrived, and that the Samians were now shut up with a close leaguer on every side, Pericles, taking with him sixty galleys, sailed out into the main sea, with the intention, as most authors give the account, to meet a squadron of Phœnician ships that were coming for the Samians' relief, and to fight them at as great distance as could be from the island ; but, as Stesimbrotus says, with a design of putting over to Cyprus; which does not seem to be probable. But whichever of the two was his intent, it seems to have been a miscalculation. For on his departure, Melissus, the son of Ithagenes, a philosopher, being at that time general in Samos, despising either the small number of the ships that were left or the inexperience of the commanders, prevailed with the citizens to attack the Athenians. And the Samians having won the battle, and taken several of the men prisoners, and disabled several of the ships, were masters of the sea, and brought into port all necessaries they wanted for the war, which they had not before. Aristotle says, too, that Pericles himself had been once before this worsted by this Melissus in a sea-fight.

The Samians, that they might requite an affront which had before been put upon them, branded the Athenians, whom they took prisoners, in their foreheads, with the figure of an owl. For so the Athenians had marked them before with a Samæna, which is a sort of ship, low and flat in the prow, so as to look snub-nosed, but wide and large and well-spread in the hold, by which it both carries a large cargo and sails well. And it was so called, because the first of that kind was seen at Samos, having been built by order of Polycrates the tyrant. These brands upon the Samians' foreheads, they say, are the allusion in the passage of Aristophanes, where he says, —

For, oh, the Samians are a lettered people.

Pericles, as soon as news was brought him of the disaster that had befallen his army, made all the haste he could to come in to their relief, and having defeated Melissus, who bore up against him, and put the enemy to flight, he immediately proceeded to hem them in with a wall, resolving to master them and take the town, rather

with some cost and time, than with the wounds and
hazards of his citizens.   But as it was a hard matter to
keep back the Athenians, who were vexed at the delay,
and were eagerly bent to fight, he divided the whole
multitude into eight parts, and arranged by lot that that
part which had the white bean should have leave to feast
and take their ease, while the other seven were fighting.
And this is the reason, they say, that people, when at any
time they have been merry, and enjoyed themselves, call
it white day, in allusion to this white bean.

Ephorus the historian tells us besides, that Pericles
made use of engines of battery in this siege, being much
taken with the curiousness of the invention, with the aid
and presence of Artemon himself, the engineer, who, being
lame, used to be carried about in a litter, where the works
required his attendance, and for that reason was called
Periphoretus.   But Heraclides Ponticus disproves this out
of Anacreon's poems, where mention is made of this Artemon Periphoretus several ages before the Samian war,
or any of these occurrences.   And he says that Artemon,
being a man who loved his ease, and had a great apprehension of danger, for the most part kept close within
doors, having two of his servants to hold a brazen shield
over his head, that nothing might fall upon him from
above; and if he were at any time forced upon necessity
to go abroad, that he was carried about in a little hanging bed, close to the very ground, and that for this reason
he was called Periphoretus.

In the ninth month, the Samians surrendering themselves and delivering up the town, Pericles pulled down
their walls, and seized their shipping, and set a fine of a
large sum of money upon them, part of which they paid
down at once, and they agreed to bring in the rest by
a certain time, and gave hostages for security.   Duris the
Samian makes a tragical drama out of these events,

charging the Athenians and Pericles with a great deal of cruelty, which neither Thucydides, nor Ephorus, nor Aristotle have given any relation of, and probably with little regard to truth; how, for example, he brought the captains and soldiers of the galleys into the market-place at Miletus, and there having bound them fast to boards for ten days, then, when they were already all but half dead, gave order to have them killed by beating out their brains with clubs, and their dead bodies to be flung out into the open streets and fields, unburied. Duris, however, who even where he has no private feeling concerned, is not wont to keep his narrative within the limits of truth, is the more likely upon this occasion to have exaggerated the calamities which befell his country, to create odium against the Athenians. Pericles, however, after the reduction of Samos, returning back to Athens, took care that those who died in the war should be honorably buried, and made a funeral harangue, as the custom is, in their commendation at their graves, for which he gained great admiration. As he came down from the stage on which he spoke, the rest of the women came and complimented him, taking him by the hand, and crowning him with garlands and ribbons, like a victorious athlete in the games; but Elpinice, coming near to him, said, " These are brave deeds, Pericles, that you have done, and such as deserve our chaplets; who have lost us many a worthy citizen, not in a war with Phœnicians or Medes, like my brother Cimon, but for the overthrow of an allied and kindred city." As Elpinice spoke these words, he, smiling quietly, as it is said, returned her answer with this verse, —

Old women should not seek to be perfumed.

Ion says of him, that, upon this exploit of his, conquering the Samians, he indulged very high and proud thoughts of himself: whereas Agamemnon was ten years a taking a barbarous city, he had in nine months' time vanquished and taken the greatest and most powerful of the Ionians. And indeed it was not without reason that he assumed this glory to himself, for, in real truth, there was much uncertainty and great hazard in this war, if so be, as Thucydides tells us, the Samian state were within a very little of wresting the whole power and dominion of the sea out of the Athenians' hands.

After this was over, the Peloponnesian war beginning to break out in full tide, he advised the people to send help to the Corcyræans, who were attacked by the Corinthians, and to secure to themselves an island possessed of great naval resources, since the Peloponnesians were already all but in actual hostilities against them. The people readily consenting to the motion, and voting an aid and succor for them, he despatched Lacedæmonius, Cimon's son, having only ten ships with him, as it were out of a design to affront him; for there was a great kindness and friendship betwixt Cimon's family and the Lacedæmonians; so, in order that Lacedæmonius might lie the more open to a charge, or suspicion at least, of favoring the Lacedæmonians and playing false, if he performed no considerable exploit in this service, he allowed him a small number of ships, and sent him out against his will; and indeed he made it somewhat his business to hinder Cimon's sons from rising in the state, professing that by their very names they were not to be looked upon as native and true Athenians, but foreigners and strangers, one being called Lacedæmonius, another Thessalus, and the third Eleus; and they were all three of them, it was thought, born of an Arcadian woman. Being, however, ill spoken of on account of these ten galleys, as having afforded but a small supply to the people

that were in need, and yet given a great advantage to
those who might complain of the act of intervention,
Pericles sent out a larger force afterward to Corcyra,
which arrived after the fight was over. And when now
the Corinthians, angry and indignant with the Athenians,
accused them publicly at Lacedæmon, the Megarians
joined with them, complaining that they were, contrary
to common right and the articles of peace sworn to
among the Greeks, kept out and driven away from every
market and from all ports under the control of the Athenians.   The Æginetans, also, professing to be ill-used and
treated with violence, made supplications in private to
the Lacedæmonians for redress, though not daring openly
to call the Athenians in question. In the mean time, also,
the city Potidæa, under the dominion of the Athenians,
but a colony formerly of the Corinthians, had revolted,
and was beset with a formal siege, and was a further occasion of precipitating the war.

Yet notwithstanding all this, there being embassies
sent to Athens, and Archidamus, the king of the Lacedæmonians, endeavoring to bring the greater part of the complaints and matters in dispute to a fair determination, and
to pacify and allay the heats of the allies, it is very likely
that the war would not upon any other grounds of quarrel
have fallen upon the Athenians, could they have been
prevailed with to repeal the ordinance against the Megarians, and to be reconciled to them. Upon which account,
since Pericles was the man who mainly opposed it, and
stirred up the people's passions to persist in their contention with the Megarians, he was regarded as the sole cause
of the war.

They say, moreover, that ambassadors went, by order,
from Lacedæmon to Athens about this very business,
and that when Pericles was urging a certain law which

made it illegal to take down or withdraw the tablet of the
decree, one of the ambassadors, Polyalces by name, said,
"Well, do not take it down then, but *turn* it; there is
no law, I suppose, which forbids that;"* which, though
prettily said, did not move Pericles from his resolution.
There may have been, in all likelihood, something of a
secret grudge and private animosity which he had against
the Megarians.   Yet, upon a public and open charge
against them, that they had appropriated part of the
sacred land on the frontier, he proposed a decree that a
herald should be sent to them, and the same also to the
Lacedæmonians, with an accusation of the Megarians; an
order which certainly shows equitable and friendly proceeding enough.   And after that the herald who was
sent, by name Anthemocritus, died, and it was believed
that the Megarians had contrived his death, then Charinus proposed a decree against them, that there should
be an irreconcilable and implacable enmity thenceforward
betwixt the two commonwealths; and that if any one of
the Megarians should but set his foot in Attica, he should be
put to death; and that the commanders, when they take
the usual oath, should, over and above that, swear that
they will twice every year make an inroad into the Megarian country; and that Anthemocritus should be buried near the Thriasian Gates, which are now called the
Dipylon, or Double Gate.

On the other hand, the Megarians, utterly denying and
disowning the murder of Anthemocritus, throw the whole
matter upon Aspasia and Pericles, availing themselves of
the famous verses in the Acharnians,

* The word for *taking down*, in the literal sense, is also the techni-
cal term for revoking, or repealing; hence the Spartans play upon the
two senses. "If you may not take it down, turn it, with its face to the
wall."

To Megara some of our madcaps ran,
And stole Simætha thence, their courtesan.
Which exploit the Megarians to outdo,
Came to Aspasia's house, and took off two.

The true occasion of the quarrel is not so easy to find out. But of inducing the refusal to annul the decree, all alike charge Pericles. Some say he met the request with a positive refusal, out of high spirit and a view of the state's best interests, accounting that the demand made in those embassies was designed for a trial of their compliance, and that a concession would be taken for a confession of weakness, as if they durst not do otherwise; while other some there are who say that it was rather out of arrogance and a wilful spirit of contention, to show his own strength, that he took occasion to slight the Lacedæmonians. The worst motive of all, which is confirmed by most witnesses, is to the following effect. Phidias the Moulder had, as has before been said, undertaken to make the statue of Minerva. Now he, being admitted to friendship with Pericles, and a great favorite of his, had many enemies upon this account, who envied and maligned him; who also, to make trial in a case of his, what kind of judges the commons would prove, should there be occasion to bring Pericles himself before them, having tampered with Menon, one who had been a workman with Phidias, stationed him in the market-place, with a petition desiring public security upon his discovery and impeachment of Phidias. The people admitting the man to tell his story, and the prosecution proceeding in the assembly, there was nothing of theft or cheat proved against him; for Phidias, from the very first beginning, by the advice of Pericles, had so wrought and wrapt the gold that was used in the work about the statue, that they might take it all off and make out the just weight of it, which Pericles at that time bade the accusers do.

But the reputation of his works was what brought envy upon Phidias, especially that where he represents the fight of the Amazons upon the goddesses' shield, he had introduced a likeness of himself as a bald old man holding up a great stone with both hands, and had put in a very fine representation of Pericles fighting with an Amazon. And the position of the hand, which holds out the spear in front of the face, was ingeniously contrived to conceal in some degree the likeness, which, meantime, showed itself on either side.

Phidias then was carried away to prison, and there died of a disease; but, as some say, of poison, administered by the enemies of Pericles, to raise a slander, or a suspicion, at least, as though he had procured it. The informer Menon, upon Glycon's proposal, the people made free from payment of taxes and customs, and ordered the generals to take care that nobody should do him any hurt. About the same time, Aspasia was indicted of impiety, upon the complaint of Hermippus the comedian, who also laid further to her charge that she received into her house freeborn women for the uses of Pericles. And Diopithes proposed a decree, that public accusation should be laid against persons who neglected religion, or taught new doctrines about things above,* directing suspicion, by means of Anaxagoras, against Pericles himself. The people receiving and admitting these accusations and complaints, at length, by this means, they came to enact a decree, at the motion of Dracontides, that Pericles should bring in the accounts of the moneys he had expended, and lodge them with the Prytanes; and that the judges, carrying their suffrage from the altar in the Acro-

* " Supera ac coelestia," as Cicero translates the words *meteōra* and *metarsia*, whence we have formed our *meteorology.* The whole Greek religion was based on certain conceptions of such phenomena, any tampering with which was, therefore, quickly resented.

polis, should examine and determine the business in the
city. This last clause Hagnon took out of the decree,
and moved that the causes should be tried before fifteen
hundred jurors, whether they should be styled prosecu-
tions for robbery, or bribery, or any kind of malversation.
Aspasia, Pericles begged off, shedding, as Æschines says,
many tears at the trial, and personally entreating the
jurors. But fearing how it might go with Anaxagoras,
he sent him out of the city. And finding that in Phidias's
case he had miscarried with the people, being afraid of
impeachment, he kindled the war, which hitherto had lin-
gered and smothered, and blew it up into a flame; hoping,
by that means, to disperse and scatter these complaints
and charges, and to allay their jealousy; the city usually
throwing herself upon him alone, and trusting to his sole
conduct, upon the urgency of great affairs and public
dangers, by reason of his authority and the sway he
bore.

These are given out to have been the reasons which
induced Pericles not to suffer the people of Athens to
yield to the proposals of the Lacedæmonians; but their
truth is uncertain.

The Lacedæmonians, for their part, feeling sure that if
they could once remove him, they might be at what terms
they pleased with the Athenians, sent them word that
they should expel the "Pollution" with which Pericles
on the mother's side was tainted, as Thucydides tells us.
But the issue proved quite contrary to what those who
sent the message expected; instead of bringing Pericles
under suspicion and reproach, they raised him into yet
greater credit and esteem with the citizens, as a man
whom their enemies most hated and feared. In the same
way, also, before Archidamus, who was at the head of the
Peloponnesians, made his invasion into Attica, he told the
Athenians beforehand, that if Archidamus, while he laid

waste the rest of the country, should forbear and spare
his estate, either on the ground of friendship or right
of hospitality that was betwixt them, or on purpose
to give his enemies an occasion of traducing him, that
then he did freely bestow upon the state all that his land
and the buildings upon it for the public use. The Lacedæmonians, therefore, and their allies, with a great army,
invaded the Athenian territories, under the conduct of
king Archidamus, and laying waste the country, marched
on as far as Acharnæ, and there pitched their camp, presuming that the Athenians would never endure that, but
would come out and fight them for their country's and
their honor's sake. But Pericles looked upon it as dangerous to engage in battle, to the risk of the city itself,
against sixty thousand men-at-arms of Peloponnesians
and Bœotians; for so many they were in number that
made the inroad at first; and he endeavored to appease
those who were desirous to fight, and were grieved and
discontented to see how things went, and gave them good
words, saying, that "trees, when they are lopped and cut,
grow up again in a short time but men, being once lost, cannot easily be recovered." He did not convene the people
into an assembly, for fear lest they should force him to
act against his judgment; but, like a skilful steersman or
pilot of a ship, who, when a sudden squall comes on, out
at sea, makes all his arrangements, sees that all is tight
and fast, and then follows the dictates of his skill, and
minds the business of the ship, taking no notice of the
tears and entreaties of the sea-sick and fearful passengers,
so he, having shut up the city gates, and placed guards
at all posts for security, followed his own reason and
judgment, little regarding those that cried out against him
and were angry at his management, although there were
a great many of his friends that urged him with requests,
and many of his enemies threatened and accused him for

doing as he did, and many made songs and lampoons upon him, which were sung about the town to his disgrace, reproaching him with the cowardly exercise of his office of general, and the tame abandonment of every thing to the enemy's hands.

Cleon, also, already was among his assailants, making use of the feeling against him as a step to the leadership of the people, as appears in the anapæstic verses of Hermippus.

> Satyr-king, instead of swords,
> Will you always handle words?
> Very brave indeed we find them,
> But a Teles * lurks behind them.

> Yet to gnash your teeth you're seen,
> When the little dagger keen,
> Whetted every day anew,
> Of sharp Cleon touches you.

Pericles, however, was not at all moved by any attacks, but took all patiently, and submitted in silence to the disgrace they threw upon him and the ill-will they bore him; and, sending out a fleet of a hundred galleys to Peloponnesus, he did not go along with it in person, but stayed behind, that he might watch at home and keep the city under his own control, till the Peloponnesians broke up their camp and were gone. Yet to soothe the common people, jaded and distressed with the war, he relieved them with distributions of public moneys, and ordained new divisions of subject land. For having turned out all the people of Ægina, he parted the island among the Athenians, according to lot. Some comfort, also, and ease in their miseries, they might receive from what their enemies endured. For the fleet,

---

* Apparently some notorious coward.

sailing round the Peloponnese, ravaged a great deal of
the country, and pillaged and plundered the towns and
smaller cities; and by land he himself entered with an
army the Megarian country, and made havoc of it all.
Whence it is clear that the Peloponnesians, though they
did the Athenians much mischief by land, yet suffering
as much themselves from them by sea, would not have
protracted the war to such a length, but would quickly
have given it over, as Pericles at first foretold they
would, had not some divine power crossed human purposes.

In the first place, the pestilential disease, or plague,
seized upon the city, and ate up all the flower and prime
of their youth and strength. Upon occasion of which,
the people, distempered and afflicted in their souls, as well
as in their bodies, were utterly enraged like madmen
against Pericles, and, like patients grown delirious, sought
to lay violent hands on their physician, or, as it were, their
father. They had been possessed, by his enemies, with
the belief that the occasion of the plague was the crowd-
ing of the country people together into the town, forced
as they were now, in the heat of the summer-weather, to
dwell many of them together even as they could, in small
tenements and stifling hovels, and to be tied to a lazy
course of life within doors, whereas before they lived in
a pure, open, and free air. The cause and author of all
this, said they, is he who on account of the war has
poured a multitude of people from the country in upon
us within the walls, and uses all these many men that
he has here upon no employ or service, but keeps them
pent up like cattle, to be overrun with infection from
one another, affording them neither shift of quarters nor
any refreshment.

With the design to remedy these evils, and do the enemy some inconvenience, Pericles got a hundred and fifty

galleys ready, and having embarked many tried soldiers, both foot and horse, was about to sail out, giving great hope to his citizens, and no less alarm to his enemies, upon the sight of so great a force. And now the vessels having their complement of men, and Pericles being gone aboard his own galley, it happened that the sun was eclipsed, and it grew dark on a sudden, to the affright of all, for this was looked upon as extremely ominous. Pericles, therefore, perceiving the steersman seized with fear and at a loss what to do, took his cloak and held it up before the man's face, and, screening him with it so that he could not see, asked him whether he imagined there was any great hurt, or the sign of any great hurt in this, and he answering No, "Why," said he, "and what does that differ from this, only that what has caused that darkness there, is something greater than a cloak?" This is a story which philosophers tell their scholars. Pericles, however, after putting out to sea, seems not to have done any other exploit befitting such preparations, and when he had laid siege to the holy city Epidaurus, which gave him some hope of surrender, miscarried in his design by reason of the sickness. For it not only seized upon the Athenians, but upon all others, too, that held any sort of communication with the army. Finding after this the Athenians ill affected and highly displeased with him, he tried and endeavored what he could to appease and re-encourage them. But he could not pacify or allay their anger, nor persuade or prevail with them any way, till they freely passed their votes upon him, resumed their power, took away his command from him, and fined him in a sum of money; which, by their account that say least, was fifteen talents, while they who reckon most, name fifty. The name prefixed to the accusation was Cleon, as Idomeneus tells us; Simmias, according to Theophrastus; and Heraclides Ponticus gives it as Lacratidas.

After this, public troubles were soon to leave him un-
molested; the people, so to say, discharged their passion
in their stroke, and lost their stings in the wound. But
his domestic concerns were in an unhappy condition,
many of his friends and acquaintance having died in
the plague time, and those of his family having long
since been in disorder and in a kind of mutiny against
him. For the eldest of his lawfully begotten sons, Xanthippus by name, being naturally prodigal, and marrying
a young and expensive wife, the daughter of Tisander,
son of Epilycus, was highly offended at his father's economy in making him but a scanty allowance, by little
and little at a time. He sent, therefore, to a friend one
day, and borrowed some money of him in his father
Pericles's name, pretending it was by his order. The
man coming afterward to demand the debt, Pericles was
so far from yielding to pay it, that he entered an action
against him. Upon which the young man, Xanthippus,
thought himself so ill used and disobliged, that he openly
reviled his father; telling first, by way of ridicule, stories
about his conversations at home, and the discourses he
had with the sophists and scholars that came to his house.
As for instance, how one who was a practiser of the
five games of skill,* having with a dart or javelin unawares against his will struck and killed Epitimus the
Pharsalian, his father spent a whole day with Protago-
ras in a serious dispute, whether the javelin, or the man
that threw it, or the masters of the games who appointed
these sports, were, according to the strictest and best
reason, to be accounted the cause of this mischance. Besides this, Stesimbrotus tells us that it was Xanthippus
who spread abroad among the people the infamous story

* These are recorded in a pentameter verse by Simonides.

Halma, podokelēn, discon, aconta,   Leaping. and swiftness of foot,
  palēn.   wrestling, the discus, the dart.

concerning his own wife; and in general that this differ-ence of the young man's with his father, and the breach betwixt them, continued never to be healed or made up till his death. For Xanthippus died in the plague time of the sickness. At which time Pericles also lost his sister, and the greatest part of his relations and friends, and those who had been most useful and serviceable to him in managing the affairs of state. However, he did not shrink or give in upon these occa-sions, nor betray or lower his high spirit and the greatness of his mind under all his misfortunes; he was not even so much as seen to weep or to mourn, or even attend the burial of any of his friends or relations, till at last he lost his only remaining legitimate son. Subdued by this blow, and yet striving still, as far as he could, to maintain his prin-ciple, and to preserve and keep up the greatness of his soul when he came, however, to perform the ceremony of putting a garland of flowers upon the head of the corpse, he was vanquished by his passion at the sight, so that he burst into exclamations, and shed copious tears, having never done any such thing in all his life before.

The city having made trial of other generals for the conduct of war, and orators for business of state, when they found there was no one who was of weight enough for such a charge, or of authority sufficient to be trusted with so great a command, regretted the loss of him, and invited him again to address and advise them, and to re-assume the office of general. He, however, lay at home in dejection and mourning; but was persuaded by Alci-biades and others of his friends to come abroad and show himself to the people; who having, upon his appearance, made their acknowledgments, and apologized for their untowardly treatment of him, he undertook the public affairs once more; and, being chosen general, requested that the statute concerning base-born children, which he himself had formerly caused to be made, might be suspended; that so the name and race of his family might not, for absolute want of a lawful heir to succeed, be wholly lost and extinguished. The case of the statute was thus: Pericles, when long ago at the height of his power in the state, having then, as has been said, children lawfully begotten, proposed a law that those only should be reputed true citizens of Athens who were born of such parents as were both Athenians. After this, the king of Egypt having sent to the people, by way of present, forty thousand bushels of wheat, which were to be shared out among the citizens, a great many actions and suits about legitimacy occurred, by virtue of that edict; cases which, till that time, had not been known nor taken notice of; and several persons suffered by false accusations. There were little less than five thousand who were convicted and sold for slaves; those who, enduring the test, remained in the government and passed muster for true Athenians were found upon the poll to be fourteen thousand and forty persons in number.

It looked strange, that a law, which had been carried so far against so many people, should be cancelled again by the same man that made it; yet the present calamity and distress which Pericles labored under in his family broke through all objections, and prevailed with the Athenians to pity him, as one whose losses and misfortunes had sufficiently punished his former arrogance and haughtiness. His sufferings deserved, they thought, their pity, and even indignation, and his request was such as became a man to ask and men to grant; they gave him permission to enroll his son in the register of his fraternity, giving him his own name. This son afterward, after having defeated the Peloponnesians at Arginusæ, was, with his fellow-generals, put to death by the people.

About the time when his son was enrolled, it should

seem, the plague seized Pericles, not with sharp and violent fits, as it did others that had it, but with a dull and
lingering distemper, attended with various changes and
alterations, leisurely, by little and little, wasting the
strength of his body, and undermining the noble faculties
of his soul. So that Theophrastus, in his Morals, when
discussing whether men's characters change with their circumstances, and their moral habits, disturbed by the
ailings of their bodies, start aside from the rules of virtue,
has left it upon record, that Pericles, when he was sick,
showed one of his friends that came to visit him, an amu-
let or charm that the women had hung about his neck;
as much as to say, that he was very sick indeed when he
would admit of such a foolery as that was.

When he was now near his end, the best of the citizens
and those of his friends who were left alive, sitting about
him, were speaking of the greatness of his merit, and his
power, and reckoning up his famous actions and the number of his victories; for there were no less than nine trophies, which, as their chief commander and conqueror of
their enemies, he had set up, for the honor of the city.
They talked thus together among themselves, as though
he were unable to understand or mind what they said,
but had now lost his consciousness. He had listened, however, all the while, and attended to all, and speaking out
among them, said, that he wondered they should commend and take notice of things which were as much
owing to fortune as to any thing else, and had happened
to many other commanders, and, at the same time, should
not speak or make mention of that which was the most
excellent and greatest thing of all. "For," said he, "no
Athenian, through my means, ever wore mourning."

He was indeed a character deserving our high admiration, not only for his equitable and mild temper, which
all along in the many affairs of his life, and the great

animosities which he incurred, he constantly maintained ; but also for the high spirit and feeling which made him regard it the noblest of all his honors that, in the exercise of such immense power, he never had gratified his envy or his passion, nor ever had treated any enemy as irreconcilably opposed to him. And to me it appears that this one thing gives that otherwise childish and arrogant title a fitting and becoming significance ; so dispassionate a temper, a life so pure and unblemished, in the height of power and place, might well be called Olympian, in accordance with our conceptions of the divine beings, to whom, as the natural authors of all good and of nothing evil, we ascribe the rule and government of the world. Not as the poets represent, who, while confounding us with their ignorant fancies, are themselves confuted by their own poems and fictions, and call the place, indeed, where they say the gods make their abode, a secure and quiet seat, free from all hazards and commotions, untroubled with winds or with clouds, and equally through all time illumined with a soft serenity and a pure light, as though such were a home most agreeable for a blessed and immortal nature ; and yet, in the mean while, affirm that the gods themselves are full of trouble and enmity and anger and other passions, which no way become or belong to even men that have any understanding. But this will, perhaps, seem a subject fitter for some other consideration, and that ought to be treated of in some other place.

The course of public affairs after his death produced a quick and speedy sense of the loss of Pericles. Those who, while he lived, resented his great authority, as that which eclipsed themselves, presently after his quitting the stage, making trial of other orators and demagogues, readily acknowledged that there never had been in nature such a disposition as his was, more moderate and reasonable in the height of that state he took upon him, or more grave and impressive in the mildness which he used. And that invidious arbitrary power, to which formerly they gave the name of monarchy and tyranny, did then appear to have been the chief bulwark of public safety; so great a corruption and such a flood of mischief and vice followed, which he, by keeping weak and low, had withheld from notice, and had prevented from attaining incurable height through a licentious impunity.

FABIUS.

HAVING related the memorable actions of Pericles, our history now proceeds to the life of Fabius. A son of Hercules and a nymph, or some woman of that country, who brought him forth on the banks of Tiber, was, it is said, the first Fabius, the founder of the numerous and distinguished family of the name. Others will have it that they were first called Fodii, because the first of the race delighted in digging pit-falls for wild beasts, *fodere* being still the Latin for to dig, and *fossa* for a ditch, and that in process of time, by the change of the two letters they grew to be called Fabii. But be these things true or false, certain it is that this family for a long time yielded a great number of eminent persons. Our Fabius, who was fourth in descent from that Fabius Rullus who first brought the honorable surname of Maximus into his family, was also, by way of personal nickname, called Verrucosus, from a wart on his upper lip; and in his childhood they in like manner named him Ovicula, or The Lamb, on account of his extreme mildness of temper. His slowness in speaking, his long labor and pains in learning, his deliberation in entering into the sports of other children, his easy submission to everybody, as if he had no will of his own, made those who judged superficially of him, the greater number, esteem him insensible and stupid; and few only saw that this tardiness proceeded from stability, and discerned the greatness of his mind, and the lionlikeness of his temper. But as soon as he came into employments, his virtues exerted and showed themselves; his reputed want of energy then was recognized by people in general, as a freedom of passion; his slowness in words and actions, the effect of a true prudence; his want of rapidity, and his sluggishness, as constancy and firmness.

Living in a great commonwealth, surrounded by many enemies, he saw the wisdom of inuring his body (nature's own weapon) to warlike exercises, and disciplining his tongue for public oratory in a style comformable to his life and character. His eloquence, indeed, had not much of popular ornament, nor empty artifice, but there was in it great weight of sense; it was strong and sententious, much after the way of Thucydides. We have yet extant his funeral oration upon the death of his son, who died consul, which he recited before the people.

He was five times consul, and in his first consulship had the honor of a triumph for the victory he gained over the Ligurians, whom he defeated in a set battle, and drove them to take shelter in the Alps, from whence they never after made any inroad nor depredation upon their neighbors. After this, Hannibal came into Italy, who, at his first entrance, having gained a great battle near the river Trebia, traversed all Tuscany with his victorious army, and, desolating the country round about, filled Rome itself with astonishment and terror. Besides the more common signs of thunder and lightning then happening, the report of several unheard of and utterly strange portents much increased the popular consternation. For it was said that some targets sweated blood; that at Antium, when they reaped their corn, many of the ears were filled with blood; that it had rained red-hot stones; that the Falerians had seen the heavens open and several scrolls falling down, in one of which was plainly written, "Mars himself stirs his arms." But these prodigies had no effect upon the impetuous and fiery temper of the consul Flaminius, whose natural promptness had been much heightened by his late unexpected victory over the Gauls, when he fought them contrary to the order of the senate and the advice of his colleague. Fabius, on the other side, thought it not seasonable to engage with the enemy; not that he much regarded the prodigies, which he thought too strange to be easily understood, though many were alarmed by them; but in regard that the Carthaginians were but few, and in want of money and supplies, he deemed it best not to meet in the field a general whose army had been tried in many encounters, and whose object was a battle, but to send aid to their allies, control the movements of the various subject cities, and let the force and vigor of Hannibal waste away and expire, like a flame, for want of aliment.

These weighty reasons did not prevail with Flaminius, who protested he would never suffer the advance of the enemy to the city, nor be reduced, like Camillus in former time, to fight for Rome within the walls of Rome. Accordingly he ordered the tribunes to draw out the army into the field; and though he himself, leaping on horseback to go out, was no sooner mounted but the beast, without any apparent cause, fell into so violent a fit of trembling and bounding that he cast his rider headlong on the ground, he was no ways deterred; but proceeded as he had begun, and marched forward up to Hannibal, who was posted near the Lake Thrasymene in Tuscany. At the moment of this engagement, there happened so great an earthquake, that it destroyed several towns, altered the course of rivers, and carried off parts of high cliffs, yet such was the eagerness of the combatants, that they were entirely insensible of it.

In this battle Flaminius fell, after many proofs of his strength and courage, and round about him all the bravest of the army; in the whole, fifteen thousand were killed, and as many made prisoners. Hannibal, desirous to bestow funeral honors upon the body of Flaminius, made diligent search after it, but could not find it among the dead, nor was it ever known what became of it. Upon the former engagement near Trebia, neither the general who wrote, nor the express who told the news, used straightforward and direct terms, nor related it otherwise than as a drawn battle, with equal loss on either side; but on this occasion, as soon as Pomponius the prætor had the intelligence, he caused the people to assemble, and, without disguising or dissembling the matter, told them plainly, "We are beaten, O Romans, in a great battle; the consul Flaminius is killed; think, therefore, what is to be done for your safety." Letting loose his news like a gale of wind upon an open sea, he threw the city into utter confusion: in such consternation, their thoughts found no support or stay. The danger at hand at last awakened their judgments into a resolution to choose a dictator, who, by the sovereign authority of his office, and by his personal wisdom and courage, might be able to manage the public affairs. Their choice unanimously fell upon Fabius, whose character seemed equal to the greatness of the office; whose age was so far advanced as to give him experience, without taking from him the vigor of action; his body could execute what his soul designed; and his temper was a happy compound of confidence and cautiousness. ·

Fabius, being thus installed in the office of dictator, in the first place gave the command of the horse to Lucius Minucius; and next asked leave of the senate for himself, that in time of battle he might serve on horseback, which by an ancient law amongst the Romans was forbid to their

generals; whether it were, that, placing their greatest
strength in their foot, they would have their commanders-
in-chief posted amongst them, or else to let them know,
that, how great and absolute soever their authority were,
the people and senate were still their masters, of whom
they must ask leave.   Fabius, however, to make the
authority of his charge more observable, and to render
the people more submissive and obedient to him, caused
himself to be accompanied with the full body of four and
twenty lictors; and, when the surviving consul came to
visit him, sent him word to dismiss his lictors with their
fasces, the ensigns of authority, and appear before him as
a private person.

The first solemn action of his dictatorship was very
fitly a religious one: an admonition to the people, that
their late overthrow had not befallen them through want
of courage in their soldiers, but through the neglect of
divine ceremonies in the general.   He therefore exhorted them not to fear the enemy, but by extraordinary
honor to propitiate the gods.   This he did, not to fill
their minds with superstition, but by religious feeling to
raise their courage, and lessen their fear of the enemy by
inspiring the belief that Heaven was on their side.   With
this view, the secret prophecies called the Sibylline Books
were consulted; sundry predictions found in them were
said to refer to the fortunes and events of the time; but
none except the consulter was informed.   Presenting
himself to the people, the dictator made a vow before
them to offer in sacrifice the whole product of the next
season, all Italy over, of the cows, goats, swine, sheep,
both in the mountains and the plains; and to celebrate
musical festivities with an expenditure of the precise
sum of 333 sestertia and 333 denarii, with one third of
a denarius over.   The sum total of which is, in our
money, 83,583 drachmas and 2 obols.   What the mystery

might be in that exact number is not easy to determine,
unless it were in honor of the perfection of the number
three, as being the first of odd numbers, the first that
contains in itself multiplication, with all other properties
whatsoever belonging to numbers in general.

In this manner Fabius having given the people better
heart for the future, by making them believe that the
gods took their side, for his own part placed his whole
confidence in himself, believing that the gods bestowed
victory and good fortune by the instrumentality of valor
and of prudence; and thus prepared he set forth to
oppose Hannibal, not with intention to fight him, but
with the purpose of wearing out and wasting the vigor
of his arms by lapse of time, of meeting his want of resources by superior means, by large numbers the smallness
of his forces. With this design, he always encamped on
the highest grounds, where the enemy's horse could have
no access to him. Still he kept pace with them; when they
marched he followed them; when they encamped he did
the same, but at such a distance as not to be compelled
to an engagement, and always keeping upon the hills, '
free from the insults of their horse; by which means
he gave them no rest, but kept them in a continual
alarm.

But this his dilatory way gave occasion in his own
camp for suspicion of want of courage; and this opinion
prevailed yet more in Hannibal's army. Hannibal was
himself the only man who was not deceived, who discerned
his skill and detected his tactics, and saw, unless he could
by art or force bring him to battle, that the Carthaginians, unable to use the arms in which they were superior, and suffering the continual drain of lives and treasure in which they were inferior, would in the end come
to nothing. He resolved, therefore, with all the arts and
subtilties of war to break his measures, and to bring

Fabius to an engagement; like a cunning wrestler,
watching every opportunity to get good hold and close
with his adversary. He at one time attacked, and sought
to distract his attention, tried to draw him off in various
directions, endeavored in all ways to tempt him from
his safe policy. All this artifice, though it had no effect
upon the firm judgment and conviction of the dictator,
yet upon the common soldier and even upon the general
of the horse himself, it had too great an operation: Minucius, unseasonably eager for action, bold and confident,
humored the soldiery, and himself contributed to fill
them with wild eagerness and empty hopes, which they
vented in reproaches upon Fabius, calling him Hannibal's
pedagogue,* since he did nothing else but follow him up
and down and wait upon him. At the same time, they
cried up Minucius for the only captain worthy to command the Romans; whose vanity and presumption rose so
high in consequence, that he insolently jested at Fabius's
encampments upon the mountains, saying that he seated
them there as on a theatre, to behold the flames and deso-
lation of their country. And he would sometimes ask the
friends of the general, whether it were not his meaning,
by thus leading them from mountain to mountain, to
carry them at last (having no hopes on earth) up into
heaven, or to hide them in the clouds from Hannibal's
army? When his friends reported these things to the
dictator, persuading him that, to avoid the general obloquy, he should engage the enemy, his answer was, "I
should be more fainthearted than they make me, if,
through fear of idle reproaches, I should abandon my

---

* Hannibal's footman, might perhaps give the jest more correctly.
The pædagogus of the ancients
was merely the slave appointed to
be in constant attendance, especially out of the house, upon the
young boys of the family, and, in
particular, to take them to school
and bring them home again.

own convictions. It is no inglorious thing to have fear
for the safety of our country, but to be turned from one's
course by men's opinions, by blame, and by misrepresen-
tation, shows a man unfit to hold an office such as this,
which, by such conduct, he makes the slave of those
whose errors it is his business to control."

An oversight of Hannibal occurred soon after. Desirous to refresh his horse in some good pasture-grounds,
and to draw off his army, he ordered his guides to conduct him to the district of Casinum. They, mistaking
his bad pronunciation, led him and his army to the town
of Casilinum, on the frontier of Campania which the
river Lothronus, called by the Romans Vulturnus,
divides in two parts. The country around is enclosed by
mountains, with a valley opening towards the sea, in
which the river overflowing forms a quantity of marsh
land with deep banks of sand, and discharges itself into
the sea on a very unsafe and rough shore. While Hannibal was proceeding hither, Fabius, by his knowledge of
the roads, succeeded in making his way around before
him, and despatched four thousand choice men to seize
the exit from it and stop him up, and lodged the rest of
his army upon the neighboring hills in the most advantageous places; at the same time detaching a party of
his lightest armed men to fall upon Hannibal's rear;
which they did with such success, that they cut off eight
hundred of them, and put the whole army in disorder.
Hannibal, finding the error and the danger he was fallen
into, immediately crucified the guides; but considered
the enemy to be so advantageously posted, that there
was no hopes of breaking through them; while his soldiers began to be despondent and terrified, and to think
themselves surrounded with embarrassments too difficult
to be surmounted.

Thus reduced, Hannibal had recourse to stratagem; he

caused two thousand head of oxen which he had in his
camp, to have torches or dry fagots well fastened to
their horns, and lighting them in the beginning of the
night, ordered the beasts to be driven on towards the
heights commanding the passages out of the valley and
the enemy's posts; when this was done, he made his
army in the dark leisurely march after them. The oxen
at first kept a slow, orderly pace, and with their lighted
heads resembled an army marching by night, astonishing
the shepherds and herdsmen of the hills about. But
when the fire had burnt down the horns of the beasts to
the quick, they no longer observed their sober pace, but,
unruly and wild with their pain, ran dispersed about, toss-
ing their heads and scattering the fire round about
them upon each other and setting light as they passed to
the trees. This was a surprising spectacle to the Romans
on guard upon the heights. Seeing flames which appeared to come from men advancing with torches, they
were possessed with the alarm that the enemy was
approaching in various quarters, and that they were being
surrounded; and, quitting their post, abandoned the pass,
and precipitately retired to their camp on the hills.
They were no sooner gone, but the light-armed of Hannibal's men, according to his order, immediately seized the
heights, and soon after the whole army, with all the bag-
gage, came up and safely marched through the passes.

Fabius, before the night was over, quickly found out
the trick; for some of the beasts fell into his hands; but
for fear of an ambush in the dark, he kept his men all
night to their arms in the camp. As soon as it was day,
he attacked the enemy in the rear, where, after a good
deal of skirmishing in the uneven ground, the disorder
might have become general, but that Hannibal detached
from his van a body of Spaniards, who, of themselves
active and nimble, were accustomed to the climbing of

mountains. These briskly attacked the Roman troops who were in heavy armor, killed a good many, and left Fabius no longer in condition to follow the enemy. This action brought the extreme of obloquy and contempt upon the dictator; they said it was now manifest that he was not only inferior to his adversary, as they had always thought, in courage, but even in that conduct, foresight, and generalship, by which he had proposed to bring the war to an end.

And Hannibal, to enhance their anger against him, marched with his army close to the lands and possessions of Fabius, and, giving orders to his soldiers to burn and destroy all the country about, forbade them to do the least damage in the estates of the Roman general, and placed guards for their security. This, when reported at Rome, had the effect with the people which Hannibal desired. Their tribunes raised a thousand stories against him, chiefly at the instigation of Metilius, who, not so much out of hatred to him as out of friendship to Minucius, whose kinsman he was, thought by depressing Fabius to raise his friend. The senate on their part were also offended with him, for the bargain he had made with Hannibal about the exchange of prisoners, the conditions of which were, that, after exchange made of man for man, if any on either side remained, they should be redeemed at the price of two hundred and fifty drachmas a head. Upon the whole account, there remained two hundred and forty Romans unexchanged, and the senate now not only refused to allow money for the ransoms, but also reproached Fabius for making a contract, contrary to the honor and interest of the commonwealth, for redeeming men whose cowardice had put them in the hands of the enemy. Fabius heard and endured all this with invincible patience; and, having no money by him, and on the other side being resolved to keep his word

with Hannibal and not to abandon the captives, he despatched his son to Rome to sell land, and to bring with
him the price, sufficient to discharge the ransoms; which
was punctually performed by his son, and delivery accordingly made to him of the prisoners, amongst whom many,
when they were released, made proposals to repay the
money; which Fabius in all cases declined.

About this time, he was called to Rome by the priests,
to assist, according to the duty of his office, at certain
sacrifices, and was thus forced to leave the command of
the army with Minucius; but before he parted, not only
charged him as his commander-in-chief, but besought and
entreated him, not to come, in his absence, to a battle with
Hannibal. His commands, entreaties, and advice were
lost upon Minucius; for his back was no sooner turned
but the new general immediately sought occasions to
attack the enemy. And notice being brought him that
Hannibal had sent out a great part of his army to forage,
he fell upon a detachment of the remainder, doing great
execution, and driving them to their very camp, with no
little terror to the rest, who apprehended their breaking
in upon them; and when Hannibal had recalled his scattered forces to the camp, he, nevertheless, without any
loss, made his retreat, a success which aggravated his
boldness and presumption, and filled the soldiers with rash
confidence. The news spread to Rome, where Fabius, on
being told it, said that what he most feared was Minucius's success: but the people, highly elated, hurried to
the forum to listen to an address from Metilius the tribune, in which he infinitely extolled the valor of Minucius, and fell bitterly upon Fabius, accusing him for want
not merely of courage, but even of loyalty; and not
only him, but also many other eminent and considerable
persons; saying that it was they that had brought the
Carthaginians into Italy, with the design to destroy the

liberty of the people; for which end they had at once
put the supreme authority into the hands of a single person, who by his slowness and delays might give Hannibal
leisure to establish himself in Italy, and the people of
Carthage time and opportunity to supply him with fresh
succors to complete his conquest.

Fabius came forward with no intention to answer the
tribune, but only said, that they should expedite the
sacrifices, that so he might speedily return to the army
to punish Minucius, who had presumed to fight contrary
to his orders; words which immediately possessed the
people with the belief that Minucius stood in danger of
his life. For it was in the power of the dictator to
imprison and to put to death, and they feared that Fabius,
of a mild temper in general, would be as hard to be
appeased when once irritated, as he was slow to be provoked. Nobody dared to raise his voice in opposition;
Metilius alone, whose office of tribune gave him security
to say what he pleased (for in the time of a dictatorship
that magistrate alone preserves his authority), boldly
applied himself to the people in the behalf of Minucius:
that they should not suffer him to be made a sacrifice to
the enmity of Fabius, nor permit him to be destroyed,
like the son of Manlius Torquatus, who was beheaded by
his father for a victory fought and triumphantly won
against order; he exhorted them to take away from
Fabius that absolute power of a dictator, and to put it
into more worthy hands, better able and more inclined
to use it for the public good. These impressions very
much prevailed upon the people, though not so far
as wholly to dispossess Fabius of the dictatorship. But
they decreed that Minucius should have an equal authority with the dictator in the conduct of the war; which
was a thing then without precedent, though a little later
it was again practised after the disaster at Cannæ; when

the dictator, Marcus Junius, being with the army, they chose at Rome Fabius Buteo dictator, that he might create new senators, to supply the numerous places of those who were killed. But as soon as, once acting in public, he had filled those vacant places with a sufficient number, he immediately dismissed his lictors, and withdrew from all his attendance, and, mingling like a common person with the rest of the people, quietly went about his own affairs in the forum.

The enemies of Fabius thought they had sufficiently humiliated and subdued him by raising Minucius to be his equal in authority; but they mistook the temper of the man, who looked upon their folly as not his loss, but like Diogenes, who, being told that some persons derided him, made answer, "But I am not derided," meaning that only those were really insulted on whom such insults made an impression, so Fabius, with great tranquillity and unconcern, submitted to what happened, and contributed a proof to the argument of the philosophers that a just and good man is not capable of being dishonored. His only vexation arose from his fear lest this ill counsel, by supplying opportunities to the diseased military ambition of his subordinate, should damage the public cause. Lest the rashness of Minucius should now at once run headlong into some disaster, he returned back with all privacy and speed to the army; where he found Minucius so elevated with his new dignity, that, a joint-authority not contenting him, he required by turns to have the command of the army every other day. This Fabius rejected, but was contented that the army should be divided; thinking each general singly would better command his part, than partially command the whole. The first and fourth legion he took for his own division, the second and third he delivered to Minucius; so also of the auxiliary forces each had an equal share.

Minucius, thus exalted, could not contain himself from boasting of his success in humiliating the high and powerful office of the dictatorship. Fabius quietly reminded him that it was, in all wisdom, Hannibal, and not Fabius, whom he had to combat; but if he must needs contend with his colleague, it had best be in diligence and care for the preservation of Rome; that it might not be said, a man so favored by the people served them worse than he who had been ill-treated and disgraced by them.

The young general, despising these admonitions as the false humility of age, immediately removed with the body of his army, and encamped by himself. Hannibal, who was not ignorant of all these passages, lay watching his advantage from them. It happened that between his army and that of Minucius there was a certain eminence, which seemed a very advantageous and not difficult post to encamp upon; the level field around it appeared, from a distance, to be all smooth and even, though it had many inconsiderable ditches and dips in it, not discernible to the eye. Hannibal, had he pleased, could easily have possessed himself of this ground; but he had reserved it for a bait, or train, in proper season, to draw the Romans to an engagement. Now that Minucius and Fabius were divided, he thought the opportunity fair for his purpose; and, therefore, having in the night time lodged a convenient number of his men in these ditches and hollow places, early in the morning he sent forth a small detachment, who, in the sight of Minucius, proceeded to possess themselves of the rising ground. According to his expectation, Minucius swallowed the bait, and first sends out his light troops, and after them some horse, to dislodge the enemy; and, at last, when he saw Hannibal in person advancing to the assistance of his men, marched down with his whole army drawn up. He engaged with the troops on the eminence, and sustained their missiles; the combat for some time was equal; but as soon as Hannibal perceived that the whole army was now sufficiently advanced within the toils he had set for them, so that their backs were open to his men whom he had posted in the hollows, he gave the signal; upon which they rushed forth from various quarters, and with loud cries furiously attacked Minucius in the rear. The surprise and the slaughter was great, and struck universal alarm and disorder through the whole army. Minucius himself lost all his confidence; he looked from officer to officer, and found all alike unprepared to face the danger, and yielding to a flight, which, however, could not end in safety. The Numidian horsemen were already in full victory riding about the plain, cutting down the fugitives.

Fabius was not ignorant of this danger of his countrymen; he foresaw what would happen from the rashness of Minucius, and the cunning of Hannibal; and, therefore, kept his men to their arms, in readiness to wait the event; nor would he trust to the reports of others, but he himself, in front of his camp, viewed all that passed. When, therefore, he saw the army of Minucius encompassed by the enemy, and that by their countenance and shifting their ground, they appeared more disposed to flight than to resistance, with a great sigh, striking his hand upon his thigh, he said to those about him, "O Hercules! how much sooner than I expected, though later than he seemed to desire, hath Minucius destroyed himself!" He then commanded the ensigns to be led forward and the army to follow, telling them, "We must make haste to rescue Minucius, who is a valiant man, and a lover of his country; and if he hath been too forward to engage the enemy, at another time we will tell him of it." Thus, at the head of his men, Fabius marched up to the enemy, and first cleared the plain of the Numidians; and next fell upon those who were charging the Romans in the rear, cutting down all that made opposition, and obliging the rest to save themselves by a hasty retreat, lest they should be environed as the Romans had been. Hannibal, seeing so sudden a change of affairs, and Fabius, beyond the force of his age, opening his way through the ranks up the hill-side, that he might join Minucius, warily forbore, sounded a retreat, and drew off his men into their camp; while the Romans on their part were no less contented to retire in safety. It is reported that upon this occasion Hannibal said jestingly to his friends: "Did not I tell you, that this cloud which always hovered upon the mountains would, at some time or other, come down with a storm upon us?"

Fabius, after his men had picked up the spoils of the field, retired to his own camp, without saying any harsh or reproachful thing to his colleague; who also on his part, gathering his army together, spoke and said to them : "To conduct great matters and never commit a fault is above the force of human nature; but to learn and improve by the faults we have committed, is that which becomes a good and sensible man. Some reasons I may have to accuse fortune, but I have many more to thank her; for in a few hours she hath cured a long mistake, and taught me that I am not the man who should command others, but have need of another to command me; and that we are not to contend for victory over those to whom it is our advantage to yield. Therefore in every thing else henceforth the dictator must be your commander; only in showing gratitude towards him I will still be your leader, and always be the first to obey his orders." Having said this, he commanded the Roman eagles to move forward, and all his men to follow him to the camp of Fabius. The soldiers, then, as he entered, stood amazed at the novelty of the sight, and were anxious and doubtful what the meaning might be. When he came near the dictator's tent, Fabius went forth to meet him, on which he at once laid his standards at his feet, calling him with a loud voice his father; while the soldiers with him saluted the soldiers here as their patrons, the term employed by freedmen to those who gave them their liberty. After silence was obtained, Minucius said, "You have this day, O dictator, obtained two victories; one by your valor and conduct over Hannibal, and another by your wisdom and goodness over your colleague; by one victory you preserved, and by the other instructed us; and when we were already suffering one shameful defeat from Hannibal, by another welcome one from you we were restored to honor and safety. I can address you by no nobler name than that of a kind father, though a father's beneficence falls short of that I have received from you. From a father I individually received the gift of life; to you I owe its preservation not for myself only, but for all these who are under me." After this, he threw himself into the arms of the dictator; and in the same manner the soldiers of each army embraced one another with gladness and tears of joy.

Not long after, Fabius laid down the dictatorship, and consuls were again created. Those who immediately succeeded, observed the same method in managing the war, and avoided all occasions of fighting Hannibal in a pitched battle; they only succored their allies, and preserved the towns from falling off to the enemy. But afterwards, when Terentius Varro, a man of obscure birth, but very popular and bold, had obtained the consulship, he soon made it appear that by his rashness and ignorance he would stake the whole commonwealth on the hazard. For it was his custom to declaim in all assemblies, that, as long as Rome employed generals like Fabius, there never would be an end of the war; vaunting that whenever he should get sight of the enemy, he would that same day free Italy from the strangers. With these promises he so prevailed, that he raised a greater army than had ever yet been sent out of Rome. There were enlisted eighty-eight thousand fighting men; but what gave confidence to the populace, only terrified the wise and experienced, and none more than Fabius; since if so great a body, and the flower of the Roman youth, should be cut off, they could not see any new resource for the safety of Rome. They addressed themselves, therefore, to the other consul, Æmilius Paulus, a man of great experience in war, but unpopular, and fearful also of the people, who once before upon some impeachment had condemned him; so that he needed encouragement to withstand his colleague's temerity. Fabius told him, if he would profitably serve his country, he must no less oppose Varro's ignorant eagerness than Hannibal's conscious readiness, since both alike conspired to decide the fate of Rome by a battle. "It is more reasonable," he said to him, "that you should believe me than Varro, in matters relating to Hannibal, when I tell you, that if for this year you abstain from fighting with him, either his army will perish of itself, or else he will be glad to depart of his own will. This evidently appears, inasmuch as, notwithstanding his victories, none of the countries or towns of Italy come in to him, and his army is not now the third part of what it was at first." To this Paulus is said to have replied, "Did I only consider myself, I should rather choose to be exposed to the weapons of Hannibal than once more to the suffrages of my fellow-citizens, who are urgent for what you disapprove; yet since the cause of Rome is at stake, I will rather seek in my conduct to please and obey Fabius than all the world besides."

These good measures were defeated by the impor-

tunity of Varro; whom, when they were both come to
the army, nothing would content but a separate command, that each consul should have his day; and when
his turn came, he posted his army close to Hannibal, at a
village called Cannæ, by the river Aufidus. It was no
sooner day, but he set up the scarlet coat flying over his
tent, which was the signal of battle. This boldness of
the consul, and the numerousness of his army, double
theirs, startled the Carthaginians; but Hannibal commanded them 'to their arms, and with a small train rode
out to take a full prospect of the enemy as they were
now forming in their ranks, from a rising ground not far
distant. One of his followers, called Gisco, a Carthaginian of equal rank with himself, told him that the
numbers of the enemy were astonishing; to which Hannibal replied, with a serious countenance, "There is one
thing, Gisco, yet more astonishing, which you take no
notice of;" and when Gisco inquired what, answered,
that "in all those great numbers before us, there is not
one man called Gisco." This unexpected jest of their
general made all the company laugh, and as they came
down from the hill, they told it to those whom they met,
which caused a general laughter amongst them all, from
which they were hardly able to recover themselves. The
army, seeing Hannibal's attendants come back from
viewing the enemy in such a laughing condition, concluded that it must be profound contempt of the enemy,
that made their general at this moment indulge in such
hilarity.

According to his usual manner, Hannibal employed
stratagems to advantage himself. In the first place, he so
drew up his men that the wind was at their backs, which
at that time blew with a perfect storm of violence, and,
sweeping over the great plains of sand, carried before it
a cloud of dust over the Carthaginian army into the

faces of the Romans, which much disturbed them in the fight. In the next place, all his best men he put into his wings; and in the body, which was somewhat more advanced than the wings, placed the worst and the weakest of his army. He commanded those in the wings, that, when the enemy had made a thorough charge upon that middle advanced body, which he knew would recoil, as not being able to withstand their shock, and when the Romans, in their pursuit, should be far enough engaged within the two wings, they should, both on the right and the left, charge them in the flank, and endeavor to encompass them. This appears to have been the chief cause of the Roman loss. Pressing upon Hannibal's front, which gave ground, they reduced the form of his army into a perfect half-moon, and gave ample opportunity to the captains of the chosen troops to charge them right and left on their flanks, and to cut off and destroy all who did not fall back before the Carthaginian wings united in their rear. To this general calamity, it is also said, that a strange mistake among the cavalry much contributed. For the horse of Æmilius receiving a hurt and throwing his master, those about him immediately alighted to aid the consul; and the Roman troops, seeing their commanders thus quitting their horses, took it for a sign that they should all dismount and charge the enemy on foot. At the sight of this, Hannibal was heard to say, "This pleases me better than if they had been delivered to me bound hand and foot." For the particulars of this engagement, we refer our reader to those authors who have written at large upon the subject.

The consul Varro, with a thin company, fled to Venusia; Æmilius Paulus, unable any longer to oppose the flight of his men, or the pursuit of the enemy, his body all covered with wounds, and his soul no less wounded with grief, sat himself down upon a stone, expecting the

kindness of a despatching blow. His face was so disfigured, and all his person so stained with blood, that his
very friends and domestics passing by knew him not.
At last Cornelius Lentulus, a young man of patrician
race, perceiving who he was, alighted from his horse, and,
tendering it to him, desired him to get up and save a life
so necessary to the safety of the commonwealth, which,
at this time, would dearly want so great a captain. But
nothing could prevail upon him to accept of the offer; he
obliged young Lentulus, with tears in his eyes, to remount
his horse; then standing up, he gave him his hand, and
commanded him to tell Fabius Maximus that Æmilius
Paulus had followed his directions to his very last, and
had not in the least deviated from those measures which
were agreed between them; but that it was his hard
fate to be overpowered by Varro in the first place, and
secondly by Hannibal. Having despatched Lentulus
with this commission, he marked where the slaughter was
greatest, and there threw himself upon the swords of the
enemy. In this battle it is reported that fifty thousand
Romans were slain, four thousand prisoners taken in the
field, and ten thousand in the camp of both consuls.

The friends of Hannibal earnestly persuaded him to
follow up his victory, and pursue the flying Romans into
the very gates of Rome, assuring him that in five days'
time he might sup in the capitol; nor is it easy to imagine what consideration hindered him from it. It would
seem rather that some supernatural or divine intervention caused the hesitation and timidity which he now
displayed, and which made Barcas, a Carthaginian, tell
him with indignation, "You know, Hannibal, how to
gain a victory, but not how to use it." Yet it produced
a marvellous revolution in his affairs; he, who hitherto
had not one town, market, or seaport in his possession,
who had nothing for the subsistence of his men but what

he pillaged from day to day, who had no place of retreat
or basis of operation, but was roving, as it were, with a
huge troop of banditti, now became master of the best
provinces and towns of Italy, and of Capua itself, next
to Rome the most flourishing and opulent city, all which
came over to him, and submitted to his authority.

It is the saying of Euripides, that "a man is in ill-case
when he must try a friend," and so neither, it would
seem, is a state in a good one, when it needs an able
general. And so it was with the Romans; the counsels
and actions of Fabius, which, before the battle, they had
branded as cowardice and fear, now, in the other extreme
they accounted to have been more than human wisdom;
as though nothing but a divine power of intellect could
have seen so far, and foretold, contrary to the judgment
of all others, a result which, even now it had arrived, was
hardly credible. In him, therefore, they placed their
whole remaining hopes; his wisdom was the sacred altar
and temple to which they fled for refuge, and his counsels, more than any thing, preserved them from dispersing
and deserting their city, as in the time when the Gauls
took possession of Rome. He, whom they esteemed
fearful and pusillanimous when they were, as they
thought, in a prosperous condition, was now the only
man, in this general and unbounded dejection and confusion, who showed no fear, but walked the streets with an
assured and serene countenance, addressed his fellow-citizens, checked the women's lamentations, and the public
gatherings of those who wanted thus to vent their sor-
rows. He caused the senate to meet, he heartened up
the magistrates, and was himself as the soul and life of
every office.

He placed guards at the gates of the city to stop the
frighted multitude from flying; he regulated and confined their mournings for their slain friends, both as to

time and place; ordering that each family should perform
such observances within private walls, and that they
should continue only the space of one month, and then ·
the whole city should be purified. The feast of Ceres
happening to fall within this time, it was decreed that
the solemnity should be intermitted, lest the fewness, and
the sorrowful countenance of those who should celebrate
it, might too much expose to the people the greatness of
their loss; besides that, the worship most acceptable to
the gods is that which comes from cheerful hearts. But
those rights which were proper for appeasing their anger,
and procuring auspicious signs and presages, were by the
direction of the augurs carefully performed. Fabius Pictor,
a near kinsman to Maximus, was sent to consult the oracle
of Delphi; and about the same time, two vestals having
been detected to have been violated, the one killed herself, and the other, according to custom, was buried alive.

Above all, let us admire the high spirit and equanimity
of this Roman commonwealth; that when the consul
Varro came beaten and flying home, full of shame and
humiliation, after he had so disgracefully and calamitously
managed their affairs, yet the whole senate and people
went forth to meet him at the gates of the city, and
received him with honor and respect. And, silence being
commanded, the magistrates and chief of the senate,
Fabius amongst them, commended him before the people,
because he did not despair of the safety of the commonwealth, after so great a loss, but was come to take the
government into his hands, to execute the laws, and aid
his fellow-citizens in their prospect of future deliverance.

When word was brought to Rome that Hannibal, after
the fight, had marched with his army into other parts of
Italy, the hearts of the Romans began to revive, and they
proceeded to send out generals and armies. The most
distinguished commands were held by Fabius Maximus

and Claudius Marcellus, both generals of great fame,
though upon opposite grounds. For Marcellus, as we
have set forth in his life, was a man of action and high
spirit, ready and bold with his own hand, and, as Homer
describes his warriors, fierce, and delighting in fights.
Boldness, enterprise, and daring, to match those of Hannibal, constituted his tactics, and marked his engagements.
But Fabius adhered to his former principles, still persuaded that, by following close and not fighting him,
Hannibal and his army would at last be tired out and
consumed, like a wrestler in too high condition, whose
very excess of strength makes him the more likely suddenly to give way and lose it. Posidonius tells us that
the Romans called Marcellus their sword, and Fabius
their buckler; and that the vigor of the one, mixed with
the steadiness of the other, made a happy compound
that proved the salvation of Rome. So that Hannibal
found by experience that, encountering the one, he met
with a rapid, impetuous river, which drove him back,
and still made some breach upon him; and by the other,
though silently and quietly passing by him, he was insensibly washed away and consumed; and, at last, was
brought to this, that he dreaded Marcellus when he was
in motion, and Fabius when he sat still. During the
whole course of this war, he had still to do with one or
both of these generals; for each of them was five times
consul, and, as prætors or proconsuls or consuls, they
had always a part in the government of the army,
till, at last, Marcellus fell into the trap which Hannibal
had laid for him, and was killed in his fifth consulship.
But all his craft and subtlety were unsuccessful upon
Fabius, who only once was in some danger of being
caught, when counterfeit letters came to him from the
principal inhabitants of Metapontum, with promises to
deliver up their town if he would come before it with

his army, and intimations that they should expect him.
This train had almost drawn him in; he resolved to
march to them with part of his army, and was diverted
only by consulting the omens of the birds, which he
found to be inauspicious; and not long after it was discovered that the letters had been forged by Hannibal,
who, for his reception, had laid an ambush to entertain
him. This, perhaps, we must rather attribute to the
favor of the gods than to the prudence of Fabius.

In preserving the towns and allies from revolt by fair
and gentle treatment, and in not using rigor, or showing
a suspicion upon every light suggestion, his conduct was
remarkable. It is told of him, that, being informed of a
certain Marsian, eminent for courage and good birth, who
had been speaking underhand with some of the soldiers
about deserting, Fabius was so far from using severity
against him, that he called for him, and told him he was
sensible of the neglect that had been shown to his merit
and good service, which, he said, was a great fault in the
commanders who reward more by favor than by desert;
"but henceforward, whenever you are aggrieved," said
Fabius, "I shall consider it your fault, if you apply yourself to any but to me;" and when he had so spoken,
he bestowed an excellent horse and other presents upon
him; and, from that time forwards, there was not a faith-
fuller and more trusty man in the whole army. With
good reason he judged, that, if those who have the government of horses and dogs endeavor by gentle usage to
cure their angry and untractable tempers, rather than by
cruelty and beating, much more should those who have
the command of men try to bring them to order and
discipline by the mildest and fairest means, and not treat
them worse than gardeners do those wild plants, which,
with care and attention, lose gradually the savageness of
their nature, and bear excellent fruit.

At another time, some of his officers informed him that one of their men was very often absent from his place, and out at nights; he asked them what kind of man he was; they all answered, that the whole army had not a better man, that he was a native of Lucania, and proceeded to speak of several actions which they had .seen him perform. Fabius made strict inquiry, and discovered at last that these frequent excursions which he ventured upon were to visit a young girl, with whom he was in love. Upon which he gave private order to some of his men to find out the woman and secretly convey her into his own tent; and then sent for the Lucanian, and, calling him aside, told him, that he very well knew how often he had been out away from the camp at night, which was a capital transgression against military discipline and the Roman laws, but he knew also how brave he was, and the good services he had done; therefore, in consideration of them, he was willing to forgive him his fault; but to keep him in good order, he was resolved to place one over him to be his keeper, who should be accountable for his good behavior. Having said this, he produced the woman, and told the soldier, terrified and amazed at the adventure, "This is the person who must answer for you; and by your future behavior we shall see whether your night rambles were on account of love, or for any other worse design."

Another passage there was, something of the same kind, which gained him possession of Tarentum. There was a young Tarentine in the army that had a sister in Tarentum, then in possession of the enemy, who entirely loved her brother, and wholly depended upon him. He, being informed that a certain Bruttian, whom Hannibal had made a commander of the garrison, was deeply in love with his sister, conceived hopes that he might possibly turn it to the advantage of the Romans. And hav-

ing first communicated his design to Fabius, he left the
army as a deserter in show, and went over to Tarentum.
The first days passed, and the Bruttian abstained from
visiting the sister; for neither of them knew that the
brother had notice of the amour between them. The
young Tarentine, however, took an occasion to tell his
sister how he had heard that a man of station and
authority had made his addresses to her, and desired her,
therefore, to tell him who it was; "for," said he, "if he
be a man that has bravery and reputation, it matters not
what countryman he is, since at this time the sword
mingles all nations, and makes them equal; compulsion
makes all things honorable; and in a time when right is
weak, we may be thankful if might assumes a form of
gentleness." Upon this the woman sends for her friend,
and makes the brother and him acquainted; and whereas
she henceforth showed more countenance to her lover
than formerly, in the same degrees that her kindness
increased, his friendship, also, with the brother advanced.
So that at last our Tarentine thought this Bruttian
officer well enough prepared to receive the offers he had
to make him; and that it would be easy for a mercenary
man, who was in love, to accept, upon the terms proposed,
the large rewards promised by Fabius. In conclusion,
the bargain was struck, and the promise made of delivering the town. This is the common tradition, though
some relate the story otherwise, and say, that this woman,
by whom the Bruttian was inveigled to betray the town,
was not a native of Tarentum, but a Bruttian born, and
was kept by Fabius as his concubine; and being a coun-
trywoman and an acquaintance of the Bruttian governor,
he privately sent her to him to corrupt him.

Whilst these matters were thus in process, to draw off
Hannibal from scenting the design, Fabius sends orders
to the garrison in Rhegium, that they should waste and

spoil the Bruttian country, and should also lay siege to Caulonia, and storm the place with all their might. These were a body of eight thousand men, the worst of the Roman army, who had most of them been runaways, and had been brought home by Marcellus from Sicily, in dishonor, so that the loss of them would not be any great grief to the Romans. Fabius, therefore, threw out these men as a bait for Hannibal, to divert him from Tarentum ; who instantly caught at it, and led his forces to Caulonia ; in the mean time, Fabius sat down before Tarentum. On the sixth day of the siege, the young Tarentine slips by night out of the town, and, having carefully observed the place where the Bruttian commander, according to agreement, was to admit the Romans, gave an account of the whole matter to Fabius ; who thought it not safe to rely wholly upon the plot, but, while proceeding with secrecy to the post, gave order for a general assault to be made on the other side of the town, both by land and sea. This being accordingly executed, while the Tarentines hurried to defend the town on the side attacked, Fabius received the signal from the Bruttian, scaled the walls, and entered the town unopposed.

Here, we must confess, ambition seems to have overcome him. To make it appear to the world that he had taken Tarentum by force and his own prowess, and not by treachery, he commanded his men to kill the Bruttians before all others ; yet he did not succeed in establishing the impression he desired, but merely gained the character of perfidy and cruelty. Many of the Tarentines were also killed, and thirty thousand of them were sold for slaves ; the army had the plunder of the town, and there was brought into the treasury three thousand talents. Whilst they were carrying off every thing else as plunder, the officer who took the inventory asked what should be done with their gods, meaning the pictures and statues; Fabius answered, "Let us leave their angry gods to the Tarentines." Nevertheless, he removed the colossal statue of Hercules, and had it set up in the capitol, with one of himself on horseback, in brass, near it; proceedings very different from those of Marcellus on a like occasion, and which, indeed, very much set off in the eyes of the world his clemency and humanity, as appears in the account of his life.

Hannibal, it is said, was within five miles of Tarentum, when he was informed that the town was taken. He said openly, "Rome, then, has also got a Hannibal; as we won Tarentum, so have we lost it." And, in private with some of his confidants, he told them, for the first time, that he always thought it difficult, but now he held it impossible, with the forces he then had, to master Italy.

Upon this success, Fabius had a triumph decreed him at Rome, much more splendid than his first; they looked upon him now as a champion who had learned to cope with his antagonist, and could now easily foil his arts and prove his best skill ineffectual. And, indeed, the army of Hannibal was at this time partly worn away with continual action, and partly weakened and become dissolute with overabundance and luxury. Marcus Livius, who was governor of Tarentum when it was betrayed to Hannibal, and then retired into the citadel, which he kept till the town was retaken, was annoyed at these honors and distinctions, and, on one occasion, openly declared in the senate, that by his resistance, more than by any action of Fabius, Tarentum had been recovered; on which Fabius laughingly replied: "You say very true, for if Marcus Livius had not lost Tarentum, Fabius Maximus had never recovered it." The people, amongst other marks of gratitude, gave his son the consulship of the next year; shortly after whose entrance upon his office, there being some business on foot about provision for the war, his

father, either by reason of age and infirmity, or perhaps out of design to try his son, came up to him on
horseback. While he was still at a distance, the young
consul observed it, and bade one of his lictors command
his father to alight, and tell him that, if he had any business with the consul, he should come on foot. The
standers by seemed offended at the imperiousness of the
son towards a father so venerable for his age and his
authority, and turned their eyes in silence towards Fabius.
He, however, instantly alighted from his horse, and with
open arms came up, almost running, and embraced his
son, saying, "Yes, my son, you do well, and understand well what authority you have received, and over
whom you are to use it. This was the way by which we
and our forefathers advanced the dignity of Rome, preferring ever her honor and service to our own fathers
and children."

And, in fact, it is told that the great-grandfather of our
Fabius, who was undoubtedly the greatest man of Rome
in his time, both in reputation and authority, who had
been five times consul, and had been honored with several triumphs for victories obtained by him, took pleasure
in serving as lieutenant under his own son, when he went
as consul to his command. And when afterwards his
son had a triumph bestowed upon him for his good service, the old man followed, on horseback, his triumphant
chariot, as one of his attendants; and made it his glory,
that while he really was, and was acknowledged to be,
the greatest man in Rome, and held a father's full power
over his son, he yet submitted himself to the laws and
the magistrate.

But the praises of our Fabius are not bounded here.
He afterwards lost this son, and was remarkable for bearing the loss with the moderation becoming a pious father
and a wise man, and, as it was the custom amongst the

Romans, upon the death of any illustrious person, to have a funeral oration recited by some of the nearest relations, he took upon himself that office, and delivered a speech in the forum, which he committed afterwards to writing.

After Cornelius Scipio, who was sent into Spain, had driven the Carthaginians, defeated by him in many battles, out of the country, and had gained over to Rome many towns and nations with large resources, he was received at his coming home with unexampled joy and acclamation of the people ; who, to show their gratitude, elected him consul for the year ensuing. Knowing what high expectation they had of him, he thought the occupation of contesting Italy with Hannibal a mere old man's employment, and proposed no less a task to himself than to make Carthage the seat of the war, fill Africa with arms and devastation, and so oblige Hannibal, instead of invading the countries of others, to draw back and defend his own. And to this end he proceeded to exert all the influence he had with the people. Fabius, on the other side, opposed the undertaking with all his might, alarming the city, and telling them that nothing but the temerity of a hot young man could inspire them with such dangerous counsels, and sparing no means, by word or deed, to prevent it. He prevailed with the senate to espouse his sentiments ; but the common people thought that he envied the fame of Scipio, and that he was afraid lest this young conqueror should achieve some great and noble exploit, and have the glory, perhaps, of driving Hannibal out of Italy, or even of ending the war, which had for so many years continued and been protracted under his management.

To say the truth, when Fabius first opposed this project of Scipio, he probably did it out of caution and prudence, in consideration only of the public safety, and of the danger which the commonwealth might incur; but when he found Scipio every day increasing in the esteem of the people, rivalry and ambition led him further, and made him violent and personal in his opposition. For he even applied to Crassus, the colleague of Scipio, and urged him not to yield the command to Scipio, but that, if his inclinations were for it, he should himself in person lead the army to Carthage. He also hindered the giving money to Scipio for the war; so that he was forced to raise it upon his own credit and interest from the cities of Etruria, which were extremely attached to him. On the other side, Crassus would not stir against him, nor remove out of Italy, being, in his own nature, averse to all contention, and also having, by his office of high priest, religious duties to retain him. Fabius, therefore, tried other ways to oppose the design; he impeded the levies, and he declaimed, both in the senate and to the people, that Scipio was not only himself flying from Hannibal, but was also endeavoring to drain Italy of all its forces, and to spirit away the youth of the country to a foreign war, leaving behind them their parents, wives, and children, and the city itself, a defenceless prey to the conquering and undefeated enemy at their doors. With this he so far alarmed the people, that at last they would only allow Scipio for the war the legions which were in Sicily, and three hundred, whom he particularly trusted, of those men who had served with him in Spain. In these transactions, Fabius seems to have followed the dictates of his own wary temper.

But, after that Scipio was gone over into Africa, when news almost immediately came to Rome of wonderful exploits and victories, of which the fame was confirmed by the spoils he sent home; of a Numidian king taken prisoner; of a vast slaughter of their men; of two camps of the enemy burnt and destroyed, and in them a great quantity of arms and horses; and when, hereupon, the Carthaginians were compelled to send envoys to Hannibal to call him home, and leave his idle hopes in Italy, to defend Carthage; when, for such eminent and transcending services, the whole people of Rome cried up and extolled the actions of Scipio; even then, Fabius contended that a successor should be sent in his place, alleging for it only the old reason of the mutability of fortune, as if she would be weary of long favoring the same person. With this language many did begin to feel offended; it seemed to be morosity and ill-will, the pusillanimity of old age, or a fear, that had now become exaggerated, of the skill of Hannibal. Nay, when Hannibal had put his army on shipboard, and taken his leave of Italy, Fabius still could not forbear to oppose and disturb the universal joy of Rome, expressing his fears and apprehensions, telling them that the commonwealth was never in more danger than now, and that Hannibal was a more formidable enemy under the walls of Carthage than ever he had been in Italy; that it would be fatal to Rome, whenever Scipio should encounter his victorious army, still warm with the blood of so many Roman generals, dictators, and consuls slain. And the people were, in some degree, startled with these declamations, and were brought to believe, that the further off Hannibal was, the nearer was their danger. Scipio, however, shortly afterwards fought Hannibal, and utterly defeated him, humbled the pride of Carthage beneath his feet, gave his countrymen joy and exultation beyond all their hopes, and

"Long shaken on the seas restored the state."

Fabius Maximus, however, did not live to see the prosperous end of this war, and the final overthrow of Hannibal, nor to rejoice in the reëstablished happiness and

security of the commonwealth; for about the time that
Hannibal left Italy, he fell sick and died. At Thebes,
Epaminondas died so poor that he was buried at the public charge; one small iron coin was all, it is said, that
was found in his house. Fabius did not need this, but
the people, as a mark of their affection, defrayed the
expenses of his funeral by a private contribution from
each citizen of the smallest piece of coin; thus owning
him their common father, and making his end no less
honorable than his life.

COMPARISON OF FABIUS WITH PERICLES.

WE have here had two lives rich in examples, both of
civil and military excellence. Let us first compare the
two men in their warlike capacity. Pericles presided in
his commonwealth when it was in its most flourishing
and opulent condition, great and growing in power; so
that it may be thought it was rather the common success
and fortune that kept him from any fall or disaster. But
the task of Fabius, who undertook the government in
the worst and most difficult times, was not to preserve
and maintain the well-established felicity of a prosperous
state, but to raise and uphold a sinking and ruinous commonwealth. Besides, the victories of Cimon, the trophies
of Myronides and Leocrates, with the many famous
exploits of Tolmides, were employed by Pericles rather
to fill the city with festive entertainments and solemni-

ties than to enlarge and secure its empire. Whereas Fabius, when he took upon him the government, had the frightful object before his eyes of Roman armies destroyed, of their generals and consuls slain, of lakes and plains and forests strewed with the dead bodies, and rivers stained with the blood of his fellow-citizens; and yet, with his mature and solid counsels, with the firmness of his resolution, he, as it were, put his shoulder to the falling commonwealth, and kept it up from foundering through the failings and weakness of others. Perhaps it may be more easy to govern a city broken and tamed with calamities and adversity, and compelled by danger and necessity to listen to wisdom, than to set a bridle on wantonness and temerity, and rule a people pampered and restive with long prosperity as were the Athenians when Pericles held the reins of government. But then again, not to be daunted nor discomposed with the vast heap of calamities under which the people of Rome at that time groaned and succumbed, argues a courage in Fabius and a strength of purpose more than ordinary.

We may set Tarentum retaken against Samos won by Pericles, and the conquest of Eubœa we may well balance with the towns of Campania; though Capua itself was reduced by the consuls Fulvius and Appius. I do not find that Fabius won any set battle but that against the Ligurians, for which he had his triumph; whereas Pericles erected nine trophies for as many victories obtained by land and by sea. But no action of Pericles can be compared to that memorable rescue of Minucius, when Fabius redeemed both him and his army from utter destruction; a noble act, combining the highest valor, wisdom, and humanity. On the other side, it does not appear that Pericles was ever so overreached as Fabius was by Hannibal with his flaming oxen. His enemy there had, without his agency, put himself accidentally into his power, yet Fabius let him slip in the night, and, when day came, was worsted by him, was anticipated in the moment of success, and mastered by his prisoner. If it is the part of a good general, not only to provide for the present, but also to have a clear foresight of things to come, in this point Pericles is the superior; for he admonished the Athenians, and told them beforehand the ruin the war would bring upon them, by their grasping more than they were able to manage. But Fabius was not so good a prophet, when he denounced to the Romans that the undertaking of Scipio would be the destruction of the commonwealth. So that Pericles was a good prophet of bad success, and Fabius was a bad prophet of success that was good. And, indeed, to lose an advantage through diffidence is no less blamable in a general than to fall into danger for want of foresight; for both these faults, though of a contrary nature, spring from the same root, want of judgment and experience.

As for their civil policy, it is imputed to Pericles that he occasioned the war, since no terms of peace, offered by the Lacedemonians, would content him. It is true, I presume, that Fabius, also, was not for yielding any point to the Carthaginians, but was ready to hazard all, rather than lessen the empire of Rome. The mildness of Fabius towards his colleague Minucius does, by way of comparison, rebuke and condemn the exertions of Pericles to banish Cimon and Thucydides, noble, aristocratic men, who by his means suffered ostracism. The authority of Pericles in Athens was much greater than that of Fabius in Rome. Hence it was more easy for him to prevent miscarriages arising from the mistakes and insufficiency of other officers; only Tolmides broke loose from him, and, contrary to his persuasions, unadvisedly fought with the Bœotians, and was slain. The greatness of his influence made all others submit and conform themselves

to his judgment.   Whereas Fabius, sure and unerring
himself, for want of that general power, had not the means
to obviate the miscarriages of others; but it had been
happy for the Romans if his authority had been greater,
for so, we may presume, their disasters had been fewer.

As to liberality and public spirit, Pericles was eminent
in never taking any gifts, and Fabius, for giving his own
money to ransom his soldiers, though the sum did not
exceed six talents.   Than Pericles, meantime, no man
had ever greater opportunities to enrich himself, having
had presents offered him from so many kings and princes
and allies, yet no man was ever more free from corruption.   And for the beauty and magnificence of temples
and public edifices with which he adorned his country,
it must be confessed, that all the ornaments and struc-
tures of Rome, to the time of the Cæsars, had nothing to
compare, either in greatness of design or of expense,
with the lustre of those which Pericles only erected at
Athens.

END OF VOL. I.

APPENDIX.

The Lives in the first volume were translated for Dryden's edition, as follows:—

THESEUS, by R. Duke, Fellow of Trinity College, Cambridge, (to whom two pages are given by Johnson in his Lives of the Poets).

ROMULUS, by Mr. James Smallwood, Fellow of Trinity College, Cambridge.

LYCURGUS, by Knightly Chetwood, Fellow of King's College, Cambridge.

NUMA, by Sir Paul Rycant, (the Turkey merchant, and author of the History of the Turks).

SOLON, by Thomas Creech, of Wadham College, Oxford, (the translator of Lucretius).

POPLICOLA, by Mr. Johnson.

THEMISTOCLES, by Edward Brown, M. D.

CAMILLUS, by Michael Payne, Fellow of Trinity College, Cambridge.

PERICLES, by Adam Littleton, D. D.

FABIUS, by John Caryl, Esq.

The following notes may be added to those given with the text:

LIFE OF THESEUS, page 1. — *Beautiful and far-famed*, or *famed in song*, are current epithets of Athens, originally given by Pindar. The two verses just above are from the scene in the Seven against Thebes of Æschylus, where Eteocles considers what captains he shall post against the assailants at each of the gates.

Page 2. — *Both warriors, that by all the world's allowed*, is from Iliad, VII. 281, said by the heralds of Ajax and Hector, when they come to part them after their single combat.

Page 4. — The Abantes of Eubœa *wearing their hair long behind*, are mentioned in the Catalogue, Iliad, II. 543; and Strabo speaks of Arabians, companions of Cadmus, who went into Eubœa.

Page 11. — The hamlets of Marathon, Œnoë, Tricorythus, and Probalinthus, formed the *Tetrapolis* or *Four-towns*, which is reckoned with Sphettus, Aphidna,

Eleusis, and others, in the list of the twelve old Attic towns or townships, all independent of each other.

Page 18. — *Theseus, Pirithoüs,.mighty sons of gods,* is from Odyssey, XI. 630.

Page 25. — The pillar is mentioned by Strabo, who says it was removed when the Dorians of Peloponnesus invaded the Ionian country, and settled themselves in Megara. The translation should be altered; the original does not refer to the inscription as a still existing thing.

Page 32. — *Cora,* or the girl, is another name for Proserpine; the whole account being (like the story of Taurus), a late transformation of fable into something that might seem like history

Page 35. — *Æthra* and *Clymene* are the two handmaids who attend Helen (*Iliad, III.,* 143) from her chamber, when she goes to seek Priam and the elders of the city upon the walls at the Scæan gate.

LIFE OF ROMULUS, page 49. — Remuria or Remoria is the name found elsewhere, instead of Remonium or Rignarium. The line from Æschylus below is out of The Suppliants (223).

Page 56. — *Sextius Sylla, the Carthaginian,* was one of Plutarch's personal friends. He is one of the two speakers in the Dialogue on Controlling Anger; and in the Symposiaca (*VIII.* 7) he gives a dinner of welcome on Plutarch's returning, after some absence, to Rome. Plutarch says, *Greek words not yet being overpowered by Italian,* on the theory that the early language was Greek, which was gradually corrupted. By the *Questions* he means his little book of inquiry into points of Roman antiquity, his Roman Questions.

Page 64. — *Caius Cæsar* is the emperor Caligula.

Page 66. — *Periscylacismus,* from *peri,* around, and *scylax,* a dog.

Page 69. — *The wood called Ferentina,* should be *the gate.* There was a wood (*hulē* in Greek), a Lucus Ferentinus, as well as a gate (*pulē*), but there seems no reason to change the latter into the former.

Page 74. — The story of Aristeas comes from Herodotus (*IV.* 14, 15), that of Cleomedes, the hero of the islet of Astypalæa, is told also by Pausanias (*VI.* 9), who says the thing happened in the 71st Olympiad, 496 (B. C.). The passage from Pindar is quoted by Plutarch at greater length elsewhere (in his Consolation to Apollonius on the death of his son), as a part of one of his Funeral Odes. "These all with happy lot attain the end that releases from labor. And the body, indeed, in all cases, is taken by overmastering death; but a living shape (or image or form) yet remains of the life; (or of the unending existence;) this alone being from the gods; while our limbs are stirring, it slumbers, but when we sleep, in sundry dreams it foreshows good and evil things to come." Fragment 96, in Boeckh. Another piece which he quotes just before from these funeral songs or *Threni,* describes the Blessed as *walking in their beautiful flowery suburb, diverting themselves with horses and gymnastics, games of draughts and the harp, and with converse on what has happened, and what is.* — Fragment 95.

Page 79. — COMPARISON. The philosopher Polemon, one of the early successors of Plato, was the author of this *definition* of love; so Plutarch tells us, quoting it again in one of his Essays (*Ad Principem Ineruditum,* c. 3).

LIFE OF LYCURGUS, page 88. — Creophylus is the correct name, which the copies of Plutarch change into Cleophylus, and Dryden's coadjutor miswrote or misprinted *Cleobulus.* Creophylus was spoken of already in Plato's time as *the companion of Homer.* — (*De Republica*, *X. p.* 600.)

Pages 90 and 92. — Plato's criticisms are in the third book of the Laws, pages 691, 692.

Page 113. — The passage of Pindar is from a lost and unknown poem. *One of their own poets* is Alcman.

Page 122. — For the reference to Plato, see the Timæus, p. 38, where the divine Creator, desirous to add to his works the resemblance of eternity, proceeds to create " this which we call Time."

LIFE OF NUMA, page 132. — Plutarch speaks more at length of this *distinction of the wise Egyptians* in one of the Dinner Conversations. — On the sixth of Thargelion they kept the birthday of Socrates, and, on the seventh, met again to celebrate that of Plato. Apollo himself, according to the story, had been born on this seventh day ; *and it had been no disparagement to the god,* said one of the company, *to attribute to him, as many had done, the mortal procreation of one that had been, under the tuition of Socrates, a greater healer of human maladies and diseases than ever Æsculapius* (Apollo's mythological son) *had become under that of Chiron.* And he referred, at the same time, to the warning which Ariston, Plato's acknowledged father, was said to have received in a dream, forbidding him the company of his wife during the ten months preceding Plato's birth. To this another of the party opposes the incorruptible nature of the godhead : *yet that by some creative, not procreative, power, the eternal and unbegotten God is the father and maker of the world and all begotten things,* Plato, he adds, *himself admits, nor can we limit the modes in which such divine intervention may operate ;* and then he gives the Egyptian dogma. — (*Symposiaca, VIII.* 1).

Page 138, Note. — The Greek would, however, not be *Aimulos* or *Æmylus,* but *Haimulos.*

Page 139. — *The stone bridge,* the Pons Æmilius or Lapideus, seems to have been built, for the actual traffic, close alongside of the original wooden bridge, the Pons Sublicius, which was allowed to remain for religious purposes, but was not otherwise used. Dionysius of Halicarnassus says it was still remaining in his time.

Page 148. — Dacier, in his note on *the Egyptian wheels,* refers to a passage in Clement of Alexandria, to the effect, that the Egyptian priests gave those who came to the temples to pray, a wheel, which they were to turn, and flowers, both of them emblems of change and instability.

Page 152. — The correct name is not *Mercedinus* but Mercedonius.

Page 155. — The verses are from a Pæan, or song of triumphal rejoicing, of Bacchylides. The complete passage is found in Stobæus ; it is Fragment 13 of Bacchylides, in Bergk's Poetæ Lyrici.

Page 156. — *The saying which Plato ventured to pronounce,* is the famous demand made with such fear and trembling in the fifth book of the Republic (p. 473) for the rule of the king-philosopher. It is repeated in the fourth book of the Laws, from which latter place come the words of the next sentence, *the wise* man *is blessed in himself, and blessed also are the auditors who can hear and re ceive the words that flow from his mouth.*

Page 163. — COMPARISON. *These with the young men, &c.,* is from the Andromache of Euripides, (597). *She also, the young maid,* on the next page, is referred by some to the Hermione, by some to the Reclaiming of Helen, both of them lost plays of Sophocles. It is the Fragment No. 791 in Dindorf.

LIFE OF SOLON, page 168. — *Hand to hand as in the ring,* literally, *like a boxer, hand to hand,* is from the Trachiniæ of Sophocles (441); the line just above is the eighth of the Bacchæ of Euripides.

Page 170. — *Work is a shame to none, the shame is not to be working,* is the 309th line of Hesiod's Works and Days.

Page 179. — Munychia was best known to the Athenians of Plutarch's time, as one of the strong-holds invariably occupied by the garrisons by which the kings of Macedon had controlled the city.

Page 188. — *The Tragedy* is probably the Philoctetes, one of the lost tragedies of Euripides. Plutarch quotes it more fully elsewhere: " What bride, what young virgin would accept thee ? Truly," &c.

Page 193. — *The end and the beginning of the month,* occurs twice in the Odyssey (*XIV.* 162, *XIX.* 307).

Page 199. — For *Homer's Ulysses,* see the fourth book of the Odyssey (235– 264), where Helen relates, at Sparta, to Telemachus and Nestor's son, how Ulysses entered Troy, as a spy, in the dress of a beggar, and was recognized by her alone, and returned after killing many and procuring much information.

Page 201. — Plato, on the mother's side, claimed relationship with Solon, so that in this way, the story of the Atlantis *came with some title to him.* See the Timæus, pp. 21 to 26.

LIFE OF THEMISTOCLES, page 232. — The Lycomedæ or Lycomidæ were an ancient Attic priestly family. Phlya is one of the Attic demi or townships; and the record found in Simonides was probably an epigram inscribed in the chapel.

Page 240. — The two lines from Pindar are quoted by Plutarch in three other places; they are one of the Fragments of his lost and uncertain poems, (*Boeckh, Fragment 96*). Olizon is one of the places whose warriors, in Homer's Catalogue, (*Iliad, II.* 716–718), are led by Philoctetes, — " The dwellers in Methone and Thaumacia, and the inhabitants of Melibœa and rocky Olizon, these Philoctetes commanded, skilful with the bow."

Page 243. — The guides in the time of Pausanias showed figures in a colonnade in the market-place of Trœzen, which they said were the representations of these Athenian women and children, erected in remembrance of their stay in the town, (*Pausanias, II.* 31).

Page 247. — The verses are the 347th and following of the Persæ.

Page 249. — *Simonides says* it probably in an ode on the victory at Salamis, similar to those of which some fragments remain, on the battles of Artemesium and Thermopylæ. A few of the words — *was ever known more glorious exploit on the seas,* are pretty certainly a part of the original, but it is impossible to restore the verse.

Page 253. — The passage in Aristophanes is the 812th line of the Equites.

Page 259. — *Nicogenes* in Diodorus is called Lysithides, under which name the same account is given of his entertainment of Themistocles.

Page 267. — Plato in the Meno, arguing the question whether virtue or excellence is a thing that can be learnt or attained by training and practice, or, on the contrary, comes to us by divine allotment, points out how Aristides and Pericles, and all the great Grecian statesmen, had failed to impart their political wisdom to their sons. *You have often heard it said that Themistocles taught his son Cleophantus to be such an admirable rider, that he could stand upright on horseback, and could throw a javelin standing upright ; — the son obviously was not without ability ; — but did you ever hear it said by any one, that Cleophantus showed any virtue, skill, or wisdom in the same sort of things as did his father ? Yet he, undoubtedly, had virtue been a thing to be taught, would have taught his son the virtue and wisdom in which he himself excelled, (pp. 93, 94).* Nothing is known beyond what is here said, of the *Address* of Andocides to *his Friends.* But the Friends, or rather Companions, are evidently the members of the oligarchical associations or clubs, who united under that name towards the end of the Peloponnesian war.

LIFE OF CAMILLUS, page 273. — Matuta is quite confidently identified with Ino or Leucothea, by Ovid in the Fasti, (*VI.* 475–562),

> Leucotheë Graiis, Matuta vocabere nostris.

The words, *they embrace their brothers' children instead of their own*, ought perhaps to be, *they take their sisters' children . . . . up in their arms to present them to the goddess.* Ino had been kinder to her sister's children than to her own. Thus Ovid says,

> Non tamen hanc pro stirpe sua pia mater adoret:
> Ipsa parum felix visa fuisse parens:
> Alterius prolem melius mandabitis illi:
> Utilior Baccho quam fuit ipsa suis.

Page 288. — *The twenty-fifth* of Boëdromion, the day of the battle of Arbela, should be the twenty-sixth; and the day which *the Carthaginians observe, the twenty-first* of Metagitnion, should, perhaps, be corrected to the twenty-second. Hesiod's account of fortunate and unfortunate days is appended to his Works and Days, from whence Virgil took the hint for his in the Georgics.

Page 290. — The Greek gives the past tense in the sentence, *Others say that this fire* was *kept burning*, &c.; but it should, probably, be altered all through into the present.

Page 291. — Doliola is the Latin name of the *place* called the *Barrels.* "It was thought best," says Livy (*V.* 40), "to bury them in barrels in the chapel adjoining the house of the flamen of Quirinus, in the spot where now it is considered an offence against religion to spit."

LIFE OF PERICLES, page 327. — *Plato's expression*, " so strong a draught of liberty," occurs in the 8th book of the Republic, (*p.* 562). The author of the verses that follow is unknown.

Page 328. — The quotation from Plato is from the passage in the Phædrus, where Socrates argues that the knowledge of nature, and, in particular, of the soul, is as necessary to the perfect master of rhetoric, as the knowledge of the body is to the physician. Pericles is said to *thunder and lighten* in the Acharnians of Aristophanes (530).

Page 337. — *Socrates says he heard Pericles propose to the people* the building of the long wall — more properly the middle wall, a subsequent addition to the long walls — in the Gorgias of Plato, (*p.* 456 *a*). The Odeum was burnt in the time of the siege of Athens by Sylla, to be described in Sylla's life.

Page 341. — The quotation from Plato is again out of the Phædrus, (*p.* 261). *Rhetoric is a* psychagogia — *a magic power of swaying and carrying about the souls of men by the use of words.*

Page 348. — *The brazen wolf* at Delphi was famous. *A man who carried off some treasure from the temple, went to hide it in the thick woods of Parnassus. A wolf fell upon him and killed him; and for many days after came daily into the city and howled. At last the people followed him, discovered the gold, and set up this image of the wolf.* — (*Pausanias, X.* 14.)

Page 353. — Aristophanes's line about the Samians is from his lost comedy of the Babylonians.

Page 354. — Most likely the engineer was called *Periphoretus,* or the *carried-about,* for the very reason that the name was already familiar from Anacreon's verses.

Page 356. — Cimon is said to have given these names to his sons in honor of the states whom he represented, as *Proxenus,* at Athens.

Page 358. — The story of Anthemocritus is not alluded to by any contemporary writer. Yet Pausanias also relates it, and speaks of his monument as still remaining on the Sacred Road, going to Eleusis; just as described here, outside the Dipylon. *The famous verses in the Acharnians* are the 524th and following.

Page 368. — *Sold for slaves* may have been Plutarch's expression, but the fact itself cannot be believed; and it would not be difficult to correct the one word in which the assertion is made.

Page 370. — *Olympus, where they say the gods have their ever secure abode,* occurs in the Odyssey (*VI.* 42), and the phrase of the *secure abode* or *seat* is repeated by Pindar, (*Nem. VI.* 3).

LIFE OF FABIUS, page 393. — This is probably a fragment, of which no more is known. No existing line of Euripides can very well be identified with it.

Page 400. — This brazen *colossal statue of Hercules* was the work, we are told by Strabo (*VI. c.* 3), of Lysippus. He speaks of it as still standing in his time in the Capitol, as the offering of Fabius Maximus, the taker of the city.

Page 404. — " *Long shaken on the seas restored the state,*" is said of Œdipus, in the beginning of the Œdipus Tyrannus.

www.ingramcontent.com/pod-product-compliance
Lightning Source LLC
Chambersburg PA
CBHW031054110726
47900CB00003B/926